Kill! Kill!

Battle of Fallujah

Kill! Kill! Battle of Fallujah

Copyright © 2019 by Chance Nix

Published 2019 by Grunt, Ink.

Book Design © Jennifer Teamann Nix

ISBN-13: 978-1-7340884-0-3

Kill! Kill! Battle of Fallujah is a work of creative historical fiction. While a majority of the content is fictional, some events are reflections based on actual experiences or conversations as interpreted by the author. All names and identifying details have been changed to protect the privacy of the people involved.

Discover other titles by Chance Nix by visiting the author's webpage.

www.gruntink.com

This book contains mature language, humor, sexuality, and violence. All Arabic language in this book is a rough translation by the author and the internet translate.

This book is dedicated to two very important people in my life:

To Jennifer and Whit –

For different reasons and both know why.

Chance
Nix

GRUNT, INK.

a novel

KILL! KILL!
BATTLE OF FALLUJAH

CHAPTER ONE

FIRST TO FIGHT

'From the halls of Montezuma

To the shores of Tripoli;

We fight our country's battles

In the air, on land, and sea;

First to fight for right and freedom

And to keep our honor clean;

We are proud to claim the title

Of United States Marine.'

-First stanza of the Marine Corps Hymn-

March 29th, 2003-

The camera's digital screen flickered and came to life. With his chest bare and bleeding, a young Marine in tattered desert trousers kneeled in the center of the frame. An eagle, globe, and anchor decorated his right arm; Captain America's shield etched into the skin of his left. Two silver dog tags clanked around his neck as the young man lifted his head. Without emotion, his blue eyes haunted the camera lens.

Two men flanked the Marine, their faces concealed with black head wraps. One clutched a machete while the other pressed the barrel of an AK-47 to the Marine's head. Walking with superior confidence, a third man entered without hiding his identity. A mangled scar stretched over his left eye, crossed the bridge of his nose, and came to a stop beneath his chin. He halted next to the injured hostage, shoving a piece of paper at him.

The battered Marine squinted through swollen eyes at the single sheet of white paper, then turned to the camera to draw in a slow, deep breath, doing nothing. Scarface insisted his captive take the paper, shaking it in front of his face, but still the Marine refused. In an act of defiance, he looked from the leader to the man with the machete, then to the one holding the AK. The Marine assumed with the safety disengaged, a round was in the chamber. It was familiar to the hostage, from the contours of the brass casing to the pointed tip of the copper round. He wondered if there were any markings to personalize it, to make it unique among the other bullets in the world.

A dusty sandal slammed into his shoulder, breaking the Marine's train of thought. He fell forward, resting on his hands, and fought to control his rage. The dirt floor collected drops of blood from his wounded face. Before he could climb to his knees, Scarface placed the paper beneath him.

"State name, rank, and read the message," Scarface demanded in broken English. The Marine spat a stream of blood into the loose dirt. His dirty crimson fingers clamped the edge of the paper, and he rose to meet their gaze.

Scarface waited for the Marine to speak, but nothing came. With a puff of frustration, which flapped his mustache, the leader nodded to the AK insurgent. Cold steel pressed hard into the back of the Marine's skull. The Marine pushed against the barrel, daring the insurgent to do something. The pressure eased, but then came a hard thud. The Marine rocked forward, but unlike the previous kick, this one did not drop him.

"State name as it appears on dog tags." Scarface spat through clenched teeth, but the Marine's distant stare defied his commands. The insurgent's nostrils flared as the camera adjusted on the American's bruised face.

Taking a deep breath, the Marine raised his head. The taste of copper streamed down the back of his throat, but he didn't grimace. Instead, a smile graced his face and the hostage said, "Gunnery Sergeant John Basilone."

His echo boomed in the small room; his chest expanded with pride.

Wrinkles furrowed the leader's brow as his face contorted with dissatisfaction. Hate radiated from his enlarged eyes as he seized the Marine by the chin and unleashed a solid punch. The captive's head snapped to the side, slinging blood which landed on the AK insurgent's foot. It seeped between his toes, repulsing him.

A deep belly laugh exploded from within the Marine as he tongued the tear in his lip. He checked for any loose teeth, which there were none, and spat more blood on the ground.

"I don't know this Basilone, but this not your name. State name as it appears on dog tags." Scarface spoke with a rapid tongue. He grew impatient watching the Marine rub the side of his jaw, massaging a lump growing under the skin.

"My name is…" His chest heaved up and down. "Gunny Carlos Hathcock."

He hoped the other captured Marines could hear him. He prayed the names of heroic Leathernecks would encourage them to resist and fight. Scarface squeezed the American's throat, digging his dirty nails into the soft flesh, forcing the airway shut. The Iraqi's rotten breath soured his stomach but never did the Marine wince or show signs of pain.

"I grow tired of this. Your real name or we will kill you."

"You'll kill me anyway, so in the words of my forefathers," the Marine gritted his blood-stained teeth, "fuck you."

The audacity of this particular warrior brought a sense of humor to Scarface. His deceptive eyes, blue and hollow, engulfed the insurgent in dread and discomfort. The jarhead's attention never wavered from the leader. The corners of his mouth curled up in a minute angle that, although he would never admit it, frightened the head insurgent. Scarface motioned to the machete man, who raised the bladed weapon above his head.

Using every muscle fiber in his back, shoulders, and arms, the machete sailed down through open air.

A heartbeat elapsed. The Marine held his stance. The blade neared and forced the parting air to caress the Marine's neck. Images of beheaded reporters danced through his mind. Their long-since silenced screams vibrated his ears and their terror-stricken eyes haunted his memories. The Marine's superior combat knowledge recognized the need to get the drop on his enemy. If he had any chance of saving his fellow captured comrades, he had to move quick. A sinister intent blazed in the Marine's eyes, festering the leader with paranoia.

Scarface sensed a wrath in this Marine and feared what he could do if it was unleashed. The blade moved too slow for the leader whose speculated horror came to fruition as the razor-sharp edge missed its target. The Marine ducked, losing only a few severed strands from his high and tight. Metal bit into metal as the machete struck the barrel of the AK. A vibration screamed up the length of the rifle and in his panic, the insurgent squeezed off two rounds. Both projectiles impacted the dirt floor between the Marine's head and Scarface's feet.

With the commotion of both the recoil and the vibration, the insurgent lost his grip on the rifle. The buttstock struck the ground and fired more rounds into the concrete ceiling. Dirt and chucks of cement rained down on them as the rifle settled into the dirt behind the insurgents. It ceased its fire and an alarming silence seized the room. Such resistance had never stood in front of them before.

Mustering whatever strength his battered body could, the Marine rose like a demon from the pits of Hell. His stance swept an equal jolt of shock and confusion over the three insurgents. The man with the machete thrusted the blade at the hostage. In one fluid motion, the modern-day Spartan twisted and locked the weapon-wielding arm of the insurgent before smashing his face. The filthy man dropped the bloody weapon to clutch his shattered nose.

Standing stunned, Scarface didn't react until a front kick floored him and stole his air.

The other man dove for his rifle, digging in the dirt to gain traction to reach the weapon. The Marine pivoted and rotated the machete up and over his shoulder. As in chopping a piece of wood, he brought the machete down, burying it deep into the man's side. With little opposition and a sickening thud, the blade chopped through the third and fourth ribs, striking the left atrium of the heart and separating it from the left ventricle.

The insurgent's fingertips graced the stock of his rifle. There was hope in his eyes before his body twitched and, in his mind, he grabbed the weapon. His trigger finger jerked back against the air. With blood gushing from his wound, he died before his body nestled into the dirt.

The Marine ripped the machete free. Spots of blood and bits of flesh splattered across the wall and ceiling. The machete's former owner charged at the Marine, who didn't hesitate. The sight of the ferocious man, covered in his own blood, only encouraged the Marine to act. He swiveled and drove the point of the blade into the insurgent's stomach. The man halted as fear and pain overtook him. Forcing the blade down, the Marine sawed open his abdominal cavity, spilling out a hot mess of blood and intestines.

The disemboweled man dropped to his knees, struggling to wail, and frantically scooping up his guts. The hot and slimy organs slipped through his fingers. His head grew light from the loss of blood, and his vision blurred a moment before he slumped to the ground. He was still collecting his guts when he slipped silently into the next life.

On his hands and knees, Scarface scurried across the floor to the rifle. As his finger brushed the sand-smoothed wooden stock, the Marine punted the rifle away. The tip of the machete caressed the leader's neck and the pin-point notion of pain froze him. Scarface looked up at the man who glared down at him like a god would his minions.

Aside from a snarling grin, the blinding light behind the Marine shielded his features.

"Who are you?" Scarface graveled. His voice shook, and his body trembled at the thought of dying with urine filling his pants.

"A Marine." His calm voice lacked any hint of compassion. Endorphins masked the pain as his chest swelled and deflated. His busted lips didn't hurt, his swollen eyes saw clearly, and his broken nose flared wide. Exhaustion never plagued the warrior's mind as he towered over the coward. The machete was steady in his hand as drops of blood fell from the tip, making dark circles in the dirt.

A whimper escaped Scarface as he pleaded with his former hostage. Scarface dropped his head and closed his eyes, praying to Allah to spare him from this fate.

"Don't do that," the Marine ordered, showing no sympathy. Moving the tip of the machete under Scarface's chin, he forced the insurgent's head to rise.

"Please." Scarface cried. As if lacking sleep, his eyes flashed bloodshot, and large tears rushed out.

"When you get to Hell, tell them, Jack Campbell—" He paused, shaking his head as if an unseen person whispered in his ear. "No, you tell them the Berserker sent you."

Sobs flowed from the leader like a child awaiting punishment. His pain and suffering filled the Berserker with pleasure. Gripping the plastic handle with both hands, the Marine lifted the blade.

"This is your zero hour." The Berserker hissed. Scarface glanced up, his hands out in front to protest his decapitation. Not once did he wonder if the men he had beheaded felt the way he felt now. A flame found only in the Devil's eyes burned in the Marine's, and he snarled, "Embrace it, motherfucker."

It took one swing and the insurgent's head fell from his shoulders and rolled across the grimy floor. "Embrace it."

CHAPTER TWO

OSCAR MIKE

Come on, you sons of bitches! Do you want to live forever?

-Gunnery Sergeant Dan Daly, USMC – Battle of Belleau Wood, 6 June 1918

I

June 6th, 2004-

Deployment Departure T-Minus 11 hours and 55 minutes and counting-

"How could you? How could you!" Jennifer Campbell kept repeating. With each syllable her anger grew. Jack imagined the last evening with his wife going in a different direction. She sat on the couch, her hands trembling, and a heaviness settling upon her chest. He yearned to hug her, to kiss her, to show her it would be OK, but he knew she'd reject his touch.

"I'm sorry, but please understand that I had to."

"Even after last time, why would you go back?" Her tone swelled with every word until she was shouting. She had known he was leaving for some time, but now that it was upon them, reality was setting in.

"It's not that I want to." The pain was evident in his voice. "It's I *have* to. I have to go back."

"I don't understand. Why would you want to go back? Why would you want to leave before—" She stopped herself from completing her own sentence and rubbed her stomach. "I don't understand."

Jack sighed. He realized there was no reasoning with her. She had every right to be upset, and he didn't blame her.

"Listen." He refrained from screaming, but with no carpet, his volume escalated. At the sound of his echo, he paused, took a deep breath, and lowered his head so they were eye to eye. "I don't want to, but I gotta see this thing through."

"You volunteered. God damn it, you volunteered." She threw her hands up in defeat. "I can't believe you'd choose this."

She shot up from the couch, and Jack slipped to the side like a boxer to avoid a collision of their heads. Jennifer pushed past him, pacing the living room. A weakness from the pregnancy overtook her, but she fought it. She didn't know where she wanted to go or what she wanted to do. Jennifer sat down; she stood up.

Jennifer wanted to lie down; she wanted to leave. The strong craving for a cigarette nipped at her, but she wouldn't give in to it. No matter how much her world was falling apart, she was still pregnant and needed to look out for the unborn child. The ache for a cigarette aroused the urge for a beer. Jack crossed his arms and leaned against the archway of the kitchen, watching her walk a trail in the carpet before the couch.

"I had to." His voice softened. "How could I live with myself if one of those guys died and I wasn't there to prevent it? I couldn't look myself in the mirror after that. Sure, things went bad my first tour, but the only reason I can wake up every morning is that I did all I could."

"Things went bad your first tour? That's putting it mildly. You can't sleep. You scream at night from what happened your first tour." She hit a nerve, forcing Jack to turn away.

He forced the memory down before it could take hold, but a single image slipped through. Jack glanced in the direction of the garage and hoped there was beer in the refrigerator. He tried to find the words, but she was right. The problems from his last tour haunted him, and it was a burden she carried as well.

"What about the next tour and the one after that?" The springs in the old couch moaned as she plopped down. "And I'm sure there's one after that."

The couch was no good. Jumping from it, she leaned on one of the wooden stools at the kitchen's bar. It made a loud squeak as it scooted across the tile floor. Jack's heart skipped at the thought of his pregnant wife falling.

"I swear it's the last tour. Once it's over, I'm out and done with the Corps."

"Bullshit." Jennifer came off the stool and jabbed a finger at him. She gasped for air while tears rolled down her red face. "You won't get out. There's no out once you're in. You love that damn Corps more than me."

"That's not true. I love you, and I wanna be there for the birth, but this is something I gotta do. These young Marines need me."

"Damn you and damn the Marines. Damn the Corps. I need you. God damn the Berserkers." Jennifer wanted to hurt him; she wanted her words to stick like knives, so he felt the pain she did. "You're not doin' this for them or me. You're doin' this because you're scared of a normal life. You like the action, the thrill of it. But most of all, you like the attention. The idea of these men worshipping you. You have a god complex, Jack."

Jack laughed, rolling his eyes.

"It's not a god complex. I want these men to come home. What if they were our son, wouldn't you want someone there that could lead them?"

"Don't you dare use our child in this?" She placed a hand on her stomach.

"I want you to understand. Men may die if I'm not there."

"Why can't you admit you love their admiration?" She dropped down on the sofa, completely at a loss, and folded her arms across her chest. She turned away, the very sight of him disgusted her. "You love it more than you love me."

Jack settled to his knees and clutched her legs. She fought to avoid his hypnotic blue eyes.

"I worship you and love you more than life itself, but I can't live with myself if I don't go. I couldn't wake up next to you or be honest with myself if I left these guys to die. I gotta go back one more time. After this, I'm done. I swear it. Then I'll get some desk job that's safe and boring. But please understand, I have to do this." Jennifer untangled his arms from her legs and allowed them to drop to the floor as she rose.

"Go. I can't change your mind but know this, I won't cry for you." She left the room, frightened for their future.

II

Deployment Departure T-Minus 09 hours and 22 minutes and counting-

Roberto Carlos smeared the condensation on his mug as he lifted the beer for a toast. Rodney Vinson, John Ashmore, and Philip Simpson mimicked him and the three leaned in to hear Carlos in the crowded bar and grill.

"Here's to the Berserkers," Carlos said. The other three Lance Corporals grinned. "If we don't come home alive, may we all dine in Valhalla."

Clinking of glasses followed, and the four men downed their beers in several quick gulps. Carlos knew about combat and questioned if these three men were as prepared as they thought they were. Even with the endless training in California, they couldn't fathom the reality of it. *It ain't like in the movies.*

"OK, who would you rather bang, Christina Aguilera or Britney Spears?" Vinson asked.

"Britney Spears," Ashmore said, sipping his beer.

"Why?"

"She seems nice. Like you could bring her home to mom. I'd like to wreck that." Vinson's laugh collided with his beer, choking him. This amused Ashmore, who replied, "What about you?"

"Christina," Vinson said, clearing his throat.

"Why?"

"That tight little body. Man, that's where it's at."

"Naw, she got Mexican in her. She'll blow up after one kid," Ashmore said. All eyes dropped on Carlos who stared over his mug.

"Fuck you, man. She ain't Mexican."

"Whatever. Simpson, what about you?"

"Those two bitches are annoying. Give me that Destiny's Child booty, and now we talkin'."

"Which Destiny's Child?" Vinson asked.

"Motherfucker, who cares? Any of them. Hell, all of them." With a deep bellowing laugh and a mouth caked in foam, the large Marine wiped his face with his forearm looking like a Viking at a feast.

"What about you?" Vinson asked Carlos.

"Which one?"

"Britney or Christina?"

"Neither. Give me Jennifer Lopez. Now that's a Mexican booty."

"I'd tap that." Ashmore tapped his mug against Carlos's and said, "Man, we should go get the Berserker symbol tattooed after this."

"What's the Berserker symbol?" Vinson asked. Ashmore motioned to Carlos, who rolled up his sleeve to reveal a red Nordic tattoo on his upper bicep. "Kind of looks like an evil fuckin' spider. Shit, I'm in. Let's get one."

"Do all the old joints got'em?" Simpson asked.

"Yeah. We all got it when we got back from our last tour. You should see Jack and Kyle's. Crazy."

"Who?" Vinson asked. Carlos laughed.

"Corporal Campbell and Corporal Dillon to you, boot." Ashmore and Simpson found humor in insulting the younger Marine, themselves having dropped in the platoon one month earlier. Vinson rolled his eyes while sipping his beer with the suspicious nature of a minor.

"Fuck yeah." Ashmore took a large gulp, wiping away the beer mustache and burped. "Let's go get tattoos, go to a strip club, and find some ladies to take back to the hotel."

"Live it up tonight, motherfuckers. For the next seven months, your asses are gonna be doing nothing but watching bugs in the sand." Arching his brow, Carlos spotted a waitress and signaled for another pitcher.

"Come on, you're telling me we ain't gonna see combat?" Vinson asked. Carlos leaned over and eyed Vinson's clothing.

"Fuck no. And wearing fuckin' combat boots with that ridiculous collared shirt, you ain't ready to go to war."

"I like this shirt." Vinson adjusted the collar for it to stand taller. The table laughed.

"Hell, the war's pretty much over anyway. It ain't like it was in Nasiriyah."

"Nasiriyah? Isn't that where Corporal Campbell killed those—" Ashmore started, but Carlos interrupted, holding his hand up and shaking his head to silence his fellow Marine.

"We don't talk about that, Devil Dog." The three younger Marines gawked at Carlos, silently pleading with him to tell his tale. He sipped his beer like an old sea dog gearing up to spin a yarn of faraway adventures. They leaned in and all other voices faded from their realm of consciousness.

"I know you guys haven't been with the unit long, and I'm sure you're dying to ask Jack about what happened in Nasiriyah, but don't. Corporal Campbell is indeed a bad motherfucker. He's the original Berserker, Jack the Ripper, you dig? And that's all you need to know. But on the up and up, I'll let you in on a secret. He lost his kid brother there, and then they tried to kill him. That man unleashed chaos that none of you've ever seen. You wanna stay on Jack's good side, you dig?"

Unknowingly, the three Marines nodded their head in unison, entranced by Carlos's tone.

"Never mention it," Carlos continued. "I was there, and when he came to rescue my ass, he was a god damn walking nightmare. I thought El Diablo was coming for me. Jack's a hard charger, you hear. Makes the real Jack the Ripper look like a fuckin' doctor or some shit. And if I ever hear any of you disrespecting him, I'll kill you myself."

A pitcher of beer slammed on the table, breaking the hold Carlos's warning had on them. Their attention shifted to the woman in skimpy shorts. Ashmore leaned back in his chair, popped his pectoral muscles like a peacock would its feathers, and rubbed his bald head. She smiled at his faux pas gesture of masculinity, then hurried to another table of gawking young men. Ashmore glowed, pouring himself a beer.

"Fuck that, though, I better get to kill somebody over there." He offered to pour Vinson another glass, but Vinson waved it off.

"Gotta piss. I'll be back." He pushed away from the table and made his way toward the restroom in the far corner of the restaurant. Snaking through the growing crowd and excusing himself with each foot he advanced, he tried hard not to run into anyone. A large biker in a black leather vest, unaware of Vinson, stepped back and slammed into the Marine. The biker's sausage fingers lost its grip on his beer bottle and it shattered on the bare cement floor. Eyes of other patrons locked onto the two men.

"You made me drop my beer." The biker postured up to the smaller Marine, stroking his beard, and snarling. Vinson read the name 'Chet' on his vest and registered the beam of hatred Chet had for him.

"I didn't do anything. You ran into me." Vinson attempted to move around Chet, but five obese digits plucked at his arm. He looked at Chet's hand, then glared at the biker with an equal measure of hate and discontent. "Get your hand off me."

"You better buy me another one, little man." Chet poked Vinson's chest. Vinson eased his head away from the stagnant smell of the biker's breath.

"Look, man, I see you ride motorcycles. By your appearance and stench, I take it you don't wear helmets or shower, but that's beside the point. What I'm getting at is I doubt your IQ level's high enough to understand this, so I'll explain it to you as simple as your pea-sized brain can understand." The other bikers stood from their table, but Vinson continued, "You dropped your beer from your hairy paws as you stepped back into me. Should I draw you a picture? You can paint it by numbers."

Chet grabbed Vinson by the collar. Vinson reared back, ready to slug the biker when someone hooked the crook of his elbow. A smaller version of Chet locked Vinson's arms behind his back.

"Shit, we gotta go." Simpson urged the other two while vaulting from his seat. His chair toppled over, catching the attention of those around, as he made a beeline for Vinson. Carlos and Ashmore downed their beers and followed the massive black Marine into the sea of people.

Chet grinned, revealing a row of discolored and cavity-riddled teeth. He closed his fist and pulled it back. Chet loved to fight, but when Vinson looked up at him with a demented glow of insanity, Chet hesitated. Vinson whipped his head back, smashing the nose of the smaller biker. To Vinson's disappointment, blood stained the back of his pretty-boy collared shirt. The tight hold on his arms released. The skinny biker stumbled back, toppled over a table, and crashed to the floor.

Before Chet could punch Vinson, Vinson planted his tan combat boot into the man's knee, forcing him to double over to nurse the injury. While crouching, Vinson shifted forward and landed an uppercut to his bearded jaw. Chet grimaced and rocked on his heels. He forgot about his knee as two blacken teeth flew out, landing on the plate of a watching customer. Something hard hit Vinson on the cheek and he stumbled into a table full of attractive females. He surprised them, and flashing his baby face pearly whites, they blushed.

The restaurant's attention went from the fight on TV to the bar fight near the restroom. Another biker, who seemed barely out of puberty, seized Vinson. He tugged, ripping the back of Vinson's shirt, and pulled him away from the women. Before he could punch Vinson, Simpson boosted him into the air like a pro wrestler. Two men with long braided beards ran at Simpson, but Ashmore and Carlos intercepted them. Vinson, ignoring the rest of the fights, clenched Chet by the vest, and jabbed him three times in his face.

"I just wanted to take a piss." Vinson smashed the biker's nose, sending him slithering to the floor. Simpson tossed the pubescent biker into the crowd. More men joined the fight. Punches hit the bikers, punches hit the Marines, and a few fought whoever they could. A bouncer took hold of Ashmore while grappling with another man in a headlock. Ashmore dropped the puny bearded biker and elbowed the bouncer.

"We gotta get the hell out of here. They're calling the cops," Carlos shouted. The four Marines burst out the front door and scanned the streets for any approaching cops. Red and blue lights pierced the night in two different directions.

"So, tattoos?" Ashmore said, and the four men ran down the street in fits of hysteria.

III

Deployment Departure T-Minus 09 hours and 12 minutes and counting-

Kyle Dillon sat on his surfboard, floating alone off the coast of California. His hands dangled lethargically at his sides, allowing the water to pass between his fingers. A shiver ran up his back, causing his jaw to quiver uncontrollably. He didn't pay any mind to his body's reaction to the cold. The ocean was his first love; the ocean at night, his first mistress.

There was nowhere in the world that brought him more peace. In the distance, the sound of waves crashing on the rocks muffled the noise polluting his head.

He glanced over his shoulder at the beach party in full swing. A stereo sent a dance vibe through the crowd occupying his beachfront bungalow. Surfboards stood like pillars along the shore, their owners having retired from the water before the sun went down. They were Kyle's friends, the radical ones who lived for the perfect wave, a remnant of his old Bohemian life.

His hair, once long and kissed blond by the sun, was now kept short, a regulation high and tight. The years of forced shaving in the military erased his baby face. Even the thought of a beard caused him to scratch at his neckline.

The moon hung full and reflected off the ocean. It allowed Kyle to see the contours of an eagle, globe, and anchor tattoo, and the battle scars adorning his body. The rough texture on his chest read like braille, transporting his mind to a place thousands of miles away. A land lacking water, but abundant in death.

Horrible experiences attacked him with such clarity, he failed to register the water surrounding him. The exhaust of Humvees filled his nose and mortar explosions drowned out the ocean. In his memory, he saw the small arms fire and rocket-propelled grenades that brought his convoy to a halt.

It wasn't hard for Kyle to remember the AK round puncturing Captain Larson's neck, the corpsman that worked to save the convoy commander's life, or how the Captain bled out in the street. There was no time to mourn as enemy rounds peppered their Humvee. Sitting behind the passenger seat, he crawled over the midsection to escape gunfire. A bone-rattling explosion rocked him as an assortment of fire and black smoke engulfed the Humvee in front of his.

A hand seized Kyle's flak jacket and jerked him from the vehicle. A silhouette of his best friend, Jack Campbell, leaned over the hood, returning fire. Together, the two Lance Corporals assembled a few Marines to counterattack the enemy. More barbarian-like than civilized, the Marines relished in the glory of a fight. They infiltrated the Iraqi Soldiers' fighting holes, outclassing and outfighting Saddam's Republican Guard.

On his board in the water, the splashing of the surf reminded him of the blood spraying in his face. The forgotten copper smell of blood caused a chill to run the length of his spine. His index finger twitched at the phantom weight of an absent trigger. His eyes spotted the long-ago fired round entering the enemy's head.

The order to return to the Humvees falsely echoed in his ears. Another attack came from the opposite side of their convoy. *Who gave the call to retreat?* Kyle wondered. *It had to be the Lieutenant; only he would give up his men when they were winning the fight.* With the enemy approaching, he hurried to climb over the body of Captain Larson and into the Humvee. Kyle didn't want to be disrespectful, especially of the dead, but his life was at stake.

He climbed on top of the Captain and managed to close the door, but not before something shocked the back of his leg. It felt like the worse snap of the hardest rubber band, but the pain burned like liquid fire. He had only a moment to grunt as an explosion blackened everything.

Kyle closed his eyes, his body swaying with the ocean, and forced the rest of the memory to stop. He didn't want to think about the jail or the screams of his men as someone removed their heads. Kyle looked out onto the distant horizon of the ocean and a peaceful feeling washed over him. The water held that alluring power, making the bad things in his life fade away.

"Kyle." Voices came from the shore. "Come in, bro."

Kyle waved to them. They wanted to party one more time because in the morning, he'd be heading back to the biggest sandbox in the world. No one said it, but everyone knew he might not return. Kyle knew this better than any of them. *Live or die, you can't lose sleep over it.* He'd miss the ocean, but Kyle was a Marine, and he had a job to do. He spun the board around and paddled toward the shore.

IV

June 7th, 2004-

Deployment Departure T-Minus 00 hours and 30 minutes and counting-

Corporal Jack Campbell pushed his digital eight-point cover back and kissed his wife. Her blonde hair gave off a shine that was heaven sent, and Jack felt a ping of heartache for leaving her. There were no words he could find to describe the beauty he saw in her. Jack placed a hand on her belly covered by a pink shirt and said, "You take care of this one."

He was strong and calm about leaving for Iraq, but Jennifer could sense he was forcing it. Her smile eased his troubled mind, but the nurturing glow she cast brought him more guilt for leaving. Jack admired the fact she kept her promise not to cry. She was strong; it was the only word he could think to describe her in this moment. The air felt clearer as if every word said the night before was a dream. He looked into his wife's brown eyes for there was warmth in them.

"She's gonna be something special." Jack kissed her again.

Marines said goodbye to their loved ones and boarded the buses. A selected few loaded large woodland hiking packs, dubbed 782 gear, and green sea-bags into the cargo section of the buses. They all wore the same cammies with digital tanned squares to blend in with the desert surroundings of Iraq.

"How do you know it's a girl?" Jennifer asked, scrunching her nose while rubbing her still flat pregnant belly.

"I got a feeling."

"Well, you come home to us safe and sound. She's gonna need her daddy someday." He kissed her again. Jack didn't want to stop kissing her, for he was afraid he would never have the chance again.

"Hey Campbell, you piece of shit, let's ride, brother." Corporal Kyle Dillon beckoned from the steps of the bus. Jack nodded, picked up the camouflage backpack known as a daypack, and slung it over his shoulders. He turned to the elderly gentleman standing next to Jennifer and shook his hand.

"You do as she said, boy. Come home alive. You already got a Purple Heart. You don't need another one." The elderly man's slow southern draw mimicked that of a John Wayne western.

"Yeah, but I couldn't leave Kyle in charge of these new guys." His sarcasm brought his father, Joseph Campbell, to laughter. As quick as it started, the laugh disappeared and his stern, sun-hardened gaze fell on Jack.

"No need to play hero, Jackie boy. You come home safe." He wasn't an affectionate person, and Jack felt strange at the sensation that they were going to hug. They shared this feeling, and in declining to hug, they shook hands. Mary Campbell stood next to Joseph with a tissue to her nose and tears streaming down her face.

"Come on, mom, don't cry," he said as he embraced her.

"I know, but I can't help it. As soon as you're there, you send your address, and I'll send some cookies." He gave her another hug and kissed her on the cheek. There was nothing he could say to comfort her, and so he stepped away from his parents, pulling Jennifer with him.

"I'm going to miss you," Jack said. Jennifer nodded, doing her best at holding back the tears.

"Write me as soon as you get there," Jennifer said. She wrapped both arms around his neck and kissed her husband as hard as she could. "I love you, Jack Campbell."

"And I love you." With one last kiss, Jack tore away from her. Pulling his daypack up higher on his shoulder, he turned away, not wanting to see them again for he was sure to cry. Excusing himself, he snaked through the crowd on his way to the bus. He smiled at one lady, nodded at a father in near tears, and wished everyone would get out of his way.

The bump came as a surprise, although it wasn't hard. The pretty blonde with a Navy rank on her eight-point cover dropped a backpack at her feet.

"I'm sorry," she said. Jack picked up her bag and handed it back to her. The nametag stitched on her blouse read, 'Greene'.

"It's all right."

"Is this the admin bus? I'm a corpsman with Headquarters."

"No, that's my squad's bus. Admin is up the way, near the front." She thanked him, but the pleasantness in her face faded as a lanky Marine placed an arm around her shoulders.

"Hey Skyler, our bus is this way. These buses at the back are for those poor grunts."

"Excuse—" Jack started but before he could finish, the Marine was leading the corpsman away. He shrugged it off and climbed the steps of the bus, turning one final time to wave good-bye. The sun gleamed down on his wife, and he hoped to keep the memory of her angelic appearance for the rest of his life. In her face, he saw the weight of his decision and the toll it was taking upon her. Sighing deeply, he climbed the stairs of the bus with the air conditioner banging in his ears. He didn't mind. It felt better here than standing out in the sun.

"Berserkers, is everyone here?" Corporal Jack Campbell passed the bus driver and threw his daypack into an empty seat. The bus erupted with grunts and barks as Jack took the seat next to Kyle. The smell of stale air, sweat, and young men's body odor hit Jack in the face. He hated how accustomed he was to these foul things. Every bus in the Marine Corps had the same stench, and Jack couldn't wait for this part of his job to be over. *One more year.*

Kyle stared out the window, marveling at the families kissing and waving goodbye to their loved ones. No one was there for him and a part of him preferred it that way. No one to mourn, no one to miss.

"And here we go." Jack relaxed.

"Yeah, here we go." Kyle pulled a can of dip from his cargo pocket and gave it two quick shakes. His index finger thumped off the top of the can, packing the dip within. Tossing a small pinch into his lower lip, he spat into an empty bottle, and said, "Finish the game, right?"

"Yeah, finish the game. Kind of feels nice to be getting back over there."

"You're hella-crazy, bro." Kyle handed Jack the can of dip, and Jack repeated the packing process while cutting his eyes at Kyle.

"Why?"

"Command would've let you out of this one. Hell, your time's almost up. A kid on the way and what you did last time, they fuckin' owe you that much."

"And what? Let you have all the fun? Screw that. If I'm not there, you might get your fool head blown off."

"Fuck you, Jack."

"Fuck you, Kyle." The two chuckled.

"Whatever. You'll be the one with your fucking head blown off." Kyle spat into an empty plastic bottle. He held it up for Jack to see before shoving it in the pouch on the back of the seat in front of him. "Don't drink this."

"Oh, thanks," Jack replied. The window tint made it hard for anyone outside to see in the bus, so no one saw Private First Class Stephen Jenson standing on his seat, drooling.

"Wow, whose sister is that?"

"Which one?" Carlos asked.

"Better not be my sister." Ashmore growled.

"Naw, Ash, it's your mom," Simpson said.

"That chick in the pink Marine shirt." Jenson pawed at the window. The other Marines traced the crowd of families until they located who the boot was talking about. One by one, they returned to what they were doing, lowering their eyes to avoid the situation. "What a hot piece of—"

"Of what?" Kyle interrupted, silencing the entire bus. The humor faded from Jenson's face. A sinking feeling attacked his stomach as if he'd went over a large hill on a roller coaster. Only Jennifer Campbell wore a pink shirt with 'Marine' inscribed across her chest. "Go ahead, boot. Say what you gotta say about Corporal Campbell's wife?"

Jenson was speechless, unsure of what to say and looked to his fellow Marines for some help, but no one offered. Jack slowly climbed to his feet and faced the back of the bus as a shudder crept its way up Jenson's spine.

"Please boot, continue." Jack motioned with a slide of his hand.

"I… I…I was just saying—" Private First Class Jenson stuttered.

"You weren't saying shit, motherfucker." Kyle snapped, standing in his seat and jabbing a knife hand in Jenson's direction. "What's your name, boot?"

The eyes of the entire squad darted between the two corporals at the front of the bus and the lone boot at the back.

"Jenson."

"Oh, you got a rank?"

"Private First Class."

"I guess we're old drinking buddies from back on the block. How about a *Private First Class Jenson, Corporal?* Address me by my rank, fucktard."

"Check, Corporal."

"Check? Check. Did you hear that Corporal Campbell? It's payday, I guess. What the hell is this check shit?" Despite wanting to laugh, Jack held his composure while Kyle continued to rant. "I hope you like working parties, you boot motherfucker, with your check ass shit. I'll fuckin' check your ass out the fuckin' window."

Kyle didn't remove his eyes from the panicked private first class as he called for Lance Corporal Carlos.

"Square away this boot piece of shit."

Carlos ran to the back of the bus, barking commands and insults at the new Marine. The bus watched with gleeful amusement as Lance Corporal Carlos reamed Jenson.

"This motherfucker." Kyle, still holding out his knife hand, lowered into his seat. At the front, a stout man with Gunnery Sergeant chevrons on his collar climbed the steps of the bus. His eyes, concealed by dark aviator sunglasses, scanned the faces.

"Corporal Campbell." Gunny didn't ask but demanded Jack to reveal himself.

"Yes, Gunny." Jack stood to address his platoon sergeant.

"Get a head count. Make sure everyone's accounted for. We roll out in five mikes."

"Roger that, Gunny," Jack replied. Gunny Wolf turned and descended the steps. Jack reached into his cargo pocket for his NCO issued green monster notebook. "All right, Berserkers, lock it the fuck up."

A silence fell over the bus, and their collective attention turned to their squad leader. Jack opened his book and searched for his list of names. He knew them by heart, knew each one of their faces, and for the most part, he knew something about them. The few new guys were still questionable to his memory, but he did his best to learn their names and faces. The rhythmic spitting into plastic bottles grew deafening to him. He hurried to speak in order to break the annoyance.

"Listen for your name and sound off like you got a pair. You got me, Berserkers!" The squad of Marines barked in unison. As their echoes faded, Jack read off the names. Jack understood accountability was important in the Corps. Losing one man could mean losing a dozen. "Lance Corporal Ashmore."

"Kill Babies!" The large, bald Marine at the rear of the bus shouted. His bottom lip protruded away from a massive pinch of tobacco, and he spat with great force into his bottle. The answer generated a few laughs, and Jack placed a checkmark in his green monster notebook. Next to Ashmore's name was his assigned weapon - the belt-fed, fully-automatic M249 SAW weapon system.

"Private First Class Black."

"Here, Corporal." A young Marine's voice cracked from the third row in the back and a tinge of embarrassment nipped at his spine. Paranoia clouded his mind. He could've sworn the eyes of the platoon were piercing through him, judging him, and this sickened him. Black took a breath, accepting the fact that the ridiculing would soon begin. As he exhaled, he realized no one was looking at him. No one cared if he was there or not and no one noticed his voice breaking like a pubescent boy.

M16 followed Black's name and Jack placed a check by both. Ten Marines in the Berserker's squad carried the M16. Every one of them carried the A4 version with upper receiver sliding rails designed to attach PEQ-2's and broomstick handles. The A4 had a changeable carrying handle to attach optic sights such as the ACOG or a scope.

"So, you're the new comm bubba?" Jack asked Private First Class Black.

"Yes, Corporal." The other Marines sighed and hissed. Their gestures confused Black, opening a hollow pit in him as his face produced a nervous twitch. He looked from face to face and asked, "What's up?"

"You guys get K.I.A.'ed quick as a motherfucker. Stay low and far away from me." The boys laughed and mocked the new Marine. Jack returned to his list and continued, "Lance Corporal Carlos."

"Here." Carlos held up a hand. Along with the M16, Carlos carried the Mossberg 500 pump shotgun. The other new guy, Private First Class Sutherland, was assigned the same weapons. Carlos loved the shotgun and considered it his primary weapon. It made him feel like a gangster or a real cowboy. Sometimes he wondered what the gang members he grew up with in Arizona would say if they could see him now. Most were dead, so they would have nothing to say.

Carlos looked at the young men, the fresh faces, and wondered who, if any, would make it out alive. A dark revelation came over him. *Outlaw or Marine, live by the gun, you die by it.*

"PFC Jenson. You still alive, boot?" Jack found the sulking face of Jenson who raised a hand but refused to speak. Not only did he feel embarrassed, he felt insulted. No one had ever spoken to him in such a manner and it hit his pride. Lowering his hand, he continued to stare out the window and pout. The abuse came at once. The shouting of several Marines interrupted his inner thoughts. Knife hands came from every direction, and he feared the wrath carried in their eyes.

"Sound the fuck off," Ashmore shouted.

"Sound off, you piece of shit." Vinson added. Jenson startled; he didn't know what to do. His face flushed red with frustration. He clenched his teeth; his eyes narrowed with hate.

Jenson shouted sarcastically, "Here, Cor-poral."

Jack smirked, placing a checkmark next to Jenson's name. He had dealt with plenty of rich kid assholes who thought they were tough. The other Marines settled back into their seats and waited for their names.

"Keep on, bitch. Your mouth keeps writing those checks," Jack said. Jenson folded his arms across his chest and returned his gaze out the window. Jack continued, "Jones."

"Kill." Jones's Virginia drawl allowed the word to flow poetically.

"Lance Corporal Simpson."

"Here." His deep Texas voice bounded as if coming from the end of a shotgun's double barrel. It scared Jenson. "You know, white boy, if we were in the pen, you'd be my bitch. Think about that."

Simpson winked. An uncomfortable shudder besieged Jenson and he slipped deeper into his seat to avert his eyes. Simpson leaned over and bumped fists with Jones. Jones, smiling, rolled his eyes. "My brother, leave that boy alone. You see he's scared."

"I ain't scared of nothing," Jenson said. Jones leaned forward to see the boot Marine.

"Shit, I can see it in your eyes, boy."

"Doc Sloan, where you at?" Jack said. The Navy corpsman had his head buried in a large brown MED backpack. He momentarily looked up at Jack, and raised his hand, before sticking his head back into his bag.

"Sound off, Corpseman." Jenson snarled, mispronouncing corpsman.

"It's not corpseman, dumbass. It's pronounced core-man. You're not a part of the Marine corpse, are you?" Doc Sloan didn't bother looking up from his bag.

"Whatever, squid." Jenson failed to insult the uninterested corpsman, but his antics were quickly squashed by the snapping of Jack's knife hand.

"You shut your fuckin' mouth, boot, and show some respect. He's an HM2, which is an E-5. Open your fuckin' cock-slurping hole again without permission, and I'll have Lance Corporal Simpson fuck your world up. Do you get me?"

"Aye-Aye Corporal." It killed Jenson to show Jack respect, but he didn't like the way Simpson smiled while licking his lips.

"I like me the white meat, boy." Simpson played up the southern drawl as good as he could. He pulled out a large hunting knife from the sheath attached to the far side of his web belt. "Cut you up, real good. Make home cookin' for everyone here."

Jenson sat straight up, mustering the courage to speak in a derogatory slave accent, "Like yo momma used to."

Simpson drove the knife into Jenson's armrest. Jenson flinched away, forcing himself against the window. If the window was down, he would have crawled out to avoid the large Marine.

"Stow that knife, Marine," Jack ordered and returned to the next name in his notebook. "Private First Class Sutherland."

"Here, Corporal." In the last row, Private First Class Sutherland sat up like a young pupil called on by his teacher. The dim light overhead reflected off his freshly shaved scalp. With wide eyes behind his black rimmed BCG's, Sutherland studied the Marines, not knowing where he fit in. He didn't know who these Marines were or if they shared a familiar background with him. They didn't know him, and he didn't know them.

Jack marked a check next to his name.

"Lance Corporal Thompson."

"Fat chicks." Thompson cried out. The bus couldn't contain the Marines and their hysteria. Thompson amused himself at the sight of the Marines trying not to lose their dip as they laughed over their spit bottles. He was the third fire team leader, and despite being only a lance corporal, he had plenty of experience as a leader. He once outranked Jack until his fist met the face of a first sergeant in a bar. Thompson didn't lose any sleep over it because no matter what he did, he was proud of himself.

"Sick fuck." Jack checked his name.

"Lance Corporal Vinson."

"Here." Vinson didn't look up from his book. Jack marked off his name, and with each man accounted for, returned to his seat.

"Lance Corporal Vinson," Sutherland said with an unsteady whisper, tapping Vinson on the shoulder. He was only a private first class, and like most young Marines, he feared to speak with anyone who held a higher rank. The isolation was sickening. Having been in the fleet for only three weeks, Sutherland was the outsider to most of the platoon. No one knew the quiet guy in the back, and he was sure no one cared.

He tried to make friends with the two other new boots in the squad, but Black was an introvert, and Jenson was obnoxious. Sutherland couldn't relate to either of them. The rest of the guys were friendly enough, but Sutherland wasn't yet accepted by them. Always seeming to be standing on the outside, he never felt a part of the conversation.

"Can you tell me something?" Sutherland asked. Vinson continued reading without acknowledging the private first class. Sutherland tapped him again. With an annoying sigh, Vinson marked his place in his book. He closed it and turned to face the newer Marine, Vinson himself senior by only a couple of weeks.

"Look, the sky is blue, the grass is green, don't run with scissors, and always remember to drink your milk and tip your waitress. Remember those things boot, and you'll do fine in this life." Vinson returned to his book. Sutherland, confused by what Vinson said, shrugged and proceeded to ask his question.

"I was wondering what kind of guy Corporal Campbell is. Is he a dick or a laid-back kind of guy? I haven't gotten to know him yet."

"Check it, man." The story Carlos told Vinson returned to him, giving him a certain authority over the younger Marine. "Campbell will bring your sorry ass back home alive, roger that? Everyone that was in combat with him, said he saved their asses more times than they can count. Don't get it wrong, he ain't no medal seeker. He's a real hard motherfucker who is saltier than you'll ever be. I heard he got the Navy Cross for killing a hundred men or some shit. So, listen to him and move when he tells you to."

Sutherland sat back in his seat and wondered what had made this one Marine so powerful in the eyes of so many. "Yeah, my Drill Instructor—"

"Fuck your D.I.," Vinson interrupted. "He ain't got shit on Campbell. The motherfucker will buy you a drink, put a boot in your ass, and take a bullet for you. He'll do all that and never ask for anything in return except for hard work. They say he got shot like six times, stabbed six times, and blown up six times. A real devil, like nothing can kill him. They call him Jack the Ripper. Frostiest motherfucker you'll ever know. Salty. Real Berserker."

Sutherland nodded, unable to find words, leaving Vinson to his book.

Kyle pulled out his headphones and looked over at Jack who was staring out the window. A low rumble growled as the sky grew dark with overcast. Small pellets of rain beat lightly against the roof of the bus, but this didn't deter the families from waving goodbye.

"From the rear," Jack's voice boomed inside the bus. "Count off."

The Marines counted. Simpson snapped out the number six, turned to Jenson, who mindlessly stared at the crowd. It took the back of Simpson's hand slapping Jenson across the shoulder to bring his attention around. A wave of confusion washed over his face before it hit him that the bus was doing a count off.

"Six," Jenson shouted. The bus moaned and bitched.

"From the rear," Jack sighed.

"I'll kill you, boot," Carlos shouted.

"You dumb motherfucker, pay attention."

"Count off," Jack said. This time, the Marines finished without a mistake, but eyes still pierced into Jenson. The bus jerked, lurched forward, and with a snail's crawl, pulled out of the parking lot.

"We're Oscar Mike." Thompson cheered. A few of the guys joined him with claps and shouts. Jenson leaned over to the other new guy, Black, and tapped him on the shoulder.

"What's Oscar Mike mean?"

"On the move." Black rolled his eyes and went back to the book he had fished out of his daypack. Jack stared out the window without hearing the other conversations going on in the bus. He looked at Jennifer. She was crying.

CHAPTER THREE

STEEL RAIN

It's better to check out of this world than to go home all fucked up.

-Lance Corporal Chance Nix in Fallujah, 2004

I

September 4th, 2004-

Delta Iraqi National Guard, Forward Operating Base - A.K.A. The Ding

Al-Karma, Iraq-

"INCOMING!" The words echoed across the compound as three mortars plummeted from the sky. Marines scattered in every direction, sprinting for the safety of a hardened structure. Metallic shells hit with solid punches, shaking the earth beneath the Marine's feet. Large clouds of dust heaved up, blanketing the sun from the sky.

Shrapnel cut through the air, danced across the dirt, embedding into anything it could. Marines toppled over like toy soldiers. Screams of pain exploded as hot pieces of metal lodged into human flesh, and in a moment, the fog of war engulfed them.

Private First Class Sutherland was in the middle of reading the *Short-Timers* by Gustav Hasford when the mortars hit. His chest pounded with the hard thuds of a war drum and action plans flooded his mind. He had to run. He had to get to a hardened structure, but he found he couldn't move. A heavy stiffness settled into his muscles and bones and froze him on his rack like a statue. He watched others move with a terror-stricken fear that he may be paralyzed.

"Come on, Sutherland." Vinson shouted back to him, disappearing through the wooden door. Men swarmed, grabbing flak jackets and rifles as they headed outside. Sutherland blinked, the adrenaline kicked in, clearing his mind, and he hopped off the top rack of his twin bunk bed. In one fluid motion, he slipped his arms into his combat loaded flak jacket and slammed his helmet on his head.

The heavy vest of woven Kevlar fibers hung open as he snatched his rifle and bolted for the door with the other Marines in his squad. For the first time since boot camp, he noticed the weight of his weapon. It pulled at his arms and he had to look down at it to reassure himself he didn't mistakenly grabbed a cinder block instead.

He didn't let this stop him, for he was ready to have his chance at the enemy soldiers and test his grit in combat. The Kevlar helmet bobbed on his head, and the unbuckled chin strap slapped at his neck. Sutherland pulled back the rifle's charging handle, allowing it to launch forward, chambering a round. His thumb rested on the safety switch, ready to flip it to semi-auto while charging out into the fading light of day.

Dust kicked up behind the Marines as their feet pounded the hard ground of Iraq. With minds educated on war movies, they expected the enemy to flood their lines with the hunger to cut out their hearts and remove their heads. Butterflies swarmed Sutherland's stomach. Like most of the new guys, he was naive. The idea of war was enticing and romantic, but he was quickly understanding that the movies didn't get it right. He was scared. They were all scared.

The Marines scanned the compound, moving up to a fighting position. The rhythmic clicking of safety switches bounded down the line as they prepared for the onslaught that was sure to follow the mortar attack. The world zoomed in and out with the throbbing of their pulses and their eyes darted from one spot to another, anticipating the entry point.

The enemy wasn't there. A stillness crept over the compound. There were no kamikaze suicide runs, no rapid gunfire, no mass attack.

The silence yielded to the screams of wounded men. Men and women hid within large concrete structures, afraid to exit for fear of expected falling mortars.

Corporal Jack Campbell strolled out of the shower trailer, eyeballing the situation. Wearing only combat boots, and with a green towel draped around his neck, he shouldered his rifle which carried his black hygiene bag around the barrel. Jack stood exposed to the world, catching eyes as people ran by, but held no shame. His breathing was easy, his pulse didn't race, and his hands held a cigarette steady as he fired it up. Behind dark aviator glasses, he surveyed, amused by nothing.

"Lance Corporal Jones." Jack's voice boomed over the screams of the injured. Jones, waiting under a concrete structure, peeked out with several other Marines. He jittered, fearing the next round of deadly mortars to descend.

"Yes, Corporal."

"Get a head count on the Berserkers. I want to make sure everyone's solid."

"Roger that, Corporal," Jones said. He then vanished.

Jack observed the panic engulfing the base. Corpsmen rushed to the injured, while some stayed shielded under concrete structures. The faint aroma of gunpowder burned in the air, and the smell of destruction excited Jack. A wall crumbled and men screamed. The chaotic sounds were a soft, beautiful melody.

Still naked and unashamed, Jack entered the Berserker's tent and didn't like the sight he saw. Many of his Marines blinked unyielding eyes, rubbing their necks or roaming hands through their hair, jumping at the slightest sound. They watched him for guidance and clarification, and he forgot that many had yet to experience combat. They stood in their gear, rifles at the ready, waiting for some massive attack that never came. Many of them took on the appearance of young boys playing dress-up.

"Welcome to the suck, boys." Grinning, he walked over to his rack and tossed his hygiene gear down, hanging his rifle off the bedpost. Kyle sat at a makeshift table constructed of old plywood in their corner of the room, feet propped up next to a thirteen-inch television and leaned back without care of the world around him.

"How's the shower?" Kyle asked.

"The steel rain or the water one?"

"Water?"

"Not bad. Felt right at home. Middle of washing my ass, a fucking mortar attack. Shit don't change." Kyle looked back to find the Marines still staring at the two corporals. The large red tattoo on Jack's chest amazed Sutherland. Some of the guys had gotten similar tattoos, the mark of the Berserker, but none as impressive or as large as this one. Jack slipped into a fresh pair of desert cammies as Kyle sighed, rising from the table.

"Listen up. All this panicking shit you hear out there, I don't want to hear it from you guys. For the ones who don't know this, I'll give you a heads up. If you hear the explosion, you're OK. If you don't hear the explosion, then you're dead, and you're still OK." The Marines nodded like children as if Kyle was sharing the secrets of life. "Now go see if anyone needs help and stop fucking eyeballing Jack's nuts."

"They're beautiful nuts, though." Jack called out to the guys as they moved about their tent. Kyle kicked his legs up on the table and returned to his movie.

"You hear from Jennifer?"

"Nope, but you know how slow the mail is." At the front of the camp, the zip of a fully automatic interrupted their conversation. The gunfire lasted for several seconds without a pause. Jack stood tall in front of his men and grabbed his rifle from the bedpost.

"Time to earn your combat action ribbon. Let's get some." Jack barked at the men still inside the tent. With rifle in hand, Kyle rushed out the room, being the first to lead the charge. Jack waved the remaining Berserkers through the door and into the hopes of glory.

At the front post, Lance Corporal Ashmore leaned into the 240G. His left hand settled atop the buttstock as he lodged the weapon tight into his shoulder. A belt of 7.62 caliber rounds hung out the side of the weapon. With one eye closed and resting his cheek across his hand, the bulky Marine wrapped his index finger around the cool steel of the trigger.

The bells in Ashmore's brain housing group chimed as a small white car made an aggressive move toward the compound. The driver targeted the front gate, not noticing the Marine in the elevated post. The situation was new for Ashmore and he wished someone had been there to tell him what to do. Rounding the first turn of Concertina wire, the car picked up speed, cutting sharp around the serpentine barrier.

The sun laid low in the sky, blinding the driver, and concealing Ashmore from his view. In turn, its rays reflected off the front windshield of the car, causing Ashmore to squint. He shook his head, clearing his vision as the car moved into the second turn of the serpentine barrier. The excitement clouded his mind, and Ashmore forgot what his rules of engagement were. The 240G was locked, cocked and ready to rock. He lined the sights up with the front of the car.

What if the guy is coming for help?

Ashmore dismissed this notion. No one coming for help drove in this manner. The engine revved and the tires kicked up dirt as the car swung into the third turn. Ashmore worried, if he killed this guy, would his command have his back or throw him under the bus. Dealing with the ROE was a tricky thing, and he kicked himself for not paying better attention to the briefings.

The sinister man bared his teeth, allowing Ashmore to make up his mind as he brought the fully automatic weapon to life. The belt sucked through the left side of the weapon and empty brass and belt links shot out the right. Marines poured from buildings looking for a fight as the 7.62 rounds of the 240G impacted the dirt in front of the car. The bumper deflected two rounds, but Ashmore was quick to find his mark on the engine block.

"Die, motherfucker, die." Ashmore sang while applying pressure to the trigger. He didn't bother with the drill of six to eight round burst. At the speed which the car was moving, Ashmore knew this fight would be over quick for one or both of them. He held back the trigger and spat rounds at the car. The tendons in his neck stretched at the force of his unleashed war cry.

The driver swerved around another row of Concertina wire. Holes peppered the hood, white smoke puffed out, but the puncturing rounds in the windshield veered off to the passenger side. Ashmore walked the weapon back to the intended target. The man's glaring face appeared clear through the smoke, gritting his yellow teeth with a determination to kill the Marines in the compound.

His hands twisted the steering wheel as if revving the throttle of a motorcycle. He ignored the spiderweb cracks stretching out from the bullet holes in the windshield. The car straightened, pointing directly at the front gate a mere twenty meters away.

"Get some, motherfucker!" Ashmore yelled at the same moment the driver let out an aggressive shout. Three 7.62 rounds shattered the windshield into the face of the driver.

BANG. BANG. BANG.

Recoil, Recoil, Recoil,

The weapon system rocked back and forth, but Ashmore held on, placing the rounds into the man's chest. Gritting his teeth, he pushed down the buttstock, raising the muzzle, and opening holes in man's skull. The impact forced the driver from his seat, initiating an explosion underneath the vehicle.

Ashmore didn't have a chance to release the trigger under his own willpower. The force of the explosion ripped him from his weapon, sending him flying from the front post. The massive fireball caused the camp's personnel to duck for cover. The engine block landed in front of the shower trailer. Pieces of car shrapnel rocketed to the ground like a sadistic metallic rainfall. Windows on a nearby bus blew out, injuring the civilian occupants.

A portion of the rear bumper struck a man out on an afternoon stroll, killing him. As the fireball morphed into a black cloud of smoke,

Jack and Kyle hurried to Ashmore, who laid on the ground motionless. His helmet rolled across the dirt.

III

HM2 Skyler Greene had been in the country for three weeks and already missed home. *Be careful what you wish for*, she thought. Her mother wanted her to go to college, marry her rich fiancé, and have children. Skyler wanted those things, but not at that exact moment. She needed something for herself, something that would allot a certain credit to her life.

Although her mother had strict expectations of how her life was going to go, it was her dying grandmother who changed her fate. The ailing woman pleaded with Skyler to live her life despite what her domineering mother had planned. She didn't want her granddaughter to turn into a brainless zombie whose only passion was to shop and look pretty.

"You only get one shot, so you better live it up before it's all over. Believe me, life happens too fast. Before you know it, you're an old woman on your deathbed talking to your granddaughter." A week after her grandmother died, she entered a Navy recruitment office on her own accord. With her grandmother's dying words echoing in her mind, she signed the recruitment papers.

Her mother disapproved of Skyler's decision. Having raised her to be the ideal beauty of southern society, she gave Skyler no skillsets useful outside of modeling. At least, her father was supportive, and he even forced his wife to the graduation ceremony. Although it might have killed her, her mother admitted she was proud of her sailor daughter.

"Well, what are you going to do now?" Her mother asked at her graduation. Skyler beamed with excitement as she told them she had joined the medical field of the Navy.

"There will always be sick people needing help," she said. Never did she fathom that by joining the medical field, she'd end up in the heart of the Sunni triangle. A place riddled with vast fields of dirt and where the absences of trees disappointed her. She longed for the swaying of branches in the cool breeze on a hot southern day.

Her recruiter told her it would be nothing more than giving shots and handing out pills. The sight of her first mangled body was something she hadn't prepared her mind for. She vomited before fainting, and although the sight of blood and deformities still troubled her, she managed. In time, they lost their gruesome nature.

Her mother enjoyed writing to her about the things she was missing, while her father wrote letters of encouragement. Skyler couldn't put the war into words for them. Despite the pain they caused, she welcomed the familiarity from home. It was only the letters of her rich fiancé, Anthony Ambrose, which annoyed her.

She had every intention not to give him her address in Iraq. Without a doubt, Skyler knew it was her mother who informed him of her whereabouts to torture her more. Anthony was a kind and well-respected man in their community. Ladies drooled over him, and her mother adored everything about him. The problem was, he was a part of her old life and she was growing to love her new life of independence.

Skyler was lost in this thought when the explosion of the car shook her room. Her body jerked and tensed, but the fortification of her building reassured her peace of mind even as dust sprinkled down on her. She heard the screams coming from outside and knew she had to do her job. Skyler threw on her flak jacket and grabbed her MED bag while rushing out into the heat of the day, looking to help.

IV

A trickle of blood, no larger than a bead of sweat, seeped from a laceration above Ashmore's eyebrow. Kyle ripped open Ashmore's flak jacket, easing the weight off his chest, and allowing his lungs the room to expand. A gathering crowd circled, and Doc Sloan dropped his MED bag next to the downed Marine.

"Ash, wake up brother." Jack patted the side of Ashmore's face as Doc Sloan rummaged through his medical gear. The longer he went without locating what he needed, the more his hands would shake.

"Doc," Jack said, seizing the corpsman by the hand. Doc stopped, baffled at why the corporal would postpone treatment. "Calm the fuck down and get the smelling salts."

He took a breath, easing the tension in his body, and pictured where the smelling salt was in his bag. From the outer pouch, he pulled the small tube and after cracking it, waved it back and forth under Ashmore's nose. The Marine flinched, jerking his head away from the corpsman's hand. Doc Sloan continued to wave the tube under his nose until Ashmore slapped it away.

"Doc, if you put that shit up my nose one more time, I'll kick your ass." His head throbbed from where the blood seeped, and he had no recollection of exiting the post. The circle of faces staring down at him made Ashmore feel as if he was in his own grave. It gave him the creeps. "Is there something on my face or am I that sexy?"

A few of the Marines laughed.

"Then what the hell are you fuckers staring at?"

"Dude, you got blown out of the post, like twenty fuckin' feet." Jones proclaimed.

"No shit?"

"No shit."

"Yeah, regular fuckin' Peter Pan," Jack said, as he and Kyle helped him to his feet. His legs wobbled like a hard-fought boxer after several grueling slugfest rounds. He touched a hand to his temple and hissed at the pain. The post above them stood in shambles, the roof was missing, and the 240G laid destroyed on the ground, having taken a large piece of shrapnel that would have cut Ashmore in two. He tried to remember being thrown out, but like a skip in a film, there was a large void in his memory.

"What the hell happened?" Ashmore asked. Jack slapped a good-natured hand on his back. A puff of dust leapt from the Kevlar fibers and sent stinging vibrations into Ashmore's head. He winced.

"You earned your CAR motherfucker, that's what happened." Jack patted the bald Marine on the back again. Through the hurt, Ashmore's face glowed until he couldn't contain the excitement and had to laugh.

"Are you fucking serious?" The others nodded. He wanted to jump and cheer, but the ground felt unsteady beneath him. Ashmore looked back at the now ramshackle post and winced at the strain in his body. "First kill, and I don't even know what the hell happened. Fuck me."

He had dreamed about this moment as most Marines did. He envisioned the feeling, the squeeze of the trigger, and the reality of ending the life of his enemy. Now he would have to hear the story of his first kill from other people. Ashmore paused and thought about it for a moment. A rolling laugh came forth. It's one thing to tell your own story, it's another to have others do it.

"You're gonna be OK, Ash?" Jack asked.

"Yeah, Corporal. I'll be fine. Just a little dizzy."

"I'll clean this wound and he'll be back in a few." Jack and Kyle handed Ashmore off to Doc Sloan and proceeded to their room with the rest of the squad.

The Berserkers threw off their gear and returned to the activities that made their lives seem somewhat normal in Iraq. Several Marines amused themselves with various card games. A couple Marines pulled out pictures of their own Susie Jane Rottencrotchs' and wrote letters. They missed their girls and feared some Jody was waiting in the bushes for the moment to slip his way into her pretty pink panties with his devilish art of seduction and compassion.

Vinson plopped down on his rack and turned on a small CD player. Sutherland positioned himself on the opposite bed, pulling out a chess set and situated it on a box of water. The two shared a can of dip while studying the game laid out in front of them. Sutherland, only having taken up the dirty habit a couple weeks prior, had grown to love the sensation of nicotine running through his blood stream.

"You call home yet?" Vinson asked without looking up from the board. The game of chess occupied their minds as they scrutinized each move, helping to dull the sense of numbness and boredom that was everyday life in Iraq.

"Last time we went to Camp Fallujah." Sutherland tossed a thumb over his shoulder in the direction of the main camp located a mile away. He then moved a black pawn. "Got my parent's answering machine."

"Why didn't you call that fine little pink Susie you got a picture of?"

"Sophie? Oh, I'm sure she's banging Jody by now. Don't matter; we weren't that serious anyhow. I mean she's looking to get married—"

"Married?" Vinson interrupted. "That sounds pretty serious, bro."

"*She* wants marriage, but I ain't ready for any of that."

Vinson moved his white queen.

"Don't worry about it, when we get home, *all* the ladies gonna wanna jump us. A combat Marine in uniform is guaranteed to get you laid. I mean it; they see these combat ribbons, panties instantly wet."

"Yeah, that's if we get to see combat." Sutherland's chest rose and a hard sigh came out as he moved his king. Vinson nodded in agreement. He too hated the lack of conflict and worried if they would get to see any real resistance.

"Smile dickheads." Lance Corporal Thompson's voice came from the foot of their racks. Simultaneously, they looked up from their game and gave a one-finger salute to his camera. Thompson pushed his cowboy hat back on his head and frowned. "Fucking Grunts. Can't one person look at the camera without flipping it off?"

"And Sutherland, a man of the book." Thompson nodded to the Bible on Sutherland's rack. Sutherland glanced down at the book, touched it, then returned to his game. "I'd figured you'd have more respect."

Sutherland didn't look up this time to flip him off, to which Thompson rolled his eyes, grinning. He shadowed his camera, narrating every step, and documenting their lives. He zoomed in on a table between Jones and Simpson's racks. Jones and Black occupied one rack while Carlos and Kyle sat on the adjacent one.

"You know what I miss?" Carlos said, rearranging the cards in his hand. "The smell of my girlfriend after we have sex."

"Yeah, I miss the smell of your girlfriend after we have sex, too," Kyle said, slamming down a card on the table.

"Fuck you, Kyle."

"I prefer, fuck you, Corporal."

"Oh, my apologies."

"Who's winning?" Thompson tried to view the cards in each man's hand but failed to do so.

"Dig it, we are." Carlos motioned to himself and Lance Corporal Jones.

"Yeah, because you're some cheating ass sonsofbitches," Kyle said.

"Motherfucker. We ain't cheating." Carlos reached for his shotgun leaning against the rack. Before he could bring it up to his shoulder, Kyle's 9mm rested on his thigh, aiming in at Carlos's nuts.

"I beg to differ." Kyle's eyes motioned down to his pistol.

"Motherfuckin' Corporal got some balls." Carlos chuckled and returned the shotgun to its place against the rack. He eased his hands away from the weapon in a non-threatening manner. Kyle smirked, nodding his head in agreement, and holstered his sidearm. Thompson leaned in closer to see Jones's hand, and Jones flinched away.

"Damn it, Thompson. Get that fuckin' camera out of my face."

"Jones, another man of the good book, over here cussing and shit." Thompson shook his head. "Sad. What would the good Lord think of that?"

Kyle smirked and laid down his cards before saying, "Motherfucker, like God cares about your soulless ass, you ginger cowboy, shit-kicking motherfucker."

"Fuck you, my hair's cherry blond."

"Cherry blond. Motherfucker, you're a fire crotch. Don't lie."

"Damn," Jones said, causing the four players to share a hearty laugh.

"Fuck you, Black. What the fuck are you laughing at?" Thompson asked. Black shrugged, to which Thompson replied, "I'll kick your fuckin' ass."

"Just don't touch me. I don't want to get *ginger*-vitis." Kyle locked eyes with Carlos, and the two seized at the hysterical stitch in their sides. Thompson let slip a snort, admitting the new guy got a good one over on him.

"Fuckin' new guy got some jokes. Good to go——" Before Thompson could finish, Simpson's deep bass voice echoed through the room, interrupting him.

"No, you can't." Simpson shouted at Jenson. They stood near a pile of water bottle boxes at the back of the room, pointing at one another.

"Yes, you can. That's stupid." Jenson shrugged off Simpson. Simpson turned to the rest of the room which by now was staring at the two.

"Jones, Carlos, come tell this motherfucker the reason it's called the impossible sit-up is that you can't do it." Simpson half snarled at Jenson, looking at the boot as if he was an idiot, and jabbed a finger in Jenson's chest. "It can't be done, boot."

Jenson batted Simpson's hand away and shook his head as the room crowded near. He rolled his eyes, fed-up with his life in the Corps. These men weren't the intelligent warfighters he had hoped to be serving with. Instead, they were overgrown man-children with too much testosterone and guns.

"Yes, you can, you dumb ape," Jenson said.

"Who you calling an ape?" Simpson towered over the smaller man with a beam of hatred burning from his eyes, but Jenson didn't back down. The room hissed and cackled.

"You're telling me I can't do a sit-up with my eyes closed. That's absurd."

"I don't know what absurd means, but you're fucking retarded," Simpson said. A few of the Marines chimed in, trying to convince Jenson that Simpson was telling the truth. Jenson waved them off, calling them a collective name for ignorant people.

"Then fine." Simpson had cast the bait, and now he was ready to set the hook. A slight grin appeared on his face, and he leaned in close to the boot. "Lay on your back and try to do one. Just one with your eyes blindfolded. I'm telling you, you won't be able to do it."

"Fine, if this will shut you up, I'll do it. I'll do an impossible sit-up." The pressure of anticipation reached a near boiling point for the gathering crowd. They fidgeted as the energy pulsated through them. Teeth held lips shut in order to refrain themselves from making any noise.

"What's the impossible sit-up?" Sutherland asked Vinson.

"Just watch." Vinson pointed at Jenson as he lowered himself to the dirty wooden floorboards of the tent.

"Impossible sit-up," Jenson snickered. "Give me a break."

He placed his hands behind his head and readied himself for the challenge. Jones kneeled, and Jenson launched a finger in his direction.

"Don't try nothing, Jones."

"I ain't, man. I'm only gonna cover your eyes so you can't cheat. I don't want you saying you did a sit-up which we all know you can't do." Jenson resumed the position and Jones placed an OD green shirt over his closed eyes. A few Marines waved a hand in front of Jenson's face to ensure he couldn't see.

"OK, don't cheat. Keep your eyes closed and on the count of three, let's see you try to do the impossible sit-up," Jones said. Jenson couldn't wait to show them how stupid they were.

"One." The count electrified the room. PFC Black giggled, and cupped his hand over his mouth to stifle it; he looked alarmed at his fellow Marines. Vinson punched him in the arm, giving him the hateful eye to shut up.

"Two," Jones barked. Jenson adjusted his shoulders and hips, ready to prove Simpson and the rest of the Marines wrong. Jones bit his lower lip and turned his head away, trying to choke off the giggles. The eyes of the Marines widened.

"THREE!" Jones shouted, and all the standing Marines gasped. Jenson threw himself upwards with all the strength in his abdominal muscles. His upper body propelled to a forty-five-degree angle without any means of stopping. As he neared the seventy-degree angle, he kept his eyes closed tight while the shirt slid free. His face stretched out in front of the rest of his body; head tilted upwards.

At the thought of his success, a smirk graced Jenson's face, and there wasn't a moment of doubt that crept into his mind. *Impossible sit-up, what a joke.* He rose, with fear fading, and prematurely rejoiced at the thought of proving that these Marines were of lesser intelligence than he. Then, without warning, he met resistance from something large, soft, and foul smelling. His nose buried deeper, his eyelids parted, and Jenson saw only darkness.

Light reflected off the object, and Jenson realized it wasn't darkness he stared into, but Simpson's large naked ass. Simpson sneered, tightened his abdominal muscles, and released a grotesque fart. The warm air surrounded Jenson's nose, assaulted his skin and eyes, and he screamed. Hysteria erupted throughout the room as Jenson shoved Simpson forward. Toppling over his trousers, Simpson fell hard to his knees before rolling over to his back. The wooden planks that made up the floorboard strained under his weight but held. Pains of laughter attacked his sides, and Simpson didn't care about his pants as he tried to draw in a breath.

Jenson scrambled to his feet, slapping at his face, trying to rid it of the pungent stench which plagued it.

"Fuck you, man. Fuck all of you." He rushed to his rack to douse his face with a large bottle of water. His fellow Marines collapsed, cackling. Jenson stomped out the door toward the shower trailer with soap in hand.

"Somebody should tell him he forgot his rifle." Simpson managed to say, gasping for air. Jack nudged Kyle, holding up a bottle of mouthwash. Inside the container, brown liquid sloshed about, and Kyle knew it wasn't mouthwash. With everyone occupied in their humor, Jack and Kyle slithered to their corner for two plastic cups and a can of cola written in Arabic.

"To the zero hour." Jack held up his plastic cup with a shot of whiskey in it. Kyle touched the brim of his cup to Jack's.

"And may the Devil meet you there," Kyle added. They drank and Jack tapped two fingers to his lip, motioning for a cigarette. Kyle looked back at the men as he slipped into his green rifle sling. They were still laughing and retelling the impossible sit-up story. "God, I love this."

The derange humor of the Marines was intoxicating and Jack had to agree with Kyle.

"You know you're going to miss this when you get out."

"Yeah, maybe." Taking the bottle of whiskey and the sodas, Jack headed for the door as Doc Sloan popped his head into their tent. Jack tried to squeeze around Doc, but Doc prevented the two from exiting.

"Hang on, Gents. I need to speak with the squad," Doc said, and Jack called them in. The Marines gathered, staring at Doc who wasn't accustomed to their undivided attention. He felt naked in front of a crowd, and for a moment his throat tightened up. He cleared it, but the nervous feeling didn't subside. His knees shook under his trousers and a childhood fear of standing before a class returned. Eyes pierced into him, judging him, and twisting his stomach into knots. He froze and felt nauseous until Jack nudged him back to reality.

"Um, I came here to give you guys something," Doc said.

"If it's herpes, don't worry, Simpson already has it." Jones shouted from the back of the huddle, bringing the room back to humor. Simpson stuck up his middle finger to Jones while simultaneously blowing him a kiss.

"Got it from your mom." The crowd went crazy with side-splitting laughter once again.

"No, it's not that." Doc Sloan continued, unamused by their childish behavior. He pulled a box of tampons out of his bag and the laughter died at once. The Marines stared with blank expressions as he placed two in their palms.

"Sorry Doc, I'm late for my period, so I don't think I need these anymore. Try me again in like seven months," Jack said.

"I'm not giving you these for menstruation. I want everyone to put these in their I-FAK to keep." A few grabbed their individual first aid kits from their flak, but the majority hesitated.

"What the fuck for, Doc?" Carlos asked.

"Because if you get shot, the hole is about the size of a dime." Doc enclosed his thumb and index finger until a small opening remained. He held the sanitary product high for all to see. "This will stop the bleeding. It may save your life."

"Check it, Doc." Jack slammed the two tampons into the corpsman's palm. "I get shot, bandage me the old way. Save this new shit for these younger Marines. Roger that?"

Doc didn't respond as Jack walk out of the tent, the makeshift wooden door slamming closed behind him. Doc looked to Kyle but only received a shrugged shoulder. Kyle followed Jack out into the fading sun that casted an orange and purple glow in the sky. Shadows gripped the elongated clouds and the heat of the day gave way to a pleasant chill.

Two small wooden benches sat across from one another with an ammo can between them. Cigarette butts poured out of the can and littered the ground. Jack fired two up, passing one to Kyle, and the two resided to a comfortable spot on the benches.

"Pals," Kyle said, and the two tipped their cups toward each other.

"Pals," Jack repeated. They drank. They smoked. When Kyle went to speak, a faint noise broke through the night, interrupting him. The whistling grew louder, bringing their eyes to the sky. The dryness of Jack's lips refused to release the cigarette butt. It hung from his gaping mouth as he identified the noise. Kyle was running by the time Jack shouted, "INCOMING!"

* * *

Letter to Jack Campbell from Jennifer Campbell,

Dated August 20th, 2004 -

Dear Loving Husband,

I hope this letter finds you safe and sound. I'm sure it would please you to know that the baby and myself are doing great. He keeps kicking me and my stomach's getting larger. I feel fat. In case you missed it, surprise, surprise, it's not a girl, but a boy. I wish you were here to experience this with me. Next time, I guess.

I'm proud of you, and I miss you a lot. How's everything going over there? What's it like this time around compared to the last time? How are the men holding up?

I hope your deployment is boring and you count the days until you can be home again in my arms. Your parents come by every day. Your mother brings me more food than the baby or I can eat, but she's so sweet about it. Your father is unlike his normal self.

You should see him. I've never seen him act this way before. He's such the grandfather type now. He came by the other day to install safety devices all over the house.

I feel like they think I can't do anything. I'm not that large yet. I can still do stuff, but your mother comes over and insists on doing the dishes and other things around the house. It's funny. Things are going well here. I can't wait to hear from you. Hurry and write me.

I ran into an old friend of ours the other day, Steve Tomes. I was shopping for groceries, and he saw me. He looked happy, and he's back from college. He was surprised that you were off at war. It's nice to see someone from the old days. What happened to all our friends? I swear we used to have a lot of friends.

Anyways, I love you and miss you so much, Jack Campbell, my big bad Marine. I'm enclosing some photos for you. No, I won't send those photos, these are of the baby. Enjoy and come home safe to me. I love you more than anything else in life and miss you so much. Take care. Many hugs and kisses.

Your Adoring Wife,

Jennifer

V

A high pitch whistle sailed through the sky as incoming rockets broke the sound barrier a few seconds before slamming into the far side of the compound. Kyle and Jack flung their drinks and rushed for a hardened structure. The earth jolted, and the concussion of the blast forced them to the ground. They covered their heads while hot pieces of shrapnel showered the area. With their faces buried in their arms, they waited with clenched teeth for what was to come.

There came a nip at the back of Jack's thigh. An electrical pulse screamed through him and escaped his mouth in the form of profanities. He found a small tear in the back of his service trousers and hot, sticky blood drenched the material.

"You hit, man? You need a tampon?" Kyle laughed in Jack's face.

"Fuck you, Kyle." Another rocket struck a generator and illuminated the delight in Kyle's eyes. Kyle's own humor ended abruptly as a piece of shrapnel dug into the side of his right shoulder. He winced and reared back, before dropping flat to the dirt. The metal burned into his flesh and he found it hard to breathe from the pain. Cackling laughter penetrated Kyle's ears, and he looked up to see Jack's smiling face.

"Oh, you need a tampon, bitch?"

"Fuck you, Jack." Kyle, grasping the side of his shoulder, flipped the bird in Jack's direction. Marines and Corpsmen scrambled to help the wounded.

"Fuck, this shit burns." Kyle moaned with blood soaking his shirt and staining his hands. The ringing in their ears made knots in their stomachs.

"Are you two hurt?" The voice was soft and gentle as a mother's touch. Kyle reared his head around, and the beauty of the female corpsman took his breath away. Her gorgeous brown eyes were enhanced by the non-military issued glasses and tossing aside her awkward helmet, freed long flowing strands of blonde hair. A breeze picked up, tussling and tossing her hair, captivating Kyle with a halo that adorned her head. He noticed the absence of makeup and thought her beauty was as natural as spring water.

While leaning forward to pull gauze from her MED bag, her flak jacket opened, and Kyle couldn't avert his eyes from looking down her loose shirt.

"Yeah, I got hit in the leg, but my friend here—" Jack slapped Kyle on the uninjured shoulder. "Well, he got hit in the penis."

With great alarm, her attention shot to Kyle, but before she could grope at his pants, he brushed her hand away.

"He's fucking lying, Doc. I'm fine. It's in the shoulder, but it's only a flesh wound." The last five words came out with a British accent.

"Monty Pythons." Jack chuckled. The Corpsman paid no attention to their joke.

"I'm HM2 Greene, let me have a look at those wounds," she said as she removed Jack's hand to access his injury. Blood trickled out of a small jagged gash under his butt cheek.

"It doesn't look like anything's embedded. Looks like it's only a laceration."

Skyler wiped away the blood and secured a piece of gauze to the wound with two pieces of medical tape.

"Hold pressure there and it should be good," she said. She then leaned over Kyle, who took in her pleasant smell. Skyler didn't notice the ecstasy on his face as she glanced into his wound. "I can see a piece of shrapnel in there, but I can't get it here. We have to go back to my room."

"Your room?" Kyle's voice squeaked, amusing Jack.

"Yeah, my room."

"Well, we just met, Doc, and you're already inviting me back to your quarters. I'm flattered." Kyle flashed her a smile and she giggled nervously.

"It doubles as the med room and it's not that great." Skyler took a handful of gauze and placed it firmly on Kyle's wound. He hissed, and she flinched. "Sorry. Hold this here."

Helping both Marines up, she passed by Kyle, and he took another deep whiff of her fragrance. It pleased him to learn that she indeed smelt wonderful, and it wasn't his imagination. Iraq smells like shit and a building full of men reeked like a hot locker room. Her scent was a small comfort in an uncomfortable world. He wasn't sure what she had on, but it enticed his senses, making him yearn for her. He would follow her to the end of the world, but she only had him follow her thirty feet.

She tossed the brown MED bag on her rack at the back of the room. Kyle scanned his surroundings, coming to the conclusion that the Navy had it better than the Marines. She motioned for him to sit on the small operating table in the center of the room.

"Nice digs," he said.

"Sure. If I would've known I'd have a guy over, I would've cleaned up."

Kyle spotted the male hygiene products littered on several racks. Her lone cot in the back was the only one with a sense of order to it. "You bunk with guys?"

"Unfortunately, yes. You wanna take off your shirt?" Kyle slung off his ruined shirt, and for the moment it covered his head, Skyler marveled at his muscular body. The contour lines of intersecting muscles made her knees weak. She had seen plenty of military men without their shirts on. Like most, Kyle was skinny, but unlike most, he kept himself in near bodybuilder shape. Her eyes read across the small scars dotting his chest and wondered what they were from.

Before he freed himself from his bloody clothing completely, she struggled to keep her facial expression neutral. Under the large medical lamp, she examined his wound. "Not much room for women to bunk out here. Shit, not many women out here to bunk with."

"How's that going for you?" He asked.

"Sharing a room with guys? It sucks." She touched the metal tweezers to the wound on his deltoid muscle, and Kyle hissed. Skyler winced along with him, feeling bad about causing him pain. "Sorry, almost got it. Yeah, sharing a room with men stinks."

"I understand that. I miss having a place of my own, too."

"No, I mean it actually stinks. They have the worst body odors and are always passing gas. It's gross in here." With a quick sleight of hand, she plucked the small metal from his flesh and quickly applied direct pressure with a stack of small gauze. The pain eclipsed his laughter. Blood saturated the small strip of sterilized material, and she had to apply more in hopes of controlling the bleeding. "You'll get the purple heart for this."

"Won't be my first." Controlling most of the bleeding, she secured a small bandage on his injury.

"Sorry to hear that. How did you get one already?"

He motioned to the dots on his chest and shrugged.

"Back in '03. Got hit by shrapnel and shot in the leg. Ended up in a bad place. You know the kind of place with bad people, and where you do bad things. The kind you get medals for." She removed her glasses and threw the surgical trash into the wastebasket. From a small fridge, she handed Kyle a bottle of water and opened one for herself before sliding the rolling stool back in front of him. "You've been over before?"

"No, this is my first tour," she said.

"How do you like it so far?" He took a drink and sighed. The chilled water sent a refreshing, cooling sensation down his spine.

"I don't." She confessed with solemn eyes dropping to the bottle in her hands. Skyler hadn't told anyone how she felt about being in Iraq, but for some reason, it came out with this Marine. She looked up with a half-hearted smile as if trying to tell him not to worry. "I thought I would. It's amazing to see this stuff, but it would be nice if the war wasn't going on. All these mortars and rockets and that explosion at the gate earlier, it's unsettling to me. I guess I'm starting to miss home more than I thought I would."

Her southern accent amazed Kyle and he wished she would speak forever.

"I understand. Where's home at?"

"Louisiana. You?"

"California. I didn't catch your name?"

"Oh, I'm HM2 Greene."

"No, your first name." One corner of his mouth curled up and she felt embarrassed to look into his eyes.

"Skyler," she said. Kyle stood up from the table and extended his hand.

"Well Skyler, I'm Corporal Dillon, but you can call me, Kyle." The two shook hands. "I've gotta get going, but do you drink?"

He picked up his blood-soaked shirt, examined it, and concluded it was beyond saving. As if reading his mind, Skyler pointed to the trash bin next to the table, and he tossed the shirt in.

"Alcohol?"

"Yeah."

"Sure, but I thought it was illegal in this country." Her answer caused him to crack up.

"I'm a Marine. If I don't break the rules, I'm not living up to my title. The next time you're off, come by my room, and we'll have us a drink." Kyle pulled a pack of cigarettes out of his front pocket and tossed one into his mouth, never losing his grin.

"All right, maybe I will." She couldn't deny his handsomeness or the physical attraction between them.

"Maybe you will." Kyle backed out of the room, refusing to take his eyes off her. He disappeared into the cool night of Iraq without saying farewell. Skyler found herself blushing at the image of the shirtless Marine who had been in her room. Erupting in goosebumps, she envisioned running her hands over his chest and feeling his lips upon her neck.

She didn't know what caused these thoughts. Perhaps it was the fact she'd been away from a man's touch for some time. She didn't care for any of the men she was serving with, but she wasn't serving with Kyle. Somehow, he was different. She didn't know how, but he was.

"Dreaming of me, Doc?" Skyler's joy vanished. Her shoulders slumped at the smirking face of Corporal James Harvey. It wasn't that she hated Harvey, but she couldn't tolerate the sight of him either. His head was long and skinny, and his glasses were too large for his face. His voice not only startled her but caused her skin to crawl. She hated his constant attention. He was annoying and it irritated her that he interrupted her fantasy about Kyle.

Harvey leaned against the wall, crossed his arms over his chest, and pushed his glasses farther up the bridge of his nose. In his mind, the sight of him after an attack was thrilling to her.

"Not really. What can I help you with?" Skyler asked, shuffling papers, trying to look busy so he wouldn't stay long.

"Just came by to check on you."

"I'm good."

"Yeah." He continued, not hearing her response. "I was in the C.O.'s office, doing my work with the officers when the rockets came in. I didn't pay it no mind. I mean, the C.O.'s office is heavily sandbagged, not like the rooms of those stupid grunts."

Most of him repulsed her, but it was his laughter that came out in large puffs of air which irritated her the most. She couldn't tell if he was gasping for oxygen or humoring himself. Skyler buried her head in her paperwork.

"You know, if there's ever anything you need, you can come to me, and I'll get it for you. I got that kind of pull around here." His bragging brought bile to the back of her throat, and although she wanted to gag, she withheld the urge.

"No, I'm good, but I have a lot of work to do."

"I understand that. I love working too. I guess I'll see you around." He snapped his fingers, pointed at her, and gave her a wink as if he was the Fonz. Harvey strutted out of the room like God's gift and Skyler shivered as she rolled her eyes. The thought of him in her room was near violating, and she had the overwhelming need to shower.

Corporal Kyle Dillon

Purple Heart Recipient

For Wounds Received on September 4th, 2004

Al-Karma, Iraq, Al-Anbar Province

Corporal Jack Franklin Campbell

Purple Heart Recipient

For Wounds Received on September 4th, 2004

Al-Karma, Iraq, Al-Anbar Province

* * *

From the pages of Jack Campbell's Journal-

Steve Tomes, that scum-sucking Jody motherfucker. Steve's tried to get with Jennifer since high school, and I guess he now has his chance with me out here. Motherfucker! When I get home, I'm going to pop out his eyeballs and skull fuck him. Why would Jennifer write me about this?

She knows I don't like the guy. Did she do this to fuck with me? Is she cheating on me? I can't take this shit. Next phone call, I'm gonna tell her to stay away from that prick. It's been slow over here, and God knows I don't need this stuff on my mind. This place is a shit hole.

It's kind of strange to see how much the war has changed since '03. A lot of the civilians are friendly, but you still have to watch your back around them. You never know where the insurgents are waiting to ambush you. Every day we're hit by rockets or mortars and somehow, always at 0700 and 1500.

Strange the Iraqi National Guard are never on base at these times. Fuck 'em. We do patrols throughout the city, but there isn't any real action going on. These men are itching for a fight. Luckily, their morale is high, and they haven't beaten the shit out of one another… yet. It's hard to stay motivated in this place when all I want to do is go home to my wife.

Iraq still smells like shit. It's dirty and hot, and there's trash all over the place. Everything's a fucking bomb out here. This time around, it's hard to tell who the enemy is. They're not military combatants, but dress like normal civilians. Is this how dad felt in Vietnam?

We accidentally burnt a man's car the other day. Fuck it. He shouldn't have left his car like that. The trunk and hood were both wide open, which according to our ROE, is a VBIED. Fuck him. Instead of risking the lives of our Marines, Gunnery Sergeant Wolf had us frag it with incendiary grenades. About five of us threw AN-M14 Incendiary Grenades into the windows of the car. These grenades burn at about five thousand degrees or some shit. We stood back and watched the whole thing burn to the ground.

About a quarter of a mile down the road, a man came running up to us with a gas can in his hand. In Arabic, we yelled for him to stop or we would shoot him. Sutherland, one of the new guys who's fluent in the language in these parts, walked up to the screaming man. He said that last week Americans burned his house down and all he had left was in his car. I guess we made an enemy this day.

The mortars and rockets won't stop. We've already sent a few guys to Germany for injuries. It sucks, I try not to think about home, but I still wonder what Jennifer might be doing. She sends me letters and I try to respond, but with what? What can I tell her about this place that will make her feel any better?

I learned my first deployment the more you think about home, the worse it gets for you here. I still can't help thinking about my wife and unborn child. Unborn child. My unborn son. It's dark here now, and it seems like everyone is asleep. The nighttime is the loneliest time in Iraq. It's a time when all is silent, and you're left with nothing but your thoughts.

I could be at home in bed with my wife, where I'm sure Steve 'Cock Sucking Jody' Tomes is at right now. Fuck no, though. I'm stuck here, listening to these motherfuckers snoring and farting. Fuck Iraq, fuck Steve Tomes and fuck my life.

CHAPTER FOUR

HELLSEEKERS

-The biggest regret I have is that my enemy has only one life to give for
his country-

I

Camp Abu-Ghraib – East of Camp Fallujah, Iraq

October 3rd, 2004-

Jack hit the concrete floor with a thud, and upon looking around, a
haze of confusion assaulted him. The dream, which was receding fast
from his mind, left the warm impression of snuggling his wife. Two
twin bunk beds, bordering the side of the small dorm-like room,
replaced the king size bed of his dream. In the center of the room was
a man-made table and he used it to push himself up to his knees. An
incessant ringing in his ears gave way only to the tickling sounds of
popping.

The noise bounced around him, mimicking the eruptions of kernels
in a microwave. Everything felt foreign and out of place and this
hindered his mind's return to reality. He shook his head, trying to rid it
of its dream-like state, as the world rushed back to him. Iraq was a
reality; home was the dream.

Jack allowed a relaxing breath to calm his body while pulling himself
up to sit on the edge of his bed. The urge for a cigarette hit him hard,
and Jack laughed at the thought he was back home instead of in Iraq.

How could one mistake this place for home? The bed wasn't as comfortable, the walls were a dreary tan color, and no one had popcorn to pop.

Jack's breathing ceased. The popping wasn't popcorn in a microwave, but something far more real and aggressive. Gunshots coming from somewhere outside washed away all remnants of sleep. On unsteady legs, he hustled out into the narrow hall. Their building had been recently acquired and it held more protection than the tent they had lived in. Men rushed in both directions of the hallway, heading for one of the two exits like students late for class. One man ran against the flow of other Marines and headed straight toward Jack.

"Jack, get your shit." Kyle shoved several men out of his way.

"What's going on?" Jack braced against the door frame to keep from falling and fought against the repulsing feeling of seasickness. Kyle ushered past him and headed for his combat gear. Weary of his swaying, Jack struggled to gather his own. The two men tossed their arms through their flak jackets as if the vest no longer weighed several pounds.

"We just got hit hard, man. VBIED and we're taking small arms fire. The goddamn Haj is attacking." The term VBIED registered with Jack: Vehicle Born Improvised Explosive Device. He didn't need Kyle to elaborate any further. His military tactic mind started putting pieces together.

The VBIED would create chaos upon the initial attack. It would hope to clear out the Marines at the front for the advancing foot soldiers. With a large enough gap, they would storm the compound like the Viet Cong during the Tet Offensive in '68. The fuzzy hum of his dream still fogged Jack's mind, and he shook his head harder to loosen it. While locking a magazine into his M16, he followed Kyle out.

The blinding sun slapped Jack in the face and the heat nipped at his skin. Sweat seeped from his pores instantly, but he paid it no attention. He oriented to the gunfire coming from the only entrance at the northside of camp. Jack and Kyle ran past Marines who were scrambling to find a place to fight. Marines positioned themselves on Humvees, sand filled Hesco barriers, large storage crates, and berms. Three Marines even took the bold risk of standing on the C.O.'s white truck, an action that would later earn them a place on a detailed working party.

The front guard shack stood mangled with twisted, burning metal and crumbling cement walls. The exploding vehicle created a vicious fire which snapped like a venomous snake. Despite the risk of personal injury, four Marines pulled two burned bodies from the destruction. Black smoke rolled into the sky as the pungent toxins of burning metal and bodies filled the area with hazardous fumes. Two large dirt mounds leaned against the inside of the surrounding concrete wall. On top, Marines returned fire from the prone position at the approaching insurgents.

In three strides, Jack and Kyle soared up one mound, flipping their weapons off safe, and plopping into the dirt. The sun burned Jack's eyes as he squinted through hawk-like vision for the enemy, wishing he had grabbed his Oakley ballistic sunglasses to aid with his light sensitivity. Scanning the battlefield, his front sight post aligned to an enemy combatant's head.

BANG. Recoil. Headshot.

His first shot of the deployment, but he didn't pause to celebrate. The round created a hole in the center of the insurgent's head and carried the man's brains out the back. Before the man hit the ground, Jack's barrel drifted to another. Rounds sailed back at Jack and Kyle's position, but this didn't bother them.

"I can't believe they're trying to overrun us." Jack fired his magazine dry, then laid his head low in the dirt to reload.

BANG. Recoil. Chest wound.

BANG. Recoil. Shoulder shot.

"I know." Kyle drilled two rounds into an enemy insurgent. The tall insurgent tumbled to the ground as he fired off several rounds from his AK-47. "I don't know if I'm ready for this crazy ass shit."

Three insurgents tossed pineapple grenades at the wall. Two hit the barrier and exploded without harming a soul. The third grenade managed to roll right in front of Kyle. He pushed at it and in the process, kicked up a cloud of dust, which blinded his vision of the small metal ball.

Kyle prayed it went over the edge of the wall and when it exploded, he sighed a breath of relief.

"What was that?" Jack asked. He had been reloading his rifle and failed to see what Kyle had done.

"Nothing really."

The enemy bound for cover behind bushes and trees, spraying 7.62 rounds as they ran toward the FOB. Bullet holes dotted the cement walls, and an RPG screamed over their heads. Jack and Kyle buried their faces in the sand as it whistled above. The agonizing explosion erupted behind them, sending dirt and rocks up as bullets continued to scatter in a synchronized chaos. The shockwave from the RPG hammered an invisible force at the Marines, zapping their energy. Another explosion ejected a Marine from a berm. Three nearby blue porta-shitters toppled over, releasing their blue contents on the ground.

"Come get some, motherfuckers." A young Marine, one neither Jack nor Kyle knew, stood atop the adjacent dirt mound. He screamed at the enemy while firing his rifle from the hip. "Yeah, fuck you…"

He pulled the trigger, waving his rifle around without aiming. The surrounding few cheered as if he was a super soldier taking on the entire enemy force single-handedly. Jack nudged Kyle and pointed.

"What the fuck is he doing?"

"I guess he thinks he's a Berserker," Kyle said.

"Bull fuckin' shit, he is."

"… Fuck you…" The Marine knocked off his Kevlar helmet and continued to pull the trigger on his M16. He squeezed off round after round as an insane laughter bellowed from deep within him. "… And fuck you too."

"Get the fuck down, you stup—" Jack shouted at the young Marine. He never finished his sentence as the young Marine's head snapped back. Sunlight glimmered through the cloud of crimson mist. His body buckled and rolled down the berm like a puppet cut from his controlling strings. There were shouts for corpsmen, but the kid was smoked.

"Stupid bastard." Jack slammed a fresh magazine into his rifle and popped three rounds off.

"How's it hanging, boys?" Skyler startled Kyle, settling down in the dirt next to him. Sensing the dismay her presence caused him, Skyler hurried to look away. He eased up the berm to shield her from any incoming rounds.

"Short, shriveled and to the left, Doc. Thanks for asking," Jack said. Kyle wasn't humored by Jack's comment. He feared for her well-being and here his friend was making wisecracks.

"So, an improvement. Changing sides?" Her humor wasn't only surprising, it was a welcoming pleasure to have a member of the opposite sex cracking jokes. Two rounds struck the dirt in front of them.

"We're fine, Doc," Kyle said. She detected the irritation in his voice and felt ashamed for being there.

"Yeah, Doc. We're discussing the politics of the Louisiana Purchase. Anything you care to add?" Jack asked before firing again. Kyle's teeth clenched, and he fired off three rounds in anger. None found their mark. Kyle wanted to pull her to the ground and keep her there until the fighting stopped. He couldn't imagine what it would be like if she caught a bullet to the grape or got dismembered by an RPG. Kyle hurried to fire at the enemy as if he alone would drive them into a full-scale retreat if only to protect her.

Another round kicked up the dirt in front of them, spraying them with rocks and sand. Kyle pulled her in close. "Keep your head down."

The dust settled, and she looked up to find the fury in his eyes staring back down at her.

"Stay down!" He pushed her under him again when she tried to get up.

"I have to go check on some other guys." As the words left her, a round impacted the concrete bricks which made up the wall directly in front of them. Jack shook the dirt off his helmet and scrambled to one knee. He fired an entire magazine as fast as his trigger finger would allow.

"We'll give you some cover, but keep your head down," Kyle said. His voice didn't hold the same fury as his eyes did, but behind his words, he breathed real compassion. There had been other men or boys who had told her how they would protect her from danger, but Kyle was the first to show it. Her lips felt full and ached to kiss him.

"What, you worried about me?" Her seductive grin cut the tension in the air.

"Go." He motioned, and they locked eyes for a moment longer. Every fiber in his body yearned to reach out for her. As Jack sprung up to throw lead down range at the enemy insurgents, Skyler turned to roll down the hill. Kyle grabbed her flak jacket, spinning her around, and the tension swelled with her chest. She couldn't release her breath as Kyle pulled her in close, and pressed his lips firmly against hers.

Their pulses synced with one another, not out of love, but out of pure passion. Despite what he had told Jack, they had never kissed before. He didn't want to die without feeling her on his lips. Then the ecstasy quickly faded into fear. *What if she pulls away mad?* Kyle thought.

That nervous, hollow pit opened in his chest and he feared he had made a mistake. *Perhaps I'm moving too fast for her or what if she only thinks of me as a friend?* He thought all these things but stopped as her lips pressed back against his. She wanted this as much as he did. The firefight faded as Kyle and Skyler drifted away together. She melted into him, surprised their first kiss was happening as rounds flew by. *How many of those beauty-queen college girls could say that back home?*

Then it was over.

"Go," Kyle shouted, causing her to flinch and run while the staccato of his cover fire echoed behind her. He fired a few shots to cover her until she was safely away from the mound. His eyes drifted to her as she approached a wounded Marine.

A loud bang echoed in Kyle's ears, his vision tilted, and his head jolted to the side. His body stiffened as a chill passed through his spinal cord. Kyle reeled around, expecting to have been shot, but feeling not the burn that came with it. Jack's fiery eyes glared at him.

"Get your fucking head in the game." Jack's voice no longer carried the lighthearted tone he had with Skyler. His slap broke the trance she held on his best friend. Kyle racked a fresh round into the chamber and advanced to one knee. A high whistle and a hard pop hit the base, followed by another, and then another. "Fuckin' mortars."

"Yeah, two o'clock." Jack looked in the direction Kyle said and spotted something he had never seen before. Mounted in the back of a small white truck was a mortar tube, and a man stood behind it, lobbing mortar shells while the truck was moving. Jack stood, hunched forward, and took sharp aim. He fired one shot.

BANG. Recoil. Chest shot.

The man in the back of the truck flew out as the vehicle sped away. Kyle nodded to Jack and said, "Hell of a shot, brother."

"Thanks," Jack replied, firing at two more insurgents hiding behind some desert shrubbery. The firing continued at the compound, but the enemy was making a hasty retreat. Three white, single cab trucks parked on the main road, providing cover fire for the insurgents.

Kyle's sights fell on one tall man. He drew in a single breath, resting his index finger on the trigger. The tall man in a red and white checkered headdress retreated to the trucks as if unconcerned by the firefight. His comrades ran in full sprint, but the arrogance of the tall man only permitted him to stroll. It was this action which caught Kyle's attention. Fear couldn't bring the egotistical insurgent to look back, for he knew Allah would protect him against the invading infidels.

Kyle's breath rolled out, relaxing his body as he eyed the black combat boots under the long tan man-dress. The insurgent hoisted his rifle over his head with both hands and shouted, "Allah Akbar."

He shook the rifle in the air, allowing Kyle to notice he lacked the pinky and ring fingers on both hands, leaving him with only six in total. Kyle steadied his rifle, aligning the front sight post between the six-fingered man's shoulders. Kyle wanted to sever his spine and make him suffer. The posture and appearance of the six-fingered man angered Kyle, and he didn't want the man to die right away. His finger increased the pressure on the trigger, and he waited for the hammer to fall.

II

Ashmore and Black stood post at the rear of the camp. Roman 6, located at the southeast corner near the trash dump, was away from the action at the front. With no cloud protection, the makeshift tin roof blistered under the sun. Ashmore spat over the side, watching his saliva drop ten feet to the gravel covered ground. He wiped the sweat from his brow. The firefight at the north gate gripped him, and he clawed at his skin, yearning to be there.

Anxiety-ridden, his nails dug at the wooden railing, while he prayed for a chance to fight. Ashmore tugged at his flak jacket's collar. It choked him and he felt like a hungry bulldog attached to a chain. He wanted his restraints cut loose, to prove he was a great Marine. He wanted glory, he wanted blood, and he wanted to kill.

Black grew annoyed with his comrade. Standing behind the 240G, he eyed the vast desert before them, while ignoring the action to his rear.

"Are you fucking kidding me?" Ashmore tore at the support beam holding up the tin roof. He shook it, wanting to break it free, and throw it at the enemy. "Come on, come back here. I want some, too. Ah, damn it!"

He punched the two by four of the makeshift threshold. The tin roof rattled but held firm. Ashmore yanked at his now constricting uniform, which suffocated him like a straitjacket. His equipment grew heavy on his shoulders, and the only thing he wanted to do was rip everything off. He kicked at a box of MRE's and tossed his weapon into the corner of the shack.

The SAW dropped with a heavy thud, startling Black. He grabbed the wooden table in fear of the floor falling out from under him. Ashmore bit down on his first knuckle, repressing the urge to scream.

"This ain't fair. This is bullshit. Everyone else is getting some right fuckin' now, and we're stuck up here like two fucking virgins on prom night. This fucking sucks."

"Chill out, man." The annoyance in Black's voice sent Ashmore spinning around with a shocked look on his face. Rage tightened his lips, and he shot out a knife hand toward the front gate.

"Chill out? Are you fucking kidding me? There's a fucking fight going on, people are racking up kills, and we're missing out. What the fuck?" Ashmore kicked the MRE box again. His boot punctured it, and when he tried to pull his foot back, the box came with him. "Damn it."

Ashmore closed his hands into fists and compressed his teeth. He swung his leg, and the box slid across the wooden floor, slamming against his rifle in the corner. Ashmore stomped and shouted, and Black cursed his luck at being posted with a Neanderthal. He scanned the flat horizon for any signs of an approaching attack. No buildings or man-made objects stood south of Camp Abu-Ghraib, and Black found only small shrubbery and drifting sands.

A mirage of water puddles and vapors danced in the distance, and Black took a long drink of his warm water, knowing he was getting dehydrated under the hot Iraqi sun.

"Have you even engaged the enemy yet?" Ashmore knew full well that before today, he was the only one to have fired shots in country. He used the MRE box as a stool.

"Nope." Black answered because it didn't matter to him that he was missing out on a *real* Marine experience. Ashmore shoved a pinch of tobacco into his mouth and using his tongue, packed it into his lower lip. Grains of tobacco covered his stained teeth. He opened a new liter size bottle of water and drank half of it before spitting a stream of tobacco juice into it. A mixture of spit and grains danced with the water, changing the color from clear to an off-brown.

"And this doesn't bother you?" Black looked back at Ashmore's bottle, and his stomach lurched.

"Nope," Black said again. He checked the weapon system on the table. The charging handle was forward with no round locked in the chamber. He went over his order of operations for the weapon, trying to ignore Ashmore's rants. If the enemy did come to the back of the camp, Black would pull back on the charging handle. A round would strip from the belt and feed into the chamber. With his thumb, he'd push in the safety switch, while getting his sight alignment and sight picture. If the enemy progressed, he'd squeeze the trigger until it fired.

He pictured men running at them with rifles and wondered if he fired a warning shot, would they retreat.

PPUUTTHHH. Ashmore's spitting echoed. He picked up his SAW and leaned it against the corner, staring out toward the front post. The gunshots died off, and the faint screams for corpsmen and mothers began.

"What kind of Marine doesn't give a shit about missing out on a firefight? You a fucking Hajji sympathizer?" Ashmore viewed the Marine Corps as a group of badass, hellraising, death bringers, and didn't like timid guys in his uniform. PPUUTTTHHH. Spit launched across his tobacco covered lips and into the water.

"No Ash, I don't care for all the killing. It's human beings that are dying."

"No, it's fucking Hajjis. It's the enemy, man." Ashmore shook his head in disbelief, not understanding how a Marine didn't want to kill the enemy. Black didn't understand how someone thought human life didn't matter.

"Man, these people eat and sleep like you and me. They work, they have kids—"

"Who they teach to kill our kids." Ashmore interrupted. Black's loyalty to the brotherhood of Marines became suspect to Ashmore. He picked up his SAW, slung the sling over his neck, and rested the rifle across his lap. He cut his eyes at Black and wondered if he'd have to kill the kid for being a traitor to his eagle, globe, and anchor.

"Most of these people want to live a normal life, just like us," Black said.

"Normal lives? These goat fuckers don't care about living a normal life. They care about taking your life, my life, and all our brothers' lives. Don't let the bullshit media confuse you, bro. We're here to exterminate, not liberate. This country should be the fuckin' Iraqi Republic of the United States of America. England did it for six hundred years and it was OK, but somewhere along the way, we let the weak inherit the Earth. Fuckin' bullshit. Crying motherfuckers."

"People have the right to their own country, to not be ruled by foreign invaders."

"Fuck you, boot. That's the weak bullshit I'm talking about. You gotta see the world for what it really is. Just watch. This turning men into fuckin' pussies, weak-ass movement can't last. Some strong motherfucker is gonna come up and start kicking ass again and then-" Ashmore flexed his massive bicep. "The weak are gonna cry for the strong. It's only the strong who have real power. I say we raise Old Glory up on Saddam's palace and kill'em all."

Black leaned his sore back against the edge of the table as he retrieved a cigarette from his cargo pocket. The two Marines eyed one another: Black took a long drag from his cigarette; Ashmore spat into the bottle.

"Ash, we're here to free the people forced to live under the thumb of a dictator. We're here so people can go to work and school and have families without living in fear. We're here to make Iraq a better place."

"No boot, I'm here to get as many kills as I can before I have to rotate back to the real world and get some bullshit job that I hate. I'm here to build my legacy as one bad ass motherfuckin' killer. You can save that noble shit talk for story time with your kids. This is war, ain't nothing about it noble. It's us against them, what's wrong with you?"

"Why does it have to be us against them? Why can't we live together and accept one another?"

"Because they won't accept you. They will kill you. You can take all that liberal bullshit you think is saving the world and shove it up your ass. It's us against them and if you ain't against them, then you ain't with us."

III

Kyle's finger tightened on the trigger, and he waited for the recoil to slam against his shoulder. The rifle's kick wasn't hard. Kyle had seen guys firing it from their crotch when no one was around. He focused on the tip of his front sight post, blurring the target.

The six-fingered man stood in the back of a truck, shouting incoherently at the compound. None of the Marines understood his Arabic words. Resistance built behind Kyle's trigger. The six-finger man stood two hundred meters away. At this distance, there was no need to adjust for windage or elevation. Another pound of pressure and the trigger would fall back.

"Cease-fire!" The order screamed down the line. Each man who repeated it, waved a hand in front of their face to signal the end of firing operations. At once, Kyle extended his trigger finger and allowed the six-fingered man to live another day. He looked up to see two tan Humvees storming out of the front gate in a race to catch up with the white trucks. As the gunfire ended, the post-firefight silence morphed into blood-curdling screams.

The commotion on both sides of the wall reflected the opposite nature of enemies at war. Outside, the insurgents laid dying, pleading for help as their comrades fled the fight. On the inside, the Marines rallied to help their fallen brothers. The yells for corpsmen were as loud as the cries of the wounded.

Jack and Kyle had heard it before. Remaining on top of the dirt mound, they surveyed the worst part of the war which had come to infect the FOB. Neither showed an ounce of emotion. Pulling a pack of American cigarettes from a grenade pouch, Jack gave one to Kyle and lit one for himself. They lingered there for a moment without speaking. The adrenaline gave way to the holds of nicotine. Jack removed his helmet, running his fingers through his dirty hair as smoke funneled out of his nose.

"Man, what a way to wake up," Jack said. Rubbing the stumbled growth on his cheeks, the sound reminded him of the crackling of a campfire. Kyle agreed without speaking. His mind wasn't on the commotion in the compound, but on the six-fingered man whom he regretted not killing. The image of the man coming back to kill more Marines didn't sit well with Kyle.

"Corpsmen up." A Marine shouted near the bottom of the berm as he struggled to remove large pieces of stone from a pile.

"There used to be a shack there," Jack said.

"RPG took it out." Kyle reminded him, to which Jack acknowledged with a head nod. Jack took a long drag off his cigarette and glanced in both directions. He couldn't find a Navy corpsman coming their way, and with a heavy exhale, he nudged Kyle.

"What's going on?" Jack asked a young Marine as they came down the berm. Upon seeing Jack's rank pinned to his flak jacket, the Private First Class stood at parade rest. He locked his hands behind his back, feet shoulder width apart, and stared forward. Everything screamed boot about this Marine and Jack whisked a hand of annoyance at him. "Stop that. Get back to work and just tell me what happened."

Jack didn't care about the detailed regulations of the Marine Corps when someone could be hurt. The young man bent over to help another Marine lift a large piece of rock from the pile.

"I saw a boot under here, Corporal," the young Marine said. Jack shared a look with Kyle, who shrugged his shoulders and shook his head. They knew if someone was under the pile, they weren't alive. The two corporals laid their rifles against a rock and started throwing aside pieces of the rubble. Several men removed a large piece of rock and unearthed the broken hand of a fellow Marine.

The sight of the lethargic limb sent a frenzy into the men. They tossed out rocks and stones at a rate of fully automatic. As the rubble cleared, the working party took a step back. A young Marine laid covered in a layer of dust, not breathing, not moving, and not alive.

"Shit." The word rode the back of a sigh that escaped Jack's lungs. He went to one knee and checked for a pulse, which he couldn't find.

"Who is he, Corporal?" The young Private First Class asked. Jack slammed the cigarette on the ground.

IV

Corporal James Harvey kicked his feet up on his desk, trying hard to ignore the gunfight outside. With the cease-fire given, he relaxed into his chair and returned to his Maxim magazine article. The article bored him, and he hurried through the pages until he came to the bikini-clad woman in the center.

Her long blonde hair and flawless tan body complimented her pearl white bathing suit. Well-manicured fingers gripped at her hair as waves crashed upon the beach behind her. Her sultry smile hypnotized Harvey, and at once he heard the rolling of the ocean's tide and smelt the aroma of salt. Biting her lower lip suggested a desire for the reader, but her frosted blue eyes said they couldn't touch her.

He dragged his finger over her face and the model's features faded into Skyler. She swayed with the breeze, elevating his blood pressure. The bikini-clad Skyler beckoned for Harvey to take her in the sand, pleasure her in ways only he knew how. Slowly, her eyes closed, and her hand flowed from her hair to her neck. Her polished fingernails lightly scratched over her breasts, titillating her nipples before dragging down her smooth abs, and along her hips.

High in the air, seagulls soared and produced a sound resembling laughter. Mist of the ocean's breeze lapped at his face as she crested the outside of her bikini bottoms. She rolled her hands between her legs, her knees slightly bowing, drawing them in close. Her thighs grazed each other, yearning for Harvey's strong hands to pry them apart.

"Harvey." A deep voice startled him from his objectifying, delusional daydream. He fumbled the magazine, trying to catch it, but then reluctantly allowed it to fall to the floor. Gritting his teeth, Harvey rocketed from his chair, wondering what idiot disturbed him. He caught the glint of the fluorescent light reflecting off the Lieutenant Colonel's bald head. A shocking alarm zipped through his nervous system as he squinted to block the light. His hands plastered along the seams of his trousers, coming to stand at the position of attention.

"Yes, sir," Harvey said. The C.O. dropped a piece of paper on his desk, and Harvey didn't need to look at it to know what it was. A pit opened in the base of his stomach, and he wanted to excuse himself to go throw up.

"Why weren't you out there in the fight?"

"Someone has to guard the C.O.C., sir."

"I bet you enjoy guarding the cock." The C.O. motioned for attention to the paper on the desk. "Mind telling me about this?"

"It's an award citation, sir."

"Who's it for?"

"Myself, sir." The C.O. retrieved the piece of white paper with official letterhead on it. Three Marines sauntered through the handmade wooden door and froze. An officer and two enlisted

Marines didn't know where to go but remained silent. The C.O. cleared his throat and read aloud without acknowledging the other three.

"Navy Achievement Medal for actions under fire while on convoy to the Baghdad International Airport." The C.O. lowered the paper, his jaw tensed, and his eyes bulged in their sockets. "When the fuck have you ever been to the BIOP?"

Harvey ran his options around in his head and couldn't think of a way out of his current predicament. The C.O. slammed the paper down on the desk. The sound echoed through the large tent and caused Harvey to flinch.

"What? Didn't you think I'd see this? I guess you thought it'd just get put on my desk, I'd sign it without looking, and you'd have another medal?" The C.O. paused. Drawing in a deep breath, he said, "Do I look like an asshole?"

"Sir?"

"You must think of me as an asshole. I mean, hell, I just went to Annapolis, but I guess I'm just signing things without reading them because of my rank."

"No sir, but—" Harvey tried a last-ditch effort to explain himself.

"Don't fucking interrupt me, Corporal."

"Aye, sir."

"A NAM? You put yourself in for a NAM?" Over the C.O.'s shoulder, the lower rank enlisted men snickered among themselves. Their pleasure at his misfortune enraged Harvey and he wanted the C.O. to turn to see the blatant disrespect of the two lance corporals. "I tell you what, I'm going to allow you…"

The C.O. paused, and the air went out of the room. Harvey couldn't believe what he was hearing, and the joy overwhelmed him. *He's going to allow the medal,* Harvey thought. *How badass is my C.O.*

"I'm going to allow you to *earn* your medals." The C.O.'s smile rose as Harvey's faded. His heart climbed into his throat, and he wasn't sure what the C.O. meant by this. With the air-conditioning and the ability to see Skyler when he wanted, he only cared about the office job.

Nothing else would suit him in the Marine Corps. Harvey wanted to shout at the commanding officer, wanting him to explain himself.

The C.O.'s smirk lingered as he picked up the magazine from the floor. He marveled at the women inside before tucking it under his arm and pointing to the paper on Harvey's desk.

"Here, read this instead." The C.O. vanished back into his office, while thumbing the magazine, and making approving sounds. Harvey's knees buckled, and he crumpled into the office chair that was no longer his. The others in the C.O.C. watched until their jobs demanded their attention.

V

The Berserkers hung their heads as they huddled around the Marine in the rubble. They wondered if it had been quick or painful.

"I can't believe it," Sutherland said. The state of shock was prevalent on his face as he had never known a dead American before. He couldn't believe he had talked with the man this morning, who now laid in the small gravel grave. It seemed unreal because Americans didn't die in war from accidents like this; it wasn't right. Their deaths were to be glorious, a romantic dance with bullets ripping them apart. It was never to be someone they knew, but as Sutherland stared into the hole, he learned there was no romance to death.

"He looks like he's sleeping," Simpson said.

"Yeah, internal sleep, motherfucker." Vinson spat a stream of dip to the ground.

"That's eternal sleep, dumbass. Besides, fuck him." Carlos hissed, angry at the emotions welling up inside him for someone he didn't even care about. The shame caused him to turn away.

Jones bowed his head.

"Damn, the kid wasn't old enough to even buy a beer," Simpson said.

"A lot of guys who die in this war aren't old enough to buy beer," Thompson added. "That's the shitty part of it all. Guys can die for their country but are too young and immature to buy alcohol. Fuckin' bureaucrats."

The circle of men paused, allowing the cold reality to plague their minds. Any one of them could be in that hole. The wind shifted, howling past them, and all the sounds and commotions around the base ceased to disturb their ears.

"Better him than me." Their collective attention pulled away from the shallow grave and crept up to that of Corporal Dillon. Kyle's eyes locked on the Marine in the dirt, but he looked past him, staring off into a memory. His expressionless gaze floated from the dead to meet his comrades. Although they didn't question it, many couldn't believe what he said.

"Damn." Simpson worded it, but everyone else was thinking it.

"Better him than any of us." The group was silent, not knowing what to say as Kyle continued, "I'm sorry this happened to the guy, but I'm still here. Shit happens to people in war, suck it the fuck up. We haven't got time to mourn the dead. We have a job to do, so shape the fuck up, Marines. This is war. If you didn't know people were gonna die, well, I'm sorry for you too, but I'm alive, and he isn't. Dwell on it when you get home."

An onlooker came to see what the Marines were looking at and was shocked to find a dead man in the middle of their circle.

"Who was he?" the unknown Marine asked.

"Jenson, Private First Class," Kyle answered. Jack studied his Berserkers, and he didn't like what he saw. With eyes cast in despair, sorrow pulled at them. Jack's snarled, believing his warriors weren't representing themselves as they should. He had to stop it.

"Corporal Dillon's right. No use in troubling yourself over this guy's death. Shit happens, people die, get over it. For the new guys, listen up. You will maintain a warrior's discipline, and that's a direct order. More of us may die, and that's how it is. I may die, I will die. I'm prepared for that, but don't you fuckin' dare mourn for me, motherfuckers. Get over it."

"Everyone meet in our room at 1900 hours." Kyle adjusted his rifle's three-point sling on his shoulder and lit up a cigarette. He blew out the smoke and nodded at the body in the shallow grave. "Get him out of there."

Kyle and Jack turned away from the circle, allowing the Marines to carry out their order.

"Nice speech back there. I liked the no time to dwell touch," Jack said.

"Thanks. Just rehashing old shit we've all heard before."

"I know, but those guys never heard it before. These men will follow you when I'm gone."

"Enough with that dying shit, Jack."

"I mean when I check out of the Corps. These guys will need someone else to lead them or at least train the next guy before you get out."

"I can't lead the Berserkers. That's your job. You're the reason we are the Berserkers."

"Well, I'm out of here after this tour."

"Bullshit, you fuckin' lifer."

"Shit, man. I'm a short-timer now."

"What the fuck are you gonna do when you get out? You even thought of that yet?" Kyle asked.

"I don't know. Maybe get an office job."

Kyle choked on his laugh and cigarette smoke. "Fuck you. There's no way in Hell you'll survive an office job. That's not what we do."

"Oh yeah, what do we do then, Kyle?"

"We are the warriors. This is our life. That sedentary shit will kill us. We're Berserkers. What good are we without a war?"

"Well, I don't know what I'm gonna do, but I do know I'm done after this tour. Seen enough of this shit to last an entire lifetime." Jack's mind drifted to a dark corridor of a prison lit by a dim bulb, giving him enough light to make out the walls. The light swung, illuminating parts of the hall while keeping the rest in shadows. He strolled the nightmarish prison with only the ghost to comfort him. A painful wailing echoed along the limestone.

Covered in blood, some from the enemy and some his own, he moved forward with no concern. He remembered having only one purpose: to find his younger brother. With the dead insurgent's rifle held out in front of him, he struck the enemy as they appeared. The muzzle flash was blinding, but not paralyzing. The wailing cry came again from the dark recesses of his mind. A moaning grunt of digression gave Jack pause while trying to orient himself to the cry.

The memory shifted and Jack wondered if he had rounded the corner first or if the next insurgent fatally appeared in front of him. Either way, Jack remembered mowing down the mid-aged man. The cry came with another few feet and his pace stalled as he fixated on the doorless cell at the end of the hall. Jack's heart pounded against his ribcage as an unwelcoming odor slapped thick against his face. A horde of dead bodies spoiled the floor, each wearing the trousers of the United States Marine Corps.

The blood worked its way out of the cell and across the stone covered flooring of the hall. His head weighed heavy upon his shoulders as he made his way to the back corner of the cell, warm blood soaking his bare feet. The wailing struck Jack and for the first time, he realized it was his own cries. Underneath a single barred window, a mound of heads formed a horrendous pyramid. At the highest point sat the head of Josh Campbell, riddled with shock and silent in his agony.

VI

Private First Class Black entered Jack and Kyle's room already occupied with the Berserkers. He paused for a moment to eye a spot to sit. Thompson and Jack were on Jack's bottom bunk, and Jack's gear cluttered the top rack. Jones's legs hung over the top of Kyle's bunk bed, and he nestled into Kyle's gear for a comfortable place to relax. Kyle motioned Skyler over as Ashmore plopped down on the bottom rack with them.

"Jesus H. Christ, Ash. You fat motherfucker," Kyle said as the springs in the bed groaned and the three settled into the rack.

"I ain't fat, that's all man meat." Ashmore flexed his bicep, trying to impress the female corpsman.

"Jesus's middle name started with an H?" Simpson asked.

"Yeah," Jack said. "It was Howard."

"Damn." Simpson's face twisted into disappointment. "See the shit they don't teach you. I ain't ever known Jesus had a middle name."

Black pushed around Simpson and Doc Sloan at the makeshift table in the center of the room. At the sight of Skyler, nervousness ran up Black's neck, forcing him to pause. Although he had seen this lady many times eating or talking with Kyle, he didn't expect to see her among them, and he couldn't for the life of him remember her name.

"Can I help you?" Kyle asked. Black shook his head. "Then take a seat."

Sutherland scooted over to make room on a black plastic footlocker.

"Now that we're all here," Jack said. Their mouths closed and their attention gathered on him. "For some of you, this is the first time you lost a guy in country. For some of you, this is the first time you've ever known someone to die. For the rest, death has become a mistress bitch that you love, but hate."

Kyle, Carlos, and Thompson grunted and barked.

"Ain't my first death," Simpson proclaimed. "Back in my hood, muthafuckers got smoked every day."

Simpson stared at Sutherland, then held up his hand in the form of a gun, thumb cocked back like a hammer and dropped it. With a wink, Simpson said, "Bang."

"Now, the Highers wanted me to get you guys together and ask for you to share your feelings about what happened to Jenson today," Jack said. Black sat up straight and tall and raised his hand.

"If you don't mind, I'll go first Cor—"

"Yeah," Jack interrupted, throwing his hand in front of Black to silence the young Marine. "We ain't doing that shit."

A few of the Marines rolled their eyes at Black, laughing as his hand slipped into his lap.

"Good job, boot," Carlos said.

"Dumbass," Ashmore added.

Black wanted to share. He wanted to show them that they were sensitive people and not the murderous barbarians they envisioned themselves as. His face felt red as the embarrassment ran out from under his collar and he hated everyone looking at him. Black wasn't sure what he could do to get these guys to like him, and at the moment, he didn't care if they did.

"We're Berserkers, chaos incarnate, devils of the battlefield." Grunting and barking erupted from several of the Marines. Jack continued, "We don't sit here and share our feelings and cry to one another like bitches. No, that ain't how this shit goes down. We're evildoers, and this is how we cope with the death of one of our own."

Jack kicked the bottom of his footlocker, causing Sutherland and Black to leap off, and from within, he retrieved a bottle of mouthwash. Bewildered eyes watched as Kyle passed out red solo cups, and Jack opened the bottle. The room flooded with the stinging aroma of alcohol as Black and Sutherland returned to their seats.

A few of the guys smiled, eagerly accepting a cup with mouthwatering anticipation. Sutherland stared up at the cup presented to him and waved it off. Kyle's hand didn't retreat, but his eyes grew intense as he scrutinized the boot Marine. Sutherland wanted to shrink, to hide behind the footlocker he sat on as all eyes watched him.

"I don't drink, Corporal."

"You do today." Kyle forced the cup at Sutherland. The room fell silent, and Sutherland could feel their stares. "Take it."

The sternness in Kyle frightened Sutherland, and he took the cup without hesitation. He'd never acquired a taste for hard liquor, and he feared he would make a fool out of himself in front of his new friends.

"Life lesson, bro. Never trust a man who doesn't have a vice. Be that women, gambling, or drinking; never trust a man who doesn't have one. Remember that, Sutherland."

"Yeah Sutherland, you're drinking because one of your brothers ain't here to drink that. This is the drink he'll never have again," Thompson said. Jack poured each man a shot. Sutherland's gut wrenched, and he couldn't hide the grimace which appeared on his face. He had only drunk a handful of times in high school and he remembered how awful it burned going down his throat. Back then, everyone had a chaser, but among a room full of hard chargers, he found nothing to ease the bite of the drink.

To an extent, he was a sheltered child, a fact he was learning with each new day in the Marine Corps. Despite their own partying habits, his parents had forbidden him or his sister from drinking in high school. Their disappointment at learning of his few nights out was worse than the pain of drinking and he vowed not to do that again. They had plans for him, a line he was meant to walk, and when he decided to join the Corps, they were irate. The last week before he left for boot camp, his mother barely spoke with him and his father told him he would fail.

The only shining light was his kid sister, Emily, who was excited for him. Their parents were harder on her, and the thought of leaving her alone to face them weighed heavily on him. He hadn't thought of Emily for some time and wondered how much she would grow while he was gone. She was seventeen, almost eighteen, and a senior in high school. He wished he could be there to see her graduate or go to prom.

"Fuck it," Sutherland mumbled to himself. Thinking of home only unleashed a dreaded feeling in him and he hoped the burning of the liquor would stomp it out.

"What was that?" Jack asked. Sutherland looked up at him, finding it surprising he had spoken those words out loud for anyone to hear.

"Nothing, Corporal." To Sutherland's relief, Jack moved on. The notion of grief subdued until he smelled the harsh whiskey. His stomach tightened and he was unsure if he would be able to hold down the liquor. Sutherland pulled his shoulders back and sat up straight, ready to give it his best try. By the time he looked up, Jack's drink was in the air, and the rest of the room had followed suit.

Skyler scooted back on Kyle's rack, leaning against the wall as Ashmore and Kyle moved to the edge of the bed. She watched each of their faces, admiring the closeness they had together. One of her fellow corpsmen noticed her hanging out with Kyle and had informed her of the Berserkers. He warned her of their strange, barbaric ways and blood-thirsty attitudes. The male corpsman even mentioned their red occultist-like Nordic tattoos.

Kyle tilted the brim of his cup at Sutherland.

"Never trust a man that won't have a drink with you. Remember that, boot." Kyle gave him a reassuring wink.

"To Jenson," Jack toasted.

"And to the Berserkers," Kyle added before anyone could speak. The rest of the squad grunted with their cups high in the air and in one fluid motion, tossed the whiskey down their throats. Skyler didn't say anything. She didn't grunt or chug her shot with the rest of them but sat back and marveled at the tradition they shared with past warrior clans. There was something ritualistic about drinking together in war, toasting to their fallen. While fixed on this thought, she noticed Kyle staring at her with a Mona Lisa smile. Her cup was still in her hand but she had yet to drink from it.

Has he been studying me as I studied them? She thought as she emptied the whiskey into her mouth. Like several of the others, she coughed, and all but Jack winced. He took it down with a straight, solid face, keeping his eyes closed to savor the drink like an alcoholic taking his first step off the wagon. Skyler choked back another cough as a few of the guys beat their chest like apes while asking for another. Kyle obliged their request.

Sutherland grimaced. The whiskey assaulted his gut, stinging his senses, and clouding his eyes. The back of his mouth salivated painfully.

"In case y'all didn't know, people will die here," Jack said, standing before the room. "I know we like to think of ourselves as the stars of our own story, but we may die here. I may die here."

Any smiles faded from their faces.

"Most of you are new to this war shit but take the word from us old joints. People die. There's no way around it. This is war, despite what the fuckin' media wants to say. But you're Berserkers. I expected a level of discipline even in the hard times. No one's OFP in the fuckin' squad."

Sutherland leaned over to Vinson. "What's OFP?"

"Own Fuckin' Program."

"We stick together," Jack continued. "We bring each other home, dead or alive, we bring each other home."

A knock came to the door, and a few of the younger Marines attempted to hide their cups. Jack took a quick headcount and stood puzzled. Everyone who needed to be in his room was there. He nodded to Black to open the door and Black did so, but only slightly to see who was there. The young Marine hurried out of the way as Gunny Wolf barged in.

"Corporal Campbell, I need to speak with your men."

"Sure Gunny, do you want the NCO's to leave?"

"No, you need to hear this shit, too." Black closed the door behind him. Gunny stood with arms crossed over his chest, studying their faces. His nose twitched to the whiskey in the air. "What are y'all doing?"

Jack didn't speak but placed a red cup in front of Gunny Wolf and poured a shot.

"For the Marine that died today." Gunny smelt the liquid, grinned, and nodded his approval. He snarled, then threw the shot back, allowing his tongue to absorb the strong liquor. Secretly, he wished they had a chaser, but since no one did, he refused to allow them to see his repulsion. The room settled into silence.

"All right gents." He ignored the liquor burning its way down his esophagus and exploding in his gut. He tapped the brim of his cup and Jack refilled it. "I got a replacement for Jenson."

"Already Gunny, damn that's quick," Simpson said.

"What, another boot?" Thompson asked.

"Worse," Gunny said. A joint moan echoed through the room. "I'm guessing you might know what you're getting?"

"It's admin, isn't it? Please for the love of Odin, don't say it's admin." Thompson threw himself off Jack's rack and paced the floor.

"Say it ain't so, Gunny." Jack shook his head in disapproval.

"Oh, it's so, and it gets worse, Corporal."

Jack shook his head. "No. No. No."

"Indeed. A fresh corporal from the admin field." Gunny couldn't stop his continual belly laugh as curse words were tossed about. Several of the Marines asked Jack for another drink to wash down the terrible news.

"Not only an admin fucktard but a fucking NCO admin. Come on, Gunny, what the fuck did we do?" Kyle protested. Skyler sat back from the others, fading into the rack with a sneaky suspicion on who the admin corporal was.

"Yeah Gunny, don't we have a say in the matter?" Jack didn't like the idea of some new shit bird in his squad thinking he was top dog. He hurried to retrieve his Copenhagen can and threw in a dip before blurting out something he'd soon regret.

"Afraid not, word came down from the C.O. himself." Gunny took one final drink from the plastic cup, placed it on the table, and strolled over to the door. "Get him trained, boys. We got a big job coming down the wire, and you're gonna want him trained."

"What kind of big job, Gunny?" Ashmore asked.

"Big. Can't give that word yet, but believe me, it's going to be amazing." A single word ran through their collective minds - Fallujah. There had been scuttlebutt going about the camp of the possible invasion of the city. Most of the Marines were well-aware of the previous assault, which took place in April. Operation Vigilant Resource ended with the Marines being pulled out of the city.

The command then turned over operations to the newly formed Fallujah Brigade, who then turned over their U.S. issued weapons to the insurgency. Now the Marines near the city of Fallujah waited eagerly for their chance to get those weapons back.

"Thanks for the drink, boys. Semper Fi." Gunny walked out of the room. The Berserkers turned their attention to their squad leader. Jack poured himself another shot of whiskey and grunted with his lips on the brim of the plastic.

"I think we got a fight coming."

VII

Skyler watched Jack leave the room, and as the silence crept in, she found herself alone with Kyle. The other Marines had left with bellies full of whiskey and lips busy with gossip. Skyler allowed the stillness to settle in and watched Kyle refill their cups, this time adding soda.

"I can't believe you guys got whiskey out here."

"Yeah," Kyle said, returning to cozy up next to her. "Jack came up with this idea on our last tour. We have family send us whiskey in mouthwash bottles. Works like a charm."

"What if they inspect the bottles?"

"Oh, that's the clever part. We have them take off the clear wrapper along the dotted line. After refilling it, they reseal it with a thin piece of scotch tape. Unless the inspector gets really close, it just looks like a sealed mouthwash bottle."

"Pretty smart. You should patent the idea," Skyler said, amusing herself.

"Yeah, that's what I'll do when I'm out. I'll make a killing on how to get illegal booze into the country. I can see it now. I'd be a legend among Marines."

"All branches," Skyler said, eyeing him over the brim of her cup before taking a drink. The liquor went down smooth with the soda. "So, what are you going to do when you get out?"

Kyle shrugged his shoulders and drank. He hadn't put much thought into it. The only thing Kyle knew besides surfing was the

Marine Corps, but he was sure he didn't want to make a career out of it.

"I don't know. Open a surf shop or something. I like the water, so I'll stay in California when I get out."

"I have never been to the ocean off California."

"Seriously? You're stationed in California and you've never been to the ocean?"

"Yeah."

"But you're in the Navy?"

"I know, but I'm green side, not blue."

"Oh man, you gotta come out. I gotta place off the beach. You'll have to come stay when we get back."

"Oh yeah, inviting me to your house already? Moving kind of fast." Skyler mocked. Kyle shot her a cunning smile, wanting nothing more than to kiss her. His knees trembled, and he hoped she couldn't feel the vibrations of them.

"I'm just saying, you'll have a place to stay if you come out."

"Sounds nice."

"What are you gonna do when you get out?" Kyle asked.

"I don't know. I still have a couple of years before I can get out, so I don't know."

"You thinking about moving back to Louisiana?" The expression faded from Skyler's face, and Kyle wished he could retract his question. She had never mentioned her home life, and from what he could gather, things weren't peachy keen.

"I don't know." Her old life seemed vague and distant, as if someone else lived it. It was nothing like the life she had now, and she wondered if she could go back after everything she had seen. The warm fuzzy tingle of nostalgia encased her. Her mind filled with a memory of sitting under a weeping willow and enjoying an iced tea on a hot day. If she thought hard enough, she could almost hear the wind rustling the trees and lapping at her face.

But it wouldn't last. Images of mangled Marines encroached on her happy thoughts and stole her smile. She didn't know how she would go back and live without thinking of Iraq. Skyler forced a fake smile and added, "Maybe I'll come out to see you."

"Yeah, I'd like that. You come stay with me, and we'll have a good time."

"But you'll have to get a job if you're thinking about trapping me into marriage." He loved the adorable way she threw her head back when she laughed. With her neck stretched, he wanted to nibble on the smooth sides of it.

"You trying to tie me down?" Kyle leaped from the rack.

"Shit, I'm the catch here."

"What?" Kyle flexed his arm, popping the bicep muscle. Skyler laid back on her elbows and fought the urge to sink her teeth into her lower lip. His arm was attractive, but she wanted him to remove his shirt like he did the night they met. He would then crawl into the bed and kiss her, harder and with more passion than he had on the dirt mound. She laughed to conceal her blushing, causing butterflies to enter her stomach.

What if he did remove his shirt and climb into bed with me? What would I do? She had only been with Anthony Ambrose and that was a lackluster experience. Anthony insisted on missionary position, enjoying the control it gave him. He'd hover over her, grunting and slamming until finishing with no concern for her needs.

Skyler couldn't help but feel guilty when she thought that there was to be more to it than that. She stared at Kyle's muscles, confident he knew how to pleasure a woman, but insecure in her own abilities. Her legs yearned to press together, to rub against one another, and satisfy the lustful urge they craved.

"Shit, you've never even seen a guy like me." To her delight, Kyle threw off his shirt and flexed both arms, trying his hardest to imitate a bodybuilder. He turned, hitting a double bicep pose, and looked over his rounded shoulder to see if she was watching. Skyler was. She marveled, but it wasn't the shape of his arms that caught her attention. The massive tattoo, running the length of his back, put her in awe. She had never seen it before and wondered how she had missed it the night they met.

She leaned in, her hand tracing the blood-red tattoo from the small of his back to where his shoulders met his neck.

"What is that?" Skyler asked. Kyle spun around, searching the area around them, nervously looking for something.

"What is it? A bug, is it a spider? I hate spiders."

"No, your tattoo."

"Oh that. That's the symbol of the Berserker. In old Nordic times, it was also the brand of sacrifice, marked on people for blood to be spilled where other blood needed to be spilled. Berserkers wore it because they were sacrificing themselves in battle for Odin and their kind."

"I heard about this Berserker name your squad goes by. Why is that?"

"Nothing. It's just one of those crazy military nicknames."

"Crazy enough to get your back covered in the tattoo?"

"Yeah." Kyle couldn't fight back the grin. He sat down on his rack and stared at his drink.

Skyler kicked herself for changing the mood. She could tell his mind was drifting to someplace he didn't want it to go. Skyler didn't know what to do, and her body wanted to act one way, but her mind tried to play cautiously. *Screw it,* she told herself and allowed her body to react the way it wanted. Kyle brought his cup up to drink, but she stole it from him and replaced it with her mouth.

VIII

Dear Jason,

I hope everything is great. What's Iraq like? Is it hot over there? Are you scared? I know I would be if I was in your place.

Pioneer day was this past week, and the carnival was amazing, as normal. Do you remember Mrs. Conway, the English teacher? She was in the dunking booth this year. It was really funny. I wish you were here with me. I miss you so much. I still think we should have gotten married before you went. I can see it now, you in your Marine uniform, the one with the blue jacket, what's that called? Anyways, I'll be in a beautiful white gown, and it can be outside with birds and the sunshine.

It will be perfect, just like we talked about. I go to see your parents from time to time to see if they heard anything from you. They say you don't call or write too much. Why not? You should call them at least once a day. I mean, they have to have phones over there, it's not like it's the dark ages, and when you do call, call me, too. I can't wait to hear from you. I'll wait for you no matter how long it takes.

Love, Sophie

Sutherland stuffed the letter back into the envelope, but before slipping it into his personalized Bible, he inhaled the sweet fragrance rising from the folds of paper. Sophie was sweet and near innocent in her thinking of them getting married. They had talked about it before he left, but his heart wasn't where she was.

They were a hot item in school, but she didn't see past wanting to be Mrs. Jason Sutherland. He didn't know what he wanted. He felt bad for only having wrote her once when she wrote him constantly. It was a pleasure to read her letter, but once he closed the envelope, he never returned to it.

The night air swooped out of the sky and hurled across the desert grounds, sending shivers through Sutherland. He wished the ammo can, full of cigarette butts, was a warming fire, but the smoke pit was no campsite. No fire sat in front of him and the only light came from the moon above.

Sutherland sat back on a green military cot, staring up at the bright moon, and leaning against the hard, sun-dried mud wall. It was jagged and stiff, reminding him of the small adobe models he made for a class project on Southwestern Native American homes. The structure of the wall faded from his thoughts as he realized the cold wasn't bothering him. The whiskey was doing its job. He smiled drunkenly at the thought of feeling like a cowboy on the plains, a real man's man, and he didn't want the feeling to end.

But the feeling did end. No one walked near him, no voices disturbed him, and in a land he was foreign to, Sutherland felt all alone. The wide-open space crowded in on him and beat him down into a pit of fear. All the possibilities of death hammered his mind and the worse fear of all came forth. Despite being among a group of crazed warriors, Sutherland feared he'd die alone, with no one there to comfort him. Worse, he feared nothing would be there to greet him on the other side.

Sutherland unclipped the red flashlight from his shoulder pocket and opened the Bible clutched in his hand. He searched for the bookmarked section he read to replace the isolation in his mind. There had to be something nice in it, something to feel good about, but he found nothing. Sutherland sighed, not realizing he was holding his breath, and drifted from the page to the black blanket of stars glittering above, unrestrained by city lights.

He returned to the book, and the passage he was looking for was right in front of him. He read the verse in his head and heard not his voice, but the voice of a cowboy in an old western from his childhood. *And I looked, and behold a pale horse: and the man who sat upon him was Death, and Hell followed with him.*

"Whatcha readin'?" A voice came from behind and above Sutherland, spooking him. His body jolted and tensed, causing him to fumble his book. Before it could fall, he caught it and shot a look over his shoulder to find Jack standing in the doorway of their building. The dark helped to conceal Sutherland's embarrassment.

Jack's face glowed like a demon behind a dangling cigarette. He stepped out from the shadows and took a seat on the cot, the smell of whiskey emanating strongly from him. Jack flipped opened a metal cigarette case and held it out to Sutherland. Sutherland stared down at the cigarettes aligned in a perfect row. He had never smoked before, but like the whiskey, his parents weren't here to condemn his actions. Throwing caution to the wind, he drew a cigarette from the case. He wanted no part of a repeat lecture like he had after refusing the cup of whiskey.

"I said, whatcha reading?" Jack enunciated his words, trying hard not to slur them in his drunkenness.

"The Bible, Corporal." Jack fired up Sutherland's cigarette. The smoke rushed down his throat, and he choked on the first drag. Jack glared at him from the corner of his eye as smoke funneled out of his nostrils like an evil bull. Sutherland felt Jack studying him, analyzing, and questioning him, but acted as if he didn't notice.

"I didn't take you for a religious man, Sut." A small grin appeared in the corner of Sutherland's mouth. Corporal Jack Campbell had given him a nickname, and this brought more pride to him than he thought it would. He was one of the guys, and Jack Campbell confirmed it.

"I'm not. I mean, I grew up Baptist, but I don't know. What religion do you believe in?"

"Fuck religion." Jack's words were sharp on Sutherland's ears, taking him by surprise. He didn't as much say them as he threw the words into the night, hoping some deity would hear his defiance of faith. "I believe in the Constitution of the United States of America. I believe in everyone having a right to their own religion, but I also believe I can say fuck religion."

He exhaled a puff of white smoke into the night and took a swig from the bottle hidden in his hands. He didn't bother looking around to see if anyone was watching. His confidence impressed Sutherland. Jack pulled the bottle away, grimaced at the bite, and forced it into Sutherland's chest. He took the bottle, hesitating for only a moment, then drank.

"What's God ever done for you anyhow?" Jack asked. Sutherland didn't know how to answer. He was afraid he had offended his squad leader somehow. Jack grabbed the bottle and took a long pull off it. "I ain't got no use for God."

"Do you ever pray?" Sutherland asked.

"I pray every night. I pray to this." Jack held up his rifle that laid in his lap as the bottle continued to pass between the two Marines. "I pray for big titty women and live action gunfights. That's what I pray for."

"Yeah," Sutherland said, puzzled by what to say next. "I don't know if praying works."

"Look, you have every right to pray, I ain't here to stop you. If you do pray, pray that God comes down here and fights Allah so we can stop dying. I'm sick of men dying for mystical Gods."

"So, you don't believe in any God?"

"Is he going to be fighting with us on the battlefield?"

Sutherland shrugged his shoulders.

"Then what good is he?" Jack continued. "I don't know if there's a God or not and I'm not saying there is or isn't a God. All I'm saying is that if there is a God, fuck him. He either hates us, doesn't have the power to help us, or he doesn't exist. He's either evil, impotent, or not real. Besides, if I had to pick a God to believe in, I'd like to believe in Odin."

"Odin? For real?"

"Yeah, why does that surprise you? If I say I believe in Odin or Zeus, you look at me and think I'm crazy. Now if you say you believe in a man who walked on water, who died on a cross and rose three days later, I'm an asshole for not taking you seriously." Sutherland nodded, understanding that Jack had a point, and drank the whiskey that no longer burned as it crossed his tongue.

"I don't know what to believe anymore. It's all so confusing at times," Sutherland said.

"Well, I can't help you out there, young blood. Go see the Chaplin. If you want to know how to kill someone or eat pussy, I'm your guy." Jack beamed; his eyes lit by the light of the moon and the glow of the burning cigarette. "It's easier to hate the Gods if you don't believe in them. But I'm just an old drunk Marine."

Jack took a drag from the cigarette and studied the cherry burning at the end.

"You know what I want, Sut?"

"What's that?"

"I want a real fight. I want a gunfight like the O.K. Corral. You ever saw Tombstone?"

"Sure."

"Like that, Sut. I want to stand my ground while bullets fly around me. I want buckshot zipping past my head and men standing in front of me, ready to die as I am. That's what I want."

Jack took the bottle from Sutherland and stood from the cot, tossing his cigarette into the darkness. It hit the ground and red dots scattered like tiny fireflies dancing about. Sutherland waited for Jack to stumble into the building before looking down at the Bible in his hands. He opened it, but once again found nothing he wanted to read.

What if Jack is right? What if this is all bullshit?

Sutherland had never questioned the book before. The Bible was law in his house, and God was all-knowing, all-powerful. His stomach quivered. The questioning of his foundational beliefs didn't sit well with him. Sighing, he set the book down on the cot, not knowing what to do or think.

"It's only the whiskey. That's all it is." He tried to convince himself. "It's only the whiskey."

Private First Class Stephen Jenson

Killed in Action

Near Fallujah, Iraq – Al-Anbar Province

July 25th, 1985 – October 3rd, 2004

* * *

From the pages of Jack Campbell's Journal-

Today we lost a man. I wonder what his family is going through right now? I'm sure a uniformed Marine has delivered the news. Shit sucks, but this is war, not summer camp. I'll try my hardest to bring the rest of the men home alive. Home seems like a fairy tale. I don't know if I'll ever see it again. I miss my wife. I'm too drunk to write this shit.

CHAPTER FIVE

EMBRACE THE SUCK

We Marines are truly blessed. We get to enjoy the sweet taste of
freedom because we know its price.

-Marine veteran John Chipura, survivor of the 1983 Beirut bombing

I

October 4th, 2004-

The air held a pleasant crispness as the morning sun washed away
the darkness of the night. Still hours away from the real heat of the day,
the morning took on the feel of a cool Texas December. With no
vehicles roaring or gunfire threatening the Marines, the camp remained
sheltered in their slumber. Aside from a few audible voices, the
compound had the eerie feeling of being deserted. The frosty air
signaled the changing of the seasons, and bitter conditions were on the
horizon.

Jack stepped out of the small building and stretched in the morning
light. The urge to smoke attacked him as soon as he woke. Carlos
looked up at his squad leader from the green military cot, then scooted
over to allow room for both men. Jack sat his M16 against the wall and
sat down.

"You look like twenty yards of road shit," Carlos said. Jack nodded
with the heavy head of an exhausted man. He looked down at his boots
to find both were untied and unbloused.

"At least I pulled tight the laces to this one."

"Oh yeah, because that helps." Carlos took a drink from the steaming cup of coffee before passing to Jack. The bean-shaped canteen cup was hot to the touch but felt good in the cold morning air. The coffee snapped at Jack's dry lips, and he yanked his head away before the burn settled in. Returning to the cup, he proceeded with more caution than before. The heat warmed his insides, pleasing Jack as he passed it back to Carlos and fired up a cigarette.

The two remained silent, appreciating the calmness of the morning as Carlos tossed a pinch of dip in his lip. He leaned forward and spat at the ammo can overflowing with cigarette butts. The spit went wide, and the dirt quickly absorbed it, leaving behind a dark circle. Carlos opened his mouth to speak, but a tall, slender Marine stomped around the corner, interrupting him.

The tall Marine dropped his 782 gear and seabag at Jack and Carlos's feet, kicking up a swirling dust cloud the two shied away from. He pushed his over-sized glasses up his nose and scratched at his dirty barracks haircut. Not once did he acknowledge the disturbance he had caused. Stitched on his uniform was the name 'Harvey', and to their disappointment, corporal was his rank.

"Do either of you know where I can find a Corporal Campbell? I heard he lives in these..." He sighed, turning his nose up in disgust. "Barracks."

Harvey didn't look at the Marines when he spoke but surveyed the area, finding it anticlimactic. The structure failed to live up to the admin living quarters. For him, these conditions were subhuman, meant for caveman grunts, and not for someone with his intellect.

Through sharp and suspicious eyes, Jack studied the tall Marine while inhaling smoke. Almost everything about the Marine was offensive to Jack. From his non-faded haircut to his brand-new boots with no mileage walked in them, something gnawed at Jack. He knew this guy from somewhere.

"Yeah, what do you want with him?" Jack asked. Harvey cast a scornful eye as if asking, 'How dare you question me?'

"That's business I have with him and not you. So, go get the corporal and do so in a hurry." Harvey leaned forward to exert command. Amused, Carlos watched in a daze as Jack gave Harvey a blank stare. The audacity of the two Marines shocked Harvey. Once settled, he would make some busy work for them both.

Jack took a slow, long drag off his cigarette, then flicked it into the ammo can. Deliberately, he stood with the speed of an eighty-year-old man with bilateral knee replacement. Carlos leaned back, curious at what Jack was doing. Jack's eyes never left Harvey as he moved to the door leading into the small building.

"Wait a minute." Harvey barked, his eyebrows turned inward, as he bore hate at Jack. Jack found it near comical the way his eyes enlarged behind his glasses. He wasn't surprised at the posture Harvey held, but everything about the lanky man seemed odd to Jack. "Come back here."

"Hmm," Jack replied, not moving a muscle.

"I said come back here." Harvey repeated, to which Jack disobeyed. A redness crawled from under his collar and painted Harvey's face. His eyes bulged as he clenched his teeth until his gums hurt. He ripped the glasses from his face and shot a finger at the corporal chevrons on his collar. "You see this rank?"

"Hmm," Jack mumbled, knowing his insubordination would cause the admin Marine to lose his shit. Carlos's stomach hurt from holding back a laugh. He turned away before he burst and to stifle the sound, he shoved an extra pinch of dip into his lower lip.

"This says corporal. Respect it."

"Hmm." Jack played as if he didn't hear Harvey again. Harvey took a deep breath and rubbed the bridge of his nose. He would report this blatant disrespect to command as soon as he set his stuff down.

"Go find Corporal Campbell!" Harvey pointed to the door. Jack flashed him a joker smile and stepped into the building. Before the door could close, Harvey said, "And Aye, Aye Corporal or some shit."

Jack halted, cracking his neck, then vanished into the barracks. The door closed completely behind him, before springing open with a loud bang, slamming into the cot and startling Carlos. The thin plywood cracked under Jack's boot. He marched out, chest protruding, shoulders pulled back, eyes beaming at Harvey.

"I am Corporal Campbell. I hear some asshole prick is looking for me." Carlos choked on his tobacco dip. A rush of foolishness boiled inside Harvey and being belittled for other people's amusement pissed him off. He vowed not to go through life in the Marine Corps like he had in high school, being the boy everyone picked on.

"I didn't know you were Campbell."

"That's Corporal Campbell to you, pogue." Jack paused, snarling at Harvey, who stood there cowering to him like a hurt puppy. Carlos couldn't stop his head from swiveling between the two. "Aye, Aye… or some shit."

"Aye, Aye Corporal." Harvey, although reluctant to say it, allowed the words to escape.

"So listen up, dick face. You need to watch who the fuck you're talking to. You ain't in the office no more, pogue." Jack returned to his seat next to Carlos and fired up a new cigarette. He inhaled, then spat at Harvey's boots before throwing a thumb over his shoulder. "Take your shit in there and find a place to sleep."

"Well, you know, if you had your rank on—" Harvey started, but the hate radiating from Jack's fiery gaze stopped him.

"What's your name, shit bird?"

"Harvey."

"You stand at parade rest when speaking to your squad leader. Billet outranks rank." Harvey cleared his throat and stood erect. Drawing back his shoulders, he interlocked his hands behind his back.

"Corporal Harvey." He liked the sound of his own rank and name together, and it always brought a bit of joy to his expression. Carlos spat tobacco juice near Harvey's new combat boots where a small black speck landed on the toe.

"Well, I'm your fucking squad leader now." Jack flared out his nostrils and turned his lips upward as if a foul stench drifted in with the cool air. "I'm Corporal Campbell. Learn my name because I'm one of those motherfuckers you don't play with. I don't like backtalk when I give a subordinate a direct fucking order."

Harvey held up his hand, making a motion to silence Jack. He had something he wanted to say, and he felt that Jack had talked long enough. Harvey smoothed out the wrinkles of his cammie blouse and pushed his glasses up. He was afraid Jack was one of those guys who loved to hear his own voice.

Jack leaned back, shocked and offended like the guy tried to take a swing at him. The fury grew inside Jack and his hands itched to wrap around this guy's skinny neck and choke the life out of him.

"I have something to say," Harvey said.

"Are you fucking with me? Is this some fucking joke? If you don't get the fuck out of my sight on the double, I'm gonna kill you. I don't mean that as a threat. It's a god damn promise. I will fucking end your pathetic life."

"Where's the NCO room?" Harvey asked.

"Who said you're an NCO? You're a boot here, bitch." Jack growled. Harvey cut his eyes at the amused Hispanic who couldn't control himself.

"OK, Lance Corporal. If you think it's so funny, get my bags and take them to my rack." Carlos grinned at the goofy looking man and this time he didn't bother with trying to avoid Harvey's boot. The splat was loud, and Harvey's stomach turned at the sight of the large dark glob of spit on his laces.

"You dig?" Carlos wiped the spit from his mouth.

"What the fuck is that, Lance Corporal? I'll be damned if—"

Harvey didn't get to finish his sentence. In one quick movement, Jack soared at Harvey and detained him by the collar. Harvey's feet grazed the loose soil as Jack spun around and slammed him against the brick wall. Harvey's vision faded, threatening to black out from the intense pain. Raising a hand to the back of his head, there was no blood to be found, but a rather large lump was swelling.

"Fucktard, I told you to do something, and you're still here. You interrupt me, and then you try to pawn off a task on a lower ranked Marine who happens to be my friend."

"But I'm a Corporal." Harvey interrupted Jack again. A killer glint buried within Jack's eyes caused Harvey to cower. Jack drew Harvey in close and then shoved him back. The air puffed out of Harvey's lungs and a beckon of pain throbbed around his head. He opened his eyes to find Jack's cigarette inching near his face; the heat from the red-hot cherry nipping at his cheek.

"I'm fucking talking. You keep your boot mouth shut. You carry your own shit like everyone else here. I ever hear of you doing this shit again, I'll kill you. You don't know who I am, but you will." His cigarette smoke floated under Harvey's glasses, stinging at his eyes. Jack didn't care about the pain he was in as he continued, "You're no Berserker. You got no rank here. You're a boot to my boots. If my PFC's give you an order, you better fucking do it. Get the fuck out of my world on the double."

With one final shove, Jack released Harvey's collar and returned to the cot.

"Welcome to the Berserkers; we find comfort in chaos." Carlos mocked with a wave.

II

The air brakes hissed, forcing compressed air out the exhaust ports, and disturbing a layer of settled dirt on the ground. The six massive tires stopped rotating, slid over the gravel, and vibrated until the truck halted. Tremors shook dry, caked-on mud from the seven ton's undercarriage, and as the truck parked behind two other troop carriers, the rear armored doors swung open. Marines filed out both openings, descending the five-foot drop to the ground.

The Berserkers stepped off in two staggered columns with Ashmore taking point. Each man kept a dispersion of fifteen feet as they moved down the bustling streets of Al-Karma. Civilians hurried about, buying food from stands and watching children play. Cars zoomed back and forth with no regards to speed limits or safety signs, which there were few. No matter what everyone was doing, all eyes watched the Marines patrolling the street.

Jack watched as first and third squad vanished down their individual routes. He stepped off with the Berserkers, following in a few steps behind Ashmore. Having once been the squad's former point-man, Jack felt comfortable in front of the formation. The men scanned their sectors of fire, watching the rooftops and windows, the doorways and alleys. Deep craters, formed by many explosions, pockmarked the dirt covered roads.

The men baked under the sun stretching high above. Bright rays reflected off the tin rooftops of old clay and straw adobe dwellings, increasing the heat. Newly constructed brick buildings populated the denser areas, and civilians flooded the streets. Parting through the thick crowd elevated the Marines' sense of awareness. The enemy no longer wore Saddam's old guard uniform, and now, as guerrilla fighters, they looked like everyone else walking the streets. These cowards hid among the populace and disappeared as quickly as they struck.

Ashmore rounded a corner, and the Marines marched into the opening of a market sector. Children bombarded the Marines, asking for candy or whatever the Marines could give. It took Ashmore great restraint from kicking the kids away. The Marines eyed each child, hoping none of them carried a hand grenade or a weapon of any kind.

Carlos gave a candy bar to a couple of kids, hoping to nullify the problem. The two small children beamed with joy as they ran off with their special treat, trying to avoid other kids snatching at their goodie. Iraqi adults watched with suspicious eyes and a few herded their children indoors.

"Why'd you do that?" Ashmore asked Carlos.

"Most of these kids have never had candy before."

"So?"

"It's called compassion, Ash. You should try it."

Two men, with hostile attitudes, marched across the street. Their wives followed, dressed in full burkas, keeping their heads lowered to the ground. The women didn't dare look at the Marines as the men in their company shook their fist at the Americans.

"How's this for compassion," Ashmore said, flipping the two men his middle finger. Their education lacked knowledge of this gesture as it had no effect on them. "Fuck you, you punk ass motherfuckers."

"Ash, knock it off," Jack ordered.

"Fuck them," Ashmore replied before turning his attention back to the two men. "I'm sure your bitches smell like goats."

"Keep your eyes off the ladies," Jack warned his men. "I don't want anyone starting shit with us for checking out their wife."

"What, Corporal? You afraid we can't handle it if someone wants to get some?" Simpson's deep baritone laugh followed and traveled through the busy marketplace.

"No, Simpson. I don't want the media to have a field day with us. You're Berserkers. I have no doubt that you could kill everyone in this city if you wanted to." The squad grunted and hooted.

"Fuck those motherfuckers." Ashmore whistled to get the attention of the women, and when they looked his way, he grabbed his crotch. "Hey baby, you want some of this fine American meat muscle?"

"What the fuck, Ash." Jack shoved his point-man in the back. "Gaff me off again, I'll fuckin' kill you, you get me?"

"Yes, Corporal."

"Yeah, Ash. Knock it off, man." Vinson shook his head. "You tryin' to start a war?"

"News flash, dumbass. We're at war."

"Doesn't mean I wanna get shot today," Vinson said.

"Pussy."

"Lock it up," Jack grunted.

Along the curbs and against the sides of buildings, trash accumulated in disgusting piles of waste and rot. In training, Sutherland learned to be wary of garbage because of the risk of improvised explosive devices. He now understood that advice was ridiculous.

There was no way he could scan all this trash. On shaky legs, he paid special attention to where he stepped. Each placement brought the fear of coming down on a landmine buried in the soft dirt. His stomach knotted at the thought.

The Marines studied each face they saw. Any person bearing a cross look, or an evident wish of death was on their mental shit list. Ashmore turned down an alley and the men followed. Sutherland pulled the neck piece away from his throat, trying to draw in a deeper breath and relax his paranoia. Large piles of trash stacked up against the far side of the alley and Sutherland clung to the wall to avoid it.

"Sutherland, move six inches off that wall," Jack ordered without looking back over his shoulder.

A ghostly touch alarmed Sutherland, and he wondered how Jack saw him without looking back. He found none of the other men were as close to the wall as he was and he eased away from it, hoping no one saw the anxiety he was having. This wasn't his first patrol through the city, but after the death of Jenson, Sutherland came to the hard conclusion that any one of them could die next. War was no video game, it was no movie, and there were no allotted extra lives.

Jack instructed Black to watch a certain rooftop. Then he informed Jones to keep an eye on a group of men while dropping back to Sutherland.

"You know why I told you that?" Jack asked his younger Marine. Sutherland shook his head. Instantly he felt ashamed and troubled for not addressing Jack by his rank. "Walls like to funnel bullets. If someone came out shooting and the bullet hit the wall, the forward motion of the projectile would funnel down and likely hit you. Stay six inches off the walls."

"Roger that, Corporal," Sutherland said. Ashmore rounded the corner between two buildings and ventured down the large alleyway. Power lines strung overhead, crisscrossing and intersecting like the web of a spider. One by one, the men followed Ashmore down the alley, eyes drifting over and around everything. No one was present, and the vantage points for the insurgency narrowed. A calmness settled among the Marines.

CLICK.

The faint sound echoed with the volume only produced by speakers at a rock concert. The Marines came to a complete and swift halt. Their hearts pounded, demanding priority over other organs, and leaving several Marines light-headed. Adrenaline injected into their bloodstreams, heightening their senses as each checked themselves. With their safety secured, they tracked the formation until landing on Thompson at the rear.

His own heart crawled into his throat, cutting short his breathing. Thompson's blood froze in his veins and a bead of sweat trickled down the side of his face. His stare matched their own before lowering to the dirt at his feet. His rifle grew heavy in his arms, but his death grip wouldn't release it. The air escaped him in one long exhale. Half-buried under dirt and trash was a small metal device.

"Oh shit," Thompson said. His vocal cords quivered. He read the terror on their faces and the realization that they had stomped through the same location he now stood, barely missing the hidden bomb. He swallowed the hard, dry lump of a doomed man. "Get the fuck out of here."

Jack ran to Thompson and paused upon seeing the edge of the landmine poking through the dirt. His shoulders slumped, his feet anchored in place, and his chest sat heavy under the combat load.

"Get out of here, Jack."

"Can't do that, brother."

"I'm fucked, man," Thompson said. Jack still didn't move. "Get out of here, you stupid bastard."

"Let's figure this out, Devil Dog."

"Oh, don't fucking devil dog me. I'm royally screwed here, bro. Get lost, come back for whatever's left of me." Thompson shoved Jack away while making sure to keep the pressure on the landmine.

"Belay that shit and calm the fuck down. Let's figure this out." Jack knew he was blowing smoke up his own ass. His friend was as good as dead, but he couldn't leave without trying to keep a death off his conscience.

"Ain't nothing to figure out. Get out of here, or I swear to God, I'll step off this damn thing and kill us both." Thompson could see the concern in Jack's eyes. He sighed and graced his face with a pleasant smile. "Look, Jack, thanks for all the good times saving my bacon. You can't save me this time. Now get the hell out of here."

Jack didn't budge.

"Get out of here, you stupid motherfucker. God damn it." Thompson pushed Jack, who paused while the two eyed each other. Thompson motioned for Jack to leave while pulling a crucifix necklace from within his shirt. "Get out of here, man."

Jack cast his eyes down, not able to bring himself to look at his friend, and reluctant to walk away, but did so. Thompson brought the crucifix up to his dry, cracked lips and kissed it. He closed his eyes and steadied his breathing. Silently, he stated the only Bible verse that came to his mind.

The king spoke and said to Daniel, O Daniel, servant of the living God, is thy God, whom thou servest continually, able to deliver thee from the lions? Then said Daniel unto the king, O king, live forever. My God hath sent his angels, and hath shut the lions' mouth that they have not hurt me: forasmuch as before him innocency was found in me, and also before thee, O king, have I done no hurt.

"What are you doing?" Kyle asked, running up to Jack as Jack ordered his men to fall back to cover.

"Skinnin' out. Ain't nothing we can do."

"Bullshit." Kyle tried to push himself past Jack, but Jack intercepted him. "That's my friend. We can't leave."

"He's my friend, too, but we can't do anything for him." Jack pulled Kyle to cover as he resisted. Over a concrete barrier, they watched Thompson fire up a cigarette.

"And to think, I was gonna quit today."

Only Ashmore laughed as the world faded from Thompson's vision. The sweet sensation of tobacco flooded his lungs and attacked his nervous system. He didn't want to die, but he wasn't going to cry about it. If this was his zero hour, his moment to fall, he would do so in a great Marine Corps fashion. He would welcome death with his head held up and his courage intact. Within his thoughts, Thompson gave thanks to his maker.

"Stay frosty, gents." He grunted and then stepped off the landmine.

III

My Dearest Skyler,

I hope this letter finds you well. I wanted to say I miss you horribly and can't wait for you to be home again. College is going great. I'm passing all my classes. I wish you could be here instead of the Army. You're a beauty queen with a gun; it could make a cool movie.

I don't know what your thoughts were when you joined. It must've been some female empowerment thing. Well, when it's over, and you're home, we'll get things back to normal.

I know how it is; you have to get some stuff out of your system before you can settle down and have a family. I can't wait to introduce you to my frat brothers who play on the polo team with me. You'll love their girlfriends. Most of them are beauty queens, too, and come from respectable Southern families.

Well, I got class. Hope you're safe and keeping your skin moisturized under that hot Iraqi sun. Don't want to damage all the hard work your mother put into your smooth, milky skin.

Your Loving Fiancé,

Anthony

Skyler folded the letter with gentle care, cringing at the growing pile in her footlocker. He wrote her like clockwork; once every two weeks and each time he referred to her as being in the Army. She wasn't in the Army, but in the Navy, a completely different branch, and this irritated her to no end.

Each letter was a carbon copy of one another and composed to bring homesickness to Skyler. She wondered if her mother put Anthony up to this or if he was writing on his own accord. His letters spoke of new friends, classes, and parties in college, but not once did he ask what she was going through. Her manicured hands had been in the cavities of people, gripping arteries to keep them alive.

From within the footlocker, she pulled out a small gold band housing a large diamond. The light overhead brought an array of colors from within the shiny rock. Skyler wondered what style of ring Kyle would propose with. It reminded her of how much Anthony didn't know her.

The diamond was as large as a glacier, but Skyler preferred smaller, simpler jewelry. A dainty diamond would have been more attractive on her tiny finger. The gold was real, and most women would die for such a ring, but Skyler didn't enjoy yellow gold and was more of a white gold kind-of girl. Her selfishness repulsed her. The cost of the ring was more than most of her fellow service members made in several months.

Could Kyle afford such a ring? She asked herself again. Kyle was the complete opposite of Anthony. He was muscular where Anthony was fat, strong where Anthony was frail, and a man where Anthony was still a spoiled rich boy. Skyler tossed the ring into the footlocker and slammed the lid, knowing Anthony no longer held a place in her heart.

IV

The deep throaty kraa of two ravens penetrated the world as they cut through the sky without a care of what was below. A tingle ascended Thompson's spine and his muscles tensed as he shifted his weight off the landmine. The pounding of his heart muted the other noises surrounding him, and he didn't feel his legs walking. They moved automatically on their own.

The firing mechanism, a small button in the center of the landmine, sprang up once Thompson's boot abandoned it. Nothing exploded as he stepped away and it amazed him that the circular disk had failed to detonate. He held a cry at bay as his breathing accelerated, but he couldn't stop trembling. A long pause had elapsed and still no explosion.

He chuckled at the fact that the landmine was a dud. Then the detonator ignited the booster charge, firing off the main charge. The concussion blast shattered windows of nearby buildings. The velocity of the detonation blanketed the alley with dirt and smoke as pieces of concrete and trash hurled at the Marines taking cover.

Kyle gritted his teeth, holding back the urge to scream while his heart vacated his chest, and his head hung in despair. In a flash, a cloud of brown dust engulfed Thompson, stripping him from the other's view.

Jack rolled a cigarette between his lips and waited for the air to clear. He tried to remain calm and collected in front of his men, avoiding the nervous and grief-stricken demeanor of Kyle. They had known Thompson since dropping in the unit as boots and had been through some shit along the way. Jack couldn't breathe as he scanned the debris with hawk-like eyes for his old friend. Although he hid the nervousness well, his stomach soured.

Ashmore kept his eyes peeled, staring with a near pleasure-like gaze into the fog. Even though he wanted his friend to survive, a dark side of him hoped to see bits and pieces of Thompson flying, satisfying his grotesques fantasy of war. His nerves betrayed him, producing an unintentional smirk to rise at the most inappropriate time. Ashmore pictured a mangled body walking out of the smoke and collapsing like a wounded soldier in an old war flick.

Sutherland didn't want to watch and slid down behind the concrete barrier. He found himself hyperventilating and biting hard on his knuckle. His mind grasped to the only solace he knew from his childhood. Closing his eyes, he started to pray, hoping that if there was a God, he was listening. *Maybe Jack was wrong; maybe there is a God.* He prayed as hard as he could, not wanting to see the destruction of his comrade.

"Look." Ashmore pointed down the alley where the smoke was still trying to settle. In unison, everyone's head popped up like gophers from the ground. The smoke parted as Thompson stumbled toward his fellow Berserkers, a broken cigarette dangling from his mouth.

"Post security," Jack ordered, running from his covered position. Simpson, Black, and Vinson faced outbound, training their weapons on anything out of the ordinary. Watchful eyes of civilians came to see what happened, and the Marines ordered them back. Sutherland didn't want to stand and look. He squeezed his hands together, his prayers turning to thanks as he labored to breathe.

"That was gnarly." Thompson spoke, without breathing, like a man punched in the stomach. Jack caught him the moment he collapsed, and Kyle helped to ease him to the ground. Doc Sloan slung off his MED pack and knelt next to Thompson. Jones and Carlos ran past the small group, providing security on the opposite side of the situation.

"Shit…shit…shit." Each word coming out with a single breath. "I'm dying."

Thompson refused to open his eyes, frightened to find himself deformed or dismembered. Doc Sloan tore open Thompson's flak jacket and examined his chest. He searched for traces of blood and shrapnel but found none. A few pieces of hot metal lodged in the green fabric of his flak jacket, but nothing had grazed his skin.

Doc looked up at Jack in bewilderment and proclaimed, "He doesn't have a scratch on him."

The ringing in his ears made it hard for Thompson to hear. He hastily reached into his shirt for his silver crucifix.

"Thank you, Jesus, thank you." Thompson repeated over and over, interrupting himself only to kiss at the cross. His head dropped back, and he relaxed in the middle of the street, still kissing the crucifix. Word spread among the men that Thompson was unscathed, and they had to see it to believe it.

"I swear Thompson, you're the only person I know that God gives a shit about," Kyle said.

"If it ain't God watching your skinny white ass, I don't know who it is," Carlos said over his shoulder, amusing himself with a hearty laugh. "Shit, I didn't know gingers had souls to sell to the Devil."

Jack and Kyle helped Thompson to his wobbly legs, and Kyle replaced the broken cigarette with a lit one.

"Does this cause you to believe, Jack?" Thompson asked.

"Yeah, Jack," Kyle said chuckling. "Does this cause you to believe?"

"Fuck you, Kyle." Jack's lower lip gulped a pinch of dip. "And no Thompson, not at all. You're just one lucky sonofabtich."

Thompson's eyes shifted past Jack and Kyle, and his grin faded to a look of disbelief.

"What's he doing?" Their attention strolled down the alley to Corporal Harvey sitting against the wall. His helmet rested on the ground, flak jacket draped opened, giving the impression of a man on a work break. Jack's eyes narrowed to slits, and his eyebrows crunched inward as his teeth gnashed hard enough to hurt.

"What the fuck are you doing?" Jack's voice thundered down the alleyway. Harvey glanced at each man, finding it strange they were returning his gaze with a questioning scowl. Ashmore seemed to be the only one hysterically dumbfounded by Harvey's antics. A few of the Marines hung their heads in disappointment.

"What?" Harvey questioned their looks. "I'm taking a break, too."

Jack snarled. Starting slow and gradually elevating his voice, Jack spoke clear enough so Harvey could understand each word. "We aren't taking a break, you dumbass son of a bitch. Go get security or I swear I'll kill you."

Harvey hesitated. He was a corporal and couldn't accept someone like Jack talking to him in such a way, especially in front of the junior ranks. When he was slow to rise, Ashmore charged at him, jerking the corporal to his feet.

"You gaffing off my corporal, asshole?" Ashmore shouted in Harvey's face.

Stunned, Harvey didn't know how to react when his feet hit the ground. He shoved Ashmore, but his force did little to move the hulking Marine. Before a fight could break out, Jack stepped in, shoving his forearm into Harvey's chest, pinning him. Harvey tried to push Jack away and in doing so, incited the other Marines to step forward. Jack raised a hand, halting his threatening squad. One thing Harvey was sure of, as soon as they got back to camp, he was going to report Jack and Lance Corporal Ashmore for their hostility toward an NCO.

"Get moving, motherfucker, or I'll let Ashmore tear you apart. He's aching for a fight." Pieces of spit and tobacco spackled to Harvey's cheek. He winced to keep it from his eyes and flinched in anticipation of being hit by a punch which never came. Harvey fastened his flak jacket and gathered his gear, posting with Carlos and Jones.

"Damn it, Doc. Get the hell off me." Thompson batted away the light Doc Sloan tried desperately to shine in his eyes. As the smoke and falling debris completely disappeared, civilians made their way out of sheltered places to see what the damage was. Thompson glared at them, knowing one of them had planted the landmine, or at least knew about it.

"Yeah, motherfuckers. You can't kill me. I ain't gonna die in this Godless fucking country." Thompson beat hard his chest and flipped them off. Jack was one second away from ordering Thompson to stow his talk but decided the man deserved his rant. Doc Sloan steadied him, and without success, tried to shine the light into his eyes once again. Thompson shoved Doc. "Doc, get the fuck away from me."

"I'm trying to see if you're all right."

"I'm fucking walking and breathing. I'm great."

"Doc, is he good to continue with us?" Kyle asked.

"Hell yeah, I am." Thompson glared at Kyle as he pushed past, disgusted that his friend would question his judgement. The rest of the squad fell into formation and progressed out of the alley. The buzz still hummed through them, but a silence befell the squad.

As Ashmore stepped into the crowded street of onlookers and honking cars, the world shrank in on him. The situation choked off his air like a noose around his neck. He looked both ways and found each window and rooftop was an alarming vantage point for a sniper. Hyperventilating, he tried to spot any possible shooter but found it near impossible to do so. Ashmore gritted his teeth and steadied his thinking long enough to figure out which way to turn.

A scream erupted, startling the Marines. Red veins streaked across an Arabic woman's eyes whose dirty fingernails scratched at Ashmore.

V

Her eyes were too accustomed to the shade of her room and stepping out into the mellow light of the day blinded Skyler. The crisp warning of winter was fast approaching, but the heat of the desert still lingered. An urge to be far away from the letters and ring in her locker overpowered Skyler. A stack of paperwork needed the C.O.'s signature and it was the thing to get her out of her room and out of her head.

People traversed the compound, and she unwittingly searched each face for Kyle. He wasn't there, and she knew it, but she looked anyways. Kyle occupied her brain, causing a school-girl grin to caress her face as she pictured his sexy combat swag like a warrior from ancient times. It was a silly crush, but it didn't stop her from wanting it.

Kyle wasn't like her socialite friends. He was bold and full of brass without the smug aristocratic annoyance that her group of peers seemed to be born with. Her fingers brushed where he had kissed her and ignited a passion that still lingered there. Her skin tingled at her little daydream, but despite this guilty pleasure of a fantasy, she feared it was a false romanticism.

She paused before entering the center of command and released a groan of demoralizing disdain. One look at the C.O.C.'s door whisked away the thought of Kyle. Harvey would be waiting and there was no way to avoid him. She sighed as she entered the heavily fortified room. Her eyes darted from one desk to the next and to her delight, Harvey was nowhere in sight.

The air-conditioner hummed, and a cold breeze blew over her with a great deal of relief, but not even the icy bliss could compare to the joy of Harvey's absence. Skyler closed her eyes and let the near orgasmic coolness of the room stroke her flesh. The banging of the air-conditioner rattled against the empty silence of the room. Every desk was empty, and as curiosity overtook her, she heard the faint vibrations of a voice creeping out from behind a crack in the C.O.'s door. She sat down in a nearby seat and waited for someone to return who could help her.

The C.O.'s voice was muffled, and Skyler couldn't help but lean toward the thin door. She never cared to eavesdrop, but with no one around, there was little more for her to do. Skyler looked at the medical files in her hand, and then it hit her. She was alone in the C.O.C. without any supervision from the admin Marines. With a stealth-like manner, she crossed the room to the large metal filing cabinet, keeping an eye on the C.O.'s door in case someone opened it.

She prayed the drawer marked A-F was unlocked, and with a quick tug, it slid open. Her index finger danced across the file tabs, searching for the record labeled Dillon, Kyle CPL. The thrill of adventure coursed through her veins, and she knew it was wrong to be looking through these papers but couldn't refuse the excitement. She located the file, but before opening it, took a quick glance over her shoulder to ensure no one was watching. Kyle's entire military career was in this folder: awards, education, and service history. Skyler retrieved the paper marked 'Awards', and her jaw fell open as she read the list of his citations.

From	To	Code	Award
20030321	20030822	CR	Combat Action Ribbon
20030329	20030329	PH	Purple Heart
20030321	20030822	NN	National Defense Service Medal
20030321	20030822	WT	Global War on Terrorism Service Medal
20030321	20030822	SD	Sea Service Deployment Ribbon
20030321	20030822	WE	Global War on Terrorism Expeditionary Medal
20030329	20030329	PW	Prisoner of War Ribbon

Prisoner of War? The words seemed almost alien to her. Kyle had never mentioned being a prisoner of war, and grotesque images populated by movies flooded her mind. The Iraq war wasn't known for American prisoners, and the only one she could recall was a female soldier during the initial push into Iraq. She felt a slight ping in her heart as a hollowness descended on her. *What else was he not telling her?*

This is stupid, she thought. *He went through something traumatic and personal and why should he tell me anything? We aren't a couple, and besides, I have my own secrets, too. And we only kissed, it's not like we're an actual item.*

She was afraid to investigate further. She quietly slid the drawer back in until it latched. No one had seen her snooping.

"A lot of men are going to die." An unknown voice radiated out of the C.O.'s office, catching her attention. She tiptoed toward the door so she could listen easier, resisting the urge to place her ear against the thin sheet of wood.

"That's what happens in war; men die." The voice boomed, shouting back at whoever opposed the idea of men dying in war. She recognized it at once as the Lieutenant Colonel, the Commanding Officer of the battalion. "Many of our men will die, and as Commanding Officer, it's hard to send these men off like that, but I guarantee you, more of their men will die. These Marines are itching for a fight."

Her pounding heart prevented the slowing of her breathing and she feared her pulse would be audible to anyone in earshot. *Who's going to die and what were they gonna do to get them killed?* She wondered. Anxiety gripped her, curling her lower lip back between her teeth, and she chewed hard on it.

"Do you think these boys are ready for something like this?" The unfamiliar voice asked.

"Shit, yes. These boys train their entire lives for a moment like this, and it's going to be big, as big as Hue City."

"What are they calling it?"

"Operation Phantom Fury."

VI

The Arabic woman seized Ashmore by the collar and pulled him in close. Tears raced down her elongated face, which was locked in an agonizing horror, and pulsing with an unbearable pain. A deafening cry burst from her lungs and caused Ashmore's heart to skip. He planted his palm against her sternum and shoved, sending her wheeling back while simultaneously bringing up his SAW.

The buttstock cradled in the nook of his shoulder, and a small red band appeared when he pressed the safety button to the left. The rest of the squad peeled out from the formation and brought up their rifles, aiming at the woman. Ashmore's trigger finger curled around the small, but dangerous extension of his rifle. His pulse quickened, the muscles in his shoulder hardened for the recoil, and he exhaled a breath of death.

"Belay that." Jack heaved up the end of Ashmore's barrel, stepping between his Marine and the woman. She fell to her knees and clasped her hands together like a starving person begging for food.

"Sutherland, get up here," Jack ordered.

Sutherland ran awkwardly under the mounting combat gear to the front of the formation.

"What's she saying?" Jack asked.

Sutherland approached the woman who captured one of his legs with both of her arms. Her cries made her words inaudible. Her head rocked from side to side and she pointed across the street, before returning to bowing at his feet and sobbing. Sutherland motioned her to be quiet. When her tongue refused to stop spitting out words, he instructed her to remain silent with a harsher gesture.

While Jack waited for Sutherland to give him word, he noticed the rifles still trained on the woman. "Lower your weapons."

The men did as they were ordered. Sutherland glanced over his shoulder and shook his head at Jack. "It's hard to translate when she's crying, but she says something about daughter go… daughter gone, daughter is taken. She says her daughter was taken."

Sutherland spoke to the woman in Arabic, gesturing with his hands for her to calm down. Rocketing to her feet, she thrust a finger with great intensity at a house across the street.

"She says something about screams and pain coming from home…" Her tongue reached near light speed, and when she refused to silence herself, Sutherland screamed, "Oguf, Bass." *Stop, Enough.*

The woman went silent, trying to stifle her sobs to avoid any punishment by the Americans.

"She keeps saying over there, that house. That it's too done, it's too late, something like that. I can't figure it out with her fucking crying." Sutherland shrugged his shoulders and hung his head in failure. "Sorry, Corporal."

"You did good, Sut." Jack slapped him on the back, allowing him to pass.

Their gaze fell on the house across the street, and they lacked the words to match their expressions. With no trees nearby, the surrounding buildings glowed in the unrestricted sunlight, shrinking away from the cloud of darkness that was the lone house. No external entity cast a shadow over the structure, yet a dreary, hellish aura radiated from within. Boards and blankets sealed off the second-floor windows and large sheets of metal bolted to the brick siding on the lower floor. The house rose up from a pit of nightmares within the cursed ground, conjuring a stomach-churning stench which clawed out of the courtyard like invisible fingers.

The house beckoned Jack, pleading with him to come in and find his doom. The front door hung askew and gaped open like a hungry mouth readied to devour a juicy steak. An image of Jennifer and their unborn son clouded Jack's mind. If he went in there, there was a good chance he wouldn't be coming out again.

"Get her off the street," Jack ordered Vinson and Black, who ushered the hysterical woman away from the area. Simpson and Jones ordered other civilians to clear out. Trouble was brewing, and they wanted no civilians caught in the crossfire.

"We gonna get some, Corporal?" Ashmore asked, fixing his lustful gaze upon the dark house.

"Maybe, Ash." Jack marched past Sutherland who was taking up a security position next to Vinson.

"You think shit is about to hit the fan?" Vinson asked.

"I think so. That house looks fucked up," Sutherland said.

"Yeah, like Freddy Kruger lives there."

"No shit." Sutherland tossed in a pinch of dip and offered the can to Vinson.

"Sweet. Let's do this shit." Vinson threw in a pinch, wiped away a sprinkle of tobacco from the corner of his mouth, then held out his muzzle in front of Sutherland. Sutherland stuck the can of dip back into his frag pouch and snarled. He slammed the tip of his barrel against Vinson's as if they were mugs of beer instead of weapons.

"What's going on?" Kyle asked as Jack approached.

"Possible torture house. You good to check it out?"

"Hell yeah," Ashmore said, twisting his head back to gauge their reaction. The majority of the squad agreed.

"Shut up, Ash. I'm not asking you." Jack looked at Thompson. "You good to go?"

"Shit, yeah. Sign me up for some payback. Nearly shit myself after that landmine."

"All right then, let's do this. Kyle, take half the guys through the front. I'll take up security around back."

"What about me?" Thompson asked.

"You're staying out with me," Jack said. The verbal slap to the face caused Thompson to take a step back.

"Fuck that; I'm going in, too."

"No, you just stepped off a landmine—"

"And not a fuckin' scratch on me. I want some payback."

"Fine." Jack surrendered. "Go with Kyle. I'll take my men and station out back. Kill or flush them out to us."

Jack made a move to head back to the front of the formation, but Kyle stopped him.

"You ain't going in?" Kyle asked. His question found an ounce of hesitation in Jack's eyes. For the first time, Kyle saw the kink in Jack's armor. The man they knew as The Ripper, the original Berserker, allowed uncertainty to infiltrate his mind and cast doubt on his abilities. Jack didn't say anything, but Kyle knew Jack was thinking of his family back home. He pulled Jack closer so no one within earshot could hear his whispers and repeated, "You really aren't going in?"

Jack threw Kyle's hand off him, blinking away the look of worry.

"No, someone has to be on the outside. Why?" Jack asked. Kyle shrugged his shoulders and stepped past his best friend.

"Nothing. I'll take care of this."

With an itchy trigger finger, Ashmore waited for the signal to move out like a small child in need of a restroom. On Kyle's command and before Jack could get his men in place, Ashmore led the Berserkers out into the open street. Civilians fled, cowering in nearby stores or homes to watch the movement of the United States Marines.

"Kyle, wait." Jack shouted but Kyle didn't respond. The Marines hustled to the front yard of the dark house causing Jack to hurry his men around back to get security. They shuffled down a large alleyway cutting between two rows of houses and stacked up behind the dark house.

With a knife hand, Kyle directed Carlos and Harvey to provide security at the front gate. They slid in behind the cement fence, crouching down for cover, and aimed across one another's line of fire. They scanned the town's populace, anticipating any possible threat of an ambush. Ashmore glided through the dirt covered front yard and up the steps of the dark house. Kyle and Thompson stacked up behind him with Jones following.

"Go for it, Hoss." Kyle motioned to Ashmore. His cheeks stretched backward in a sadistic joker smile, with eyes wide in bloodlust. He stepped back, grunted, and planted his size eleven boot in the center of the door. It splintered under the impact, ripping off its hinges, and flew inward as the Marines funneled in. The sun abandoned the men as they crossed the threshold into the lingering darkness. A pungent odor of rotting flesh halted their advancement, causing bile to saturate their throats.

"What the fuck is that smell?" Thompson asked. Jones and Ashmore rushed the stairs to investigate the second floor, hoping the stench would dissipate the further up they went.

Despite difficulty seeing, Kyle managed to avoid walking into a table centered in the room. The quick transition from light to dark plagued his eyes with blindspots, and he couldn't see the object which caused him to roll his ankle. He stumbled, trying to regain his footing, and stuck his arm out to prevent falling. Warmth radiated off the interior dwelling, and a thick substance glued his hand to the plaster. Small rays of sunlight penetrated many cracks, revealing the blood-painted wallpaper. Kyle dropped his gaze to the severed human foot under his boot.

"Jesus fuckin' Christ." Kyle jumped back. Thompson clicked on his flashlight and illuminated the area. At the far side of the house, a long hallway stretched into a dead end. Thompson's light failed to penetrate the blank void. He stepped closer to the hall, and as if coming out of some abyss, a half-open bedroom door materialized. The shadow of a man rushed out of the darkness, catching the Marines off-guard. The initial shock caused Thompson to yank back on his trigger.

BANG. Recoil. Miss.

BANG. Recoil. Miss.

Both rounds went right over the man's head and embedded into the frame of a bedroom door.

"Oguf, bitch." Kyle screamed out, trailing the man with his rifle. The man ducked his head, shielding it with both arms as he stormed through the living room and into the kitchen. "Stop motherfucker."

VII

Jack gave the backyard a quick scan as they rounded the surrounding shoulder high cement wall and entered the rear gate. The rear of the house sat tilted, casting a drearier and more distorted structure than the front. The nightmarish dwelling brought an uneasy quiver to Jack's stomach. He hustled through the yard as two shots rang out from within the house.

Vinson and Sutherland quickly posted at the entrance of the gate, mirroring Carlos and Harvey's position at the front.

Jack dashed toward the rear door with Simpson close behind.

The blue metal door flung open and over the descending concrete steps flew a surprised young Iraqi man. His feet were far from the ground when he spotted the two combat Marines approaching. A disbelief, masked in dread, crossed his face as he tried to change trajectory in mid-air. Simpson launched over Jack's shoulder and with his large fist, struck the young man with a solid thud, rattling his brain. His feet swung up into the air, coming over his head before he smacked hard against the unforgiving ground.

The ability to breathe evaded him, preventing him from choking on the blood accumulating in his nasal passage. He gasped, labored to draw in a breath, and rolled over to his stomach. Jack snatched his wrists and pushed them upward into his shoulder blades, pinning him to the ground. The man's face flushed red, and his eyes bulged in their sockets, as he continued to struggle for air.

His lower jaw quivered to produce a sound, but nothing came. Blood leaked from both nostrils, and he wanted nothing more than to cry for help. A chain reaction of agony began in his head and screamed throughout his entire body.

"Jack," Kyle's voice echoed from within the house. "You may want to see this."

"No, I don't," Jack shouted back. There came a pause.

"Yeah, you do. Fucker."

"Vinson, Doc, watch the prisoner," Jack said. Vinson approached and placed a knee on the man's back to which the man groaned.

"I'll watch him," Vinson said. He twisted his knee hard into the man, delighting himself at the man's discomfort. Doc ushered Vinson off the prisoner's back while Jack and Simpson ventured into the house. Vinson glared at Doc and said, "What are you doin'?"

"Checking to make sure he's fine. We still have to give aid to our enemies, you know." Doc shined his penlight into the man's eyes, checking his pupils as Vinson fashioned black zip ties to his wrists.

"You have the right to remain silent," Vinson stated, pulling the zip ties tight. "Anything you say will cause me to shoot you in the head. If you have an attorney, I'll shoot that motherfucker, too. If you don't know what I'm saying to you, please speak up in your chicken scratch kind of gibberish, and I'll gladly put a bullet in your head."

Jack and Simpson pushed through the kitchen, not hearing Vinson's verbal assault. They rounded the table when the god-awful smell stopped them in their tracks.

"God damn, Corporal. What the fuck is that?" Simpson covered his nose and mouth to discourage himself from vomiting.

"That's death." The odor amplified as Jack rounded the corner of the kitchen and stepped into the thick air of the living room.

"Oh, my God." Simpson gasped at the grotesque scene which resembled something out of the medieval Tower of London. Bodies chained to the walls; their intestines touching the floor in a steaming pile. Tiny bodies of children laid scattered with bullet wounds. Shackled to the table, a man was gagged with his own amputated genitals. The dense scent of iron hung in the air as well as the cooked meat of recently burned bodies. In two of the four corners of the living room was an assortment of dismembered body parts.

"Sutherland, bring that piece of shit in here," Jack shouted over his shoulder. It wasn't long before Sutherland came through, kicking the detainee, and presenting him in front of Jack. A blood goatee smeared over the man's face.

Jack dug his fingernails into the back of the Iraqi's neck and kicked him behind the knee, causing him to buckle. In his excitement, Sutherland had failed to take in a breath. He was all smiles and wide-eyed, but when the smell hit his stomach, it lurched like that of seasickness. He rushed to relieve it in the kitchen sink.

Jack shoved the man's face within an inch of a dead ten-year-old girl. Her hollowed eye sockets and mutilated body produced a surprised scream from the man. He fought to push away, but Jack held firm.

"What'd she do to deserve this?" Spit splattered as Jack spoke. Wiping bits of bile from his chin, Sutherland translated what Jack was saying.

"He says they had to teach the parents of these children a lesson. He says their parents were traitors to Saddam and the children had to pay for that. They couldn't let the children grow up not supporting the great Saddam. He says they're better off dead."

"Better off dead? For a lesson?" Jack jerked his sidearm from its holster on his hip and spun the gun around to catch it by the barrel. He pulled the man's head back so that his spine arched in a painful manner. "Well, I got a lesson for you. I want you to remember the joy of eating without using a straw."

Jack heaved the pistol high above him and snarled as he said, "Oh, and fuck Saddam."

The man bared his teeth like a rabid dog. The pistol swung downward, striking him in the jaw, and sent broken teeth flying. He flopped back onto the sticky floor, choking on what remained in his mouth. The restraints holding his arms behind his back denied him the ability to clutch his face. Then his cries turned into a strange gurgling laughter.

The fine hair on Simpson's neck stood on end. Paranoia sent his eyes darting to every shadowy spot, trying to see if a threat was lurking. He brought up his rifle and waved it around the room until Jack captured the shaky barrel. The laughter made his blood boil, and after releasing Simpson's rifle, Jack grabbed the Iraqi man's collar.

"What the fuck is so funny?"

"I go to Abu-Ghraib prison." The man spoke in a clear English dialect. "I get medical treatment, food, shelter, and the Qur'an to pray to Allah to kill you American bastards."

"Oh yeah, funny, right?" Jack towered over the man and cut short his laughter with a series of pistol whippings to the side of his head. The man went limp, still breathing, but barely. "Still funny, motherfucker. Try reading with brain damage, bitch."

Jack spat on him and holstered his sidearm. Sutherland stared at Jack in disbelief. Kyle enjoyed seeing the Berserker side of his friend once again.

"Get his ass out of here," Jack ordered. Thompson and Simpson picked the man up off the ground. His legs were limp, but he stood as best as he could and growled at Jack. "Send his ass to the Israelis."

At once the man's demeanor changed, and the growl turned into sobs as the rest of the strength in his legs gave out. He looked up at Jack, one eye closed and swollen because of the fracture to his orbital bone and he cried red tears. His expression turned from shock to complete terror as he violently shook in protest.

"No mister, no. No Israelis." Tears flowed in full force down his cheeks. "No…no…no Israelis."

Jack's deception warmed him. His men knew he was lying; the prison would offer everything the detainee had mention. The infamous stacking of the prisoners and torture pictures changed everything. Abu-Ghraib Prison was no longer a place to fear, but rather a five-star resort for the insurgency. The treatment of the prisoners was better than the Marines on the ground. It was because of this that Jack took pleasure in lying to the now begging man.

Simpson and Thompson hoisted the man off the ground. He wailed, scared to be in the clutches of the Israelis, but never flinched a muscle in resistance. He hung his head and sobbed long after he was out of the house.

"Corporal Dillon, can you come up here?" Jones called from the second-floor landing. Exhausted at what seemed like an endless task inside this house of horrors, Kyle nudged Jack. Along with Sutherland, they sauntered up the stairs.

Kyle poked his head into the first room they came to and immediately regretted it. He wished he would've made the assumption that Ashmore and Jones had cleared out the room, but one had to check unless they knew for a fact the room was clear. There were no insurgents, but upon opening the door, a gush of heat slapped him in the face. A reeking stench far more powerful than the one downstairs blew out.

Kyle counted. He didn't know why he did, but he counted each body which hung from hooks like meat in a freezer. They were nude, males and females alike, and their heads laid tilted to one shoulder. Staring at the ground, their eyes no longer saw this world. There was a dozen of them and not one more hideous than the next.

"Room clear." Kyle eased the door close without stepping inside, having seen all he needed to.

Jack and Sutherland bypassed Kyle, moving onto the next room. Rumbling down the hall was the blood-curdling screams of a woman. The three men broke out in a full sprint with their weapons at the ready. Ashmore circled out of the room, holding his arm, and cursing at the blood oozing through his fingers. They entered to find Jones with his hands held up in a calming manner, rifle slung behind his back and a teenage girl in the distant corner.

She stood on the other side of a king size bed, a knife held out in front of her, and not a stitch of clothing to hide behind. Tears flowed down her cheeks, and each time Jones neared, she swiped the blade at him. Blood smeared the insides of her thighs and lacerations ran in patterns across her flesh, leaving a scripture of pain for all to read. The girl, younger than Jennifer was when Jack started dating her, screamed something in Arabic while slashing the knife at the men.

"What the hell is going on?" Jack asked. Jones never looked away from the victim.

"We found her unconscious by the bed. Ash woke her, and when he did, she cut him," Jones said. Ashmore stood at the door, still clutching his arm, and shrugging his shoulders.

"I've had worse."

"Go get it checked out with Doc."

"I said I'm fine, Corporal."

"And I gave you a direct order, Lance Corporal. Go and bring Doc up here to treat her when he's done with you."

"Aye, Aye, Corporal," Ashmore said before vanishing down the stairs.

"Sutherland, what's she saying?" Jack asked. Sutherland removed his glasses and rubbed at the spot where they rested on the bridge of his nose. He leaned up against the wall near the door, wiped dust free from his lenses, and replaced the eyewear on his face.

"She says she wants to go home. She never did anything and please, no more hurt."

"Tell her we're going to get her medical treatment. Reassure her we're here to help." Sutherland stepped near the bed and repeated in

Arabic what Jack had ordered. She swiped the knife at Sutherland, causing him to retreat. Jack was quick to draw down on her, but Sutherland raised his hands for Jack to lower his weapon. "Jones, go tell Black to get HQ on the hooks. Radio in for a medical truck to evac this woman to Camp Fallujah."

"Aye, Corporal." Jones peeled out of the room while Kyle retrieved a blanket off the bed to wrap around her. The hysterical girl forced the knife at him. Her screams were nails driving into Jack's ears.

"Sutherland, get her to shut up with that."

"I'm trying, Corporal."

"Well, try harder, or it's your ass." Jack demanded. Sutherland spun around, gritted his teeth, and shouted at the girl in her native tongue. To Jack's surprise, the woman closed her lips tight, only allowing small whimpers to escape. The knife dropped from her hand and bounced hard off the concrete flooring. Kyle moved like lightning to cover her shoulders with the blanket.

Her body trembled beneath the wool fabric and the fear froze her legs. Kyle gave her a gentle nudge and led the sobbing woman to the door. He held her shoulders tightly to help control the involuntary tremors. Sutherland started to follow, but Jack stopped him. His eyes fixed on Jack's hand holding his bicep, and he wanted to jerk free from it as if it was toxic. He refrained from doing so and instead, brought his dull, emotionless eyes up to meet that of Jack's.

"What did you say to her?" Jack asked.

"I told her if she didn't stop, we would allow this to happen again." Jack's mind panicked, and the urge to punch the private first class was hard to resist. Jack's blood pressure rose at the thought of this woman going to the media to tell the world that Marines were allowing this to happen if you didn't obey them.

"Why in God's name would you say that?" Jack snarled, and this time, Sutherland didn't hesitate to pull his arm free.

"God? What God would allow this?" Sutherland asked. Jack had no answer for him. Sutherland shrugged his shoulders and continued, "Besides, it got her to shut up, didn't it, Corporal?"

For the third time that day, Sutherland hung his head.

VIII

A shot of whiskey was waiting for Jack as he came in from the showers. Skyler and Kyle sat at their circular table in the NCO's room, indulging in their drinks. Jack picked up the small shot, tossed it back, and asked for another.

"What's the word?" Jack asked.

"Word is they are planning on feeding us steak and lobster or some shit for a big meal. Might be for the Marine Birthday next month." Kyle answered with his lips touching the brim of his cup.

"Doubt it's for the birthday. Same meal they give to death row inmates, right?" Kyle and Skyler nodded. Kyle poured more whiskey into Jack's cup and offered him a cola with Arabic writing on it. Jack nodded his head in approval of the soda and Kyle filled his cup. He took a sip, closing his eyes and smiling at the pleasant sensation running over his tongue. "Damn that's good."

"How's the shower?" Skyler asked.

"Still fuckin' broken and cold as shit."

"I'm sure they will have it fixed soon," Kyle said.

"I doubt it."

"I'm sorry to hear that Harvey is in your squad now," Skyler said.

"Oh, you know the guy?"

"He kind of has a thing for me. It's annoying; he's annoying."

"I'm learning that." Jack threw his shower gear on his top rack and took a much-needed seat at the table. His feet hurt and propping them on the empty chair brought about a great sigh of relief. He hadn't relaxed the entire day, and since getting back to base, he had been doing paperwork on the hell house. His mind having to replay the gruesome scene over and over as he wrote out each detail of the incident.

Jack took a sip again, and although it was missing ice cubes, it was quite refreshing. He settled into the chair, and his shoulders dropped. Finally, he allowed himself to relax. He held up his plastic cup toward Kyle.

"Thanks for the drink," Jack said, and Kyle toasted his cup in the same manner. "Pals."

"Pals," Kyle replied and drank. Skyler tossed a look between the two men as they drank their cups. A snicker escaped her.

"What was that?" she asked.

"What do you mean?" Kyle wiped at the drops of drink that clung to the stubble on his upper lip.

"Pals? What's that?"

"It's just something we've done for a long time. You ever see Young Guns?" Jack asked. There was a look of abandonment on her face as she was clueless to what he was saying. "Young Guns? Western from the 80's? Emilio Estevez?"

The look continued.

"Shit, you've never seen Young Guns one or two? Damn it, lady." Kyle said displeased. "It's about Billy the Kid. It's one of those movies we like to quote."

"Damn right," Jack said and raised his glass again. "To the game."

Kyle touched the brim of his cup to Jack's. "To the game."

"OK, what's that?" Skyler asked.

"See, there's three Chinamen playing fan-tan." Jack straightened in his chair, leaning his elbows on the table so Skyler could see into his eyes. "This guy runs up to them and says, *Hey, the world's coming to an end.* And the first one says, *Well, I best go to the mission and pray.* And the second one says, *Well, hell, I'm gonna go and buy me a case of Mezcal and six whores.* And the third one says,"

"Well, I'm gonna finish the game," Kyle proclaimed. The two men banged their cups together and downed the rest of their mixed drinks.

"Boys with guns, always want to be cowboys."

"Shit, we are cowboys. Fuckin' Berserkers and rough riders. Outlaws and warriors of a modern age." Jack stood and poured himself another drink. Kyle raised his cup and Jack poured him one too. Skyler laughed while waving off the offer to refill her drink.

"Jack, why do they call you The Ripper?"

"Because I'm Jack the Ripper, baby. I slice'em and dice'em. Shit, we're Marines. We're the first ones in and the last ones out." Jack took a long drink, not seeing Kyle's tipsy eyes on him.

"You sure about that?" Kyle questioned. Jack sat his drink down and allowed himself the full swallow before speaking.

"What's that mean?" Jack asked. Skyler unknowingly sat back away from the two as the tension grew in the room.

"Just saying, you know."

"No, I don't know."

"Hey guys, come on." Skyler tried to step in, but Jack wasn't having it.

"No...no...no. He has something he wants to say."

"Just saying, you hesitated back there at that house today."

"What? Fuck you, when?"

"Look, the Jack I know, the fuckin' original Berserker, The fuckin' Ripper, he would've been the first through that door, but you sent another team in. Just think you got something on your mind that's holding you back." His throat went dry.

"Kyle, stop—"

"No Skyler. Let's have this. Come on. I got home on my mind, so?" Jack said.

"Well, you said it."

"Yeah, I've been thinking of home, so what! I have a family now. I have to think of home."

"You were the guy that told me not to think of home because it could get you killed."

"That was the last deployment," Jack said.

"Still holds true, bro." Kyle ripped the tab off a new can of cola and poured it into his whiskey. "You keep worrying about home, you're going to get someone killed or get yourself killed."

"Oh, I'm sure you would hate that?"

"Fuck you. What the fuck does that mean?" His stomach weakened, and the uneasy sensation moved throughout his legs, preparing him for a fist fight.

"Just saying," Jack stood, leaning forward, and tapping his index finger on the plywood table. "If I'm still here, you don't have to be the leader, and God knows you don't want that job."

"I've never backed out of taking command."

"Shit, you don't want command. That's why you wanted me to go on this fuckin' tour."

"Bullshit!" Kyle shot up from the table and came nose to nose with Jack. The whiskey-fueled them both, and their faces didn't mask this fact. "You wanted on this tour because you can't hack civilian life. You had every opportunity to get out, but you didn't want it. You spend so much damn time worrying about home, why didn't you just stay there?"

"Because of the game, god damn it. Because of the game." Jack jerked his rifle from the bedpost, grabbed his journal from under his pillow, and marched to the door. He didn't pause as he said, "I will finish this game!"

He threw open the door and stormed out into the hall, never looking back to see if the door closed. Kyle slid back into his seat and took a long pull off his whiskey.

"Well, that went nice," Skyler said.

"Some things need to be said."

* * *

From the pages of Jack Campbell's Journal-

Screw this place. Today sucked; worst day since Josh died. I ain't seen anything like a house we saw today, and I'll never forget it. Some images get burned into your brain. What kind of monsters would do that? I hope the rumors are true about Fallujah. I seriously want to fuck these bastards up.

To me, all religions are bullshit. What kind of God would want people to do this shit to someone like a little girl? Religions are all the same, they kill and judge then kill some more, and it never ends. It never ends, and I'm sick of it.

I am thinking of home more. Kyle is right, and it does break one of my rules of war. How can I make it home if I don't give this place and this mission all that I have? Shit, what will I be when I get home? Is Jennifer right when she said I need this to survive, to live, and is Kyle right about me not hacking civilian life?

Can I hack it?

What am I testing myself for? Why am I doing this? I've done it all over here, why do I want to keep doing this?

If there is a God, I have questions, and he better have answers. How can you sit on the sidelines and allow this shit to happen? You have all the supernatural powers of the universe and can stop this kind of shit, but you'd rather watch like some sick psychopath and do nothing. Is there a God? Are you real?

CHAPTER SIX

5.56 JUSTICE

-This is my rifle. There are many like it, but this one is mine.

My rifle is my best friend. It is my life. I must master it as I must master my life.

My rifle without me is useless. Without my rifle, I am useless. I must fire my rifle true. I must shoot straighter than my enemy who is trying to kill me. I must shoot him before he shoots me. I will...

My rifle and myself know that what counts in this war is not the rounds we fire, the noise of our burst, nor the smoke we make. We know that it is the hits that count. We will hit...

My rifle is human, even as I, because it is my life. Thus, I will learn it as a brother. I will learn its weaknesses, its strengths, its parts, and its accessories, its sights, and its barrel. I will keep my rifle clean and ready, even as I am clean and ready. We will become part of each other. We will...

Before God, I swear this creed. My rifle and myself are the defenders of my country. We are the masters of our enemy. We are the saviors of my life.

So be it, until Victory is America's and there is no enemy, but peace!-

The Rifleman's Creed

I

Pre-dawn hours of November 8th, 2004 – City of Fallujah.

The seven-ton troop-carrier bobbed to one side and then slammed to the other. The men occupying the large vehicle shifted slightly in their cramped seats and paid little mind to the rough terrain.

Jack, sitting at the rear of the troop-carrier, caught sight of the hatch's metal handle vibrating in the moonlight. He grabbed it, fighting against the tremors in the metal, and ensured it would hold. They were crammed in the troop-carrier, shoulder smashing into shoulder, and Jack didn't want his men nor himself falling out the back.

Satisfied the metal door would hold, he flipped down his night vision goggles attached to his Kevlar helmet and peered out at the massive convoy cutting through the desert. Small red blackout lights burned bright green in his night vision, lighting up the desert for miles.

It had been the biggest convoy of military vehicles Jack had ever seen and wondered if the Marines in World War II felt like this heading to Japanese controlled islands. Inside the perimeter of Fallujah, great explosions brightened the cloudy night. The flash was lightning quick and vanished to leave behind a burning image of what had been. Field artillery cannons fired at will and without restraint. They struck various portions of the city with no regard to whom may be there.

The bright shower of destruction came to Jack in a great green form. It was blinding, but far enough away that the auto-sensor didn't switch off the goggles. Jack sat back against the uncomfortable wooden bench cutting through the middle of the truck, pleased with the destruction. His head bumped against the back of Kyle who sat behind him, facing the other direction. Kyle said nothing but watched the night on his side.

The rest of the squad occupied the remaining section of the back to back benches. Facing outbound, they kept a keen eye open for any possible attack. Yawns and boredom stretched across the men's faces despite the battle growing closer. A few kept a silent prayer and anxiously wondered how they'd perform when faced with battle. An artillery round erupted and the truck rattled, but this didn't stop some of the men from falling asleep.

"Marines sleep anywhere." Jack amused himself. A hand nudged his shoulder, and Jack managed to turn as far as his gear would permit.

The pre-dawn morning didn't allow for Jack to make out Kyle's facial features.

"Can't find my dip. Hit me up." The churning of the engine and the pounding of the tires made Kyle's voice nearly inaudible, but he shouted over the distractions. They had forgotten the argument they had over drinks three weeks prior, and neither held a grudge. Jack pulled a can of stateside dip from his grenade pouch and handed it to Kyle.

"How's things on your side?" Kyle tossed a pinch and handed the can back.

"Like watching the fourth of July," Jack replied, putting a dip in his lip before returning the can to the grenade pouch on the chest of his flak jacket.

"Would you two be quiet. Muthafucka tryin' to get some sleep over here." Carlos adjusted his helmet and nestled his head onto Simpson's shoulder.

Another flash popped, and Jack saw a few of his men were wide-eyed with fear, and he hoped his own fears weren't as obvious. The white smoke of the explosions drifted over the dark city, resembling four giant Victorian women with large butts and tiny waists. The illusion humored Jack. The giant smoke women held purses up to their chins and walked in short steps across the starless sky.

Sutherland couldn't understand why Jack was chuckling to himself. His legs were shaking uncontrollably, and he found nothing funny about their situation. His nerves betrayed him, and he hoped the Marines flanking him couldn't feel his jitters. He looked at the desert, trying to find something that would take his mind off his worries. In the distance, barely visible among the vast abyss in front of him, a strange red glow appeared, traveling fast and parallel to their convoy.

The dot, no bigger than the cherry on a cigarette, flew fast and unsteady as if riding on the back of a wave and Sutherland lost it in a small flash of fire. He eagerly scanned the desert in hopes of seeing it again, unsure of what it was he saw in the first place. A minute went by when out in the darkness, the small cherry glowed again. Sutherland nudged Vinson with his knee, startling the sleep-deprived Marine.

"What?" Vinson asked, keeping his voice low. It was dark and felt right not to speak loudly.

"What's that?" Vinson followed Sutherland's finger, like looking down the sights of a rifle until he found the red glow.

"Oh, it's a TOW missile."

"Why does it move like that?"

"You never saw a TOW before?" Vinson asked.

"No."

"It's on a wire. The guy firing it is looking through goggles, and wherever he looks, the missiles go. So, what you're seeing there is the guy breathing. Pretty cool, huh?" Vinson said. Sutherland sat back in astonishment, his fear and confusion vanishing. "You all right?"

"I don't know, man. This is crazy."

"Yeah, you got your Bible?" Sutherland pulled it out of his cargo pocket. He held it tight, so his shaking hands didn't lose it over the side. Although he carried it with him everywhere, he had yet to open it since the hell house. Sutherland didn't want to read about judgment or paradise, but the weight of the book still brought him a sense of comfort. Vinson nudged Sutherland with his elbow and said, "Just keep praying. I'm sure it'll be all right."

Another flash flamed, and the silhouettes of tall buildings glimmered before fading into the nothingness from which they came. Tracer rounds, glowing red, cut through the night like lasers. This brought back memories of the Star Wars movies to Sutherland, and the feeling of them in a futuristic space war washed away thoughts of a desert fight. A vehicle to their rear burst in a blinding flash and most of the Berserkers gasped as they looked on.

"Damn, they're firing back with mortars. Eyes open, gents." Sutherland motioned toward the fireball in the darkness. With no other rounds impacting, the other men stared with nervous eyes at the bombarded city. They knew it held their demise.

"I know, can you believe this shit? We're going into battle, man." The excitement in Vinson's voice alarmed Sutherland.

"I'm gonna puke."

"Don't do it on me, asshole. Go over the side," Vinson said on the tail-end of another explosion. "Or throw up on Black."

Black, sitting on the opposite side of Sutherland, sat more wide-eyed than the rest. His jaw hurt from clenching at each pop, and his barrel rested against his helmet as if he was praying to a cross. Vinson leaned over Sutherland to slap Black's rifle away from his head.

"You're gonna blow your fuckin' brains out like that. Lean up against something else and keep your rifle pointed outbound. Fucktard."

The white clouds of artillery burst fascinated Ashmore. Each pop, blast, or flash of light meant some other hajji just bought the farm. Ashmore interlocked his fingers together and bowed his head to pray. The others who saw this thought it odd, but unbeknownst to them, Ashmore wasn't praying for anyone's safety. He prayed all the enemy wouldn't be dead before he got his chance to kill some.

"If you can't see me, then just listen up." Jack's voice interrupted the Marines fixated on the battle unfolding before them. The periodic blast of mortars and arty shells drowned out his voice, but he shouted so all could hear despite these interruptions. "You all heard the C.O.'s talk about how big this battle is gonna be. It's gonna be the next Hue City or some shit."

The Marines nodded, whether Jack could see them or not.

"We're gonna hit the train station hard. Anyone with a weapon is an enemy combatant. You get me?" A few barks and growls came at him, but he couldn't see from who. "I want everyone to stay fucking frosty."

Jack held the armor-plate, trying to avoid taking a spill over the side as the trucks slammed into one dip after another. The Marines grunted and cheered Jack.

"Don't forget what you are; you're Berserkers. Battle's the blood within your veins. This is your time to earn your stories, earn your place in Valhalla."

On top of the seven-ton's cab, the rapid cha-cha-cha-cha of the .50 cal weapon system summoned all eyes to its massive report. Nerves broke, and Black lurched over the armor to relieve his breakfast. The convoy neared the train station as enemy rounds returned fire at the trucks. Some of the Marines flinched, ducking their heads to avoid catching a stray round. Jack stood despite the potential danger.

Enemy tracers flew past. Flares flashed glimpses of the walls, silhouetting the structure of the train station. The Marines checked their rifles as adrenaline started coursing through their veins. The seven-ton came to an abrupt halt, sliding across the loose gravel. Another flare illuminated the night sky and other trucks stopped. Marines poured out the back of the bulky vehicles, heading toward the firing line.

"You're Berserkers." Jack kicked open the back hatch and dropped to the ground, turning to wave his men forward. "Chaos unleashed."

Men hurried out of the back of the trucks and kept a low profile to avoid incoming AK rounds.

"Tear this city to the fucking ground." Jack roared with the power of a mighty lion. A frenzy overtook his men, and with war cries so fierce, they drove the enemy within earshot to retreat. No nerves failed them as their training kicked in. AK rounds dinged off the armor plating of the seven-ton trucks, and the men took up a prone position on the ground. Flipping their weapons to semi-auto, they were impatient to return fire.

Sutherland kept his head low to the ground as rounds screamed overhead. He glanced up only to spot Jack's legs running past him, pausing long enough to motion his men to follow. A small paved road wrapped around an open section of dirt and elevated up to the train station's parking lot. The higher terrain gave the insurgent a tactical superiority over the battlefield.

Jack hustled across the oval-shaped opening nestled between the berm and the road. The Berserkers followed and running full speed, fired their rifles at unseen targets. The men slammed into a steep embankment made of loose soil and rocks, thankful to find cover from enemy fire.

The winding road leading to the parking lot by the train station appeared absent of booby-traps, but no Marine was foolish enough to exploit it. A Marine from the next squad rushed up the loose dirt of the embankment, firing his M16 at targets illuminated by flares drifting down from the sky. As he reached the top of the ridge, a round struck him in the chest. His legs jerked out from under him and he tumbled down the rough and rocky mound.

Harvey buried himself in the ground as far as it would permit, wishing he had an E-tool to dig in even deeper. Rounds fired in both directions, and Harvey abandoned moving until they ceased.

"What do we do, Corporal?" Sutherland asked. Their eyes besieged Jack, capturing him, and still, they found themselves surprised at his ominous smile seen shining through the darkness of Iraq.

"Berserkers," Jack pushed himself to his feet, snorted, and spat into the dirt. "Take the fuckin' train station."

He led the charge up the embankment. At the top of the berm, he dropped to the ground, exposing only his head, rifle, and shoulders. Quickly, he assessed the situation, popping enemies at random as his men plopped into a mirroring position. Rounds zipped by, but Jack was unfazed. He fired without restraint, taking out the enemy and providing cover for his own men.

An impact punched Jack in the head a moment before he heard a round whip by. His helmet tore away, and the velocity sent him spiraling toward the base of the embankment. The Berserkers froze, watching helplessly as Jack tumbled down the dirt mound. Dust and rocks kicked up until he crashed to the level ground below.

Seeing his friend and mentor taken out on the first push sent Sutherland into a frenzy. He gritted his teeth and unleashed a fury through rapid trigger pull.

Doc and Kyle raced down the berm, their feet skimming the dirt as they flew to the aid of their comrade who laid face down. They rolled Jack over, and at once he popped up. Shaking his head and looking for his helmet, Jack stared at Kyle and Doc like a man waking from a dream. Kyle handed him his helmet with a large gash running the length of the cover. His jaw stiffened, and despite his throbbing temples, Jack slammed the helmet on his head. Blinking to clear his vision before looking up, he saw the faces of several Berserkers staring down at him.

"What? Am I sexy, you want to fuck me? What are you waiting for?" He shouted, stunning the men as he jumped to his feet and ran up the berm. "Kyle's team lay down suppressive fire. The rest of you, assault the station. Get there before anyone else beats you to it. You're Berserkers. You're Marines, first into battle, this is your destiny."

Kyle, Carlos, Ashmore, and Doc Sloan positioned at the top of the berm, firing at insurgents hiding among the train station. From behind them, the chatter of a .50 cal M2 weapon system created a steady stream of tracer fire at the buildings. There was no time to stop and admire the great action. The remaining Berserkers scrambled over the top without pausing and thundered across the paved parking lot to assault the main structure.

Large streetlight towers dotted the compound with insurgent snipers occupying the highest points. A round struck near Ashmore's foot and he dropped to one knee. Catching the flash of a sniper's rifle, he hastily aimed up and jerked back on the SAW's trigger. Sparks flew as 5.56 rounds clipped the metal railing of the streetlights and shattered glass rained down. The sniper, unable to shield himself from penetrating bullets, dropped his Dragunov rifle then slumped over the side of the fifty-foot pole.

The roar of gunfire muffled his screams, but Ashmore swore he heard the body hit hard and wet on the unyielding pavement below.

The .50 cal M2 died off, allowing more Marines to close in on the structure. Jones rounded the corner and spotted the craze-fueled eyes of an insurgent and the enormous barrel of his AK. Surprised that he didn't have to think, his finger, his arm, his instincts tapped out a hammer drill.

BANG. Recoil. Sucking chest wound.

BANG. Recoil. Chest wound.

BANG. Recoil. Head shot.

The insurgent's flight instinct demanded that he run, but the only thing he could do was fall to the ground, dead. The Marines filed into the main courtyard, screaming war cries, but found no enemy to fight.

Enemies not dead or dying fled out the back of the station and across the tracks to the towering city beyond. Each room was searched and cleared, but the only things left were dead insurgents and unsatisfied Marines.

II

Dear Anthony,

I hope this letter finds you well. I don't know where to begin. Life in Iraq is hard, not that you care. I miss seeing everyone and hope everyone is well, but I don't miss the way of life you have come to cherish. Maybe I'm writing to tell you I'll never come home again.

Or I'm writing this out of fear I'll never leave this place. I don't know for sure. I know when or if I do come home, I won't be the same pretty little princess everyone knew. I've seen things in this country you could never even dream of. You know nothing of pain and suffering, Anthony.

You're planning to live a life with someone who enjoys being outwardly superficial, but I'm not that kind of person. I love you and always will. You were the first boy I ever loved, and I thank you for the time we shared together, but I know I cannot persuade you to leave your one-dimensional way of thinking just like you cannot persuade me to return to it. I hope you look back on the time we shared together with fond memories and as a learning experience. I know I will.

I release you from your promise to wait for me, although I'm sure you have not been faithful. Even so, I don't hold it against you. Enclosed in the envelope, you'll find the engagement ring. It's a gorgeous ring, and I hope you find a beautiful finger to put it on. Live well, Anthony and follow your dreams. You only get one life, so go live it.

-Skyler

Under the military approved red flashlight, Skyler crumpled up the letter and tossed it into the floorboard of the Humvee to join the two others resting there. Sitting slumped for a while caused her back to ache and she sat up, allowing blood to drain back into her feet. They tingled from being propped up on the open door and felt as if they weighed a ton. She rubbed her stiffening neck, stepping out from the tan Humvee, and looked back at Fallujah.

Arty shells exploded about the city, painting an abstract picture, and hypnotizing her. Several Marines slept in nearby ditches, ignoring the action. The convoy, carrying personnel and supplies to the train station, waited for the Marines to secure the compound from enemy combatants.

Skyler occupied the medical Humvee with three other Corpsmen and the majority of the medical equipment. She knew the dangers and hardships were real and the wounded and dead would mount up quickly, but her thoughts were only for Kyle heading to the front lines, ready to assault the enemy at any moment. In the distance, she could see the tracer rounds and explosions directed at the train station. The noise woke the Marines and personnel in the convoy, causing them to stand and watch.

The call box on the radio squealed something inaudible to her and her vehicle commander replied, "Yes, sir."

HM1 Roe released the small black handset, allowing the taut cord to recoil back toward the base of the radio. He stepped out of the Humvee and leaned up against the hood to watch the fireworks peppering the city.

"What'd command say?" Skyler asked as she approached him, her words sounding strange amidst the backdrop of war. He didn't turn to look at her, but instead kept his eyes on the city and wondered what they were heading into.

"The Marines have taken the train station." The two other medics in their vehicle were asleep and didn't hear them speaking.

"That's good," Skyler replied.

"They're pushing into the city. We move out in five mikes. Pass the word." Before Roe could finish, word was already traveling down the line. Men gathered their gear and headed for the trucks.

"Were there any casualties?" Skyler asked as a sickening feeling washed over her. Grisly images of Kyle torn to shreds flooded her mind. His face replaced the dead troopers she had already cared for during this deployment. The sickening feeling told her the truth. Kyle laid sprawled out on the wet street, surrounded by his blood and guts. The nightmarish pictures caused her to stifle a desire to cry.

"A few, mostly the enemy. The Marines are getting ready to push into the city. Get ready because our job is about to get real hectic. Let's mount up," Roe ordered, keeping his eyes off Skyler as a single tear ran down her cheek.

III

"Get the fuck down!" Jack's voice deepened and boomed while shoving Sutherland behind a pile of rubble before several AK rounds dotted the section of the street he had occupied. The rising sun launched a full spectrum of colors, blinding the advancing Marines funneling into the city. Enemy fire rained on them as they pushed their way into Fallujah.

Dirt, mud, and pieces of street kicked up at them and they scattered to escape the enemy fire. With bullets striking nearby, Doc Sloan stood momentarily disoriented, paralyzed with fear. The cracking of a whip echoed past his head, singeing the peach fuzz on his ear, and driving panic into his heart. Doc dropped to the deck in the open.

Jack dashed through the crossfire, caught Doc by the handle of his flak jacket, and hauled him to another alley for cover.

"Are you hit?" Jack asked Doc. He could only shake his head, unable to find his voice with everything going on around him. Jack's anger flared, and he slapped Doc upside the helmet. Eyeing his men, he didn't like the breakdown he was seeing. Barking over the gunfire, Jack shouted, "What the fuck is wrong with everybody?"

Arabic voices chanted through loudspeakers situated throughout the city, encouraging insurgents to stand up to fight the invading infidels in the name of Allah. The Marines responded with their own psychological warfare as 'Ride of the Valkyries' played from American vehicles.

"Hey Sut." Ashmore sent rounds into a nearby window. He didn't count the rounds or the seconds he held the trigger down but allowed the gun to do the talking. Releasing the trigger, Ashmore dropped back to cover as enemy rounds peppered the sand colored wall behind him. "What they sayin'?"

"They're calling themselves holy warriors," Sutherland answered with a shaky voice, revealing his uneasiness. An RPG struck the building high above Sutherland and pieces of stone hailed down. The impact rocked a large satellite dish on the roof. The bolts holding the dish in place strained, and it would have held if not for a stray AK round.

The bolts ripped free and the dish came crashing to the ground in a heap of twisted metal and jagged rods. The force flattened Sutherland, and as the dust settled around him, the thought of his own mortality sent a shockwave of horror rippling across his face.

"Sut, you all right?" Ashmore stood but dropped back behind cover as rounds flew at him. The satellite debris blocked Sutherland from Ashmore, and he panicked to get over to his friend. "I'm coming, bro. Hang in there, I'm coming."

Ashmore got ready to pounce but halted as Sutherland raised a thumbs-up in the air. Relieved his friend was fine, Ashmore settled down.

"I'm good."

"You sure?" Ashmore asked.

"Yeah." Sutherland climbed to his knees, staying low behind the courtyard perimeter. "Yeah, I'm fine."

"So, holy warriors?" Ashmore tried to make light of the fact that the dish nearly crushed Sutherland.

"What? Yeah, holy warriors."

"Holy warriors? Pssh, my ass." Ashmore laughed as he spat tobacco. "Fuck it, holy warriors versus the devil dogs, title fight of the century, I'd say. Come get some."

Ashmore aimed in on targets and sprayed his weapon. The enemy returned fire and two of their rounds hit the barrier he crouched behind. Pieces of dirt and rock sprayed his face. Ashmore ducked back down and maniacally laughed as he added, "Bitches."

"We gotta get off this street. It's a choke point," Jack said a second before an enemy round ricocheted off the pavement, deflected off a light pole, and embedded itself under the flesh of his left forearm. Jack stumbled but didn't fall, clinging to a window ledge to support himself. "God damn it."

"This way," Kyle shouted as he ran past Ashmore, keeping his head low and running hunched over. Rounds hit the top of the cement walls and rocketed out into nowhere. Carlos trailed Kyle and Ashmore circled in behind him as they ran onto a front porch enclosed with rebar. Carlos knelt behind the small half wall surrounding the front porch and started popping rounds off.

As rhythmically as a guitarist picking cords, Kyle flicked off the thumb clip, pulled the pin, and tossed a green grenade through the window flanking the front door. The spoon released from the small ball as it smashed through the glass.

POP. Flash, a puff of smoke.

Dust and smoke funneled out of shattered windows. With a combination of driving knees and a smashing elbow, Ashmore splintered the cheap door, tearing it from its hinges. Like a creature from a Godzilla movie, he trampled over the destruction and stomped off into the abyss. The smoke obstructed his vision, but within the fog, the outline of an insurgent appeared. The blast had momentarily disturbed the insurgent's vision and deafened his ears and he never saw the hulking Marine advancing. Ashmore squeezed out six shots; two rounds found their mark.

BANG. Recoil. Punctured lung.

BANG. Recoil. Pierced right atrium of the heart.

In the doorway, Carlos pushed past Ashmore as another insurgent ran along the second-floor catwalk. From the hip, Carlos fired one shell from his shotgun but completely missed. Without hesitating and continuing to run, the insurgent fired three shots from his AK-47 over the steel railing.

Carlos didn't flinch as the wall showered him with fragments of plaster and bits of stone. In one smooth motion, he pumped the forend while bringing the shotgun to his shoulder. The front of his weapon led the insurgent, who broke into a full sprint for a room at the far end of the hall. Carlos fired.

BANG. Recoil. Knee shot.

The solid steel slug detached his lower leg and the insurgent stumbled. He managed to catch the handrail into his armpit, preventing his fall, but in doing so, exposed himself to the Marine below. He never heard the final report of the shotgun.

BANG. Recoil. Headshot.

The second blast separated the top of his skull like an opened lid on a can.

"Clear," Ashmore said. He strolled over to the breathless, lifeless man he had shot when entering the house. A pool of blood circled him, but this didn't stop Ashmore from sending three more rounds into his chest.

"Clear." Carlos mimicked as dark red matter dripped from the ceiling above the catwalk. The Berserkers filed into the house for safety as Kyle, Ashmore, and Carlos charged up the stairs. Quickly, each man kicked open a door and scanned it for more insurgents. Several rooms held an assortment of weapons, a cache of death, but lacked any personnel.

Jack rushed for the stairs inside the house, but before he could climb them, Doc seized his arm.

"You're hit." Jack looked down to find blood seeping out the cuff of his sleeve and landing on the floor in fat drops.

"We'll deal with it later." Jack ordered his men to advance to the roof. They stormed out into the sunlight of the early morning. The crack of enemy rifles forced them to keep a low profile. All directions seemed to buzz with activity, and it took a few minutes for them to learn the rounds weren't directed at them.

Sutherland stood to see black smoke emerging in different places throughout the city. A sonic boom shook the area as a tank destroyed another building. Sutherland saw a few Marines exchanging rapid fire with a group of insurgents on opposing rooftops. The war was finally unfolding in front of him, and he couldn't hide his smile. It is natural, for the unconditioned eye sees war as glory.

"What are we doing up here?" Vinson asked, reloading his rifle as Kyle, Black, Ashmore, and Carlos joined them.

"We need to clear out that house." Jack pointed across a four-foot gap which separated another house from their current position. "We're gonna sweep it from the top down and flush them out for Thompson to smoke."

"Where's Thompson?" Kyle asked.

"He's in the yard below with Simpson and Harvey," Jack said. Kyle didn't like any of their men being outside the safety of a cleared house, and he wished Jack would have brought them in.

Ashmore poked his head over the side of the building. The ground stuttered, rotating and spinning, before drifting away. He forced himself back. His stomach turned, and his breathing quickened. "That's like four feet across. Under all this heavy gear, we ain't gonna make it."

"It's only four feet, Devil. You'll make it." Kyle reassured Ashmore as Sutherland slung his rifle behind his back and cracked his neck.

"I'll go first." Sutherland sprinted forward, leaping over the two-story drop, and landing easily on the neighboring roof. He dropped to one knee and scanned over his rifle for any hidden threats. Once he was sure all was clear, he motioned for the others to follow.

"Ash, you're next," Jack ordered. Ashmore's blood ran cold and he battled with his gag reflex. He envisioned himself leaping and while suspended in midair, some Hajji would fire at him. Ashmore could see his outstretched arms as he missed the landing and crashed into the next house. His stomach lurched at the thought of enduring a fall that wouldn't kill him but would surely break his back. Ashmore couldn't bear the thought of himself in a wheelchair and knew he'd rather die.

"Ash, go," Jack ordered for the second time. Ashmore walked up to the edge of the building, unslung his weapon, and threw it to the waiting Sutherland.

"Come on, brother." Sutherland cheered on his friend. Ashmore started at the point that Sutherland had. A lump swelled in his throat, stripping his mouth of moisture, and making it difficult to swallow. His upper body leaned forward, but his legs were locked in place. With shaky knees, he struggled to breathe.

"Ash, move it," Jack shouted. Ashmore gritted his teeth and forced his body forward. The muscles in his quads were slow to start but picked up speed as he focused on the adjacent ledge. His body seemed heavy, and his run felt wrong. He approached the gap, only realizing his miscalculations as one roof sank away and the second fell out of range.

Like in his vision, he stretched out his arms, swatting for the adjacent ledge. His chest collided with the opposite house and the impact knocked the wind from him. Panic ran rampant across his face. Ashmore kicked furiously at the side of the house, trying to get a footing to push himself up, but found nothing. He didn't look down. The fall wouldn't kill him, he knew this, but he didn't want to be paralyzed for the rest of his life.

Jack and the Marines watched on in horror, not being able to help their friend. Ashmore's muscles strained; he wanted to quit and fall from the wall. The sting of failure engulfed him, and he knew if the fall didn't kill him, the insurgents would.

Sutherland sank his fingers into Ashmore's wrists. Pulling back, he struggled to bring Ashmore over the edge of the wall and onto the roof. Sutherland tried to hurry before the enemy noticed the helpless Marine dangling from the side of a house.

"I got you, bro," Sutherland said. He gritted his teeth, straining the muscles of his back to save Ashmore. He pulled and pulled, but through the struggles, Ashmore only moved an inch. The weight of the massive Marine and his gear was too much for Sutherland. He feared his friend would slip from his grip. "God damn it, Ash. Help me out."

The toes of Ashmore's boots scratched away at the wall and to his surprise, located a footing. A series of pre-existing holes created by misplaced bullets allowed Ashmore to use them to push with everything he had in his beefy legs. The strain prevented him from opening his eyes and he kept them closed until he sensed a large shadow blocking out the sun.

An alarm went off in Ashmore's head and he worried some insurgent had gotten the drop on Sutherland, but as he opened them to warn his friend, he found only the familiar and friendly face of Corporal Kyle Dillon staring back down at him. Taking his other arm, Kyle and Sutherland jerked and pulled as hard as they could. Ashmore's gear caught on the edge, stopping any progress.

"Fuck, Ash." Kyle grunted while placing a foot on the lip of the wall and falling back into his weight. Ashmore slid over, and Kyle darted out of the way, but it was Sutherland who became momentarily pinned under the large Marine as the two collapsed in a heap. Ashmore rolled off Sutherland, and the two stared at the overcast sky, laughing despite their fatigue.

"Damn it, Ash. Lose some fucking weight."

"Bite me, asshole," Ashmore replied. The two shared another good-humored laugh and Ashmore stomped his foot, relieved to have something solid under him again. His heavy breathing had yet to ease, and it took Sutherland pulling him to his feet to get him to stand. "Owe you one."

"You all right over there?" Jack asked. Ashmore stuck a thumb in the air, too exhausted to shout his response, but allowed Jack to breathe easier. The others leapt across the clearing without incident. Once on the second roof, they found two entry points: a locked red metal door and a hole in the roof. At the edge of the hole was a makeshift stairway leading into a second-floor bedroom.

The stairway wasn't attached to the roof but laid against the edge of the crumbling hole. Jack and Kyle crouched down, peered into the hole, and scanned the room for insurgents. Jack shook the wobbly staircase and a tingle ran up his back. *It's a welcoming to Hell,* he thought. Rocks flung upward and sprinkled back down in conjunction with the burst of an AK rifle. The cement edge chipped away, and the Marines scurried back from the opening.

"Motherfucker." Jack prepped a hand grenade and tossed it into the room.

POP. Flash, a puff of smoke.

A dying scream echoed from within the building.

"I think you hit him," Black said.

"I'm goin' in." Ashmore stuck a dip in his lip to help settle his nerves and readied himself to get back to doing what he did best - kicking insurgent ass. "Who's got my back?"

Jack stared at the opening and took a step back, unaware if anyone saw. Kyle did.

"I do." Kyle shouldered through the crowd as Ashmore stepped on the first rickety step. The staircase, made of a random assortment of wood, swayed. It moaned under Ashmore's weight but held firm, so he proceeded.

"Fat ass," Sutherland said at the noise in the wood.

"Fuck you." Ashmore flipped him off as he descended. Kyle followed and Sutherland, sensing the thrill of adventure, brought up the rear. They felt as if they were on the spinning tunnel of a carnival ride. With each step, they had to adjust their balance to keep from crashing as they hurried to the bottom.

"OSHA would be pissed to see this shitty workmanship," Kyle said, a crooked grin of sarcasm adorned his face.

There was no carpet or rug, but only cold hard cement flooring that welcomed Ashmore's boot. The room was close to bare, with an unmade queen size bed dividing the room with a small wooden nightstand on the near side. A large oak wall wardrobe laid tilted on its side at the foot of the bed, missing one of the two doors. Ashmore located the absent one as part of the wooden staircase his friends were still descending. Sporadic gunfire erupted without warning from the hallway outside the room.

"Get back…get back…get back," Ashmore shouted. Rounds splintered the bottom of the staircase sending Ashmore diving behind the bed. With nails straining to hold, the stairs careened from side to side, challenging Kyle and Sutherland's escape plan. Ashmore sprang up, spraying a volley at the door without care for his personal safety.

Sutherland hit the hard surface of the roof and spun around to assist Kyle. Their fingertips grazed one another's as the wooden stairway collapsed beneath him. The sinking feeling, like being on a rollercoaster, hit Kyle while lunging for the roof. He managed to claw his fingers onto the edge of the hole while his body swung, aching to let go. His hands slipped, inching him ever closer to the void.

Ashmore's own firing halted as the missing closet door crashed on top of him, dropping him to the ground.

Large, jagged, broken boards pointed up at Kyle, beckoning him to let go and impel himself upon them. His fingers pained, hurting to slip over the edge, then a pair of hands snatched Kyle by the forearms. Jack slid in next to Sutherland and grabbed the other arm, preventing Kyle from falling and dragging Sutherland over with him. Black watched, begging silently that Corporal Kyle Dillon would make it through this.

Under the pile of rubble, Ashmore reawakened his weapon, continuing a steady stream of covering fire. The belt zipped through his SAW and ran dry a moment after Kyle's feet cleared the opening. The insurgent wasted no time. As Ashmore's weapon stopped, the insurgent crossed the threshold and fired at the opening in the roof. Unsatisfied with missing his chance at the dangling Marine, the insurgent changed his course of fire and shot at the bed.

Mattress stuffing and cement chips from the wall rained down on Ashmore who wedged himself behind a small nightstand and the pile of broken boards. His hands fumbled with reloading his large weapon, but he managed to get the job done and return fire. None of his rounds found their mark, but they did the job he had intend. The insurgent retreated, giving Ashmore a small amount of breathing room.

"Holy shit," he said under his breath, realizing how close he was to certain death.

"That motherfucker's still alive down there and Ash is trapped." Sutherland couldn't believe his words. The Marines retreated from the hole. "What do we do, Corporal Campbell?"

Jack's mind was racing. For the first time in his military life, he couldn't clear it quick enough to form a plan under fire. The eyes of the Berserkers were on him.

"I want us off this fucking roof. Everyone back over to the first house," Jack ordered. A collective look of confusion afflicted the men. Jack took a step in the direction of the first house, but Kyle locked onto his bicep and prevented him from going.

"Fuck that, Ash is still down there," Kyle said. He forced his whisper at Jack, not wanting the men to hear what he had to say. Jack looked back at the hole, and it dawned on him what he was doing. He was preparing to leave one of his men behind because it was getting too dangerous. This terrified Jack more than any insurgent possibly could have. Carlos leaned near the opening of the roof while trying to avoid exposure to enemy rounds.

"Ash, hold tight, bro. We're coming." Carlos marched over to the locked door and kicked it as hard as he could. The door flew open with a hard-vibrating bang to reveal an enclosed stairwell concealed by shadows. He glanced back to wave his men on, to follow him before he headed into the darkness. "Let's go."

The Marines moved down the steps with their rifles pointed in front of them, ready for any insurgents. A young male in his early twenties stood outside a room, firing at Ashmore trapped inside. The deafening sound of gunfire concealed the descent of the Marines. Carlos's rifle peeked out of the stairwell, aligning his sights on the insurgent's head.

BANG. Recoil. Headshot.

The bullet tore through one temple and shot out the other. He flinched as if pinched rather than shot, but then dropped effortlessly to the floor like all the bones had vanished from his body.

"Marines…Marines…Marines…" Carlos called out a warning as he exited the stairway, not wanting to catch friendly fire. "Ash, cease-fire. We're coming in."

Ashmore stopped his burst and Carlos stepped out to an opening that looked down to the first floor. A bullet nearly took his nose off. He snapped back as a series of gunfire erupted from down below. Jack tossed a grenade over the railing. The grenade bounced with a solid thud and rolled before going off with a bang.

POP. Flash, a puff of smoke.

Three insurgents cried out in pain. Jack chewed on his lower lip, took a large breath in through his nose, and sprang out from cover. Sutherland stood next to him, ready to exchange fire with the enemy, but found only the horrors of combat. They watched the insurgents run about, swatting at their body as if they were on fire. Sutherland glanced at Jack.

"What the fuck was that?"

"White phosphorus. Burns at like 2500 degrees," he said. The cries died off from down below and the bodies collapsed.

"Shit, is that even legal?" Sutherland asked.

"Legal? We're in a fight, son. All's fair in love and war." Immediately, his mind cycled to Steve Tomes and his wife. *All except that, you fuckin' cheating cock suckin', Jody, motherfucker.*

Two more insurgents, unharmed by the white phosphorus chemical burns, opened fire. The surprise counterattack drove Jack and Sutherland to cover. Sutherland stepped back to where he had been standing, but Jack ran across the opening, dodging incoming rounds. He momentarily exposed himself at the top of the stairs but reached cover behind another wall in the second-floor hallway.

Doc Sloan and Black followed Carlos and Kyle into the room to access Ashmore. Besides a few scratches, he was without wounds and more than overjoyed to see his friends.

Jack stood in the hallway, clearing his mind, and remembering what he had to do. He counted the shots coming from the first floor below and waited for a pause. When it came, he leaned out and aimed in at the head of an insurgent taking shelter behind a couch.

Sutherland peeked out from his own cover and fired at an insurgent standing in an opening. The insurgent vanished unharmed, taking shelter deep into the house as Jack aligned his sights on the top of an Iraqi man's hiding head. His trigger finger grew with pressure and he readied himself for the small recoil many men flinched too, but he did not. Then, cold metal pressed gently to the back of Jack's head. The hair on his neck came to attention and he interrupted the squeezing of his M16's trigger.

Jack cut his eyes over to Sutherland who had not noticed the trouble his corporal was in. Sutherland stared down his sights and Jack closed his eyes. He heard but didn't see Sutherland shooting the Iraqi hiding behind the couch in the living room.

BANG. Recoil. Headshot.

The Iraqi fell over to his side, neither protesting nor fleeing. He was dead. Sutherland cheered his kill, amazed to have taken his first life. It wasn't how others had told him it would be. He didn't feel nauseated or saddened by the event but elated. This troubled him more than the kill.

"Hell yeah. Got one, Corporal." His good-humored face dropped, morphing into one of surprise and shock. His eyes stretched to their limits and his muscles froze, failing to raise his rifle in order to help. He didn't know what to do and could only utter, "Oh, Shit."

Jack didn't cower at the cold steel pressing against the back of his skull. He accepted it with closed eyes and waited for the inevitable without shedding a tear.

BANG. Recoil. Headshot.

IV

Skyler and the rest of the Corpsmen had yet to unpack when the first casualties came rolling in from the city. An empty room served as the aid station and they hurried to throw cots out for the young men. Blood soon saturated the green cots and covered the concrete floor. Grabbing IV catheters and tubing, Skyler flew, sticking a vein before moving on to the next patient. HM1 Roe followed behind, attaching the IV set tubing to a bag of Normal Saline. He hung the bags on whatever he could as Skyler hit another vein with a needle.

A medical doctor stormed into the room. Immediately, he started patching bullet wounds, plucking shrapnel, and mending broken bones. Sweat didn't just trickle but screamed down Skyler's face. Injured Marines pulled at her blood-stained hands, pleading for help and relief, screaming in madness from the pain. Some Marines called for their mothers and others called out for God.

A Marine rested against the wall, face half-charred with burns and blood running from two gut shot wounds. He tried to cover them with his burned arm. Through obvious pain, he reached a blackened hand into his cargo pocket and pulled out a crushed cigarette pack. He dumped the pack out on the ground and searched through the mess of broken paper and loose tobacco until he found a bent, but whole one. His hand trembled getting the filter to stay between his lips on the uninjured side of his face, then he sparked it.

Melted skin sealed off his left eye and bits of flesh hung from his face, revealing burnt tendons and muscles beneath. The Marine sucked on the cigarette and blew out a hefty puff of smoke. Skyler rushed to him, but he waved her off, uninterested in her help.

"You need to get those wounds bandaged. You're losing a lot of blood," Skyler said. She warned him, but the Marine took another drag and waved her off again.

"Don't waste your time on me. I ain't gonna make it," the Marine said.

"Yes, you are. We're here to help you," HM1 Roe said. The Marine shook his head and a gentle smile appeared through the horrible injury. He allowed the cigarette to dangle from the uninjured portion of his mouth as his eyes drifted off, staring at a world they couldn't see. Skyler didn't move or stir the man, but simply watched the cigarette fall. His head slumped forward, and smoke spilled into the breeze.

"He's gone," Roe shouted, trying to shove her along to the next patient. The sting of tears swelled behind her eyes, but she didn't allow herself to cry. Injured men looked at her with pleas for help on their faces and she would be damned if she let them see her cry. Skyler dragged her hand down the Marine's good eyelid to hide his blank stare before turning away.

There was no time to process. Screams echoed from another truck coming around the corner and men hurried to offload the wounded.

V

Harvey's barrel eased over the lip of the cement fence and fired at random, picking no targets to sight in on. He sat back down in the dirt and reloaded his rifle with clumsy hands. The thick wall, made of cinder blocks and mortar, gave Harvey a sense of safety and he had no interest in leaving the position. Keeping his head below the top of the fence, he again lifted his rifle up and fired without looking.

Simpson nudged Thompson, and they stopped what they were doing to stare at the admin Marine. Harvey chewed the side of his cheek and rapidly pumped his finger until the magazine ran dry. When he sat down once again, he felt their burning stares piercing him.

"Did you get them?" Thompson asked.

"What?" Harvey didn't understand the reasoning behind their judgmental stares. Simpson bellowed with laughter as he slammed a magazine against his helmet. The rounds inside the magazine seated flush against the back side in order not to jam.

"Do you know what the fuck you're doing?" Thompson continued.

"Killing the enemy," Harvey said with a 'duh' attitude injected into his voice.

"Are you sure? How the fuck do you know? You ain't watching where you're putting the rounds. Why don't you try being a Marine and pick your shots? You could wind up hitting another Marine with that kind of shit."

"I'm not sticking my head up to get shot," Harvey said. He inserted a fresh magazine into his rifle and racked back the charging handle. The thirty-round magazine popped out and landed with a puff of dirt. Thompson snatched it off the ground before Harvey could get to it.

"Sticking your head up might be the best thing you could do for the squad, Harvey." Thompson threw the magazine into Harvey's chest. He bobbled it in his hands, nearly dropping it again, but managed to get a hold on it. "At least try to fake being a Marine. If you do that Hollywood movie shooting bullshit again, I'll fucking shoot you. We watch where our rounds are going, so we don't have blue on blue fire."

Harvey inserted the magazine, his teeth gnawed his cheek, and his eyes drooped. He snorted nothing but dust and air and his shoulders hunched forward.

Thompson sighed. He didn't like the tone of his voice. Taking a breath, he counted to three before saying, "Man, I'm not trying to ride your ass, I'm just trying to look out for you and our Marines. Pick your shots. We may get into a situation where we need every last bullet, so we have to make them count. Don't waste rounds. Now let's get back into this fight."

Thompson tapped a magazine to his Kevlar and locked it in his rifle. He sprang up, spotting an enemy insurgent moving rapidly across the street with his head tucked to avoid getting shot. Thompson led his front sight post in front of the enemy's head and fired.

BANG. Recoil. Throat shot.

The insurgent tumbled forward, rolling in the street, squirming and clutching at his neck, and dying without anyone coming to his aid. Three more insurgents sprang from cover. Harvey eased up, sighting all three of the men, and pulled his trigger with ease.

BANG. Recoil. Headshot.

BANG. Recoil. Headshot.

BANG. Recoil. Headshot.

Thompson and Simpson stared without blinking as the three men collapsed to the wet pavement. Harvey sank into cover and to the astonishment of the other two, didn't gloat a single word about his kills.

VI

The cold metal felt sadistically nice against Jack's hot skin despite the inescapable death sentence it carried. He closed his eyes tight and hoped it would be quick and painless.

BANG. Recoil. Headshot.

The rifle report rang in Jack's ears and he found it amazing he could still hear. The muscles in his neck and back tensed. He expected the hard, blunt force of the bullet entering his skull, but it never came.

Vinson had squeezed off a round without hesitation. The 5.56 traveled through the insurgent's skull, separating the optic nerves, and upon exiting, lodged in the far wall. The force of the round knocked the insurgent back against the door of the room he had come from. His fingers locked around the AK as his body curled up on the floor.

"Corporal Campbell, I got him." Vinson exclaimed with boyish glee.

Sutherland's muscles unhinged, and he quickly kicked away the rifle from the insurgent. The embarrassment of freezing up took away any joy Sutherland had upon getting his first kill. He kept his face turned away from the others and stared down at the man.

"I owe you a drink when we get back." Jack squeezed Vinson's shoulder and gave him a nod of not only approval, but thanks. Vinson couldn't hide his delight. For men like Vinson, there was nothing more rewarding in combat than impressing a man like Jack.

"Shit, Vinson. He's still breathing." Sutherland stood over the injured man, keeping his rifle trained on him. Jones looked over Jack and Vinson's shoulders to stare down at the man in disbelief. His chest moved up and down despite the two holes in his head.

"How in the hell?" Vinson couldn't believe it. Jack pulled his 9mm pistol and aimed it at the man, motioning Sutherland to clear out. He pulled the hammer back, but before he could pull the trigger, he caught a side-glance of Vinson standing solemnly, staring at the pistol in his hand. Jack forced the pistol at the young Marine.

"It's your kill. You finish him."

Not wanting to appear too eager to earn his kill, Vinson said, "It's yours if you want it."

Jack leaned in close to Vinson.

"I'm the fuckin' Ripper. I've got my kills," Jack said. Vinson grabbed the sidearm from Jack, marveling at the weight of the official 9mm military issued Beretta in his hand. He looked up from the weapon to find eyes were on him, waiting to see if he had the guts to finish the injured man. Vinson aimed down the sights, steadying his hand, and pulled the trigger.

BANG. Recoil. Headshot.

The bullet struck dead center. The insurgent relaxed, and there was no more breathing. Vinson continued holding the pistol as a heavy anvil dropped into the pit of his stomach. *I've killed a man, killed a living man, who is no longer living, but dead as dead can be.* He was still thinking of this when Jack fished the pistol from his grip.

"Good work, kid." Jack slapped the top of Vinson's helmet, snapping him out of his small, guilty daydream.

"Thanks, Corporal."

"Look at you two," Jack said. He switched his glance from Vinson to Sutherland and back to Vinson. "Both you motherfuckers just popped your cherries. God damn, it's a fine day."

Vinson and Sutherland smiled, unable to hide the joy they felt at Jack 'The Ripper' Campbell's approval. Jack looked over the railing and remembered there was more to do. "All right you assholes. Let's go."

Jack lead the way down the stairs and Jones was on his heels. They aimed their rifles over the railing, scanning and sweeping across the living room to spots they had yet to see from above. Vinson watched the Marines making their way down the stairs to the living room, but he didn't want to move. The childish feeling of acceptance and approval was warm and comforting and Vinson didn't want it to leave. A backhand from Sutherland across his shoulder pulled him back into the present.

"Big hot shot, saving the Corporal like that." Sutherland teased. Vinson gave him the one-finger salute, then followed his friend down the stairs.

Tiny rays of sunlight broke through shattered windows on the first floor, uncloaking the dead insurgents scattered about. Across from the stairway, the front door stood barred by a large sheet of plywood. Jack took note of this and the opening to the kitchen immediately to his right flank. Leading with the barrel of his rifle, he cut sharply into the empty kitchen.

Jones nudged Sutherland and the two proceeded cautiously across the living room, venturing into the hallway behind the stairs. The dark hallway held three rooms before veering right at the end and continuing deeper into the house. Where it ended, Sutherland only wondered, but knew they had to clear each room before finding out.

Jack punted the kitchen table over, and Vinson hurried into the room, drawing his M16, ready to blast anyone who might be there. No insurgents hid underneath. The room was clear and void of any enemy weapon systems. Jack nodded to Vinson, who abandoned the kitchen and cut back by the stairs. He spotted Sutherland and Jones in the hallway, preparing to enter the first door and changed his course, heading away from the hallway and toward the opening across the room. Navigating through the dead bodies burned and suffocated by white phosphorus, Vinson rounded a raggedy, solo standing couch.

The unmoving eyes of a dead face stared up at him, his skull opened at the top and blood and brains funneling out. The Iraqi man was young, as young as Vinson, and Vinson wondered if perhaps their lives may have been similar in one way or another. Perhaps he had goals of going to college and living a normal life with a wife and kids. Perhaps he had a normal job but then the war started and changed the man's life forever.

The lifeless eyes spooked Vinson, and he no longer wished to stare at them. It didn't matter if the man had a wife or kids or a regular job or if he wanted to be an insurgent all his life. None of that matter now, because he was dead and nothing else mattered to him. Vinson's stomach growled and he shrugged his shoulders, continuing on to the opening that was the spare family room across from the kitchen.

DAT…DAT…DAT. AK rounds burst around the corner of the family room, and Jack dove back into the kitchen, narrowly missing the rounds which dotted the wall next to him.

The shots sent Sutherland spiraling to one knee, and his rifle came up as if on its own. He found nothing to sight in on and his eyes darted nervously to find Vinson dashing through the open space of the living room. Sutherland caught the severity dawning on Vinson but couldn't find the words to scream at him.

VII

"Ash, you lucky sonofabitch," Kyle said, assisting Black in helping Ashmore to his feet. Carlos slapped a hand hard on Ashmore's shoulder, shaking him as he did.

"Holy shit, I can't believe you ain't dead," Carlos said.

"Thanks, bro." Ashmore shook hands with each Marine that came in. Using a penlight, Doc Sloan watched his pupil reaction until Ashmore knocked the light away, and shoved Doc. "I swear to God Doc; you try to shove shit up my nose or in my eyes again, I'll fuckin' grease you, got me?"

"Man, what was going through your mind?" Carlos asked. His eyes held pure astonishment while trying to imagine what his friend had been through. Ashmore smirked, the spotlight of attention resting on him, and he liked it.

"Fuckin' crazy, man. At first, I was like, I need to provide cover for the boot and corporal, but then I just wanted to smoke the motherfucker. Who got the kill anyway?" Ashmore asked.

"Dig it," Carlos said, face beaming with joy. He tapped a finger to the side of his head. "I popped that motherfucker in the head. POW."

"Why didn't you take the shot, hippie tree hugger?" Ashmore slapped Black in the chest with the back of his hand, laughing as he did. Black stepped back embarrassed.

"Fuck you, Ash. I didn't have a shot to take."

A loud bang echoed up from down below. Kyle paused, turning back to the doorway as if listening to something the others couldn't hear.

"What is it, Corporal?" Ashmore asked.

"I don't know. Seems quiet," Kyle said. As if on cue, a hail of gunfire from downstairs broke the silence. The men ran to the railing to look down on the first floor to see Vinson caught out in the open.

Vinson didn't notice the men looking at him, and he never saw the insurgent firing from the family room. Too far from the kitchen to turn back, he made a mad dash for the hallway where Sutherland waited. Fear added additional weight to his muscles and his sprint felt sluggish like a cartoon character trying to run but only managing to stay in place. A burning pain traveled up his lead leg. At first, he thought it was an old shin splint injury coming back to haunt him until his kneecap landed on the couch.

His body pitched forward, unable to support his weight, and a second 7.62 round entered under his armpit. The brass projectile punctured a lung and separated his spinal cord. His body buckled and he opened his mouth to scream, but a third-round tore into his neck, silencing his cries forever.

"Vinson." Sutherland howled and darted forward, only to be jerked back by some unseen force. Jones wrapped his arms around

Sutherland's chest, preventing him from a suicide run, which would grant Sutherland two things: a medal and death.

"Wait, motherfucker. You'll get yourself smoked if you go out there." Jones shouted over the noise of the burst. A brief pause came as the insurgent ejected the empty banana clip from his rifle and inserted a loaded one. Vinson rose on his elbows, confused at why the rest of his body wasn't rising.

Save him now, oh God, please, save him now. Sutherland begged silently in his head.

A nervous itch attacked the base of Vinson's skull. He searched the ground around him as if looking for something he was missing. He didn't know what it was, but he had a strange feeling that he misplaced his rifle or gear somewhere. An alarm went off in his head when he tried to breath but found it difficult to draw in air.

Why won't you help him, Sutherland pleaded with a God that failed to show himself. *You're supposed to save him; I'm praying for it.*

A solid blunt kick dropped Vinson flat. When he looked to see who had done it, no one was there. Everything was confusing and as he looked about, his eyes dulled. He could no longer remember how he came to be in this place. As the insurgent commenced to firing, Vinson felt something like that of an insect biting at his arm, but he no longer held the strength to look down at his bicep.

Goddamn you, Goddamn you.

"Corpsmen up!" Sutherland shouted, but no one came.

Doc heard the call from his spot on the second-floor catwalk, but Carlos and Kyle cut him off from the stairs.

"It's no good," Kyle said. The second bout of AK rounds struck the walls and handrailing. The group on the second floor moved to cover, never once seeing the man in the family room shooting at them.

"Corpsman up." Sutherland shouted again. Still, no one came, and he was forced to watch the mutilation of his best friend.

The concrete floor felt cool to Vinson's cheek, and the warm liquid surrounding him felt comforting. He twitched with each bullet that struck him and wondered who had placed him in a hot bath before the final bullet entered his skull and ended any new thoughts.

"We have to get to him." Sutherland pleaded with Jones, hot tears running down his face.

"He's wasted, man. You wanna get yourself dead, too?" Jones pinned Sutherland to the floor.

Jack extracted a grenade from his chest rig, prepped it, and tossed it into the family room. The grenade landed with a thud on the carpet and rolled underneath an end table. Upon seeing the grenade by the couch, the insurgent stood to run. He found nowhere to go before the small metal ball detonated.

POP. Flash, a puff of smoke.

The concussion launched the insurgent into the glass china cabinet. He slammed to the floor with shards of glass and wood falling on top of him. Jack sprinted and without pausing, snatched the handle on the back of Vinson's flak jacket, dragging him to the hall where Jones provided cover. Sutherland helped Jack pull Vinson into a cleared room. In a frenzy, they removed his flak jacket and Kevlar. Blood seeped out of the bullet holes like a water fountain that someone had left running.

"He's gone," Jack said. Sutherland refused to accept this. He hurried to cover the bleeding holes, only to learn that Vinson had too many and he had too few of hands. Jack shoved Sutherland away from Vinson. "He's gone."

Sutherland pushed at Jack, but Jack blocked him from getting back to Vinson. He pinned Sutherland against the wall, holding him there until he calmed down. The realization of the incident hit Sutherland, and he didn't want to stand any longer. He didn't want to think or feel, and so he allowed himself to do the only thing he could. He sank to the floor, eyes never leaving Vinson, and hyperventilated to stop the tears.

"Stay here," Jack ordered Sutherland, who had no plans on leaving his injured friend. "Jones, let's get this motherfucker."

"Fuckin' A," Jones said, ensuring a round was inserted in the chamber of his rifle.

They advanced into the living room with eyes primed for movement and ears open for any sound. Rounding the corner, they found an unchecked hallway that Jones assumed wrapped back around to the hall they had left. Jones and Jack ignored it, instead training their weapons on a spot where they knew the insurgent would likely be. The insurgent sat on his knees, slumped over as if praying to Allah, and a small puddle of blood formed under his hovering face that he covered with both hands as he moaned.

He bounced up and down, staying within an inch margin, keeping a steady rhythm. Jack and Jones neared, the insurgent slung himself back without warning, sitting up. Jack and Jones, caught off guard, leaped back a full foot and yanked up their weapons. His hands eased away from his face and something inside Jack told him to look away. *Somethings can't be unseen,* Jack thought.

He didn't care to see the mangled remains of the man's face, but neither Jack nor Jones turned away. Small red dots, like bleeding freckles, littered his features and Jones grimaced as he leaned in to look. Two large pieces of shrapnel protruded from the man's swollen eyes, and a white, almost clear fluid leaked out of the slits. Blinded, the man felt around the floor for his rifle.

"How the fuck is he still alive, Corporal? The kill radius is five meters. The blast shoulda smoked this dude. God, look at his face. It's all maimed and shit. What do we do?"

Jack stepped up and kept his barrel three inches away from the man's temple. There was no compassion in Jack as he thought about Vinson in the other room and his brother dead in a cell. He could care less to call for a corpsman.

"Fuck'em. Fuck'em all." Jack didn't squeeze the trigger with a smooth grace, but instead, jerked back on it with great anger and hate. The 5.56 NATO round penetrated the man's brain, sending him to meet Allah.

A blast came from behind Jack and Jones. Jones launched forward from what felt like a sledgehammer slamming into his back, but stayed on his two feet, staggering like a prizefighter caught with a hard punch. Jack snagged Jones and the two crashed to the floor behind the couch.

"I'm hit. Jack, I'm hit." Jones sprawled out on the floor as a dull pain throbbed in his back, making it hard for him to breathe. The back of the couch blew out from AK rounds. Trying to stay low and out of range of the assault, Jack rolled Jones onto his side but found no blood. In the back flap of Jones's flak jacket, the large E-1 sapi plate was completely shattered. The bulletproof plating had done its job.

"You're fine. It hit the sapi." A sense and sigh of relief came over Jones. More AK rounds pierced the shabby couch as an insurgent fired from the doorway leading into another hall at the back of the house. Cotton, cloth, and wood tore from the furniture with each bullet. The two Marines hugged the floor, wishing they could dig through it to get even lower. A board inside the couch snapped and the couch tilted toward them.

They waited for the insurgent to break for a reload which seemed to never come. Their nerves chattered. A jolt ran through their bodies, spasming their limbs, as a much louder bang came from the insurgent's direction. Jack and Jones waited to feel the pain from whatever caused the bang but there was none. The loud percussion interrupted the AK fire, and a second later, another bang followed. Jones flinched, and neither man wanted to rise to see what it was.

"Get some." Sutherland screamed as loud as the blast which crumbled the insurgent. Using the hall that wrapped around the back of the house, Sutherland took the hajji by surprise. The first roar of the twelve-gauge shotgun smashed against the insurgent's back.

Sutherland loomed over the man, pumping the weapon, and chambering a fresh slug. The second blast separated the man's shoulder from his body, but still, Sutherland wasn't done. The insurgent's good arm crawled across the floor for his rifle and Sutherland removed his hand with the third blast. The Iraqi looked at the nub of a wrist that was left.

"Get some. Get some, you muj motherfucker. Get some." Sutherland released a terrifying war cry, pumping the forend, and pulling the trigger repeatedly until he had sent every round he had into the insurgent. After the last shot, he flipped the shotgun around, grasped the upper receiver and the comb of the stock, and brought it down on the man's head. The insurgent's skull broke underneath the force of the weapon. Sutherland still didn't stop.

Blood splattered upward, marking Sutherland's face and uniform with tiny red specks as the hard cracking of the skull gave way to a mushy thud. Jones and Jack rounded the couch and rushed at Sutherland.

"Sutherland, that's enough," Jack said. Sutherland didn't acknowledge him. He continued to bring the shotgun up over his shoulder, and down with the movement of someone chopping wood. He brought it down into the flattened mess where a head once was. Sutherland leaned back and repeated the process. The forced sucking of air and the audible exhale replaced the words escaping him.

Sutherland pulled the shotgun back again, and Jack ripped it out of his hands. Dazed, Sutherland turned his blood-drenched face to Jack with pieces of bone and brain matter clinging to his chin. He paused, sucking in a deep breath through his nostrils.

"They can't fight back when you splatter them on the floor like a fuckin' cockroach, Corporal." Sutherland's eyes drifted away from Jack, then he retreated down the hall from which he came. Jones entered the room where Vinson's body laid, leaving Jack in the family room with the mauled insurgent.

Jack fished out a cigarette and touched fire to the paper stick, not noticing Doc inspecting his injured arm.

"Corporal, we need to tend to this arm." Jack ignored Doc as he watched the others walk solemnly into the room which housed Vinson. He didn't know what to say or do for his men. Doc rolled up Jack's sleeve. "The bullet's lodged under the skin. I can get it with some tweezers."

"Do your thing, Doc." Jack watched his men while taking a drag from the cigarette, mindlessly repeating, "Do your thing."

Corporal Jack Campbell

Purple Heart Recipient

For Wounds Received on November 8th, 2004

Fallujah, Iraq

Lance Corporal Rodney Vinson

Killed in Action – Fallujah, Iraq, Al-Anbar Province

August 3rd, 1984 – November 8th, 2004

* * *

Letter to Jack Campbell from Jennifer Campbell,

Dated October 26th, 2004-

Dear Jack,

It's almost time for this boy to be born. Sometime next month I'm guessing. My stomach is so large that it feels disgusting. I'm glad you aren't here to see me like this, but I also wish you were.

Why did this war have to happen? I want you home. I wish you would have never volunteered to go back. I mostly understand why, but sometimes I don't. Steve Tomes is good to vent to, which I think I do a lot these days. He asks about you.

What is the date you expect to return home? I hope it's sooner rather than later. Maybe you can talk to your command about coming home earlier? There's not much news going on over here. A plane crashed killing thirteen people and looks like Bush is going to win the re-election.

Oh, there is talk that Martin Luther King, Jr, and Coretta Scott King are going to get the Congressional Gold Medal. I'm trying to find more news to tell you about, but I don't think things are as interesting over here as they are where you're at. Please come home safe. Our son, Joshua Dillon Campbell, is going to want to meet his father.

Hurry home.

Jennifer

* * *

From the pages of Jack Campbell's Journal-

Seriously, seriously! I'm going insane. My men are dying, we're in what might be the biggest battle since Hue City of '68, and the only thing I can think of is this prick ass Jody, Steve Tomes, trying to stick his meat snake into my wife. I heard women are hornier when they're pregnant but come the fuck on. Is this motherfucker fucking my wife right now?

Steve Tomes is good to vent to. Are you fucking kidding me? I can't take this. Every insurgent I shoot in the fucking face, it's Steve. Glad our ROE's are out the fucking window. Vinson is dead, my men are tired, and it's only the first day of this shit. I gotta lead and figure out a way to protect these men, and I don't need to think of my wife getting drilled by some college frat boy shithead.

Did I get Vinson killed?

My mind has been on home so much lately. What if I didn't react or do something right and now Vinson is dead? Can I lead these men? Maybe I should turn over command to Kyle, then again, I don't know if he wants to be the leader after I'm gone. I want to go home. I want to keep these men alive. I want to smash Steve in the fucking face. I know my wife is true to me and wouldn't sleep with Steve, but still, my mind troubles me. I want to hold my wife. I want…I want…I want.

I sound like a child. I hate this place.

CHAPTER SEVEN

HEAVY METAL

If you want peace, pray for war.

I

November 10th, 2004-

The Marine Corps 229th birthday-

Sutherland flapped his eyelids awake. The moon wasn't powerful enough to illuminate inside the house, but Sutherland could make out the soft silhouette of Ashmore at the front window. He posted there, lacking any visible features, for the morning hue had yet to kiss away the night. Sutherland sat up in his old camouflage poncho-liner with the cloud of sleep still lingering over him. He had a nightmare, but it didn't scare him.

Vinson was in his dream. They were returning to their game of chess, but Vinson's torn body loomed over the board. His ears took the place of the rooks, and his eyes were the knights. His fingers were the pawns, and both thumbs replaced the bishops. It was his tongue that occupied the Queen's spot and standing in for the King was his nose.

Bony white stubs pushed Vinson's game pieces around, leaving smears of blood on the board. The dream lingered a moment longer, whispering at Sutherland until he had to rise from it. Sitting in the dark living room of a stronghold they occupied, Sutherland could still hear

Vinson's haunting echo as he laid down his king and muttered, "Checkmate."

Sutherland left the poncho-liner where he laid and stood to stretch among the sea of sleeping Marines. Green poncho liners subbed for blankets and many of the Marines used their packs as makeshift pillows. He navigated through them carefully as not to step on anyone.

Sutherland staggered into the kitchen, surprised to find Jack at the table, a cigarette dangling from his fingers. He held his wrist near his face, examining the wound he uncovered in the beam of a small red flashlight hanging from a string above him. On the table was his disassembled rifle and the bandage that once covered his wound. Sutherland stared at Jack's dirty fingernails, realizing it wasn't dirt, but blood which stained and dried some time ago. He placed his hand on the back of a wooden chair and looked at Jack, nonverbally asking his approval to sit.

Jack took a drag, and while squinting through the smoke, motioned for Sutherland to join him. He slid his pack of smokes across the table. Although he was never a smoker before the service, Sutherland had to admit the Marine Corps made smoking and dipping alluring. He choked on the first drag, to which Jack found amusing. The lightheaded sensation overtook him, loosening the stiffness in his muscles, and he settled back into the wooden chair. The two warriors lingered there, enjoying the silence of the morning, and the smoke of their cigarettes.

For the first time in his life, Sutherland felt like one of the guys, like he belonged to something.

"I didn't start smoking until my first tour." Jack broke the silence which spooked Sutherland. He didn't know what to say so he sat back and continued to smoke to the best of his abilities. Jack studied Sutherland's face, then asked, "What's your story, Sut?"

"My story?"

"What did you do before the war?"

"Before the war?"

"Yeah, what's with the fuckin' echo? What did you do before the war?"

Sutherland had to take a second to recall. He hadn't really thought of his life before the Corps. He thought of people, but his actual life seemed foreign to him, as if someone else lived it. With a tapping of his thumb, he beat away the growing gray ash from the end of the cigarette and said, "I was a student."

"What did you study?"

"I was in love with English and History."

"So, you want to be a teacher?"

"No." Sutherland took a drag, stifling the urge to cough again. He looked over his shoulder to make sure no one was within earshot, and said, "A writer."

"Holy shit, fuckin' Bill Shakespeare over here. You're a writer?"

"I wanna be. As a kid, my parents were devoted to themselves more than dealing with me, so I would read a lot. I stumbled on an old typewriter and one day started writing my own stories to entertain myself. They were knockoffs of books I had already read, but it was fun."

"A writer. That's good to go. So why did you join the Corps?"

"I wanted the experience. I wanted something I could write about later in life, like Hemingway."

"And now look at you, fuckin' hard charger. I guess after this war is over, you'll have something to write about. You just better make me look good in it."

"Agreed," Sutherland said. Jack snuffed out the cigarette on the wooden table, not caring if the owner would disapprove. He smirked at the idea of the owner coming back and getting pissed at the burnt mark on the table. Chuckling to himself, he fired up another one. Jack leaned back in the chair, balancing on the two hind legs, and blew out the new puff of smoke inside his lungs.

"My brother lost his virginity to a stripper in Oklahoma," Jack said. Sutherland choked, fanning away the smoke to clear a path for him to breath. He didn't know why Jack was telling him this and Jack didn't know why he was saying it. "We were in Fort Sill for a training exercise. You ever been there?"

"No."

"Well, it's an army town and not that many Marines on the base. It's an artillery unit and we were learning some stuff on forward observing. Anyway, they have this place in Fort Sill called Dragons West. It's a nice little strip club, women are pretty good looking. The beer sucks but you can buy it in a gallon jug." Jack took a long pull from his cigarette and watched the smoke.

"There was this stripper there with these Bugs Bunny teeth," Jack continued, to which Sutherland laughed. "Just bad. Anyway, she takes my kid brother out. The next morning, he comes back and he talked about getting laid and shit, but he starts pulling at his crotch."

Sutherland's eyes widen.

"I asked him what's up and he says his dick felt raw and that he went at it bareback with this chick."

"He fucked a stripper without a condom?"

"Yeah. So, I tell him it could be bad, and he should go get checked. Have you ever been checked for the clap, Sut?"

"No."

"Well, they punch your bore with a giant cotton swab." Jack jabbed the air twice with an invisible cotton swab stick like it was a knife. Sutherland grabbed his groin and his face tensed in an uncomfortable fashion. Jack laughed and said, "Twice."

Sutherland groaned. "Jesus. That's gotta hurt."

"You know it. So, he comes back and says they didn't tell him shit. I say he has to do it again."

"No you didn't?"

"Fuck yeah, I did. And he goes." The two laughed together, trying to keep their volume low as to not wake the others. "He comes back cussing and pissed off, talking about how much it hurts. That's when I tell him he ain't got shit and he's just raw because of the friction of fuckin' too hard without a condom."

"Holy shit. That's great."

"Yeah, he was pissed at me. Told the motherfucker, he ever fucks some strange bitch without a condom again, he'd surely catch some shit that could make his dick fall off."

"Jesus. Who fuck's a stripper without a condom? That's just asking for something."

"Apparently my little brother."

"God, that's awesome. Shit, I lost my virginity in a tree house."

Jack's eyebrows tried to reach his hairline. "How young were you?"

"Sixteen. Nothing special."

"It never is." Jack leaned forward, sitting the chair back down on all four legs. His elbow settled into his hip, keeping the cigarette an inch from his lips, and he crossed one leg over the other. "Here's one for your book, did I ever tell you the story of my first cigarette?"

"No," Sutherland responded.

"A Chinese rocket came in and landed fifteen feet from me." His face never faltering, which fascinated Sutherland.

"Wait a minute. A rocket fell fifteen feet from you and you ain't dead?" Sutherland couldn't believe it.

"I know. The immortal Jack 'The Ripper' Campbell, the great Berserker." Jack rolled his eyes at the nonsense of his own legend. Sutherland suspected he spoke only to amuse himself in some fashion and as if reading Sutherland's mind, Jack waved off the notion with a snap of his wrist. "No, really though. The kill radius is like 30 meters, but some dumbass haj wired that damn thing wrong. It didn't explode. All it did was break in half and shook the hell out of the ground. Two more came in, but luckily they were forty meters away."

"What did you do?" Sutherland was unaware that his arms rested on the table. He leaned in toward Jack, soaking up the stories his leader had to tell him as if he would never be able to hear them again.

"Ran like hell," Jack said, causing Sutherland to wheeze from the smoke. Jack slung the bolt of his rifle a couple of times to make sure it was functioning properly, then carefully aligning it with his charging handle, slammed it in the upper receiver of his M16. "See, you wait for the first one to explode, so that way you know where you need to run when the second and third come in."

Locking the bolt and charging handle forward, he attached the upper receiver to the lower. The fit was flush, and he pushed in the two pins that held the weapon together as he continued, "After everything cleared, I was face down on the ground, covering my head, and scared shitless. A Marine walked up to me with a cigarette. I'll never forget what he said to me."

Jack stood the weapon up on the table, thumbed the switch to safety, and pulled the trigger. Nothing happened. He switched the safety to semi-auto, pulled the trigger, and ensured it clicked. Jack pulled back the charging handle, walked it home, and flipped the switch to three-round burst. The hammer fell, the click was audible, and Jack was satisfied with the function check of his weapon.

"This Marine looked down at me with no expression on his face. This guy wasn't scared at all, just one cool motherfucker. He simply said, welcome to the shit, bro. Then he handed me the cigarette and walked away."

"Where were y'all at?"

"Nasiriyah." The word cause Sutherland to pause. He heard scuttlebutt about the Berserkers in Nasiriyah and knew it was better not to ask about it. Jack could read the question on Sutherland's face. "You can ask."

"Ask what?" Sutherland tried to deny what his face was hinting at.

"Don't fuck with me, boot. I can see it in your eyes. You want to know what happened in Nasir." Sutherland ensured no one was listening for he would catch shit for it. Then he leaned forward, elbows resting on the table and spoke in a soft whisper.

"What happened in Nasiriyah?"

"Death." Smoke rolled from the corner of Jack's mouth as he spoke like a demon breathing the atmosphere of Hell. He relished in the wide-eyed gaze of Sutherland. "Our convoy came under attack. It was a well-placed ambush, but our LT got us lost even though I told him we were going the wrong way. Some guys in charge want to be heroes."

"That sucks."

"Gets worse. Anyways, we got captured. The LT surrendered us to the muj. A rocket hit my vehicle. Myself, Corporal Dillon, and Carlos were all knocked unconscious. When I awoke, I was in a jail cell with several of our comrades."

A dark and dank cell formed in Sutherland's mind, plagued with grimy floors and rats scavenging among the injured men. Only the movies gave Sutherland a glimpse of what a P.O.W. jail looked like, and he reckoned the real thing was much worse.

"My brother had been in the LT's truck and when I woke, I couldn't find him. At one point while I was out, our glorious LT, cowering in the corner, failed to identify himself as the man in charge. Apparently, my brother stood and said he was." Jack mentally kicked himself, taking in a hard drag. Sutherland took another cigarette from Jack's pack without asking. Jack didn't protest. "If I'd been awake, I would have fought. I would've led those guys out."

No time elapsed between snuffing out one cigarette and firing up another. Idle hands are the Devil's playthings, and Jack wanted something in his hands besides a weapon. His knee shook, and he knew regretting the mistakes he had made in life wouldn't change the past. The anxiety was his punishment to bear and he refused to release it.

"There were other cells and other men going through the same shit. An entire platoon of men and their screams echoed through the jail. The last time they came back, the LT was still in the corner."

Jack's knee nervously tapped out the rapid beat of his frustration.

"I demanded to see my brother and their leader. I told them I was Captain Campbell. That fucking prick LT was physically shaking with fear as they led me out of the cell. Some of the guys protested and started pointing and giving up the LT. He didn't even look at me as they took me away." The craving for a hot cup of coffee twisted Jack's stomach, but there was none and the cigarette would have to do.

"How'd you get away?" Sutherland couldn't break the hold his squad leader held on him, and the tale was more astonishing than he had imagined. He was like a vulture, feasting on the carnage of each word.

"They tried to behead me, so I killed them for it." The statement came in a period, harsh and flat, and any surrounding sounds vanished. Sutherland chewed on the end of the cigarette but failed to pull in a drag. He wondered what primal frame of mind did one slip into to do what Jack had done.

"They were videotaping. Gonna show the world they could kill Marines, but this *Marine*, this *Berserker* stepped up to the plate. Killed all three sonsofbitches." There had been talks of a videotape, but only a few truly knew of its existence. "I freed my men and found my brother. They had chopped his head off. I guess that's when the Berserker in me took over."

Sutherland recalled how alone and helpless he felt as the bullets tore Vinson to pieces. It was his one comparison of death he had to relate to Jack. Vinson had been his best friend and it was a title he didn't take lightly for Sutherland wasn't a man of many friends. The loss and his actions created new lines on Sutherland's face that were more suitable for a man ten years his senior.

"What did you do after you found your brother?" Sutherland asked, ready to rid his mind of guilt.

"I killed every hajji I saw. Killed every last one of them. Recovered our weapons and freed our brothers. I hunted them down. I searched in every place they could hide and killed them."

"What about the Lieutenant?"

"When I walked into that cell with weapons and other Marines, he stood up like he was finally ready to take charge." Jack slammed his fist against his chest. "His chest stuck out, and he held his chin up high. He pretty much had the attitude that I should be thanking him for all this."

"Sorry piece of shit."

"Yeah, and then he actually said this. I'm fuckin' quoting here, he said, now follow me, I'll lead us out of here."

Sutherland shot back in his chair as if Jack had punched him.

"What the fuck? Are you serious?"

"Yeah. You believe that shit? Some people."

"Please tell me you told him off."

"I handed him my brother's dog tags," Jack said. The humor dissipated as the severity of Jack's tale came to apparition. Jack inhaled deeply, watching the trail of smoke dancing from the burning end of his cigarette like a Bollywood seductress.

"What did he say then?"

"He told me I did a good job and I would get a medal for this."

"Did he give you a medal?"

"No."

"Fucking prick." Sutherland threw his arms up and shook his head. "I'm sure he took full credit for it all."

"Maybe," Jack said, shrugging his shoulders.

"I'm sure they gave him a silver star or some shit."

"I don't know what medals they buried with him."

"So, he died?" Sutherland asked, to which Jack nodded his head.

"Yeah, I'm sure your heart stops beating when a machete carves out your skull." Silence. The only sound was the burning of cigarette paper and snores coming from the other rooms.

"No one said anything?" Sutherland asked.

"What kind of man would rat on his brother that just saved his ass? 'Specially, for the one that got a lot of your brothers killed?" Jack paused to smoke and allowed the lesson to sink into Sutherland. Leaning forward on his elbows, he pointed his two fingers that held his cigarette at Sutherland. "We watch after one another."

There came another long pause between the two men.

"I got a handjob on a Ferris wheel once." Sutherland blurted out. He was unsure why he said this, but it came out before he could stop himself. Jack leaned away from Sutherland's admission.

"Well, congrats. That's good." The two chuckled, neither knowing where to go with the conversation. Both turned their attention to the men who still slept, watching as they stirred in a stupor of dreams until the approaching light of morning broke their slumber like a den of hibernating bears.

II

The day stretched on, and by noon, the Berserkers feared the fighting was over for them. Not a single engagement with the enemy occurred while clearing out house after house. Many homes stashed large caches of weapons and abandoned encampments with traces of burnt out fires and discarded food.

Each rooftop held the possibility of an unnamed sniper bullet ready to smoke one of them. Alleys were harbingers of some well-placed ambush. The dark spots were perfect hiding spaces, but all these were wasted with the lack of resistance from the insurgency. As the day drew on, fighting seemed far-fetched. Boredom laid behind each door and complacency plagued them. Their jolly tones died off and everyone moved fruitlessly in the formation.

"This sucks." Ashmore stomped over a pile of rubble in the street and rounded a row of large sand filled Hesco barriers. The men followed. "How the hell did the Haj get Hesco barriers?"

"Fuckin' stole them, duh," Simpson said.

"Go figure." He stepped over a pile of stones from a partially destroyed wall and sighed heavily. "Well, this still sucks."

"No shit," Thompson replied.

"Man, this is like Grand Theft Auto Vice City without the cars or any side missions to do. Fuckin' boring."

"Ash, this is more like Hue City than Vice City."

"Is that on Playstation 2?" Ashmore asked. Some of the others laugh.

"Ash, you fuckin' idiot. Didn't you pay attention in Marine Corps History during boot camp?" Thompson asked.

"Not really. I was trying not to pass out. You ever played Vice City?"

"No."

"Shit, Thompson. It's fuckin' awesome. Best game on Playstation 2."

"Fuck Playstation. Xbox is better." Jones called out.

"Fuck you and fuck the Xbox. It ain't got shit for games like the Playstation does."

"Fuck you. The graphics are better."

"Whatever." Ashmore continued. "Does it have Resident Evil or Grand Theft Auto? No, it doesn't. So, fuck the Xbox."

"Will y'all shut the fuck up?" Jack interrupted. "Besides, these modern games are shit. Endless continues and lives. Fuck that. Nintendo is the only real game system. Fuckin' three lives to beat an entire game and that's it. Fuck the Playstation and fuck the Xbox. Pussies."

A cheer went up among the men who agreed.

"I don't know about all that," Ashmore mumbled and kicked at the dirt. "I wish something would happen."

The squad turned down a larger road flanked by tall apartment buildings and stores that looked closer to the ghettos of Detroit than a desert city. Artillery shelling peppered the brick siding, burning, breaking, and chipping away large sections. Great mosque-like designs displayed the Muslim architecture, but several blankets, covering windows and entire sections of balconies, destroyed the image.

Storefronts held signs written in Arabic, advertising something the American Marines couldn't understand. Nearly every front was locked by an extension cage, barricading the store and its contents from possible looters. The electricity to the city had been cut long ago and anything in the store's refrigerators were surely spoiled by now. Only months prior and months after the battle, these stores would be full of people trying to make a day's wage by selling whatever they could.

The Berserkers scanned their perimeters, but most of them knew the enemy was no longer around. Their hearts didn't toy with the idea of a lingering threat nearby. They filed down the road in formation, relaxed in their movement with boots kicking at rocks and breaths flowing heavy from their chest. All were lost in their own thoughts.

Ashmore clenched his fist, signaling them to halt. On instinct, the squad dropped to one knee, bringing their rifles up to the ready. Their minds raced and their hearts pumped with adrenaline. Jack hustled up to the front of the formation.

"What the hell is going on?"

"Is that what I think it is?" Ashmore pointed farther up the road. Lying motionless in the wet street were two men wearing the battle gear and fatigues of the Marine Corps.

"Shit, keep an eye open, gents." Jack motioned them to advance. The men widened their formation, avoiding the tendency to bunch up.

"Get down." An unfamiliar voice called out from some unseen position. Within the measure of a heart beat, the crack of an AK rifle immediately followed. The noise ignited their senses and sent them diving for cover. Eyes bounced from one place to another in hopes of locating a shooter as a second series of shots kept them from regrouping.

Jack spotted two unknown Marines standing in an alleyway, frantically waving him over. With Sutherland and Ashmore tailing him, Jack accepted their invitation. He wasn't sure which men from his squad were with him, but as he entered the alleyway, he turned to see Simpson, Thompson, and Carlos plunged head-first behind a burnt-out taxi. The enemy riddled the damaged orange and white car with rounds. Simpson tried to break for Jack's location, but a burst of AK fire dotted the street at his feet. He slid to a stop, spun around, and relaunched himself behind the taxi.

"You just had to say it." Sutherland nudged Ashmore with his elbow, who shrugged his shoulders and grinned.

"Lock it up," Jack ordered, moving past the two Marines posted at the edge of the alley. "Where was the firing coming from?"

"The house at the end of the street," one of the Marines from the other unit said.

"From which one?" Jack poked his head out to see, but an enemy round drove him back.

"Did you notice how the road comes to a T-intersection?" the unknown Marine asked. Jack nodded. "The large white house at the top of the T."

"Who's in command?" Jack asked, to which the Marine thumbed in the direction behind him. At the other end of the alley, a small group huddled around someone on the ground. Jack rushed up to them with Ashmore and Sutherland acting as his personal bodyguards.

"Who's in charge?" Jack demanded.

"I am." A voice moaned from the ground. A man laid flat and winced as the Corpsman touched a wound on his leg. "Jesus, Doc. Fuckin' watch it."

The bar on his chest indicated the injured man was a lieutenant.

"Sir." Jack tried to interrupt the man's cries, but the LT wasn't listening. "Sir!"

"What is it?" The Lieutenant leaned his head back and bellowed more screams.

"I'm assuming those are your men in the street back there?"

"Yes, we were fucking ambushed. We were trying to link up with that D-9 over there." His head hooked in the direction of the massive bulldozer. "The bastards opened up on us without giving us a chance. It's not fair. It's not fair."

"Sir, none of it's fair, but sir…"

"Oh fuck me, oh shit, fuck me," the Lieutenant shouted. The men standing around the officer were rolling their eyes at his pain and agony. The wound was small, not more than a splinter of metal under his skin, and hardly bleeding. By his actions, the LT made it sound as if his leg was severed.

"Sir—"

"Oh fuck, oh Jesus."

"Sir!" Jack shouted as he grabbed the LT by the flak jacket and caused several of the Marines to flinch away.

"Jesus, Corporal. Can't you see I'm injured?"

"We're all injured, Sir, but try to maintain some fuckin' discipline." Jack turned away from the group and gathered with Ashmore and Sutherland. "We need to draw fire away from Carlos and those guys. Follow me."

One Marine standing in the huddle around the injured officer grabbed Sutherland by the arm. Ashmore paused with him.

"Who is that guy?" the Marine asked.

"That's The Ripper. Jack Campbell," Sutherland said.

"And we're the Berserkers. Remember it." Ashmore added and together, they joined their corporal at the dozer. A soldier leaned against the D-9 with armor plating and bulletproof glass.

"Is this your ride?" Jack asked.

"Yes, Sir," the soldier replied.

"I'm not an officer. I work for a living. Name's Corporal Campbell and I need your help, soldier."

"I'm supposed to be with those men." The Army soldier motioned toward the Marines standing around the injured lieutenant.

"And now you're with me. What's your name?"

"Specialist Nelson, Corporal."

"Well, Specialist Nelson, we got a house full of bad guys, and my Marines are pinned down. I'm commandeering your vehicle with or without you. Now I don't know how to drive this thing so the Army might like it if you did it, so they can have their toy back in one piece." Jack could sense the soldier's doubt as Nelson looked at the men he was assigned to. Jack rolled his tongue across his teeth, wishing he had a moment to brush them. "I'll take all the blame if your command gets mad. Tell them Marine Corporal Jack Campbell held a gun to your head."

Ashmore nudged Sutherland. "What's he doin'?"

"Stealing a D-9," Sutherland replied. Ashmore rubbed his hands together in a small cheer.

"Just like Vice City."

III

The taxi's side mirror vanished with a gong-like bang and pieces of shattered plastic and broken glass rained down on Simpson. He cursed, brushing the trash from his shoulders. Thompson rose, his head inching over the top of the taxi's hood, but more rounds prevented him from running free. Carlos pulled him back down and the three looked at one another, knowing hope was something they didn't have.

Carlos didn't like their situation and looked around to see if he could find a way out. Kyle stood in the doorway of a blown-out building with the remaining Berserkers, motioning to him to make a break for it. Three 7.62 rounds deflected off the street in front of him, keeping Carlos pinned. Kyle and the other Berserkers fired at the large white house but were unsuccessful in providing cover for the other three to run. Carlos waved his hand in front of his face, calling for Kyle and his men to cease fire.

Simpson looked past Thompson and noticed Jack, Sutherland, and Ashmore were gone from the alley with the other group of Marines.

"Where the fuck did they go?" Simpson wondered.

Thompson searched but didn't see any trace of his squad leader or the other Marines that had followed him. The absence of Jack was a shock to his system. Jack Campbell, the great Ripper, the first Berserker, didn't run from a fight, but he wasn't there.

"Don't worry about Jack." Thompson reassured his Marine. "He'll get us out of here. Trust me."

"Really, because it looks like he just fuckin' cut and ran."

"Hey," Thompson and Carlos said in unison, screaming at the younger Marine. Carlos allowed Thompson to take over as he was the fireteam leader. "Don't ever say that Jack Campbell is a fuckin' chicken. I guarantee right now he's figuring out a way to save our asses. That man saved my life. He saved Carlos's life. He saved a lot of men's lives at a great cost, so don't you ever talk shit about him again, you get me?"

Simpson nodded his head. Behind Kyle and the others, Thompson could see Doc Sloan getting his MED bag ready. This troubled him as the burnt, rusted metal of the taxi chipped away around them.

IV

A crudely painted white house, built of brick and mortar and fit for someone with money, sat at the head of the T-intersection. It loomed over the street like a devouring mouth, ready to inhale the Marines and all things in its view. Artillery bombardment destroyed sections of walls and chipped away at the bricks, but the structure was sound. Several insurgents fired from windows and doorways at the pinned down Marines.

The one blessing the trapped men had was that the insurgents had failed to complete a 'U' shape ambush position. Although they kept the Marines immobilized behind the taxi, no one outflanked them to finish the Americans off. Angry clouds slithered across the darkening sky and released a fury of rain on them.

Jack scaled the side of the dozer, unfazed by the pelleting rain, and pulled Nelson's door open.

"See my men behind that car?" Jack shouted, pointing to the taxi. Nelson nodded his head. "Don't run over them, but head for the fucking house at the end of the street."

Nelson shifted into drive and the iron rhino jerked forward, tearing down the street and crushing anything it encountered. Jack, Sutherland, and Ashmore fell in behind it, trying hard not to breathe in the exhaust. The heat pouring out of the great beast was a welcoming comfort against the chill of drizzling rain. The churning tracks ate at the pavement, shoving vehicles and discarded objects from its path like a street sweeper. A half-filled Hesco barrier burst under the dozer's weight and an overturned bicycle flatted like a penny struck by a train.

Nelson pivoted, moving alongside the charred taxi, and clipping the edge of a building. Bricks bounced off the street and the dozer, but Nelson hardly noticed it. The scoop caught the edge of the taxi's trunk and to the horror of the pinned Marines, it slowly skidded sideways, exposing them to the enemy. Rounds popped off the taxi and struck the dozer. Using the D-9's scoop as cover, the pin-downed Marines hurried to fall in with Jack.

"Nice to see you again, Jack." Thompson squeezed in next to his squad leader.

"Yeah, you can buy me round when we get back, we gotta go." The dozer crawled forward again, and the enemy concentrated on the front of it. The engine revved while idling as Nelson came to a sudden halt. The Marines tucked in close for protection while taking a knee. Jack mounted the back of the hot dozer, accepting the burns rather than exposing himself to enemy fire.

"What the fuck are you doing?" Jack yelled at the bulletproof glass.

"They're firing at me." Nelson complained.

"You're in a goddamn armored bulldozer. Run through that fucking house." Jack screamed over the noise of the engine. The dozer kicked forward, and Jack jumped off the back to cram in next to the five other Marines.

Hoping to stop the large bulldozer, the enemy unloaded magazine after magazine at the D-9. Nelson winced at each round that left a black burn on his inch-thick windshield. The gears churned, and the bucket rose a foot off the ground, ready to plow through the six-foot-high concrete wall surrounding the house. From an open window screamed a single RPG.

Nelson leaned back, but there was nowhere for him to hide. The rocket impaled into the dozer's scoop and erupted in a great fireball. The white flash blinded Nelson, and he didn't see the D-9 destroy the fence and rip through the large front yard. In a desperate attempt, the insurgent focused the bulk of their fire on the D-9's front glass. Spiderweb cracks flashed in several spots, but nothing penetrated. Nelson increased the height of the bucket, cuing the insurgents to leap from any opening they could.

From each side of the dozer, the Marines peered out and opened fire on the fleeing insurgents. Three fell at once, and two made it to the side fence before falling dead. Another two insurgents weren't immediately killed but got hit exiting the house. One managed to fall back to a stone section of a wall that had fallen, but the other took a series of 5.56 rounds to the knees. He crawled, digging his nails into the rain-drenched dirt in hopes of getting away, but the dozer didn't stop. Nelson, still fighting back the flashes in his vision, didn't see the man on the ground as his dozer ran over him.

It was Thompson who stepped in the man's remains and complained as if he stepped in a pile of dog shit. A pineapple grenade flew out from behind the wall, trying to get past the D-9 and kill the Marines. The Hajji's final act of insurgency failed. Simpson peeled out from behind the dozer and released a grenade of his own.

POP. Flash, a puff of smoke.

The Berserkers cheered at the sight of their fallen enemy. Jack relished in their victory, leaning up against the bulldozer and removed his helmet. None of his men were hurt. Grinning, he said, "Happy Birthday, Marines."

* * *

Letter to Jack Campbell from Jennifer Campbell,

Dated November 4th, 2004-

Dear Jack,

I'm sorry this letter's short, but I'm extremely tired and wanted to write before I went to sleep. Joshua Dillon Campbell has entered this world and is one healthy baby. I've enclosed a picture of him. I can see in his eyes he wants to meet you. He weighed six pounds and eight ounces and was nineteen inches long. The labor was intense, but it was much harder without you being here. So many people have come up to the hospital to see us.

Your father slept here in the waiting room, just in case we needed something. He's been a big help, and it's kind of funny to see him with Joshua. His rugged cowboy demeanor has faded to a soft, cuddly old man and I think he enjoys the fact that he's a grandfather. I'm tired. Please come home soon. Please write me. We love you so much. I can't wait to start our lives without the worry of deployments.

Love your wife and son.

CHAPTER EIGHT

GET SOME

There are only two kinds of people that understand Marines; Marines and the enemy. Everyone else has a second-hand opinion.

-General William Thornson, U.S. Army

I

The men chowed down on MRE's and indulged themselves with bad tasting cigarettes. Brands like Royal and Crown flowed between the Marines, and they agreed the smokes taken from dead insurgents tasted like shit but were cigarettes nonetheless. Jack laid a map out on a kitchen table of a two-story house they occupied and plotted their next route. Sutherland offered Jack some of his MRE, turkey with potato chunks and gravy, but Jack declined, hitting his cigarette instead.

A ray of sun broke through the window, catching a circular disk on the counter, and ricocheted a beam into Jack's eye. He picked up the CD, and a long-forgotten memory rushed back to him. Basking in the warmth of a Texas spring day, his father blared the radio in the old family Camaro as a ten-year-old Jack hung his arm out the window, surfing on the back of a rushing wind.

"Black, you got your CD player?" Black walked in from the living room, where many took up a spot to eat or catch some sleep and produced his silver portable disk player with external speakers.

"What's that?" Kyle spun a chair around at the table and sat backward while smoking a cigarette.

"Sam Cooke," Jack said. Simpson strolled in with Jones and Sutherland.

"Who's Sam Cooke?" He asked. Jones's eyebrows curved inward with disbelief, questioning Simpson before slapping him in the back of the head.

"Man, you don't know shit about Black history. Sam fuckin' Cooke. One of the greatest singers of all time." Jones wasn't sure, but he could have sworn steam was coming out of his nose.

"Did he ever tour with Pac?"

"Tupac? Man, I'm going to slap the shit out of you again, you ignorant motherfucker. Shut up and listen. This is R&B back when it was rhythm and blues. Back when it had soul in it." A soothing voice from the 1960's poured from the small speakers as the Berserkers fixated on the CD player like it was a television.

"I'm surprised there's a Sam Cooke CD here."

"I guess even the Haj has to like good music," Jones said. Jack leaned back to smoke and the two shared a nod of agreement.

"Wish we had some Pantera," Sutherland said.

"I thought they broke up," Thompson added.

"Fuck you. They'll get back together. Best fuckin' metal band there is. They put on the best show."

"I'm a Korn fan, myself," Kyle said.

"I'm old school punk rock. Like the Ramones or the Misfits. They got a song called Bullet about killing JFK in Dallas fuckin' Texas." Ashmore shook his head and stuck a dip into his lip.

"Fuck you, man," Jack said. Ashmore smirked.

"Where you from, Corporal?"

"Where you think?"

"Dallas?"

"Yeah."

"Oh, well, y'all killed Kennedy."

"Hey, hey, hey. We've killed a lot of people, not just one president. Now shut the fuck up and listen to the music." Everyone went silent.

Scanning the somber faces of his men, dirty and rugged, Kyle thought of the zero hour. He thought how this could be their last minutes together. At any moment, any one of them could buy the farm. No matter the dread of a possible short future, these killers of men who stood smack dab in the middle of a combat zone, were allotted a moment of peace. This thought, although morbid, made Kyle chuckle. *All the money in the world couldn't buy something this precious and rare,* he thought.

"Hey, let's get a group photo before we head out again." Kyle pulled a small digital camera from his daypack. With the sun blanketing their faces and the music grooving, the Berserkers crowded into the frame while Kyle sat the timer. Smiles and snarls painted a few faces, and some held the blunt attributes of warriors with their fists clenched in the air. Cigarettes burned in nearly every hand except for two. Each man took on the persona of the saltiest dogs on earth.

In the center of the back row, with smirking heads held high, Jack draped his arm around Kyle's shoulder and Kyle reciprocated. Kyle thrust his rifle in the air before the flash. A moment captured in digital history followed by an abrupt end as reality came streaming back into focus.

"Cut that off," Carlos said in a tone no louder than a whisper. He glided, hunched over through the kitchen and into the living room. Black smashed his finger down on the stop button, nearly knocking it off the table. Taking a cue from Carlos, the Berserkers crouched as if some imminent robotic threat was scanning the building for life forms. Carlos flowed stealthily to the front window, and Jack and Kyle moved past the rest of the men to follow.

Two white cars, untouched by the war, centered in the small alley-like street in front of the house. The two cars, parked headlight to headlight, shielded a gathering of insurgents unaware of the Marines in the adjacent house. Stone steps led up to the front door of the building like apartments from the slums of New York City rather than a city in

Iraq. A metal trash can stood next to the steps and Jack half-expected to see a grouchy puppet emerge from within. The thought nearly made him smirk, but the situation was too serious to do so.

Carlos tried to calculate how many more men were in the building behind the nine, but the enemy combatants kept rotating positions, walking from one window to another, moving in and out of view, until Carlos gave up trying to finalize the unknown number of hidden fighters.

Hovering over a map pinned down to a car hood, three men discussed ambush plans in their native tongue. On their hips, they carried pistols, indicating authority in the Arab world. A plan formulated in Jack's mind. At the end of the narrow, alley-like street, a great wall created a dead-end. This limited the insurgent's movement to only three directions: retreat out behind their currently held building, sneak out the side where the street wraps a hard-ninety-degree turn around the apartment, or the insurgents could charge across the street at the Marines.

Whoever designed this section of the city must have been drunk or stoned or created this dead-end purposely to lure Marines in, Jack thought. He whirled away from the window, and much to the surprise of the others, he was grinning.

"Those bastards have no idea we're in here. I say we surprise these motherfuckers. Sneak attack these pricks like they've been doing to us." The collective herd of Marines pulsed with excitement. "Kyle, you see that house over here?"

Staying out of sight of the window, Kyle eased up next to Jack to see what he was pointing at. Across the way, past the hard-ninety-degree bend in the road, sat a two-story house with a blue tin roof and structure damage from artillery bombardment.

"From the looks of it, that house over there will give us a clear view of the back and the side of their building. Take a team." He ticked off his finger at Doc, Carlos, Harvey, Simpson, and Jones. "Get to that house quick."

"So, you want us to flank them?"

"Yeah, have some men covering the back of the house, so if they try to retreat, you can smoke'em. You let us start the show and when they come running your way, mow them the fuck down. Go," Jack ordered.

Kyle rounded up his assigned men, and they disappeared out the back door. Sutherland and Ashmore hurried to a window, while Thompson moved into the next room. Black disappeared up the stairs without calling attention to himself.

"Ash, when I say, I want you to pop up in that window and let loose with your SAW."

"Wanna play talkin' guns, Corporal?" Eager to replace the small pouch of tobacco in his lip, Ashmore pulled out his can of dip and shook it. It was empty.

"No, smoke the motherfuckers," Jack said.

"Shit. I'm out of dip. Got any?" Ashmore asked. Jack shook his head but tossed him a cigarette.

"Ash. Rain hell on them." Ashmore agreed while spitting out a brown wet plug of dip from his lip. He moved to his assigned window to wait anxiously for the time he could squeeze the trigger on his SAW and raise his body count. The Marines checked their rifles, inserting fully loaded magazines while crouching down. They stayed low, keeping out of sight while itching for some action.

II

Kyle's men peeled out the back and ran across several yards, leaping over cement walls and avoiding damaged debris. Kyle eyed each passing roof, looking for the particular blue tin covering that signaled their assigned house. He found it and ushered his men in. The floor was covered in broken pieces of cement bricks from a wall which crumbled under the artillery attack. Jabbing a knife hand at the stairs, Kyle ordered Jones and Carlos to clear out the top floor while reminding them to maintain noise discipline.

Carlos responded with a nod, but Jones kept his attention on the high ceiling. Dangling from a chandelier by the neck, with eyes closed and a dry, rigid tongue protruding from its mouth, was the rotating corpse of a black cat.

"Sick bastards," Jones whispered, but Carlos didn't stop to stare at the cat. He nudged Jones to get him moving, and the two men sailed up the stairs. They stayed an inch from the wall so the floating concrete steps wouldn't moan under their weight. With a systematical check, they cleared each room. Jones paused long enough to admire a Persian rug covering the floor in the master bedroom. Despite the destruction of the house, not a speck of dirt or a single rock laid on this beautiful hand-woven piece of art.

Carlos motioned for Jones to move and Jones eased up next to the last door in the hallway. A foot-wide gap allowed him to peer inside, and he spotted the back of an insurgent posted up at the window, looking out on the targeted structure. Focused solely on providing security for the meeting across the street, the young man was oblivious to the Marines moving into the room.

Jones slid the M16 to his side, allowing the three-point sling to hold it there. From the front of his flak jacket, he unsheathed his Ka-bar knife, and treaded heel to toe, gliding like a ghost while controlling every muscle in his body with the utmost discipline to avoid making a sound. A scream from the insurgent would alert the others to the Marines' presence and allow the insurgency to escape with minimal damage. This would not do, so Jones held his breath.

The insurgent stirred, pulling the rifle strap from around his neck and laid the AK-47 across his lap. Jones paused as the insurgent lit up a cigarette. His heart pounded in his ears, his body twitching from the adrenaline, and he was sure the insurgent could hear him. The insurgent moved, stretching his arms wide while releasing a large puff of smoke. Jones's heart settled, his grip tightened on the knife's handle, and he leaped forward. In his relaxed demeanor, the insurgent startled when Jones kicked the AK from his lap.

The rifle struck the wall and fell out of reach. The man didn't have time to stand or react. The only thing he managed to do before Jones had a hold of him was to drop his cigarette, scorching his shirt. His eyes widened and he tried to scream, but Jones yanked back his head and drug his blade across the man's throat, muting him.

The insurgent kicked the window ledge, fell backward, and pinned Jones to the floor. Jones didn't relent. He fought hard to hold onto the struggling man's head as blood greased his grip. The man squirmed, fighting to wiggle free, but Jones wrapped his legs around the man's waist to keep him from spinning off. Jones arched his hips and reared back with his arms. The laceration widened, spewing a flood of blood out of both the jugular and carotid artery. The man stretched for his rifle, but it was just out of reach.

He thrashed, driving elbows into Jones's ribcage in hopes to get free. His lungs hurt for air and if only he could get away from his attacker, he could catch his breath.

A sharp, thin elbow jabbed at Jones's hip, and Jones pulled harder. He raised the seven-inch blade above them, then plunged it into the man's chest, driving it to the hilt.

"Shhh," Jones whispered into his ear, trying to calm him and stifle the fight. "It's all over soon."

The insurgent's fingertips brushed the cool metal of his rifle, and he stretched out one more time to get it. He lifted his arm, but it was too heavy, so he tried kicking, fighting on until there was no life left in him. Jones drove in the blade three more times before rolling off the insurgent and shoving him away. The sun coming in through the window beamed down on the insurgent, and Jones went gray.

Carlos whispered to him, but Jones didn't move, for his eyes were locked on to something unexpected.

III

Skyler ducked out of the makeshift hospital room to lean up against a desert stained wall. She found it hard to wash the red film from her arms and sleep was a distant memory. Exhausted, she removed her glasses and squeezed the bridge of her nose for relief. Her eyelids were heavy, and she closed them, finding a moment of reprieve from the chaotic world. Her breathing calmed and settled in her ears but died quickly to the haunting screams of dying men.

She jumped, half expecting to see a bunch of ghosts or dead men standing around her, trying to get at her, but when she opened her eyes, she found only the wind blowing.

"This helps," a voice said from behind her. A man lay on a gurney, his chest bare, and his abdomen wrapped with a saturated field dressing. An IV hanging from a screw in the wall, connected to his arm as he held out a burning cigarette.

"I don't smoke." Skyler informed him with a pleasant smile as if saying thanks but no thanks. She returned her glasses to her face.

"It helps." He forced the cigarette at her until she took it. The rising smoke stung at her nose and drifted under her glasses, burning her eyes, causing them to water. The filter was bitter and dry as her tongue graced the end of it.

"Breathe it in," the Marine said. Skyler did and the smoke burned in her throat, but she invited it. Her chest filled with the toxic air that gripped the nerves of her spinal cord with a pleasant tingle. The troubles of her world felt fleeting as the ecstasy of the nicotine embraced her. She wanted to kiss, to take another drag and make love, but more importantly, she felt like forgetting the war. Skyler wished the cigarette was Kyle's lips, soft and full of passion.

The filter stuck, refusing to break their connection. Upon opening her eyes, she found the young man staring at her with a wide grin on his face. She returned the smile and pushed the cigarette back toward him, but he refused.

"Keep it. Looks like you need it more than I do." Skyler took another drag. She squatted where she stood, leaning against the wall, and running her hand through her dirty hair. Her lungs didn't burn. Her mind went back to Kyle. She could see his face and wanted only to touch him.

He was handsome, more so than the boys back home and her father would love him, even if her mother might judge him for being a Marine. Skyler wished they had been together, made love at least one time before he left for the front. Her heart ached at the thought of not seeing him again. She stared listlessly at a pile of equipment near the entrance of the hospital room. Boots, flak jackets, and other gear laid tossed into a growing heap, covered with blood. A helmet sat on top, the inside drenched in a matter she could only assume was brains. A shiver crawled down her spine at the sight of the gear belonging to the dead.

IV

Carlos pulled at Jones's arm, only then seeing the dead man on the floor, was in fact, a thirteen-year-old boy. Carlos sighed heavily, unable to find the words as he pulled Jones away from the body.

"Shit, bro, he would've smoked us if we gave him the chance." Jones didn't react. "Jones. Snap out of it, brother. Dig it, he had a weapon. He was a combatant, and that's fair game, amigo."

Carlos forced their retreat down the stairs, pushing Jones to regroup with the others.

"Why aren't you posting upstairs?" Kyle asked. Carlos released his hold on Jones and Jones floated away from the two, heading closer to a window that looked out on the meeting of insurgents.

"He knifed a kid up there," Carlos fired up a cigarette and blew the smoke away from the face of Kyle. "I think it Sectioned-Eight him."

"Great, that's what we need, a basket case out here." Harvey shook his head disapprovingly before Kyle flung a knife hand in his direction.

"Stow that shit," Kyle barked as he marched up to Jones. "Snap out of it, Marine, or I swear I'll shoot you right here."

Jones stared at Kyle but didn't respond. His eyes drifted past Kyle to something outside the window. Without concern for his safety, he stomped forward, pushing past Doc and Harvey.

"We need to have that high ground coverage," Kyle said. "Simpson, you and Harvey go up there and post where you can see the back of that building. In case they try to exit out the rear, kill them."

"Shit." Simpson shook his head. "Why do I have to be stuck with the fuckin' pogue?"

"That's an order, Simpson."

"Come on, Admin." Simpson led the way up the stairs with Harvey following. Simpson hated the look of the Iraqi boy lying dead on the floor. "Grab a leg and let's move him."

"I don't want to touch him."

"Muthafucker, grab a leg, or I'll kick your fuckin' ass and call it blue on blue." Harvey did as the larger Marine instructed and together, they drug the body into the hallway. With the corpse gone, they posted at the window where the kid had been sitting alive only five minutes before. A pop crackled in the distance and was immediately followed by several more.

Simpson eased up to the window to see insurgents scattering.

"Get ready, men. Wait for them to start running and then fuck them up."

V

Ashmore sparked the cigarette. He had been waiting for this moment, and the eyes of his squad were on him. Hoisting his SAW into his shoulder, Ashmore stepped out in front of the window.

"Let's rock-n-roll." He unleashed a fury with the SAW. The velocity of the rounds shattered the glass in front of him as the belt of ammo zipped through the weapon. Empty belt rings and brass casings ejected out the opposite side. The filter of the cigarette mashed between the teeth of his grinning face. Ashmore envisioned himself as a prohibition gangster, cutting down an opposing gang. As pieces of building chipped away, and the enemy fell or scattered, Ashmore's chuckle bellowed into laughter.

With the first few shots, the majority of the insurgents froze even as two of their men buckled to the ground. A series of war cries erupted from the neighboring buildings. When several more rifles joined in, the insurgents scrambled for cover. The Marines tore apart the adjacent structure without opposition. A full thirty seconds elapsed before a single insurgent returned fire.

A whistle broke the sound barrier and a trail of white chem smoke appeared from the insurgent's roof. A hard impact struck the second floor above Jack and Sutherland. The house shook, kicking loose dust and tiny pieces of concrete to rain down on them. Jack angled out, leveling his rifle at a running insurgent, and fired three shots.

BANG. Recoil. Sucking chest wound.

BANG. Recoil. Shoulder wound.

BANG. Recoil. Headshot.

An insurgent crept into view at a second-floor window, body half shielded by the plaster of the wall. Jack lifted his head from the stock of his rifle and scanned the building without looking down the iron sights. The insurgent brought forth a rocket-propelled grenade, aiming it at Jack's window. AK rounds struck the window panel, flinging glass at Jack who flinched away from the shards. Time appeared to slow to a crawl and the worst vision came to Jack's mind. He pictured his men blown to bits by the RPG.

VI

It only took one man trying to escape for Jones to march up to the window. The words came screaming out his throat, "You motherfuckers!"

He drove the barrel of his M16 through the window and rapidly pumped his trigger finger. Selecting targets at random, he swayed his barrel back and forth without pause.

"Sending kids, you pieces of shit."

Jones screamed a vicious war cry while throwing round after round at the enemy.

Kyle popped up and shot off a couple of rounds before dropping into cover. He cussed, pissed that Jones had jumped the gun before a larger group of insurgents had tried to make a break for it. Kyle looked at Doc and Carlos, who stared at him as if they had never seen a firefight before.

"Start fuckin' fighting."

Doc came up with grit and determination. His rifle planted into his shoulder and he eyed the scene for an insurgent to shoot. Before he could get a shot off, the glass in front of him fractured. An AK round slammed into the center of his chest, sprawling him out on the cement floor with a thud.

"Doc!" Carlos peeled out from his window and ran to the corpsman. Doc clutched at his chest, gasping for air, face flushed red as his eyes bulged in their sockets. He spun on the hard tile floor, uselessly trying to draw in air as his mouth fluttered like a fish on the deck of a boat. The impact felt like he had taken a direct punch from Mike Tyson. He sat up and with great relief, tore open his flak jacket. The pressure eased from his chest, allowing air to funnel back into his lungs.

Carlos reached Doc as two rounds broke through the walls. He grunted as the first round skidded off the back of his helmet, rocking his head, and causing the room to spin. Carlos took a sideways step, trying to maintain his balance, but spiraled to the floor as the second bullet hit him in the neck.

VII

Jack steadied his breathing and achieved sight alignment and sight picture. Despite the debris flying around him, he squeezed the trigger.

BANG. Recoil. Headshot.

A shower of pink mist blossomed. The enemy combatant vanished from the window, but not before his RPG rocked the insurgent-held building.

"Holy shit," Sutherland said. Jack rolled to the side, stepping out of view from the insurgents. "Nice one, Corporal."

Jack didn't share in Sutherland's boyhood excitement. It was another dead insurgent, another death on his record, another notch to carve into the handle of his knife. Jack slammed a new magazine against his helmet, ensuring a proper seating of rounds.

Two insurgents stormed the front gate but managed only to funnel themselves into Ashmore's kill zone. He sprayed a belt of ammo at an alarming rate, and as one insurgent fell, another appeared. The brown dirt turned dark with blood. Ashmore gritted his teeth, the muscles in his neck tightened, and he let out a fear-provoking war cry.

"Hey, Jack." Sutherland flipped his head in the direction of the war-crazed Ashmore. "True Berserker."

"Indeed," Jack replied, failing to conceal his grin. A feeling of pride overcame him, and he was certain his men would survive this day.

VIII

Simpson and Harvey took the time to aim in at their targets. The insurgents hurried out the back of the building, trying to cover their heads. Neither Harvey nor Simpson sprayed rounds at the men running in sandals and man-dresses. They took their time and picked off each one — one shot, one kill.

Both had no inclination that Carlos was soaking in his own blood a floor below. His fingers stained as he clamped a hand to his neck.

Doc, who completely forgot about his own pain, rushed to Carlos. With the burning intensifying, Carlos kicked and squirmed. Doc pulled Carlos's hand away from the wound and blood drizzled out, but it wasn't in spurts. Carlos jerked his hand free from Doc to recover his wound.

"You got to let me look at it," Doc shouted over the gunfire and slapped Carlos's hand away. He quickly examined the wound and replaced Carlos's hand. To Doc's relief, the bullet had missed the jugular entirely and simply sliced across the side of his neck.

"Patch me up, Doc. I got to get back to the fight," he said through clenched teeth, trying to rise.

"Hold on, Marine." Doc pushed him back down and slapped a pressure dressing on the wound. "We need to med-evac you."

"Fuck you, Doc. Not happening."

Kyle scrambled over to Carlos, reloading his M16 as he moved in a crouching stride. Carlos climbed to his feet, placed his helmet on his head, but allowed the chin strap to remain unlatched - John Wayne style.

"Carlos, stay down," Kyle ordered, but Carlos strolled up to the window.

"Fuck that," Carlos said, firing a couple of shots at the enemy. "And let you all have all the fun. Not on my Marine Corps birthday."

Lance Corporal Roberto Carlos

Purple Heart Recipient

For Wounds Received on November 10th, 2004

Fallujah, Iraq, Al-Anbar Province

* * *

From the pages of Jack Campbell's Journal-

Today should have been a happy day. It's the Marine Corps birthday, and normally we're all getting decked-out in our dress blues for the ball. Tonight should've been full of drinking and fun. Then again, we're doing what Marines do best: kicking ass and dropping bodies.

One of the shittier parts of this job happened today. I was told by a Marine in Sergeant Whitmire's squad that some friends of mine bought the farm. Fucking smoked on the Marine Corps' birthday. Shame. I've known two of these guys since before my first tour. I mean, shit, we killed some hajjis together and now they're dirt farmers. Sucks, an entire fire team wiped out.

Corporal Mark Houston, Corporal Craig Lawrence, Lance Corporal Scott London, and Private Brian Welsh fought bravely to the bitter end. From what eyewitnesses and the after-action report is saying, it was a bad situation from the get-go. The new guy, Welsh, entered the house from the front door and caught a bullet in the neck. Fuck, Carlos got hit in the neck today but managed to make it. Damn.

Hell, Welsh was only nineteen. Houston and Lawrence moved around to the back, where they kicked in the door and tossed in a frag. They rushed in, smoked two insurgents in the dining room. I'm guessing they entered the living room where they saw Lance Corporal London lying dead on the floor. The report said his hand was on the handle of Welsh's flak jacket.

London had tried to pull his comrade to safety and died for it. Shots and drinks to you, Marine. Lawrence and Houston were on the stairs when a pineapple grenade came rolling down. Houston shoved Lawrence down the stairs and absorbed the majority of shrapnel in his back. A piece lodged in his neck, slicing through his spinal cord, killing him instantly. Lawrence took some shrapnel as well.

The next team in the house said it looked like Lawrence had been crawling for his unattached weapon. He must have lost it when Houston pushed him. The team entered to see an insurgent standing over Lawrence. The Haj placed three rounds into his face. They smoked the motherfucker, but four of our brothers are dead. Good guys who bought the farm way too early in life. Fuck, I hate this war. I got more dead friends than I do live ones.

Shots to all you Marines. Farewell, brothers.

I want to go home. Can I go home? Jennifer deserves better than I can give her.

CHAPTER NINE

SEMPER FI

One of the reasons why it is so easy to march men off to war is that each of them feels sorry for the man next to him who will die.

-Ernest Becker

I

November 12th, 2004-

Sutherland aligned behind Ashmore, flanking the front door of a single-story house. His clothes were filthy; he stank of sweat and dirt and wanted nothing more than to take a shower. The skin on the back of his neck crawled. It itched with sweaty residue despite the cold chill blowing in the air.

"I got a bad feeling about this door." Ashmore glared intensely at Jack. Jack leaned around Sutherland and surveyed the ordinary looking door. Jack trusted his men and the look in Ashmore's eyes gave a reason for concern.

"Wha'cha feelin'?" Jack asked.

"I don't know. But something ain't right here."

"Move around to the side. Find an entrance," Jack ordered. One by one, they peeled away, following Ashmore through a small pathway running between the house and a concrete fence. The tight path forced Ashmore sideways. He scanned the wall to find a suitable entry point and came across a large opening created by either artillery or a tank round.

"Frag the motherfucker." Ashmore pointed to the hole, moving past it to provide security. While Jack kneeled and provided rear security, Sutherland pitched a grenade through the three-foot hole.

Pop. Flash, a puff of smoke.

To the amazement of the Marines, after the small explosion, a larger one followed. Ashmore's face brightened with an 'I-told-you-so' attitude.

"Makes me all gitty inside," he said before climbing through the three-foot hole. Dust particles danced through the smoke made visible by rays of sunlight coming in the opening that was once the front door. Despite the light, Ashmore couldn't identify the room he was in due to the heaviness of the shadows.

He aimed his barrel to the left, and as he stepped a foot into the house, he swept around to scan each spot the best he could. The dismal light obscured his vision, casting one shadow to be darker than the next without revealing an object's true form. Secretly, with the lack of visual certainty, Ashmore hoped for no insurgents. He tucked his head and entered the room completely, then froze. Standing in what appeared to be a doorway was the silhouette of a man.

Ashmore's whole body locked up, and he knew he was as good as dead. He could see what appeared to be a rifle or a weapon system in the man's hand. There was no time to think as his finger jerked the trigger and buzzed four rounds at the figure.

The flash of the man's barrel appeared simultaneously and then the dark figure shattered into a hundred tiny pieces. Ashmore collapsed against the wall, slid down, and before taking a breath, rolled out of the hole. Sutherland and Jack hurried to his side.

"What the hell was that?" Sutherland asked. He stuck his head in, expecting to see a dead insurgent but found only a ransacked bedroom.

"Shot...myself...mirror...explain later...all clear." His chest heaved up and down. He closed his eyes to settle the world and let his blood pressure return to normal. Jack laughed at Ashmore as he and Sutherland helped the Marine to his feet.

"Let's go," Jack said. They followed him back around the corner of the house to where the front door laid bent and twisted in the yard. He bypassed it to check out the threshold. The hinges that had held the door to the frame stood separated, mangled and jagged on the doorjamb. Mounted next to the jamb was a small device with burnt wires and charred metal plating. Pieces of the adobe wall broke away, revealing the straw and rock-hard mud used to create its structure.

"Booby trap." Jack pointed at the device with Sutherland and Ashmore looking over his shoulder. Sutherland cast a side glance at Ashmore, who stood tall with that same large smirk on his face, touching his index finger to the tip of his nose.

"Don't doubt this nose. I can smell a booby trap a mile away," Ashmore said. Sutherland rolled his eyes.

"Yeah, but your eyes can't tell the difference between your reflection and a fuckin' haj." Sutherland added. To this, Jack laughed and lead the way into the house. Nothing inside moved except a small amount of smoke which had yet to dissipate. The Marines searched the mundane house of some family who looked as if they had a little money. Religious items decorated the walls with strange Arabic cursive, but there was no children's artwork hanging on the refrigerator, no family portraits, and no excessive media components for their entertainment.

They searched the two-bedroom home with no signs of the insurgency still occupying. The unanimous conclusion was that the enemy had fled long before the Marines blew off the front door.

Ashmore strolled into the kitchen and stopped like hitting an invisible wall. He ushered a gasp and stared wide-eyed at the large, pyramidal pile of white powder situated in the center of a cheap plywood table. Three corners of the kitchen held stashes of weapon caches and littering the countertops were an assortment of ammunition canisters. The white powder held Ashmore's gaze so that he didn't notice the weapons around him.

"Holy shit, we've hit the mother of them all." Jack and Sutherland ran into the kitchen, alarmed to find Ashmore dancing around the table like a man who had won the lottery. His greedy fingers itched to plunge deep into the white powder, but Jack grabbed him by the wrist.

"Ash, no. We don't know what that is."

"What? It's cocaine." Their lack of excitement bemused Ashmore.

"It could be anthrax," Jack said. Ashmore's face arched in a disapproving gesture as he pulled his hand free.

"Anthrax? Bullshit. That's fucking coke, bro."

Sutherland ran to the front door to signal that the house was 'all clear' and called in the rest of the squad. Kyle came into the kitchen, his attention shifting between Jack and Ashmore, then on the table.

"Is that cocaine?" Kyle asked.

"Fuck yeah." Ashmore's excitement was bursting at the seams.

"We don't know that. It could be anthrax. We need to call this shit in," Jack ordered, pointing to Black who held the radio pack on his back. Simpson stepped around Sutherland, moving closer to the table.

"That ain't anthrax. It's coke. You don't grow up in my hood without knowing what some snowflakes look like." Simpson marveled at the mound of powder. "Goddamn, I don't think Tony Montana saw this much blow in his life."

A few of the guys agreed with blazing excitement. Black brought the radio's handset up to his ear, but before he could depress the thumb button on the side, Ashmore snatched it away.

"You know what the street value for this shit is? We can keep it, figure out a way to send it home and make a lot of money."

"I'm with Ash on this one. I mean, guys were doing this shit back in Vietnam," Simpson said.

"This ain't Viet fuckin' Nam," Jack proclaimed.

"Yeah, what the fuck you two talking about?" Thompson interrupted. "We ain't keeping this shit. You wanna do drugs or sell drugs and shit, do that back on the block when you're out of my Corps."

"Your Corps? You're one to talk, Thompson, as many times as you've been busted down." Simpson laughed. Thompson took a step forward, not intimidated by Simpson's massive frame, and looked him square in the eyes.

"You got a fuckin' problem, Simpson?"

"Get the fuck out of my face, Thompson." The two snarled at one another, ready to swing, but then a loud bang ripped their attention away from one another. The table slammed over, smacking the hard floor with enough force it broke one of the legs, and the white powder sifted in the air before sprinkling on the dirty floor. Everyone startled, bringing their rifles to the ready as a few covered their mouths and noses to avoid breathing in whatever the white substance was. Sutherland lowered his leg and shrugged at the rest of the Berserkers.

"Oops, argument over. Let's go." Sutherland ventured outside as Simpson and Ashmore watched in stunning disbelief.

"Balls." Simpson sighed, amazed by Sutherland's courage.

"Check it." Jones broke the tension in the room. A small white puppy sniffed at Jones's gloves, and Jones took a piece of MRE pound cake out of his pocket to feed to the dog.

"Jones, leave the dog. We gotta move," Jack ordered.

"Oh, come on Jack, he likes me. I'm going to name him Cannonball." Jones petted the dog, and the dog licked his hand. Thompson moved up beside him to pet it. "He's friendly. I can't leave him behind, Corporal. He reminds me too much of my dog back home."

"Square this shit away. What the fuck, Marines?" Jack kicked at the table in frustration. "Fuckers trying to sell coke; Jones and Thompson drooling over a puppy, and we got a city falling down on us. What the fuck, Marines?"

"Check this out," Black said from across the room.

"What now? What the fuck now?" Jack threw up his hands. Their collective attention turned to the boot Marine pointing at several dirty syringes scattered about the floor.

"I guess it was dope. I heard some guys talking about this. The muj injects it into their heart and then goes on a warpath trying to kill as many grunts as they can before their heart pops. Fucked up shit." The radio squawked, and Black picked it up while everyone else stared at the needles.

"See, it is coke," Ashmore added.

"Corporal Campbell." Black held the handset up to his ear, staring at Jack.

"What is it?"

"Command said to burn the house."

"You heard it. Move out, Berserkers. We burn it to the ground and Jones, if that pup gives away our position, I'll shoot him and you for it, roger?"

"Roger." The men filed out of the house with Simpson and Ashmore hanging back. They stared longingly at the wasted product on the floor, but with deep sighs, both men followed their comrades. Sutherland, Black, and Carlos tossed in incendiary grenades and waited to see the flames engulf the house. Dark smoke funneled into the blackening sky.

"Nice job, Sutherland. We could've kept that shit."

"Shut up, Ash. It's over, let it go." The squad advanced across the street to another alley.

"Lock it the fuck up. Keep your eyes open and your fuckin' cock-holsters shut." Jack ordered, having had enough of everyone's talk for the moment. There were some perks to being in charge, and the men followed his orders.

The Berserkers traveled down the road without passing another word between them until the sky opened with little pellets of rain. Jack sighed, chuckling with an eye roll as the men moaned and complained. They came to the end of the alley, and Jack held up his fist. He peeked around the corner and caught a glimpse of something he thought he'd never see on the field of battle.

Situated in the middle of the street, two large sheets of armor plating stood against a six-foot high mound of sandbags. Reaching out between the two plates were the twin barrels of a Soviet era ZU-2. The anti-aircraft weapon system wasn't pointed at the sky but leveled with the ground.

Terror engulfed Jack as the weapon rotated toward his alley. He scrambled back to safety as chunks of the wall peppered him like a swarm of bees. In large whooping puffs, the 114mm caliber rounds decimated the walls, punching large holes in the concrete, compromising the structure of the building.

"What the fuck is it?" Kyle's voice was barely audible over the roar of the weapon they had only seen in World War II movies. More holes appeared in the walls and the rain couldn't stop the small alley from filling with smoke and debris that choked the Marines as they retreated.

"AA gun," Jack said as the anti-aircraft weapon system came to a halt. Jack turned, facing back down the alley, and forged a plan. Kyle shuffled up next to him as well as Sutherland. "We have to flank it."

The words no more left his lips when his body launched backward as if someone had tied a rope around him and pulled. Jack let out a grunt, slammed against the wall, and smacked hard off the ground. The report of a rifle echoed around them.

"Fall back," Kyle ordered, and with the help of Sutherland, they drug Jack by the handle of his flak jacket. Men moved away from the alley, taking cover behind a building away from enemy fire.

II

Carlos didn't need to look back to know Jack was smoked. His last order was to flank the anti-aircraft weapon, and Carlos was going to see the order carried out. He didn't cry or scream; he only charged head-first into his mission. Not waiting for support, Carlos circled the building and came up behind the Soviet AA gun.

A main road cut through the middle of the city. The four lanes were full of trash, junk, half-burnt cars, and all sorts of discarded objects used to create barriers against the invading Marines. A large median divided the four lanes and situated in the center was the Soviet AA gun-hut, standing like a stationary fortress. Two additional armor plates guarded the rear of the weapon and the sandbags piled high and tight protected those inside.

Carlos didn't think the hut was big, but when the twin barrels rose skyward and rotated, his heart stopped. Horror scratched at his soul and a burning image of the weapon sighting in on him ceased his breathing. His feet ached to run, to flee the area, but Carlos's spirit wouldn't allow it. The twin barrels rotated a quarter of a circle, inching their way around, but stopped before coming to Carlos's position.

They lowered and locked in place, aiming at the building the rest of the Berserkers were hiding behind. Still taking cover, Carlos was sure the insurgents were unaware of him as they cranked up the AA gun again. Concrete, glass, and rubble blew out like the guts of the building. The sound of the machine gun, along with the whirlwind of debris, created a destruction that Carlos had never seen before.

Mesmerized by the onslaught, Carlos contemplated the legality of using such a weapon on ground troops. *It has to be against the Geneva Convention's articles of war,* he thought, but doubted the insurgency cared for such articles. Lost in the carnage, he barely had time to flinch as a burst came from a concealed RPK hidden within the hut.

Startled by the surprise gun blast, Carlos flinched, and his boots slid out from under him on the slick ground. He didn't notice the pain in his elbow as he crashed to the street. More rounds sailed overhead, and he rolled over, scrambling for more cover behind the corner of the building.

"What was it?" Ashmore asked, coming up behind Carlos. Carlos looked up, glad to see the large Marine, and pushed himself to his feet. The coldness in the air stung at his throat and both men squinted through the rain to see one another.

"The AA gun's heavily protected on all sides by armor plating and some fully-auto inside is covering the rear. Didn't get eyes on it though. Damn thing nearly took my fucking head off." The soggy bandage around his neck drooped and Carlos tore it free, tossing it to the ground.

"What do you wanna do?"

"I wanna get a grenade in there," Carlos said.

"You think you can throw one that far?"

"No. Opening's too small and too far away."

"Opening's too small? Story of my life." Ashmore grabbed himself and smiled playfully.

"Give me cover. I need to get closer." Carlos fished a grenade out of the pouch on his flak jacket, and Ashmore squeezed by him to crouch at the corner. Staying on one knee, he waited for a signal that would indicate Carlos was ready. Carlos tapped Ashmore on the helmet, and Ashmore leaned out with his SAW pointed at the armored hut. The sly grin appeared on his face again, and he squeezed the trigger, unleashing a fury of rounds. Sparks dinged off the armor plating and sand blew out of the green sandbags. The brown clouds of dirt were soon trampled down by the rain, making a large mess outside the hut.

Carlos bee-lined to the half-exploded car. The rain and dirt created an uneasy run across the slick street and Carlos took a tumble. He slid across the wet pavement and slammed hard against the side of the car. Flashes erupted from inside the dark hut, sending tracers flying at Ashmore. Carlos's elbows throbbed at the points that had twice struck the hard ground. He pushed himself up against the car, keeping low enough to avoid rounds screaming at him.

"You all right, bro?" Ashmore shouted between momentary pauses of gunfire. Carlos shook his head, gave him a thumbs-up, and steadied his breathing.

Ashmore fired at the opening of the armored hut, but a return series of 7.62 rounds drove him back around the corner. Carlos started to his feet and the RPK shifted to his direction. Several bullets punched through the weak metal of the car and Carlos eased away, hoping the rest of the car held up. Ashmore brought the RPK's attention back to him, but the report of the weapon lasted only a moment longer.

The pause came and Carlos was ready. He sprang up, rushing for the small pathway cutting between two buildings on the opposite side of the road. As he cleared the car, exposing himself to all the dangers the war had to offer, he pivoted long enough to hurl the grenade into the hut. The grenade blew, but Carlos failed to see it as he squeezed into the pathway.

POP. Flash, a puff of smoke.

The AA gun stalled, and two insurgents stumbled out the rear opening of the hut. They wobbled on shaky legs and indiscriminately fired their weapons in every direction. Carlos leaned out of the small pathway to return fire but jumped back as a few AK rounds cracked past his skull.

BANG. Recoil. Left shoulder.

BANG. Recoil. Left lung punctured.

Ashmore ceased his fire only long enough to watch one of the insurgents take both rounds and collapse against the pile of sandbags. The second insurgent, with a chest full of shrapnel, spun and bent at the waist. He brought up the RPK in Carlos's direction.

III

More rounds popped, reverberating Sutherland's eardrums. His eyes followed his barrel, searching to find the hidden location that the shots rang out from. New holes dotted the wall next to him.

"You're up high, aren't you?" Sutherland said only to himself. In a building two hundred meters away, in a third story window, was the tiny silhouette of a shooter. He was no bigger than the targets at the rifle range in Camp Pendleton, California. "You're mine, motherfucker."

A light breeze blew in, carrying with it the falling rain, slapping at Sutherland's unyielding face. He adjusted his rifle accordingly. The insurgent fired and the bullet beat by Sutherland's head, going twice the speed of sound. Time crawled, a second passed, and the rifle's report thumped Sutherland. He was quick with his shot, hoping to nail the insurgent before the enemy could leave his position.

The round struck the windowsill, driving the insurgent from view. Sutherland kicked himself for being so eager. Wet hands, moist with rain, had attributed to the miscalculation. He adjusted his rifle into a better position against his shoulder. Sutherland achieved perfect sight picture and alignment as the insurgent reappeared to return a volley at the retreating Marines.

Enemy rounds bounced around Sutherland, but Sutherland didn't flinch. He relaxed, took a breath, and allowed the front sight to drop from his intended target. Upon exhaling, the tip rose and settled on the insurgent's head.

BANG. Recoil. Headshot.

The puff of red mist from the open window pleased Sutherland. Without hesitation, Sutherland scanned the other windows and rooftops for enemy combatants, finding none.

IV

Bullets blew past Carlos as he threw himself into the frame of a door that wouldn't open. The space was small, and he leaned his head back, pressing against the door to narrow his body. The intense velocity from the rounds caused him to drop his M16. They seemed never-ending. Carlos clenched, waiting for the series of rounds to finish him off, but they ceased.

Ashmore fired wildly at the man holding the RPK, slicing deep into the back of the insurgent's thigh, and taking his attention away from Carlos. Cradling the large RPK under his arm to steady it, he continued to fire while walking the weapon to Ashmore. Rounds rapped against the burned car like a drummer banging a cymbal.

Carlos peeked out. Finding the attention off of him, he scooped up his M16 and fired a round.

BANG. Recoil. Side shot.

The insurgent spun again, his attention divided in two directions, and sprayed rounds over Carlos's head. Carlos pulled the trigger on his rifle again, but nothing happened. A 5.56 casing stood in the ejection port like a smoke pipe. The insurgent forced his barrel down to level with Carlos. He pulled the trigger, releasing a hollow click. The two men, Marine and Insurgent, locked eyes. The insurgent feverishly tossed the RPK aside to fetch his partner's AK.

Carlos yanked back on his charging handle to free the smokestack casing. The charging handle stuck, but Carlos overpowered it, locking it to the rear. The casing was hot to his cold fingers as he jerked the round out of the ejection port. Carlos released the charging handle on an empty magazine and a hollow chamber.

The other insurgent, lying on the sandbags, used his elbows to drag his body across the road. His AK sat in the open, a mere three feet from his reach. As his fingers brushed the wooden buttstock, his friend pulled the rifle away from him. Carlos eyed the two men and decided he had no time to reload his weapon. He allowed it to fall to his side, swinging around his shotgun from his back.

The insurgent fired before aiming, missing Carlos, but caused him to wince. Carlos side shuffled away like a fighter and flew in behind a small concrete barrier. Taking a tight grip on the shotgun, he fired it over his head and without looking. He pumped the scatter blaster, fired again, and drove the enemy back.

Ashmore pulled the pin on a grenade and tossed it in the direction of the insurgents. The grenade rolled by the crawling man, who threw himself into the hut for protection. The small green ball came to a rest at the heels of the standing insurgent.

A grazing round of buckshot struck the man in the chest and he stumbled backward. A sharp snap flared up his ankle as his foot rolled over the metal ball. He only had a second to acknowledge his sprained ankle before the grenade burst.

POP. Flash, a puff of smoke.

The insurgent flipped over, landing on his shoulder and head. His right foot detached completely and both legs were mangled below the knees. Despite his injuries, the insurgent pressed on, creeping his hand out for his AK and impressing Ashmore.

BANG. Recoil. Hipshot.

BANG. Recoil. Kidney shot.

BANG. Recoil. Heart shot.

As the mangled insurgent succumbed to his injuries, the surviving man rushed from the hut with a machete. His mouth opened, ready to scream, but before he could release his war cry, Carlos blasted the insurgent.

BANG. Recoil. Side shot.

The blast knocked the insurgent off his feet like a truck had hit him. He toppled over the sandbags, falling flat to the street. The insurgent reared back, pushing away from the ground, gasping for air as one lung collapsed. His fingers dug into the handle of the machete as he used the sandbags to get to his feet.

BANG. Recoil. Shattered femur.

BANG. Recoil. Punctured liver.

BANG. Recoil. Chest shot.

The punch-drunk insurgent staggered but managed to stay standing. The rounds ate at the street around him and he swayed, moving away from the sandbags with the machete over his head.

"Don't you ever fuckin' die?" Carlos marched out from behind the concrete barrier, pumped a round into the chamber of the shotgun, and fired.

BANG. Recoil. Separated spinal cord.

A blanket of gray and black clouds hung overhead, and the insurgent looked up in hopes of finding a clear section of sky. The darkness of Carlos's twelve-gauge barrel lingered in front of him, blocking his view. With an exhausted sigh, he surrendered his fight on the wet street. He didn't look away, for his pride wouldn't allow that.

"See you in Hell, cocksucker." Carlos pulled the trigger, delivering the coup de grâce.

"Fuckin' A, man."

"Goddamn terminator hajjis." Carlos laughed, shaking his head and stepped under an awning. He fired up a cigarette and handed it to Ashmore who was shaking the rain off his head.

"What now?" Ashmore asked.

"I don't know. I can't believe Jack's wasted."

"No shit," Ashmore said, exhaling hard and hanging his head in despair. Carlos took the cigarette back.

"Come on, let's get going." The Marines returned to their platoon, surprised to find the men huddled around Jack, sitting in a blown-out section of a building, smoking a cigarette. His flak jacket hung open and around his feet were black shards of a broken sapi plate.

"Did you get'em?" Jack asked.

"Got'em," Carlos said. Jack nodded his approval.

"Let's move out." Jack flicked his cigarette at the ground in front of him and fastened his flak jacket. A knot formed in his chest muscles and although it hurt to move, he led the men back down the alley. As the clearing approached, Jack couldn't help but pause out of fear. The twin barrels of the abandoned AA gun were silent, but full of much horror. An uncontrollable terror gripped his mind.

The wind screamed across the wet streets, chilling the Marines, and in the distance, black smoke battled its way through the downpour. The rain drummed off tin metal roofs, creating a musical rhythm only nature could produce. Jack swallowed, forcing away his anxieties. When he was ready, he gave Ashmore and Sutherland the green light to move across the street.

The two sprinted through the opening with their heads tucked, and their eyes up. They entered the adjacent alley, each taking a corner, and aiming down opposite sides of the street. Jack and Kyle scampered across like squirrels, stopping only when safe on the other side. Jack signaled for the next set of men to join them.

The sky pitched gray through the filter of rain clouds that lacked the boom of thunder or flashes of lightning. Simpson took a moment to admire the cool and refreshing sensation of rain washing the dirt from his face.

"It's a nice day," Simpson said, watching Thompson and Jones making it safely to the opposite alley. Jones and Thompson immediately took up security and waved Black, Harvey, and Simpson over. The three remaining Marines rushed out into the slick street. Harvey, who had been waiting anxiously, tucked his head and ran. His foot struck the back of Simpson's ankle, tripping the rather large Marine.

"Harvey, you fucktard," Simpson cried out as his knees struck the street. CRACK. The sound echoed through the weather, and no one mistook it for lightning.

V

Tink…tink…tink. The rain beat against the concrete buildings and abandoned metal train cars populating the train station stronghold. Skyler failed to notice the drops falling in fat splashes as her hair laid plastered to her face and the burning cigarette between her fingers extinguished, turning the white paper brown. Goosebumps littered her flesh from the cold creeping into her bones, savagely shaking her muscles.

Her eyes, haggard and aged with stress, didn't see the wetness darkening the dirt colored wall in front of her. She didn't hear the commotion of the rain dancing on the train cars or the men walking briskly from one building to the next, trying to avoid getting wet. Her mind shut down to all of this and projected things she never cared to see again.

The pleading faces of a dozen men who she failed to save while air still filled their lungs, stood in front of her. Not one reached out for her or spoke. Their faces hung in agony, with silent death screams. Their grotesque nature refused to give death the pleasure of their cries. They gathered around her, horrid and ragged, the evidence of their demise written on their bodies, yet they stood with discipline. They stood, in ghostly shades of wind and light, with honor.

Then they changed. A collection of moans rose deep within their hollow frames, growing to a dull growl. She covered her ears with convulsing hands, attempting to block out the white noise. She paused, understanding they weren't pleading with her, but beckoning to her. They taunted her to join their ranks, to become one of the dead.

The rain didn't touch the dead, and they weren't afflicted by the cold for they felt nothing. The dead only wanted to collect their own.

The drenched cigarette dropped from her fingertips and broke against the soaked ground. Skyler stepped forward, allowing her hands to fall to her side, and walked through the flock of phantom men who parted for her like Moses in the Dead Sea. Men rushed back and forth across her path, hurrying to get out of the weather. She no longer tried to determine if they were alive or dead. To her, they were all dead, just some had yet to accept it.

Skyler walked into a small room where a large wooden cross hung from the wall, and she crashed to her knees before it. Fastening her hands together, she bit down on her knuckle, trying to find the strength to pray. Her eyes rose to the cross, hoping an answer stood there. Tears mingled with the drops of rain running down her face, tinted red by spattered blood.

"We have never spoken before, and I don't know if you're real, but if you are, help me." Her head bowed, forehead touching the knuckle of her index finger, and she wept. She squeezed her fingers hard around one another and the pain from the cold radiated up her arms. "Help me."

"He hears you, sailor." A voice came from behind her, surprising Skyler. A Chaplain, with the rank of a captain on his collar, stood in the doorway of the makeshift chapel. Skyler didn't bother with standing or giving a proper greeting, and the Chaplain didn't trouble her with the formalities.

"I know him not, sir," Skyler said. It was the truest statement she had ever made for herself. Although raised in the church, Skyler knew she wasn't a true believer.

"He knows you. He hears you." The Chaplain walked deeper into the chapel and stood behind Skyler. Together their gaze returned to the large wooden cross.

"Can he make this war stop? I've seen enough, sir."

"No, he can only show men how to stop the war." He laid a hand on her wet scalp. The shivering in her body ceased, but not from the warmth of his touch, but at the boiling of her blood. Skyler stood from underneath his hold, moving past him to the door.

"Then why should I worship a God that can't stop this misery." She left the room, drifting back into the rain and the ever-growing crowd of the dead.

VI

Simpson had fallen due to Harvey, and palmed his face in disappointment, but while climbing to his knees, a bullet ripped through him. The force knocked him over, and he came to rest with his face against the cold street. A growing circumference of blood mixed with the fresh rainwater stretching out from him. It hurt to open his eyes, and he found himself confused at why he couldn't lift his head to look down at his body. He knew he was hurt but didn't know how bad. For some strange reason, he had the urge to call out for his mother, wanting the comfort only she could give.

He remembered being young, five or six, and hurting his knee after falling off his bike. Never wanting anyone to help him, he ran into his room and stayed there until she came. Hiding under a blanket, and with his knee throbbing, she kissed away the tears burning his cold cheeks. His mother made it all better. She bandaged it and embraced his head against her chest. He longed for that warmth as he laid in the freezing street.

His legs were absent, and a pain burned its way up his back, spreading over his upper body. A raindrop clung to the end of his nose, itching at him to knock it away, and Simpson feared he wouldn't be able to. He couldn't remember any rifle noise or mortar blast, or even the injury which had buckled him. The itch on his nose became unbearable and he swatted the drop of rain away.

Oh, thank God. My arms still work.

At the sight of Simpson crumbling to the ground and hearing the rippling wave of the unseen rifle shot, Sutherland's arm went rigid and clutched the Bible in his cargo pocket. *Oh God, oh no, please stop this. Not again. Stop this now.*

Harvey and Black darted past Thompson as the report of the rifle echoed through the area. They were deep in the alley when Simpson crashed to the ground. Thompson shoved them out of the way and dashed out into the street with no concern for a sniper. Doc slung off his MED bag and was hot on Thompson's heels. Thompson nabbed the handle of Simpson's flak jacket and lifted with everything he had to keep from dragging Simpson's face across the pavement.

"Cover fire!" Ashmore shouted and without waiting for the men to back him up, threw lead downrange in the possible direction of the shooter. Carlos and Sutherland joined him, giving Doc cover as he moved up next to Thompson.

In the midst of the 5.56 rattle, another loud crack rang out. The cold rain on Thompson's face was whisked away by the heat of Doc's blood. Doc stumbled against Thompson and crumbled to the ground. Thompson didn't bother with wiping the blood from his face. He pushed backward on his toes and drug Simpson out of the street, left with no choice but to leave Doc in the open. The ground around Doc chipped away, spraying bits of wet street into the air. Carlos leapt forward, but Jack stopped him.

"We gotta get'em." Carlos cried out, trying to push Jack away. "Doc, hang in there. We're coming."

"Wait!" Jack screamed, but Carlos refused to listen. Another round hit Doc's body, causing him to twitch. Carlos shoved Jack.

"Aw shit, he's getting shot out there. We gotta get'em."

"Wait! It's a fuckin' sniper. That haj will waste you, too." Jack tried to reason with Carlos, but he continued to push forward. Kyle and Jones assisted in restraining Carlos, keeping him from running into a shower of death.

"Oh fuck. I'm hit. I'm fucking hit." Simpson cried as the rain struck his face and blocked his breathing. Jones released Carlos, grabbed Doc's MED bag, and sprinted to Simpson. Black and Sutherland waited by his side to help. Ashmore peppered the scene with rounds from his SAW, trying to locate the sniper but having no luck. Another round struck Doc, and his body jerked from the impact, but he did nothing to cover up the wounds.

"Fuck, we gotta get to him." In his panic, Ashmore fumbled around the belt of ammo, sloppily forcing the reload of his SAW.

"What do we do, Corporal?" Sutherland shouted over Ashmore's assault. Jack wanted time to think, but the situation didn't allow it.

"Jack." Kyle slapped him on the arm. "What do you want to do?"

"I want smoke, now," Jack ordered, fighting back the urge to panic. He had made the mistake of wanting to abandon one of his own before, and he wouldn't do that again. "Snap to it, Berserkers."

Sutherland pulled a smoke grenade from his flak and tossed it to Jack as Kyle readied one of his own. Together, the two Corporals lobbed the grenades near Doc. The cylinder canisters popped, and gray smoke screamed out the top, screening Doc from the sniper.

"Harvey," Jack yelled, getting his attention. "Let's go."

"I ain't going out there with a sniper shooting at us." Harvey protested, leaning against a wall, eager to run the other way. Jack yanked Harvey by the neck strap on the front of his flak jacket.

"You do what I say, or I'll fuckin' kill you myself." Jack warned as he pulled Harvey to the entrance of the alley.

"Why would you want me to go out there with you anyway?"

"He needs someone to shield him from the sniper while he gets our Doc." Thompson snarled. The smoke fought against the weather to shield the area. Jack nodded to Ashmore, who opened with another fury of cover fire. Kyle joined Ashmore, while Jones, Sutherland, and Black worked to save Simpson. Jack and Harvey pounced into the gray smoke with rounds echoing around them.

A small chunk of the street kicked up and pelted Harvey in the face as another round ricocheted near Jack's boot. Harvey turned back to the direction he believed he had come from but before he could leave, Jack pushed him closer toward the injured sailor. Cutting through the gray smoke, a dark object appeared curled up in the street.

Jack forced Harvey to take the handle of Doc's flak jacket while Jack grabbed Doc's shoulder. They pulled with enemy rounds continuing to deflect nearby. One bounced next to Jack, but he ignored it. Harvey's biceps stretched in agony, and he wanted to release the corpsman. The two men pulled and with the forward momentum, slung the downed corpsman into the alleyway, his body sliding through the gathering water.

Carlos rolled Doc over, and everyone gasped at the concaved, hollowed opening that was once Doc's face. Shreds of flesh, bone fragments, and blood filled the woodland Kevlar helmet. A puddle gathered in the crevice, and for each clear drop of water which fell in, a red droplet bounced out.

"I'm going to die…I'm going to die…" Simpson repeated over and over. Jack hustled toward him.

"Stow that shit, Marine. Have some fucking discipline."

"Roger that, Corporal." Simpson fought through the pain and Jack took his hand.

"You can hack it, brother. You ain't gonna die. Before you know it, you're gonna be back on Virginia Beach, hitting up all the little split-tails," Jack said. Simpson looked him dead in the eyes with rain falling on his face.

"Fuck you, Jack. I can't feel my legs." Each Marine, soaked to the core, shivered, except for Simpson, who remained motionless despite the weather.

Lance Corporal Philip Simpson

Purple Heart Recipient

For Wounds Received on November 12th, 2004

Fallujah, Iraq, Al-Anbar Province

Hospital Corpsman 2 David Sloan

Killed in Action Fallujah, Iraq, Al-Anbar Province

October 24th, 1978 – November 12th, 2004

* * *

Letter to Jack Campbell from Jennifer Campbell,

Dated November 5th, 2004-

Dear Jack,

Our son is heading home today, and he's doing great. Joshua is a healthy baby, and I think he has my chin. Everyone's been real nice. The hospital staff was incredible, but everyone asked where you were. It's funny to see their reactions when I say that you're in Iraq and everyone says to be safe and get home quick.

I wish you were here to see how beautiful our son is when he's sleeping. I can't believe we made him, and I think when you see him, it may restore your faith in God. I'm sure every parent says the same thing, but just watching him move and sleep is one of the most amazing things in the world.

I'm glad that most people brought diapers at the baby shower. He goes through them so fast, it's incredible. This kid is going to be a lot of hard work, and your parents have been helping me out so much. You need to write them and thank them. You need to write them, period. They long to hear from you.

I long to hear from you, too. You haven't written in some time, and I'm starting to wonder if everything's all right? Be careful and come home soon. Your son will want to watch baseball with his dad.

Love,

Your Wife and Son

* * *

From the pages of Jack Campbell's Journal-

The seven-ton trucks dropped us off at the train station. We're in desperate need of ammo, and we had to get Simpson back for a medevac. Doc is dead, wasted trying to save Simpson. He might have taken a bullet for Thompson. Simpson's done, waiting on word about the extent of his injuries.

I've been around death for so long that it doesn't seem real anymore. I'm down on men and moral. Simpson was a big guy, in body and heart. He was a driving force in the unit, and many of the guys looked up to him. Same with Doc. He was older, but friendly to the younger guys and I just can't believe they're gone. My brothers are wasted. How many more will die? I can't keep doing this. When will it end? I can't sleep.

CHAPTER TEN

RELOAD

A Marine should be sworn to the patient endurance of hardships, like the ancient knights; and it is not the least of these necessary hardships to have to serve with sailors.

-Field Marshal Bernard Montgomery

I

Jack's eyes fluttered and tried to focus on the ever-changing blur high above him. The glimmering sun pitched off the rotating ceiling fan, combating the shadows against the white painted walls. They danced and moved, creating a growing picture of war and struggle, of men fighting and men dying. Jack brought his arm up to help shield his unaccustomed eyes to the brightness. The warmth of the room washed away the coldness which had settled in his bones. The thought that he was dead came across his mind, and he was fine with this conclusion.

In the shadow war that raged across the bedroom walls, he saw a large figure, massive in size going face down in the middle of a street. Jack watched as each one of his men perished to the enemy's imaginary fire. A dismembered dark head screamed in silent agony as it rolled into a pile of dead bodies like a bowling ball into pins. Jack's stomach soured, and he shifted to the other side of his body, hoping the shadow war would not follow.

At once, the terrible images faded at the sight of a woman sleeping peacefully under ivory sheets. The outline of her body, curves concealed by silky fabric, portrayed an image of his wife. A gentle hue radiated from within her skin and the sun reflected off her blonde hair like a halo from heaven. His fingertips lightly traced the soft surface of her exposed shoulder. A breeze blew in from an open window, flapping the pearl curtains over the bed, and waking Jennifer.

"Good morning, sunshine," Jennifer said. Her flawless lips stretched back over her perfectly aligned teeth, but Jack didn't speak. He only stared, pleasantly overwhelmed, until she nudged him.

"I've missed you," Jack whispered, scared to disturb the silence in the room, as if the strong vibration of his voice would cause it to melt away. A perplexing look swept over Jennifer's face.

"Missed me? Where did you go?"

"Iraq," he said. A laugh, both tender and graceful, escaped her, and she shook her head.

"Bad dream. That's been over for some time." Although baffled by this, he forced a grin, which morphed into a genuine smile. Jack kissed her forehead, then her lips. He swept the hair from her face, tucking it behind her ear. His hand trailed down, across her neck and shoulder, and from there, he journeyed to her flat and soft stomach.

"The baby?" Jack asked. With a head nod, Jennifer motioned to the foot of the bed where the top of a wooden cradle swayed. Jack started to sit up, but Jennifer pulled him back down to the comfort of their bed.

"No, let him sleep." She was his angel, and there was no refusing her wishes. He wanted to cry at how good he felt, but then a sadness invaded his expression. "What is it?"

"It's not real, is it?" Jack asked. He knew the truth before she could speak. The room wasn't the one he shared with his wife in their home, and although it lacked familiarity, it was the most beautiful room he had ever seen. Everything was bright; everything was warm. There was no pain, no aches, and no depressing thoughts. "Is this heaven?"

Jack feared her answer because he knew he didn't belong there.

"No." Her radiant smile faded as grief seeped into her eyes.

"I want to see him. I want to see Josh."

"But you can't. You have to go now," she whispered, fastening her hands to Jack's face and stroking it lightly.

"I don't want to go. I want to stay here with you," Jack said. She ran her hand down the sandpaper stubble of his face, sparking the nerve endings. He embraced the pleasure of her touch until it was too overwhelming and he pulled away. The gentle breeze coming in through the window turned into a gale force, and the sun dimmed as a chill attacked Jack.

"You have a job to do. Your job is more important than us. You don't get to see us again. This is not your place. We are not your home," Jennifer said. Jack released her hand and crawled toward the foot of the bed. "Please don't."

Her voice called from behind him, echoing outward like a past dream drowning by awakening. The cradle, still swaying, was five times larger than it had been before. Jack's eyes widened in dismay as he found not a child in the crib, but a bath of blood. The crimson liquid filled to the brim and something moved under the surface. Jack sunk his hands into the hot substance, allowing it to wash over his arms until he pulled out a large object.

Immediately the air rushed from his lungs, and it left him breathless. He cringed at the sight of his dead brother staring back at him with a lifeless expression. Jack wanted to vomit, to throw the head, to cry, to fight, to kill, to explode. Every emotion he ever felt came screaming at him. Turning, he found Jennifer propped up against the headboard, a dime-size hole dotting the center of her forehead where he had placed a kiss.

The room lurched and jerked about him as if on the Tilt-A-Whirl ride at a carnival. Blood seeped from the corners of the ceiling, painting the white walls to a dark red. Decapitated heads, driven down on spikes, surrounded the bed like demonic guards standing watch. The faces, unveiling the last agonizing moment of their death, were the Berserkers. Bodies littered the floor, and underneath the walls oozing blood, the plaster cracked, revealing the tan stone color of an Iraqi home.

"I told you not to look," Jennifer said without moving a single muscle in her mouth. Something warm trickled down his head, and the taste of iron filled the air. Blood pooled on the floor, engulfing the dead bodies, and spilling over the edge of the bed like a wave cresting over the side of a sinking ship.

"Why?" Jack cried.

"Because you brought this on us," the corpse of his wife confessed. "You are the Berserker. You bring death with you."

The bedroom door burst open, and two men wearing ski masks rushed in firing AK's. Jack dove off the bed, submerging himself in the tide of blood as his wife's voice, taking on a near demon-like quality, drifted to him from some other realm. "Your suffering will echo in the halls of Hell."

II

November 13th, 2004-

The jolting surge awoke Jack in a room with arctic cold air coming in from a broken stained-glass window. There was no blood, no severed heads, and no dead wife. A dreary color decorated the walls and the sounds of men snoring disturbed the silence of the dawn. Jack rose, muscles stiff from war and cold, and slipped into a pair of white socks. He paused, shaking the grogginess from his head before cramming his feet into his combat boots.

His pack of cigarettes rested on top of his gear, and he drew one out. Sparking it and taking a drag, he caught sight of Sutherland leaning against the opposite wall, mirroring himself. In one hand, Sutherland held a burning cigarette, in the other, a bean-shaped canteen cup. Steam scaled over the brim, and Sutherland held the silver metal cup up, inviting Jack over for a drink. Jack accepted the offer.

He took the canteen cup from Sutherland and sat down on the cot next to him. The steam was pleasant to his cold face, but the metal was hot to the touch. Jack blew away the spiraling vapor before sipping. Hot liquid scorched his cold lips and the coffee rushed down his throat, warming the rest of his body.

"Awe, the nectar of the gods." Jack confessed. After his second drink, he handed the oddly shaped cup back to Sutherland and noticed the Bible in Sutherland's lap.

"Been reading the good book?"

"Not really," Sutherland said, shaking his head and sipping the coffee.

"Just wanted it out?" Jack asked. Sutherland shrugged; he didn't know why it was out. He felt the familiar urge to read it, but the will wasn't there.

"I've been thinking something, Corporal." Sutherland took a drink, and Jack puffed on his cigarette, cutting his eye over to the younger Marine. "You know how they say the muj will get like fifty virgins."

"Seventy-two and yeah, so?"

"Well, as we know, most of these guys over here, their first sexual experience is with another man, like eighty percent of these guys. They view women for only having babies."

"What the fuck are you talkin' about, Sutherland?" Ashmore sat up on one elbow and with sleep still in his eyes, took the coffee from him.

"Just listen," Sutherland continued as Ashmore passed the cup to Jack. "So, they believe men want pleasure and women are only good for procreation. They think that if I'm a man and I want pleasure and he's a man, and he wants pleasure, then together, we want pleasure."

"Get on with it, Sut," Jack demanded while enjoying the coffee.

"What if, the fifty virgins —"

"Seventy-two," Jack corrected.

"The seventy-two virgins that this entire time we've been thinking are scantily clad women, in fact, are scantily clad boys." As his words settled into their minds, Sutherland smiled at their discomfort.

"Are you saying they're fags?" Ashmore blurted out.

"Jesus, Ash, I got a cousin who's gay," Sutherland said.

"Well, I don't."

"Well, then, yeah. In asshole terms, they're fags. But that's beside the point. I'm saying that maybe we've been thinking of their goal all wrong."

"This conversation is too much for me."

"I'm just saying."

"And I'm just saying that this is the best sleep I've had in over a week and I'd like to get back to it." Ashmore laid back into his cot and pulled his green sleeping system up over his head. Within a few minutes, Sutherland and Jack could hear the large, bald Marine snoring.

"You're one sick fuckin' thinker, Sut, and I have only one thing to ask." The flat surface of the coffee caught Jack's eyes; the steam was dying down. "Where did you get warm coffee from?"

Sutherland, sitting proud, motioned to the head of his cot. On the floor was a small, green one-burner propane stove.

"Where'd you get that?"

"I *acquired* it from the supply boys." Sutherland took a drink, and Jack could do nothing but laugh as he patted Sutherland on the shoulder.

"You stole it?"

"Nope. Acquired it. Only one thief in the Marine Corps—"

"Yeah, yeah, yeah. Everyone else is just trying to get their shit back. Man, and to think, when you first got to the unit, I thought you were just another college kid. But I guess I was wrong. Looks like we'll make a Marine out of you after all." Sutherland took a drag and tipped his head to say thank you while the cup passed between the two of them.

"I've never been to college," Sutherland admitted.

"What?" Jack looked surprised at Sutherland, who didn't bother to return his stare. Sutherland smoked and wondered what the next question would be.

"I've never been to college."

"But I thought you had gone to school and came from some rich family," Jack confessed.

"No, my family is middle class, I guess. Shit, I barely went to a party before joining up. Hell, I can count on one hand how many beers I ever had in my life, and it wouldn't take all the fingers to do it. So yeah, my family ain't rich, and if I wanna to go to college, I figured I'd better join the Corps."

"Shit, I thought you said you were going to school for English or writing or some shit."

"No, Corporal." Sutherland felt ashamed for leading Jack on. "I only graduated from high school two years ago. I worked in a factory and lived with my parents. I turned nineteen in boot camp and twenty before coming over here."

"Damn, Sut. I didn't realize that. Sorry, I assumed you were some rich kid. I mean when you got here, you were like, I don't drink and shit. You weren't like the other guys."

"Yeah, my parents didn't allow drinking. Maybe because my father was an alcoholic. I guess it was my mother who didn't allow it. She was more of the disciplinarian in the family. She didn't want me or my sister to end up like my dad."

"Mean drunk?" Jack asked.

"Funny drunk. Everyone loves my old man when he's drinking. I guess I was nervous to drink hard liquor in front of you guys. I didn't want to embarrass myself."

"Where you from, Sut?" Jack asked.

"Paynesville, Texas." Jack had never heard of it, and his facial expression gave it away. With only a slight pause, Sutherland continued, "A small town, kind of like Mayberry with nice, pleasant people."

Jack liked the idea of pleasant people and he longed to be somewhere that apple pies and baseball games were the norm. He wanted real Americana.

"Never been there. I'd like to see that, a town where people are nice to one another. I grew up in a bad area. It'd be nice to raise my children in a nice town."

"If you go there, stop by Granny's Grill for pancakes, best in Texas." Sutherland's Texas drawl was prominent in his words and brought back a sense of home to Jack. He then handed the cup back and stood up before grabbing his green fleece pullover, tan watch cap, and his rifle.

"I gotta hit the head. What's the word on showers?"

"Baby-wipes only here and still broken back at the rear."

"Damnit. Could really use a real fuckin' shower one day. Fuckin' ass hurts."

"No shit."

"Whatever. Make some more of that coffee, if you please." He tossed Sutherland his canteen cup and headed for the door.

Outside the air felt clean, but bit with the harshness of winter. The chill lacked a breeze but was cold enough to make Jack zip up his fleece pullover until it became a turtleneck. Several Marines from different companies moved about the train station, paying no mind to the corporal as he headed for the restroom.

Three tall stalls made up the restroom, and each one was occupied. Jack gave a disapproving grunt as his bladder knotted up. If he didn't relieve it soon, it would relieve itself in his pants. He headed around the corner, away from the main population of the train station, and propped his rifle up against a stone wall. His cold fingers fumbled with the buttons on his trousers, and he feared pissing himself before undoing them.

He managed to pull the two remaining buttons open, the third having fallen off some time back, and hurried to free himself. Quickly the urine splashed on the dry dirt next to the base of the wall and a pleasant relief settled on Jack. He looked to his right to see the sun coming up over the horizon with all its glory. He had never seen a sunrise as beautiful as this, and it was happening in Iraq.

Then he noticed something that didn't belong in his world of war. Something that was out of place in this great sandbox. Standing a mere ten feet away and gaping at Jack was a female reporter. The offensive nature in her face didn't stop Jack from continuing his business, and he did so with a waving of his hand and a projection of his middle finger.

Her face changed from shock to disapproval to disgust. He shrugged his shoulders and returned to his attention to relieving his bladder, but she still didn't walk away. When he finished, Jack buttoned up and cinched down his web belt, taking notice at how far over it went. *Damn, how much weight have I lost?*

He ran his hand down the front of his body and could feel his ribs protruding out farther than they ever had. Jack tried to guess his weight and figured he was around a hundred and forty-five pounds. The numbers vanished from his head as he released a disappointing sigh upon hearing the female reporter shout, "Sergeant Major."

III

Four cots aligned the walls in the corpsmen's room, and Kyle found Skyler sleeping on the last one. She laid curled up in her sleeping system; her body turned away from him as if hiding her face from the rest of the world. Kyle tiptoed across the room and squatted next to her cot, where he placed a light hand on her bare shoulder. The heat of his fingertips shocked her, and she spun with a look of angst while trying to recognize Kyle.

He was strange to her, a foreigner with a familiar face, a person she knew in a different lifetime. Had she loved him once? Had she known him her entire life? His face was rough and tired.

"Are you dead?" she asked through a haze of sleep, causing Kyle to lean away from her with a questioning look.

"No. Not that I know of." He reassured her. His voice sparked her memory, and she knew the man squatting there next to her. His name was Kyle, he was from California, and she loved him. "Scared you?"

"Bad dreams." Skyler stretched. Arching her back emphasized the shape of her breasts, and a yawn forced her eyes closed. Kyle couldn't pull his attention away and marveled at her beauty like a man seeing the sun for the first time after years of being in the dark. Through her yawn, she asked, "What are you doing here?"

"Got in late last night. I was wanting to see you, but I figured you were asleep. Sorry if I woke you."

"No, it's fine. I'm glad you woke me. I missed you." She desired a kiss, but having yet to brush her teeth, she feared morning breath would repel him. "I don't know why you want to see me though. I probably look like a mess right now."

Kyle disagreed with her. He pulled his collar away from his neck like releasing a pressure valve. His eyes admired her as she climbed out of her sleeping system and threw her legs over the side of her cot. Her legs were smooth, and the grooves of her muscles ran up to her high-riding short shorts.

Skyler sensed his gaze but did nothing to avoid it. Reaching in her boots, she pulled out a half-empty pack of cigarettes and threw one at her face. The cigarette launched up and she caught it between her teeth before offering Kyle the pack. He accepted a smoke but hesitated sparking it up.

"You don't smoke."

"Helps with the nerves," she said, blowing out a large puff of white smoke. Kyle sensed something was off with her, that something was going on that she had yet to tell him about. "Heard about Doc Sloan, sorry."

"Yeah, sucks. True devil doc. Died saving my Marine."

"What are y'all going to do about a corpsman?"

"They gave us some new guy, Brooks?" She didn't know the name.

"When do y'all head back into the city?"

"Tomorrow morning. Long enough for some briefings and resupply," he said. Skyler bumped the ashes from her cigarette into a half-drunk bottle of water. As she returned the bottle to the floor, her arm struck the backpack at the foot of her bed. A white piece of paper, resting on top, slipped through the air and onto the cement floor.

Skyler's hand shot out for the letter, trying to snag it off the ground, but Kyle picked it up first. As he handed it back to her, his eyes caught a glimpse of three words, 'Love, Your Fiancé.' His heart stopped with the cigarette dangling from his lips. The smoke burned his eyes, but the only pain he felt was in his chest. Her face was stricken with panic. Gravity urged him to slump forward. He didn't have the willpower to even lower the cigarette.

"Fiancé." The word felt foreign to him. Kyle stood, almost in disbelief that he even uttered it. "You're engaged?"

IV

"Excuse me, sir, I need to speak with you." The female reporter caught the attention of the sergeant major and beckoned him over. The tall, bald man, with a mouth full of dip, moaned and made his way over to the reporter. Annoyed, Jack pulled the zipper of his fleece pullover down, allowing his chest to breath. He fired up a cigarette and leaned against the wall, waiting to see what shitstorm was coming his way.

"Can I help ya?" Sergeant Major's southern accent came out with a stream of brown spit.

"Yes, is that one of your Marines?"

"He is."

"First off, I walked over here and found him urinating on the ground. Right out in the open. I know we're in a war zone, but these men are Americans and need to act civilized. There are proper places for that kind of thing, and one isn't in the open where a lady can see." She placed a hand on her chest and turned her nose upward with a smug attitude.

"And the second thing?" There was a hint of annoyance in his voice that the female reporter didn't pick up on, but Jack did.

"The second thing is he then proceeded to wave at me and then flipped me off." Jack wasn't sure, but for a moment he thought the sergeant major nearly cracked a smile. Jack tossed his cigarette and stood at ease in front of the sergeant major.

"This true, Corporal?"

"Yes, Sergeant Major. I was taking a piss, and she came up to get a free show of my junk." The reporter took a step backward, appalled by the corporal's rebuttal of accusations.

"All right." Sergeant Major held up his hand. Then he murmured a word like he was trying to find its meaning, as if it was some strange concept in his world. "Civilized?"

"I can't believe he would offend me like this. I have never."

"Civilian, don'cha interrupt me." Sergeant Major turned his attention to the corporal. "That there tittoo on ya chess…"

Jack looked down at his stretched-out collar hanging low, and the top half of his Nordic tattoo was showing.

"Ya apart of the Berserkers?"

"Yes, Sergeant Major," Jack replied. Sergeant Major stood pondering over what he knew about Jack and the infamous Berserker squad.

"Berserkers," he repeated the word to the reporter. "Do ya know what that is?"

She knew the word, but not its real meaning.

"They're anything but civilized. They're barbarian war machines, and I don't take kindly to ya callin' my Marines civilized. I don't won'em civilized. So first off lady," Sergeant Major's bark was rough and frightening, causing her to flinch. A small grain of tobacco landed on the tip of her nose, but she was too afraid to wipe it off. He drew in a deep breath. "Stop trying to catch a free show from one of my Marines when they're taking care of business. And next time ask before you try to take a peek at a Marine's dick."

The reporter stood in a state of utter discomfort. She wanted nothing more than to walk away, to run and hide, but his words rendered her immobile.

"I don't really give a good gaw damn shit where these men piss in this blasted country as long as they don't piss near my room. This is a gaw damn war zone." He spat tobacco juice on the ground. "Suck it the fuck up, little Miss. Sunshine. Ya copy?"

"I'm…I'm…I'm going…"

"Ya gonna finish that fuckin' sentence? I hate me a gaw damn stutterer." He waited for a reply which never came. "Now, if ya don't mind, I'd like to get back to takin' a shit before the gaw damn war is over."

She stood dumbfounded, lost in the brutality of his words. Sergeant Major looked over at Jack.

"Carry on, Corporal."

"Yes, Sergeant Major."

"I fuckin' hate reporters." Sergeant Major drew the curtain of the restroom. Jack responded with a motivating 'Ooh-rah.'

V

Kyle didn't respond or stop as Skyler called after him. A few servicemen looked on but returned to their own business and forgot the two making their way to the last train car. It was a dangerous spot where many servicemen didn't wander off to, but Kyle didn't care about some hajji sneaking up on him. He wanted to be alone.

With each breath, he sucked in air to his hollow chest and hated himself for falling for her. The word engagement kept circling in his head until he punched the side of the metal train car.

"Kyle, stop," Skyler shouted with tears in her eyes. He didn't respond, keeping his back to her as he escaped into an abandoned car. "Please talk to me."

"Go away. I got nothing to say to you."

"Please, let me explain." She followed him into the car.

"Just leave me alone," he pleaded. The walls reverberated his shouts and he could hear the pain in his echo.

"Please, please let me explain."

"Go ahead." Kyle threw his hands up, pacing a small circle into the metal flooring. "Go right the fuck ahead and explain to me how it's all right what you're doing. Explain to me how it's different. How if you were back home and he was over here with another person, then it would be a different story. Tell me how it's OK."

He punched the wall again and spun around, the rage in his face floated no more than a foot from hers.

"Tell me!" He paused, waiting for her to respond. She stood there, shaking her head, and it disgusted Kyle to look at her. "Tell me how it's OK for you because I'm sure if you found out he was back home with some Susie, then it'd be cheating. Explain that to me?"

The acoustics of the train car amplified his voice. Tears welled in her eyes, not out of pain for herself, but knowing she had caused him hurt.

"It's not that simple. I don't even write him anymore. He writes me."

"So, you're just leading him on, good job for you." His golf clap was sarcastic; his hurt wasn't. "And what about me?"

"What about you?"

"Are you leading me on too? When we get back are you gonna forget about me and run back to this guy?"

"No, my parents want us to get married. He wants us to get married, but I don't want that anymore."

"I'm sure he's from that same old society in the South that you are. And when we get back home, you can tell all your beauty queen friends how once, while you went to the service, you had your fun with some poor ass serviceman. Who cares whose heart gets broken, right? You got to have your fun, now leave me alone."

"It's not like that. I don't even love him or that lifestyle anymore?"

"You don't like that life? Oh, that's fucking rich."

"I'm not like that anymore," she shouted, trying to reason with him, to convince him with her hands thrown up in surrender. "I don't like that lifestyle. It's not me. I don't know who I am anymore."

"Well, what do you want?" He held back the urge to call her a spoiled little rich brat.

"I'm scared. I want the bad dreams to go away." Skyler lowered herself to the floor and placed her face in her hands. The whimpers passed through her fingers. "You don't understand. I see the dead all the time now."

She pushed her hands through her hair, gripping it in random spots to ease the tension in her scalp. Her red eyes beamed at him.

"More dead bodies than I've ever seen, even on T.V. I see them when I'm awake and when I'm asleep. I can't be that person I once was because I don't know how to go back. I'm not the same, and I can't go home after seeing the things I've seen. I don't know what to do."

Kyle wanted to kneel next to her, to touch her and comfort her, but he was unsure if he could.

"I swear I'm not in love with him. I'm not staying with him. I love you; I want you. I want you to…" She sucked back the tears, and he lost himself in her eyes. He sank to his knees in front of her, wanting to hear her words and feel her touch. "I want you to make the bad thoughts go away."

She leaned forward, clawing at his shirt, pulling him toward her. Their mouths touched, then he pulled away from her. Their eyes danced with one another, anticipating the next move. He reached up behind her head and pulled her to him, firmly smashing their lips together.

"Make me feel normal again." She ran her hands under his shirt and slipped it off. "Make me forget, make me feel normal again."

Her breath repeatedly whispered in his ear as he nipped at the side of her neck. Her legs trembled, and she pressed her thighs tightly together, so Kyle didn't notice. Her aching body subsided to a pleasant numbness. His warm breath stroked her earlobe, making her nipples hardened under her shirt.

He worked his way across her chest, firing signals of ecstasy through her. With one quick movement, he relieved her of her green skivvy shirt. Blood rushed through his body, and he wanted nothing more than to free himself of his clothes. As if reading his mind, she tore at the buttons on his pants and he unburdened her from her panties.

Straddling him, they locked together at the waist, moving on autopilot, with bodies taken over by the desire to comfort one another.

Bearing witness to the horrors of battle, they understood there was no time in taking things slow, for tomorrow was never promised. Hell, ten minutes from then wasn't promised.

She rocked, swaying her hips, and grinding into him. Her warmth overwhelmed him, and he lost his breath. Seizing the back of her head, he forced her face into his and their tongues tangoed with one another. Reluctantly separating, her chest rose, arching her back and interlocking her fingers behind her neck. Kyle sat up to greet them and captured her breasts between his lips as he stroked the tenderness of her back.

Quickening her stride, she crushed her pelvis against his. He pulled her in close, their seething bodies fighting off the chill brought in with the morning air. Her soft moans elated him. Their bodies danced in unison. She clenched her legs tight to his hips, the surge of energy and pleasure rising in her body, waiting to burst like fireworks. Her limbs snaked around his body, squeezing him to ride his wave of movement while her own ceased. He continued the work for them, not wanting to stop as he neared climax. Her teeth sank into his neck, fighting to stifle the moan emerging from deep within.

Her breathing stopped. Kyle thrust harder and harder and then with great exhaustion, her orgasm was over and his began. He grew rigorous, drawing her in closer while his body became rigid, and she surrendered to his experience. She could feel him swell inside her and then he contracted; his muscles relaxed.

Skyler nestled her head on his shoulder, and their chests heaved in rhythm with one another. Sweat drenched their bodies and exhaustion rendered them motionless. They rode the waves of euphoria together, allowing Skyler to forget the troubles in her head. Kyle kissed her on her forehead, trying to catch his breath, and together, they laughed.

VI

"Just got the word." Jack's voice caused the men to stir in their cots. Some were ready to leap to their feet and move out at a moment's notice. "We Oscar Mike in one hour. Shit, shower, and shave, and be ready to move."

The accustom groans and complaints followed, and Carlos threw down the cards he held.

"We just got here. We're already moving back out? This is bullshit."

"This ain't no luxury vacation. We got a job to do, and we gotta get back and do it. Be lucky you got to sleep the night here." Jack tossed his rifle on his cot and searched the room of faces until he located Jones, brushing his teeth and spitting into an empty water bottle. Cannonball the dog sat at his feet, gnawing on an MRE pork patty. "Oh, Jones, you got those extra lance corporal chevrons on you?"

"Yes, Corporal."

"Give them to Sutherland."

Sutherland perked up at hearing his name. He had always wanted the cross rifles underneath his solo chevron. It was the symbol which solidified being a Marine and set apart the Marines from the other service branches.

"Congrats, little bro. Picking up E-3. I think I have my extra pair somewhere in here," Jones said, taking a small white cardboard with two lance corporal chevrons out of his daypack.

"Truthfully, you don't need yours anymore, either." Jack tossed him an identical white cardboard square with two corporal chevrons pinned to it. Jones stood in disbelief, eyes tracing over the rank, and imagining the responsibilities which came with it.

"Are you serious?" Jones asked, face gleaming with pride, until glass from the painted window blew inward, and the walls shook from incoming rockets.

VII

Skyler and Kyle didn't mutter a word as they walked away from the train car. Both refused to look at one another while trying to conceal large grins. Kyle ran his hand through his hair and stopped.

"Damn, I forgot my beanie. I'll catch up with you later." He kissed her, not caring who saw, then ran back to *their* train car. Her shoulders relaxed, and she sighed. A pleasing sensation washed over her and the stress she had been carrying seemed to vanish. Skyler felt normal once again.

She didn't wait for him to disappear into the train car. Work could not wait, and while feeling anew and refreshed, she understood everything would be all right. A small satisfying smile donned her face as she walked back into the main area of the train station, assured the visions of the dead would no longer beckon to her.

Kyle bounced into the train car with a new-found energy and the ease of a child climbing a tree. His beanie laid on the ground next to the imprint of their bodies and he couldn't help but laugh at the image. The sound of his chuckle bouncing off the metal car walls soon dissipated, and his smile faded to a grimace. The filth that covered the floor now covered his body and he prayed the showers were magically working again so he didn't have to resort to a baby wipe bath before heading back to the line.

As he leaned over for his beanie, a hard tremor shook the train and threw him off his feet. He shuffled one way, then the other before slamming his head off the metal wall and opening a small gash above his eyebrow. The hard vibration was accompanied by several explosions, one after the next, and Kyle hugged the floor. The concussions wrapped around him, it's source of origin a mystery, and banged at his ears as if he was inside a steel drum.

The deafening gong of three consecutive rockets that rung the train car slowly subsided, allowing Kyle to regain his bearings. He climbed from the boxcar on unsteady legs, and with his head still spinning, he focused on what was happening. People ran, fearing another round of rockets. He shuffled forward, his legs betraying him, and he felt as if he was on an ocean liner in rough seas.

Black and gray smoke drifted by him, and he coughed, choking on the harsh chemical taste in the air. The next explosion induced in him vertigo, spinning the world in circles. He reached out to grab a hold of anything he could, but there was nothing nearby. Kyle fell hard to the pavement. Pieces of buildings and chunks of the ground kicked up in the air as more rockets exploded in the compound.

VIII

The men inside the Berserker's room scrambled for their gear while broken pieces of painted glass showered over them. Cannonball scurried under Jones's rack, peeking out to whimper at the sounds of the rockets. Jones petted the dog's head, calming the small animal while his own nerves threatened to betray him. Jack noticed half of his men weren't in the room and his first thought was of Kyle. *Where are you, you sonofabitch?*

"Corporal Jones. Get a head count. Listen up," he barked, their eyes locked on him. "Let's go help anyone that needs it."

Jack marched out the door with Sutherland tight on his six and the other men following. He pushed opened the door. Blood-curdling screams echoed around the compound, and Jack hoped the cries weren't from his Marines. *They better have greater discipline than to scream from being injured,* Jack thought.

I'm hit. I'm hit, I can't feel my legs. Simpson's words echoed back to him and Jack chewed on his bottom lip to force the sound of the recent memory from his head. Other men from different units ran back and forth, carrying bodies or attending to wounded troops.

Jack stopped, standing a foot outside of the door and blocking it from the others who collided against one another in the doorway. His heart stopped and his face drooped. In the center of the courtyard outside their room, a surge of men hustled by, and in the middle of them all was Kyle. The Berserkers moved around Jack, slowing their strides until they came to a complete stop. Dread filled their faces. The urge to rush to his friend grew in Jack, but he knew his friend wasn't there.

Blood trickled down Kyle's expressionless face and the hustling men parted from his path. In his arms rested Skyler like a bride in the arms of her groom on their wedding night. Her head nestled into his chest. In a daunting stroll, Kyle walked the walk of a dead man heading toward the electric chair. One lethargic arm hung out in front, palm facing the sky, as her dangling hand pointed the way. Small drops of blood fell from her ring finger, dotting the trail for him to follow.

Covers, helmets or eight-points, were quickly removed from the Berserker's heads and their own faces dropped to the ground. All except for Jack, who stared on, doing nothing but looking. Kyle's lifeless, dreary eyes drifted to him, blinking as if he knew who Jack was but couldn't recall from where or how. They momentarily held an empty stare until Kyle returned to his procession of death. He stepped one foot in front of the other, unknowingly heading to the makeshift chapel.

All was silent to his ears except for the echo of his boots on the hard ground. He eased through the curtain draped over the chapel's opening and found a wooden bench inside. Gently he eased her down, cradling her head to comfort her from the hard surface.

A tender breeze blew, rustling her hair. Kyle stroked a strand behind her ear before placing a kiss upon her cooling lips. With a thumb drenched in blood, Kyle drew the mark of the Berserker, the brand of sacrifice upon her brow. The Chaplin stood before them and removed his cover. Casting solemn eyes at the lifeless body of Skyler, he remembered the troubled woman he spoke with only days before.

Kyle stood without speaking, and leaving behind the chapel, ventured to the main area. Smoke swirled with the wind. Two men rushed by carrying an injured body on a cot. Kyle's sorrowful eyes met again with Jack, and this time Jack couldn't hold it. He lowered his gaze.

Destruction and chaos engulfed the area. The war was speaking to Kyle and he understood what it said. He accepted it with a nod of his head. No matter what he did or how hard he fought, no one would make it out alive.

HM2 Skyler 'Doc' Greene

Killed in Action Fallujah, Iraq, Al-Anbar Province

February 13th, 1983 – November 13th, 2004

CHAPTER ELEVEN

DEVIL DOGS

The deadliest weapon in the world is a Marine and his rifle.

-General Pershing

I

November 15th, 2004-

The Marines advanced south through the city, marching to the Euphrates River, and funneling the enemy into a kill zone. With tanks on the opposite side of the river, the insurgents had two options: die or surrender.

HM3 Brooks, the new corpsman assigned to the Berserkers, strolled along with the formation. His eyes chattered in their sockets, searching desperately for the enemy. Like many young men, Brooks boasted about wanting his chance to get in on the action, but when selected to replace the fatally injured Doc Sloan, reality slapped him with a hand of fear like a scorned lover.

The jerky habits of Brooks didn't go unnoticed by Jack and he moved up carefully next to him, not wanting to startle the new guy. The M16 jittered in his hands and several of the Berserkers cast an uneasy glance over their shoulders to ensure he wouldn't shoot them. Jack didn't like the distraction. It kept their attention off the mission and risked them missing a deadly detail.

"What's your name again?" As hard as he tried, Jack's voice still spooked the new corpsman.

"Brooks, from Maui." His vocal cords trembled. His attention didn't remain long on Jack before his head darted around.

"Hawaii?"

"Yes."

"Okay, Brooks from Maui. I'm guessing this is your first time in the city?"

"Yes, Corporal." Brooks shook his head and his helmet, too big for the smaller man, wobbled back and forth. Jack patted the guy on the shoulder to reassure him not to be so jumpy.

"Look, you'll be all right. Remember your training, and you're *our* Doc now. We got your back but keep your ears and eyes open. If someone screams for the corpsman or just simply Doc, you better haul ass as fast as you can. Copy that?" The fresh-faced Corpsman didn't speak, and Jack stifled a laugh as the large helmet shook comically on his head. "We'll have to get you a new helmet when we get back. Stay alert, stay frosty."

Ashmore poked his head around the corner of an alley, but then popped back, not sure of what he saw. He motioned for Jack, who paused a moment longer with the new corpsman.

"Stay frosty," he repeated, then ran down the ranks. Jack halted the rest of the men and oriented them to their sectors of fire. The Berserkers obeyed, taking a knee, and aimed their weapons outbound at possible enemy locations. "What's up?"

"Not sure exactly," Ashmore said. He removed his helmet and scratched at the reddening impressions on top of his scalp. "Take a look."

Jack cautiously leaned out and like Ashmore, came back puzzled. In the center of the street, a man sat in a chair wearing Marine Corps desert cammies. His weapon hung across his lap, and he was fast asleep.

"Told you," Ashmore said.

Jack called for Kyle, and the line relayed the message, but Kyle didn't respond. His eyes and mind were cast upward, lost in the gray sky above. The rain had ceased but the threat was still imminent. Jack called again, and it took Sutherland shaking his arm to bring his attention around. Kyle's face sank inward, taking on a more skull-like appearance as the flesh clung to the muscles underneath like a man burdened by insomnia. Standing without fear of snipers, Kyle sauntered to the front, kicking pebbles from his path.

Jack subdued his urge to be annoyed and thus calmed his aggravation. He worried about his best friend, but he needed Kyle on the front lines to help.

"Check this shit out," Jack said, overlooking Kyle's demeanor. Kyle looked, and his expression didn't change.

"That's odd." Kyle shrugged his shoulders; his voice toneless and flat. "I'm guessing it's a trap."

"You think," Ashmore said. Before Ashmore could get a reply, Kyle strolled into the open street. Jack reached for him but missed. "What the fuck is he doing?"

There was a sternness in Kyle. An inquisitive look of purpose replaced the dullness in his expression.

"Shit, get security," Jack ordered Ashmore, but Ashmore couldn't take his eyes off Kyle. Keeping to a whisper, Jack shouted for Sutherland and Jones to cover the opposite corner of the street.

Kyle's movement transfixed Ashmore. He saw not his friend or corporal, but a gunslinger from the Old West on a vengeance death march, ready to burn the entire town down. His rifle dangled by the green three-point sling, and his hand was far from the handle. Producing no sound as he moved, Kyle unsnapped the safety strap of his desert colored 9mm holster. His head tilted forward like a predator stalking its prey. He slid his sidearm off his hip.

Ashmore's face glowed with enthusiasm. He couldn't tear his eyes away and waited anxiously to see what Kyle's next move was.

The sleeping man didn't stir as Kyle stopped three feet from him. Kyle's head slouched to the side, studying the man who didn't wear combat boots, but instead, wore sandals. The uniform was legitimate, with tiny upside-down eagle, globe, and anchors camouflaged about the digital patterns.

The blouse lacked a name tape over the right breast pocket or rank on the collars. Kyle's head rotated along his shoulders to the other side. He didn't utter a single word; no expression crossed his face. His melancholy eyes stared blankly at the man, and his ears couldn't hear the whispers of the Marines behind him. A twitch of his thumb took the 9mm Beretta off safe. He leveled the barrel at the center of the man's head.

Cocking back the hammer awoke the insurgent with sleepy eyes. Panic gripped his heart as the Marine towered over him like a vengeful demon from his worst nightmare. The insurgent's hands flew up in a universal sign of surrender, pleading with the Marine that he meant no harm.

Kyle's head rolled back on his shoulders like a silent serial killer from a slasher film. The man shifted in his seat, hands at chest level, and he sat straight up. Kyle blinked, snarled, and squeezed the trigger. The hammer fell, striking the primer of death.

BANG. Recoil. Headshot.

The silent streets of Fallujah echoed with the report of the pistol. The insurgent's head snapped back, and brains followed the mangled bullet out the back of his skull. His body slumped in the chair, and his weapon slowly slid down his outstretched legs. Gravity pulled at the man's dead-weight, causing him to topple to the hard, wet road.

His death brought nothing to Kyle, but he marveled over the dead insurgent. Blood dripped to the wet pavement, disturbed only by the wind blowing across the road, kicking up a pile of dirt which swirled about the standing Marine. His arm lowered, but he didn't holster the smoking pistol. The kill eased the pain in his heart, but his eyes only saw Skyler lying on the dirty pavement at the train station.

The chill of the ground still left an imprint on his knees when he had placed a hand on her shoulder. She didn't stir under his touch the way she had that morning. His weight had grew too heavy and his legs came out from under him, permitting him to place her head on his lap.

The memory of her warm blood soaking through his trousers blocked out the cold wind blowing through the city. No smell assaulted his nose; no sound disturbed his ears as he stared without blinking at the man on the ground. He couldn't hear Jack walking up behind him, nor did he hear the cry of the AK rounds erupting from an elevated position.

II

The cigarette Carlos enjoyed took his mind away from the butchery of battle. An onlooker would see a man who fit the description of a person relaxing by the side of a lake on holiday, rather than sitting in the midst of battle. The report of Kyle's sidearm spun Carlos's focus back to the job. He flew to his feet along with Thompson at the rear of the formation.

"Follow me." Thompson nudged Carlos and as they ran by Harvey, Carlos grabbed him by the flak jacket, pulling him along. Harvey hesitated at first, not knowing what was going on, but as Carlos and Thompson moved away from where the gun report came from, Harvey joined them. They turned into an alley that was nearly concealed by two tall buildings. Only large enough to move in a single file, the three shuffled down the alley with rough-cut bricks snatching at their shoulders.

The sunlight extinguished in the narrow corridor and a small crack was the only opening they found in the first door they came to. Movement and voices came from within as Thompson shoved open the door and tossed in a grenade.

"Frag out," he shouted. The three Marines turned away from the opening to shield themselves from the blast.

POP. Flash, a puff of smoke.

The whispers inside turned to screams and Thompson pushed his way in. The vapors of burnt gunpowder and hot metal clouded the room. An insurgent stretched out against an overturned shelf of canned goods, looking at the invading Marines in disbelief. Blood draining from several places in his body, and he motioned to speak, but Thompson didn't grant him a final word.

BANG. Recoil. Heart shot.

Scrambling on the floor, another insurgent lay maimed by the grenade, but Carlos refused to waste ammo on him. Instead, he drove his ka-bar bayonet into the base of the man's skull. The man twitched once before flattening out as Carlos turned the blade. A set of stairs laid beyond the threshold to their right flank and to their front was a door leading into a storefront.

Thompson hustled, moving past Carlos, stepping a full foot into the store. Carlos pulled the bayonet from the man's neck and looked up. Thompson cleared the doorway a second before an insurgent sprayed his AK.

Several bullets buzzed by Lance Corporal Thompson, splintering the door jamb. Carlos shielded himself as chips of wood flew his way. Thompson ducked from the shrapnel made from flying wooden splinters and returned fire.

BANG. Recoil. Chest shot.

BANG. Recoil. Chest shot.

The insurgent fell behind a stack of boxes as a second blast came from the opposite direction. Thompson didn't hear the report of the weapon, only felt the sledgehammer-like impact to his side. The force swept him off his feet and Thompson cursed himself for not clearing the room before rushing in. The pain was dull and throbbed with a pulse of its own. Carlos stepped over Thompson and fired two shots at the enemy who had a pistol sighted in at the door. The insurgent fired too, but his rounds went wild, missing Carlos, but Carlos didn't miss.

BANG. Recoil. Sucking chest wound.

BANG. Recoil. Adjacent sucking chest wound.

Down he went, gasping for the air his collapsed lungs couldn't draw in. Carlos swept his rifle from corner to corner, finding no additional insurgents. Thompson rolled over to his back and felt his side. He wanted to cough, his face straining for relief until a violent gasp brought in a breath. He rocked from side to side, trying to escape the pain.

"I'm hit, bro." Thompson moaned. Carlos frantically searched him for an injury.

"Still lucky, motherfucker." Carlos jested, slapping Thompson on the helmet before shoving him away. Taking out two M16 magazines from a woodland pouch, he found a 9mm round had penetrated one and lodged in the other. The round stopped, nestled between two NATO bullets. Carlos was still laughing as he pulled Thompson up to his feet. More gunfire came from upstairs, dumbfounding the men. Thompson looked about, then stared at Carlos, stifling his humor.

"Where's Harvey?"

III

Rat...tat...tat. Rat...tat...tat. Kyle either didn't care or failed to notice the shit storm of rounds crisscrossing his location.

Rat...tat...tat. Rat...tat...tat. Jack and Jones kicked up dirt to get to Kyle, but he didn't care. He couldn't be bothered with them or the two men on the second-floor of an apartment building, or the couple of guys across the street on the second floor of a store. Kyle continued to stare at the man on the ground who lacked a large portion of his skull.

Rat...tat...tat. Rat...tat...tat. The hard plastic of his kneepad tore open, sending a vibration up his leg, but Kyle didn't flinch away. The incident only shifted his attention. He swung his 9mm toward the apartment windows and squeezed off the entire clip.

Jones pumped his M16's trigger, aiming at the building behind Kyle, knocking out panes of glass and pinning down the enemy on the second floor above the store. Jack moved and with a hard yank, uprooted Kyle, shoving him to the apartment building. Kyle's head snapped to face Jack, and for a moment, he didn't recognize his old friend.

"What the fuck are you doing?" Jack yelled over the explosion of gunpowder. Kyle shrugged Jack away and without explanation, ran up the three steps to the apartment's front door. Jones popped off three rounds, then three more, continuing to repeal the enemy from across the street. Jack tapped him and he followed his squad leader into the apartment, leaving Carlos and Thompson with the responsibility of the storefront insurgents.

Carlos had no idea Jack and Jones were following Kyle into the apartment across the street. Stepping over destroyed shelves and dead bodies, Carlos hit the stairs at the back of the store. He led the way with his rifle pointing upward to kill any enemy at first sight. Thompson followed close behind, stepping where Carlos had to avoid making any sound. With each step, he glanced back down the stairs to ensure no one was behind them.

Bullets struck the wall above Carlos, causing him to duck under the second level landing. He sprayed six rounds in the enemy's direction, forcing the man to jump behind a bar as Thompson moved around Carlos. Standing on the second from the top step, Thompson saw the hunched-over back of a cowering insurgent behind the bar.

BANG. Recoil. Shattered hip bone.

BANG. Recoil. Miss.

"Oh, that had to hurt, motherfucker." Thompson chuckled. The man lurched forward, screaming in pain, but avoided the second shot. Another insurgent rose from behind a stack of wooden crates. Without thinking, the two Berserkers fired at the same time.

BANG. Recoil. Chest shot.

BANG. Recoil. Headshot.

Thompson glided past the wooden crates shielding the fallen insurgent, to find him holding a primed grenade, the pin hooked around one finger.

"Fuck America. Allah Akbar." The man extended his fingers, allowing the spoon to fling into the air.

"Shit." Thompson watched as the small metal stick flipped end over end away from the grenade. He spun on his toes and dove for Carlos, who managed to leap halfway down the stairs when the grenade went off.

POP. Flash, a puff of smoke.

IV

Kyle burst through the apartment door and executed an insurgent waiting for him to enter. He moved on automatic, killing and advancing at the will of some primal instinct deep inside him. A single 30-watt light bulb illuminated the gloomy hallway, straining to keep the hall from a blanket of darkness.

Jones closed the metal door behind them, preventing more bullets from chasing the trio. Kyle turned down the 'L' shaped hallway and disappeared. Jack let out an irritated sigh but followed. Kyle bypassed several doors, and ran up the flight of stairs, knowing the enemy was on the second floor. He took the steps two at a time, rushing to a meeting with death: either theirs or his own.

Jack made haste rounding the bend in the hallway. He didn't like bypassing doors, but his concern was for his friend who was running to his certain death. Jack hardly noticed each door he passed, none being any different from any other. They looked the same, had the same frames and trims, if one could call the bricks and cement trim, and all were closed tight. Any number of insurgents could be hiding within, but all of this was absent from Jack's mind as he hit the stairs.

The one thing he did pause a thought for was the last door on the right near the base of the staircase. Boarded-up and held tight with chains and a padlock, a small amount of sunlight broke through the cracks around the door. It was the rear exit, but the haj was determined for anyone who entered to leave out the front door, either standing or being carried out dead.

Jack didn't look back to see if Jones was there. He knew he was and pointed to the first room they came to.

"Clear it." He ordered Jones and continued his search for Kyle. Failing to systematically clear out the rooms of such a large building gnawed at Jack. He preferred to have his entire squad do such a large operation, but Kyle wasn't giving him time to assemble them. Ignoring a set of stairs leading to the third floor, Jack knew where Kyle was heading.

Kyle proceeded to the end of the hall and unleashed a war cry that would've made the Gods proud.

BANG. Recoil. Sucking chest wound.

BANG. Recoil. Separated aorta.

Kyle didn't enter the room to clear it. He didn't need to. Anyone standing, anyone not a part of his beloved Corps, was mowed down. Satisfied with their deaths, he spun on his heels and collided with Jack.

"We need to regroup and have words, brother. Move out."

Kyle didn't listen. He pushed past Jack and hit the next door, kicking it open and nearly splintering the wood with his force. An insurgent rushed him from the side, a bayonet held low and thrusting forward. His eyes filled with a blood lust that Kyle could respect. The haj grabbed Kyle's rifle by the barrel, pinning him against the door, and jabbing with his blade at Kyle's hip.

Kyle swatted the bayonet away, its sharp point cutting across the back of his flak jacket. He tried to reach his other arm around, but it was pinned between his rifle and the door. The hajji pulled his blade back and thrust again, but Kyle kept his hand on the man's wrist, preventing the knife from stabbing him. The sharp tip poked at Kyle's hip, tearing a small hole into his trousers. The man screamed in Kyle's face, driven to kill the Marine, but then was jerked away.

He released the bayonet and Kyle caught only a blur as Jack and the haj flew to the floor. Jack gritted his teeth and snarled at the man underneath him; his own bayonet lodged deep into the man's throat. The Iraqi tried to push Jack away, but he was too weak to fight with blood pouring from his neck. Jack twisted the bayonet, cutting deep into the man, killing him.

"Die motherfucker." Jack stood and wiped the blood from his blade on the man's shoulder. He turned back, pointing his knife at Kyle. "Move out. That's a direct fuckin' order, Corporal."

Jack moved past Kyle and as Kyle turned, he kicked the hajji's bayonet. The sheath laid not far from them and Kyle took both, attaching the sheathed bayonet to his flak jacket. The two men moved down the hallway toward the stairs, meeting up with Jones who was coming out of the last door.

"All clear," Jones said and then pointed to the stairs leading up. "What about the rest of the floors?"

"Fuck'em," Jack moved around Jones. "We'll call in arty to blow the shit out of this fuckin' place."

The gunfire from outside dwindled to periodic shots until it diminished completely.

"What the fuck, Kyle?" Jack said, descending the stairs. They rounded the elbow of the 'L' shaped hallway. Kyle refused to answer. Jones rushed past Jack and Kyle to exit the house first and get security.

Jack stepped on the threshold leading outside, but before he could clear it completely, something hard shoved him forward. Jack tripped clear of the front porch steps and managed to stay standing. The front door sealed shut with Kyle on the inside, and when he tried to donkey kick it open, it failed to budge.

"Kyle, open the fuckin' door."

Kyle was too stunned to answer his squad leader. The door leading outside slammed just as another door, concealed upon their entering the apartment, was pushed open. It wedged into the front door, securing and locking it in place, creating a barricade between Kyle and the other Marines. An elderly man, with a long gray beard and yellow rotten teeth, emerged from the darkness encapsulating the hidden room.

Like the man upstairs, this old man held a blade, ready to plunge it into Kyle's chest. Unlike the man upstairs, he held it high over his head like a killer in an old black and white horror movie. He snatched Kyle by the flak jacket and together they stumbled back down the hall. They crashed into the wall, knocking over a small table, and destroying a mirror.

Kyle clenched the man's beard, tearing strands from his chin, as a glint of light reflected off the driving blade. Jack called from outside, but his voice was unheard during the commotion. Kyle swatted at the sharp knife but missed the man's arm and the blade lunged at his chest.

V

The grenade's deafening ring vibrated Carlos's ear canal, spinning his head, and zapping his energy. He pushed himself up from the floor, feeling drunk or exhausted as if he just fought the tenth round in a twelve round prize fight. The room swayed back and forth at the bottom of the stairs, and it took a hard shaking of his head to clear his vision. He dropped his helmet to the ground as white smoke rolled down the steps like a fog drifting in from the sea.

On unsteady legs, Carlos took one step at a time, holding the wall for support.

"Thompson?" Carlos said as if clearing his throat. Nothing but a humming silence answered back. He asked again and again nothing came. The overpowering stench of gunpowder diseased the air, and the wind screamed through the busted windows. A single drop of sweat trickled down the length of Carlos's nose. He batted it away with a heavy hand and continued to ascend the steps. At the top of the landing, a hand rested on the edge, not moving.

"Thompson," Carlos called out and still no response. He kept his rifle ready for any active enemy and cautiously moved up to the top of the stairs where Thompson laid motionless. He kneeled, scanning the room while shaking Thompson's arm.

"Hey, you OK?" His voice was a near whisper but seemed amplified to him. To his surprise, Thompson stirred. He groaned, releasing a breath that felt held in for years. Looking at Carlos through concussed eyes, he didn't try to pull himself up. The stiffness in his body worked its way into his jaw and rotating it only produced a popping noise with no relief.

"What the hell does a guy have to do to get a purple heart?" Thompson said, exhausted. Carlos smirked, relieved as he slid down the wall to sit on the top steps. He fired up a cigarette and stuck it in Thompson's mouth.

"Not a scratch?"

"Nope."

"Ginger magic," Carlos said to which Thompson flipped him off. Thompson cracked his neck and sat up.

"Harvey?"

"Not here," Carlos replied.

"What if some haj snatched him on our way in or some shit?"

The wet, dreary memories of an Iraqi jail cell flooded their minds, bringing with it a dank smell of sweat and blood.

"Shit," Thompson said, taking a large puff off his cigarette. "Let's get back to the others."

VI

The tip of the blade pierced through the material of Kyle's flak jacket. His shoulder slammed into the hard wall, knocking dirt and an empty picture frame from it. The solid impact frightened Kyle, but his sapi plate stopped the knife. Before the man could draw the knife back, Kyle quickly rolled his shoulder and shoved his palm forward, punching the old man in his wrist. The knife ejected from his hand and slid into a dark spot, not to be seen again.

Kyle reared back, bringing his elbow across the man's shoulders, and smashing the point of it into the old man's jaw. His legs buckled, and he released his hold on Kyle's flak jacket. The old man snorted, shooting out a long rope of blood and mucus which landed on Kyle's knee. Before the old man could wipe his nose, Kyle shoved his pistol upward, burying the barrel beneath the long beard.

BANG. Recoil. Headshot.

The man collapsed as his brains rocketed to the ceiling. The spray of crimson mist blanketed Kyle's face and he leaned against the wall, surprised he had survived the attack. A deep breath escaped his lungs, and he was glad this foolishness was over. Then a pineapple grenade rolled by. Without thinking, he kicked it to the end of the hall. It struck the wooden leg of a table, continued to travel around the turn in the hallway, and disappeared.

He spun, turning his face away from the flash of light. The wall shielded him from the shrapnel, but the concussion dazed Kyle. The room shifted about as his ears drummed with a ringing.

A fog, smelling of hot metal and gunpowder, expanded in the hallway. A barrel crept through the opening of the once concealed door, and Kyle, still woozy, fired his pistol. His feet were unsteady, and the small recoil had enough force to push him off balance. He tripped over his own feet while the barrel retreated at the flash of Kyle's pistol, giving him enough time to crawl for the corner.

He reached the elbow of the 'L' shaped hallway, and a solid thud brought his attention around. Another pineapple grenade landed near his boot. He kicked it back toward the hidden room and threw his body around the corner. The grenade went off, shredding plaster from the walls which showered down on Kyle. All sound became a dull vibration.

A burning pain nipped at his leg, and as he looked to ensure it was still there, Kyle caught sight of a second insurgent coming from the room. The insurgent made a grave mistake by looking eye level with the hall instead of down on the ground. Kyle fired.

BANG. Recoil. Miss.

BANG. Recoil. Gutshot.

BANG. Recoil. Gutshot.

The man dropped to his knees, grappling at his stomach.

BANG. Recoil. Headshot.

The insurgent stiffened on his knees before folding over sideways.

Kyle scurried over the first insurgent killed upon entering the apartment. Still warm, his weight released trapped air from within the useless lungs. With his vision wavering, tilting on its axis, he retrieved his M16 from around his back and propped it up on the shoulder of the fallen insurgent. Aiming at the end of the hall, he waited. Two men ran screaming and firing their rifles, casting the hallway into a blinding light. Kyle returned fire.

BANG. BANG. BANG. BANG. BANG. BANG.

RECOIL. RECOIL. RECOIL. RECOIL. RECOIL. RECOIL.

Two more bodies lay riddled with bullets piercing several vital organs. Another grenade bounced down the corridor and landed at the barrel of Kyle's rifle. He punched the grenade back the other way and buried himself beneath the carcass to shield himself from the blast. The insurgent's grenade increased the pressure in Kyle's head, and he felt as if it could burst. Dazed, he scooted deeper into the house, inching his way toward the stairs as another man rounded the corner. The insurgent receded when three M16 rounds struck the wall near his head.

Kyle ejected a magazine. He thought of throwing a grenade, but another concussion blast would drive him mad. He slammed a magazine into his rifle, and chambered a round, readying himself for a last stand, for his zero hour.

The insurgent fired blindly at Kyle. Two rounds screamed over his shoulder, causing Kyle to yell out. Confusing the cries of anger for injury, the insurgent reemerged from the corner where Kyle sprayed a three-round burst.

BANG. Recoil. Knee wound.

BANG. Recoil. Groin wound.

BANG. Recoil. Heart penetration.

The last bullet snipped the apex of the insurgent's heart, killing him. Kyle kept firing at the corner of the hallway as two more barrels appeared.

VII

Carlos and Thompson staggered down the stairs. Their minds riddle with explanations of what they were going to tell Jack about losing one of their own.

"You guys good?" Harvey stood at the door leading into the alley, smoking a cigarette. Carlos allowed his rifle to drop by his side, not believing what his eyes were telling him. In one flash movement, he crossed the gap to Harvey and slammed him against the wall.

"Are you fucking kidding me?" Carlos screamed into his face as Harvey looked on with wide-eyed terror. "You were out here the entire fuckin' time?"

"There were people shooting in there. I wasn't going in." Harvey tried unsuccessfully to pry Carlos's hands off the collar of his flak jacket. Carlos banged a quick uppercut into Harvey's jaw, but his hold on Harvey kept the admin Marine from falling.

"You motherfucker. We nearly died in there looking for your stupid ass and the whole time you were out here smoking a cigarette." Carlos released Harvey's collar, and Harvey stood tall, rubbing his jaw, but not backing down. Carlos hit him again, and Harvey's cigarette flew down the alley, where it struck a wall and extinguished in a small puddle. Thompson seized Carlos before he could unleash a fury of punches.

"Look, you can all play cowboys and Indians and try to be big heroes, but I'm going home alive. Besides, I just lost my girl, so fuck you."

"Girl? What girl?" Carlos asked.

"Doc Greene. We were in love."

"You mean Kyle's girl?"

"Kyle's girl? You don't know what the hell you're talking about. Skyler loved me."

"Motherfucker, please. She didn't give a shit about your sorry fuckin' ass, you stalkin' fuckin' pervert."

"Fuck you, wetback." Harvey turned away before Carlos could punch him again and headed back to the rest of the squad.

"Oh really, bitch."

"Yeah, and don't forget, I'm a corporal. Your ass is going up on charges for this assault against an NCO."

"You think so?" Carlos called after Harvey, who was nearing the exit of the alley. Harvey turned around to say something but stopped. The sight of Carlos's M16 barrel sent him into a full sprint. He ran for an open area, while in the apartment across the street, Kyle was easing himself into a tight position.

Kyle unloaded several shots at the enemy, which kept the insurgent at bay. Out of nowhere, the hallway flooded with a wash of sunlight coming from behind him. The padlocked back door crashed inward as Jack sailed through the air. Kyle didn't bother with turning around to see who was there. Exhaustion sent his head spinning, and he could care less if it was the enemy or not. Jones and Ashmore stepped in and fired down the hall, providing cover for Jack.

"Black's calling in a fire mission. Let's move." Jack screamed at Kyle. Kyle's legs wouldn't function. His body drained of energy, and his muscles felt useless. Jack grabbed the handle on Kyle's flak jacket and pulled him out of the apartment, while Jones and Ashmore tossed in two grenades.

POP, POP. Flash, Flash. Two puffs of smoke.

Corporal Kyle Dillon

Purple Heart Recipient

For Wounds Received on November 15th, 2004

Fallujah, Iraq

* * *

Letter to Jack Campbell from Jennifer Campbell,

Dated November 7th, 2004-

Dear Jack,

Oh, I wish you could see your son. He's so beautiful sleeping in our bed, and you won't believe how much he has to eat. I have to wake up every three hours to feed him. My nipples hurt. You're lucky you don't have to share this responsibility.

He is an amazing boy with hands so small, and he stays curled up in a ball. Sometimes he stretches, and it is impressive; truly takes my breath away. Your parents can't get enough of him. They're over here so much that I forget that they don't live here.

How are you doing? Have you not written? Have you gotten the letters I've sent? I wish you could call or just come home right now. I want to hear your voice. Please write me soon. I love you. We love you. I'm worried about you. Please write. Love Jennifer

CHAPTER TWELVE

OOH-RAH

I come in peace; I didn't bring artillery. But I am pleading with you with tears in my eyes: If you fuck with me, I'll kill you all.

-General Mattis to Iraqi tribal leaders.

I

The middle of an alley opened into a large square, intersecting with three entry points, sullied with two bulky trash canisters, several piles of garbage, and one burnt out car. Overhead, twenty power lines ran to a single transformer high on a pole. Artillery fire had destroyed many rooftops, and the Berserkers stepped cautiously to avoid rolling an ankle over busted pieces of bricks.

They regrouped away from their last scrimmage. With security posted, Jack, Ashmore, and Jones carried Kyle from the apartment building. Only Ashmore held a grin on his face; enjoying the war he had come to love.

"Fuck you, Kyle."

"Fuck you, Jack," Kyle said, exhausted.

"What the hell is wrong with you?" Jack fumed at Kyle, easing him to a sitting position. Kyle leaned against the wall and reached in his pocket for a cigarette without answering. He closed his eyes, trying to clear his rocky vision.

Frustrated, Jack kicked at a piece of debris on the ground. The weight of his M16 dug into him, and he unslung it, tossing it at Sutherland who sat it on the ground next to Kyle.

The other Berserkers faced outward, wanting to eavesdrop, but not wanting to be obvious about it. Jones sat next to Kyle and whistled for Cannonball who came running from a hidden box behind a trash can. Doc stepped forward, shining a light into Kyle's eyes, and Kyle swatted him away like an irritating fly.

"You tryin' to get yourself dead, bro?" Jack shouted, looming over Kyle who still refused to answer. Instead, he shrugged his shoulders and smoked his cigarette.

"I swear, I'll fucking shoot…" Carlos's voice traveled before anyone saw Harvey sprinting into view. Jack rolled his eyes, fed up with the drama.

"Is everyone on the fuckin' rag today?" Jack growled as Harvey ran past him, looking at Jack to rescue him from Carlos.

"I ain't done with you." Jack pointed at Kyle to which Kyle turned over his hands, showing that he didn't care. Jack stepped between Harvey and Carlos's rifle. "What the fuck is going on? Lower your weapon."

"I'm going to kill him." Carlos was eerily calm for a man who had just chased another man on foot.

"Fuck yeah," Ashmore said. "Kill that admin motherfucker."

"Stow it." Jack snapped a knife hand at the bulky Marine before turning back to Carlos and saying, "Lower your weapon, Marine."

"Screw that. Shoot the prick." Thompson steadied himself against the wall, rubbing his stiffening neck, and not seeing the hateful stare Jack cast.

"I said stand down, Marine." Jack took a step toward Carlos.

"He deserves to die. That motherfucker nearly got me and Thompson smoked."

"Lance Corporal Carlos, I'm giving you a direct order." An urge pulled Jack's hand to his sidearm. "Stow that fucking weapon, Marine."

Carlos eyed the pistol at Jack's side and rolled his tongue against the back side of his teeth. He tilted his head to see the cowering Harvey peering over Jack's shoulder like a scared child.

"Step aside, Corporal." Carlos tightened his grip on the rifle's handle, resting his index finger on the trigger. Jack eased the pistol from his holster.

"I said stand down."

"You gonna shoot me over this prick?" Carlos asked. There came a pause. Jack didn't respond. Carlos snarled as he shouted, "I've been with you for a long time, Jack."

"And that's why it will pain me to do this, but I gave you a direct order."

"You gonna shoot me over him? You gonna shoot me over him!"

"No. I'm gonna shoot you for disobeying a direct order. You're questioning my orders in front of the others. You're making me draw a line. Now lower your fucking weapon, or I'll be forced to shoot you. I won't give this order again."

Carlos snorted back a phantom drip from his nose. His teeth remained clenched, but he complied. He lowered his rifle and took a step forward, squaring off with Jack.

"I've been your brother for years, and you would shoot me over this motherfucker?" Carlos whispered in a tone loud enough for everyone to hear. "Damn you, brother. He's gonna get one of us smoked, and that'll be on your head, you dig?"

Carlos walked away, but Thompson remained, shaking his head in disappointment. Jack slipped the sidearm back into its holster.

"They're waving a white flag," Sutherland called out, training his rifle on three men walking down the alley. The man in the front held a white flag, flanked by two Iraqis with their hands at their sides.

"What do we do?" Black asked.

"What the hell do you mean, *what do we do*? We take them prisoner," Jack said, growling. His face grew red from the lack of common sense spreading throughout his squad. He pushed past Sutherland and Jones followed, waving the three Iraqis over. The man controlling the flag hesitated, allowing the other two to step past, revealing concealed pistols. They fired at the approaching Marines.

The Marines scurried for cover as the .45 caliber rounds flew. Sutherland and Jones crashed behind a trash canister as rounds rang out on the other side like a gong. Jack didn't flinch, his feet didn't move, and he didn't run for cover. The only muscle movement he made was swinging up the 9mm Beretta, not in a knee-jerk reaction, but in a smooth draw. The insurgents moved about but remained in the middle of the alley. Jack planted his feet, squaring off with them, amused at finally getting the gunfight he had dreamed about.

"Lying motherfuckers," Sutherland shouted. The flag bearer dropped the white fabric and sprinted away from the fight.

BANG. Recoil. Leg wound.

The bullet ripped through the outer muscle of his thigh, tripping the flag bearer to the ground. He screamed out in pain and agony. One of the gunmen retreated, firing his pistol until it was empty. He managed to run three feet before a round struck him in the back and sent him skidding into a pile of garbage.

BANG. Recoil. Upper rear shoulder shot.

The third and final standing insurgent stepped directly in front of Jack. The moaning of the wind drowned out all noise and both men fired. The insurgent's .45 caught a piece of Jack's trousers, and cold air rushed in as he squeezed the trigger on his 9mm.

BANG. Recoil. Chest wound.

The insurgent's knees buckled, but he remained standing. His arm drifted, and he fired again, missing wide of Jack. He forced it back, but before he could get a shot off, Jack repeatedly popped the trigger.

BANG. Recoil. Gutshot.

BANG. Recoil. Forearm wound.

The insurgent dropped his pistol, but before it could hit the ground…

BANG. Recoil. Headshot.

The insurgent tensed like a bolt of electricity rocketed through his body. Every muscle went rigid and he toppled over like a stiff board. Jack called for a cease-fire but kept his pistol on the insurgent. One by one, the Marines appeared from their places of cover to find Black lying face down in the street. Sutherland and Doc hurried to roll him over, and to their surprise, he jolted up like waking from a deep sleep.

"You OK?" Jack asked.

"Yeah." He dropped his backpack on the ground at Jack's feet. A small hole punctured the back plate of the radio, exposing wires and components. Black stretched, rubbing his throbbing back. "But the radio is dead."

"Might be but looks like it saved your life."

"Hey, Jack." Sutherland nudged him. "Tombstone, right?"

Jack looked at the body he had stood toe to toe with and a smile crept upon his face. "Yeah. Tombstone."

"Check it out." Ashmore stood over a body, holding a knife. "Fuckin' Hajji bayonet."

Across the way, lying in the garbage, the face down insurgent reached his hand out for a blade sticking out of the rubble.

"This one's still alive." Thompson nudged the man in the ribs with the barrel of his M16. "Don't think about it, buddy."

"Fuck you, American dog," the man said in rough English, lifting his head and shouting over his wounded shoulder. "Your mother's a whore. Allah Akbar."

"You met my mom? How is she?" A slight laugh jiggled Thompson's stomach and annoyed the insurgent. He spat blood, intended for the Marine, but came nowhere near. Thompson rolled his eyes at the man still reaching for the knife.

"Fuck you. Allah will welcome me. He will have my virgins waiting for me."

"No bro, that's 72 Virginians. Not virgins."

"Fuck you, Thompson," Jones said.

"Oh, my bad, Jones. Forgot you were from Virginia, bro."

"Allah will welcome me." The insurgent lunged for the knife.

BANG. Recoil. Headshot.

The insurgent deflated into the garbage.

"Tell'em the Berserkers will send him more," Thompson said. He reached down and picked up the knife the insurgent was going for. "Hey, Ash, check it."

He held a bayonet that matched the one Ashmore had found.

"Got me one, too."

The wounded flag bearer screamed at the sound of Thompson's gunfire.

"Tell us where Zarqawi is?" Sutherland pulled at the man's collar. With each tug, the man moaned more.

"I don't know. I am a student, not a soldier." The wounded man gripped the torn white flag tarnished brown by dirt and red with blood, holding it like a shield against his chest. Doc Brooks went to work on the man's leg until Kyle shoved the Corpsman out of the way, seizing the injury. He squeezed, pressing his thumb into the man's wound and the man bellowed cries of pain to the sky.

"Talk, motherfucker. Where are your friends at?" Through moments of whimpers, the man declared he knew nothing. He sat up with hands held out in front of him and repeatedly stated he was a student.

"I swear." The man cried in a trembling high pitch voice. "I got trapped in the city when the fighting started. I am a student at the university. I am a student at the university. I am a student at the univer…"

Sutherland's elbow broke the man's nose, interrupting him.

"Yeah, University of Muj, you motherfucker," Sutherland said.

"Then what were you doing with these two insurgents?" Jack strolled up to the student with his pistol in hand and smoke flowing from his nostrils. The proclaimed student eyed the weapon, and he quivered while he spoke.

"They made me hold the flag. I thought they wanted to surrender. I don't like the fighting. They told me to do it, and everything would be OK. I didn't know they wanted to kill you Americans. I swear."

"I don't trust him, Corporal. I say we smoke the cocksucker." Sutherland stood up from his kneeling position, pressing the barrel of his rifle to the man's temple. Ashmore cheered him, tobacco juice slinging from the corner of his mouth as he shook his head frantically. The man turned his face away and prayed.

BANG, Recoil. Headshot.

The man went limp in the wet street. The end of Sutherland's barrel smoked, and Jack slapped the side of Sutherland's Kevlar hard while shoving his rifle away. Sutherland's rifle report rippled out into the city as the others made quick work of searching the dead, retrieving cigarettes and permitted war trophies.

"What the fuck did you just do?" Jack screamed at Sutherland.

"Saved your life, bro." Sutherland motioned toward the student who held a small knife in his hand. Sutherland shrugged, Kyle laughed, and Jack shook his head as the blood drained from the hole in the student's skull.

II

"Sut, frag it," Jack said, trampling through the front gate and pointing at the blue metal door of a single-story house. Harvey followed behind Sutherland and they scanned corners and windows for enemy combatants. The blue door stood ajar, and as Sutherland reached for a grenade, Jack pointed to the opposite corner of the perimeter fence and told Harvey, "Fan out."

"I want to throw a grenade," Harvey said with the tone of an impatient child. Annoyed, Jack shrugged, and Sutherland moved out. Harvey pulled the pin on the grenade, smiling gleefully like a boy lighting a firecracker for the first time.

The excitement and joy were too much for Harvey, and in his eagerness, the grenade slipped from his hand. The joy vanished with the clinking of metal against concrete, and the small metallic ball landed at his feet on the wrong side of the door. He cut, boots digging into the dirt, and sprinted to the opening in the cinder block fence without saying a word.

Jack and Sutherland heard the grenade hitting the ground, and their eyes caught the blurry image of Harvey dashing to the other side of the fence. Jack had a split moment to shout, 'Grenade' before reacting. Almost instinctively, they grabbed their helmets and dove to the ground.

POP. Flash, a puff of smoke.

Something warm bled into Jack's uniform and soaked the loose dirt residing in a small drainage ditch along the base of the fence. There was no pain aside from a small ringing in the ear, and as the smoke dispersed, Jack forced himself to his feet. The military issued Camelbak hung shredded from his back. The wall supported several small dots, outlining Jack's body. If it had not been for the drainage ditch some homeowner dug long ago, he would have been killed.

"Ugh," Sutherland groaned as he sluggishly climbed from the ground. "You shoulda let Carlos smoke him."

Harvey poked his oddly shaped head around the corner of the gate. Upon seeing everything had cleared, he walked back to rejoin his fire team.

"Hey, guys." Harvey drew in deep breaths and shook his head. A chuckle left him. "Don't tell anybody, OK."

"No Harvey, we're fine. Thanks for asking." Sutherland brushed himself off and kicked the metal door open.

III

The Berserkers crowded around a table in the kitchen, studying a map of the city. Jones sat on the floor, roughhousing with Cannonball, and feeding him treats from an MRE.

"According to our time frame, we should be in this area." Jack tapped his finger on the map while the surrounding men jammed in closer to see where he was pointing. It was hard to distinguish the houses on the map. They sat nearly on top of one another and the strangling streets brought on a hint of claustrophobia.

"Corporal." Ashmore squeezed his way to the front. "I think we're further up than that."

"Farther," Thompson interrupted.

"Fuck you, Ginger."

"Cool it," Jack said.

"See this mosque." Ashmore pointed to a spot on the map. "We passed it yesterday."

"Shit, I remember that." Jack puffed on his cigarette. Ashmore dragged his finger along an invisible route and stopped at another point.

"If so, I think we're around here."

"If this is true, then we're far ahead of the other units and squads." Jack leaned back in his chair and ran a hand through his hair, feeling the grime and dirt clinging to each strand. Standing to stretch, he examined the faces of his Berserkers and found Kyle wasn't among the group.

"So, what do we do?" Carlos asked.

"Yeah, do we wait here until the other units catch up?" Jones asked as Cannonball growled at Harvey who tried to pet him on top of the head. Some of the men laughed.

"Harvey, even the fuckin' dog knows you're a piece of shit," Ashmore said.

"Our mission is to push to the river." Jack brought everyone's attention back to the map. "I like the idea of being the first ones there. Imagine, us chilling at the shore when the other units show up. What do y'all say?"

A mass unison grunt was the only reply Jack needed.

Standing at the bathroom mirror, Kyle studied the unfamiliar lines and creases forming like ridges along his eyes and mouth. His sockets sank inward, bringing about an expression of hollowness to his gaze. Shadows stretching down his face revealed a gaunt structure, both foreign and frightening to him. *Fuck, I look thirty,* he thought.

He turned on the faucet, allowing the cold water to rush through his fingers before cupping his hands to contain it. The refreshing liquid morphed from clear to a brown rust color, washing away the dirt and grime which had become like a new layer of skin in the passing days. A chill fluttered down his spine and stole his breath as he splashed water on his face.

The image in the mirror gripped Kyle's attention. The water streaming down his face carried with it traces of blood and dirt to paint a horrid piece of art.

This is the real you, a mangled image of war. It was a foreign voice that echoed in his head.

"This ain't me," Kyle whispered at the reflection. He thought of the kid he once was, sitting on his surfboard, and could almost feel the sun from his memories. He hurt to be back there.

Oh, are you sure? How do you know who the real you is anymore?

"This isn't me. This isn't me." Kyle ripped a hanging towel from a hook on the wall and dried his face. In the mirror, the dark particles of dust swirled about, creating an outline of a figure in the low light. Kyle didn't want to blink. He knew who the outline was and didn't want to waste a single heartbeat with blinking.

Skyler stood, made of smoke and darkness, drifting behind him like a phantom presence. Kyle froze, for the sight of her brought not fear, but heartache. Her ghostly hand brushed across his shoulders and traveled along his back. He ached and sighed, for his mind remembered the warmth of her touch that was no longer there. He wanted her to be real, and the thought turned his stomach to knots and caused tears to flow from both eyes.

"Then who are you?" The apparition's voice whispered sweetly in his ear. The shadowy fingers wrapped around his shoulders, and although he couldn't feel it, she kissed the side of his neck.

Yeah, who are you? A dark and foreign voice laughed maniacally.

"This isn't me." Kyle repeated as if trying to persuade himself. In death, she still looked enchanting to him with no signs of injuries. Then she flickered from his reality, in and out of existence as if caught in the static of a bad television reception.

"You're death. You and your men bring death to everyone and everything around you. This is what you are. You live in a world of the zero hour. Embrace it," Skyler said.

"This isn't me."

You're a Berserker. Show the world who you are. Let go and allow yourself to be free.

"This isn't me."

"You're like me." Skyler placed another phantom kiss on his cheek. "You're already dead."

Skyler faded, and the dark voice receded to whatever abyss it had come from. Kyle was alone. He placed a small green box on the side of the sink which contained three trays of paint: black, green, and white. He rubbed his fingers on the white strip and applied it to his face.

V

The Berserkers stopped and stared. Cannonball cowered with a whimper behind Jones. Kyle approached the table, a burning cigarette stuck between his teeth. A white base of paint crafted a skull's opaque sheen, but it was the black circles around his eyes that drifted into an obscured muddy fog, giving him a haunting look. His nose appeared hollow from the bridge down, with the same black paint cracking upon his lips. Kyle didn't bother with their stares as he took his place at the table to study the map.

No one spoke. The face was a horrible reminder of their business. They were death and Kyle was simply showing them that.

"So, what now? What's the game plan?" Kyle asked.

"We finish our mission and get to the river." Jack didn't bother with commenting on the face paint. "You with us now?"

"More than ever." Kyle's voice was stern, and his gaze focused. Jack was happy to see the energy coming from his friend, reeking with the hostility of a Berserker. A high-pitched scream interrupted Jack before he was able to speak. Heads spun to the front of the house. Black and Carlos crouched beneath a window and watched two men, carrying AK's, dragging a woman down the street.

"We got to help her." Black started for the door, but before he could open it, Jack planted his foot at the base to keep it closed.

"Wait," Jack said, and all eyes fell on him. "It could be an ambush. The interpreters all say the women of Fallujah are more evil than the men are."

Her screams echoed through the empty streets as the men tugged on her, pulling her farther down the road.

"If we don't help her, they'll butcher her. Remember the hell house in Karma?" Black said. The gore of that house flashed through their minds: butchered and burnt bodies, children, women, men, the beheadings, the rape, the torture, and all the other vile evils. "Besides, we're way ahead of everyone else. No one knows we're here and I doubt the enemy does, so how can it be a trap."

"Just because they don't speak English, doesn't mean they're stupid." Thompson rose from the table. "This whole fuckin' city is a trap."

Jones picked up Cannonball, allowing the small white creature to lick at his face.

"Get out of here." He shooed the dog away, but the small white pup came back to him. "Cannonball, you gotta go. This is gonna get bad. If we make it out of this, I'll come back for you."

The dog whimpered again and licked Jones's face. Jones smiled, nuzzled his nose against Cannonball's, and sat the dog down. Hanging his head in defeat, Cannonball trotted out of the room. Jack chambered a new round.

"Let's do it."

CHAPTER THIRTEEN

FUBAR

The tree of liberty must be refreshed from time to time

with the blood of patriots and tyrants.

-Thomas Jefferson

I

The two insurgents pushed and pulled the woman into a house a hundred meters away. Jack, Sutherland, Ashmore, and Black stacked up, but kept beneath the back-gate's ledge. The sun rode low in the sky, and an unsettling calmness crept over the land. Sutherland tapped Jack on the shoulder to get his attention and once having it, tossed his thumb back.

"The Euphrates," he said. The others turned and were in awe at the sight of the river. The sun reflected off it, and the sounds of its water rushing off to unknown places filled them with a sense of nirvana. In several sections of its bank, palm trees swayed in the wind. Their main objective was close enough that they could smell it, and a sense of accomplishment nearly overcame them. This excitement filled the others except for Ashmore.

He dreaded going back to a normal, boring civilian life, and prayed for either a quick death or a great fight.

"We ain't done yet, boys. Let's go make our money," Jack said. He stormed through the back gate. Two wings of the house faced the men, revealing the dwelling as a massive U-shaped structure. Years of harsh sandstorms had blasted away the hard mud coating in several sections until the bricks showed underneath.

Jack turned the handle freely, easing the door inward. The fading light of the sun through the windows gave the kitchen it's only light for Jack to scan his surroundings. Dust had settled over the room. Jack stopped just past the threshold, taking a knee, and ordering the others to proceed.

"Ash, Black. Take the other wing and start clearing down. Stay quiet as long as you can. We want to get the jump on these fuckers. Hopefully, we'll meet in the middle." Ashmore and Black both nodded and ran off to their objective. Sutherland followed Jack, gliding across the room, and arriving at the other door in the kitchen. The void of sound within the house gave the impression that the walls were holding their breath for some surprise.

The cold knob felt lifeless under Jack's fingers as he twisted it and pulled the door open. He forced his way into the next room, and a crystal chandelier above the large oak table caught his eye. *Whoever lives here has some money*, Jack thought.

He walked around the table, crossing in front of a chest-high rectangular window and peeked out. Overlooking the patio, Jack watched Ashmore and Black disappear down the other wing. Sutherland moved along the opposite side of the table, and while trying to peer out the window himself, he bumped into a chair. It rocked, threatening to crash hard to the floor, but Sutherland shot out a leg and caught it with his boot before it could. He looked alarmed at Jack.

Jack trained his rifle on the door in front of them, and Sutherland aimed at the other one leading out onto the patio as they waited for a reaction from within the house. Any minute now, they were sure someone would rush in, AK blazing, but to their relief, no insurgent came.

"Maybe they skinned out," Sutherland said.

"Maybe it's a trap, and they know we're here."

"I like my suggestion better." From the window, they saw Kyle and the rest of the Berserkers providing security around the perimeter. Sutherland opened a door on the right to find a wooden deck and patio set with furniture undisturbed by the war. The setting of a table and chairs, along with fake plants, reminded Sutherland of his parents' house, causing a twinge of homesickness to bother him.

A brief hiss vibrated by Sutherland's head, snapping him out of his daydream. He leaned back into the house as another set of rounds beat against the door jamb. In one quick movement, Sutherland hunched forward and squeezed his trigger three times. The first round missed and alerted the insurgent to crouch deeper into the corner of the U-shaped house. His defense did little for him as the next two rounds met their mark.

BANG. Recoil. Shoulder wound.

BANG. Recoil. Chest wound.

The last bullet struck the insurgent above the heart, separating his aorta arteries, and killing him instantly.

"Surprise is over, let's move." With his adrenaline in high gear, Jack took a large step forward and kicked the door leading into the study. It broke and ripped free from its hinges. Shadowed by Jack and Sutherland, the door flew into a room where bookshelves lined the walls, and a large desk sat in the center. Hunkered behind the desk, a twenty-year-old man crouched down with an AK in his shaky hands. Jack dove to the side as the insurgent open fired.

Sutherland never saw it coming. His head slammed to the side, the hardest punch he ever took, as the bullet bounced off the side of his Kevlar helmet. His body leaned heavily to one side, and he tried in vain to stabilize himself. The next gun blast went unheard by Sutherland as he tumbled to the swaying floor. His eyes grew heavy and despite his best effort, it felt good to close them. When he opened them again, he witnessed in a slow, blurry haze, Jack executing the insurgent with a single shot to the head.

II

Kyle maintained discipline, never averting his eyes from his sector of fire as the shots rang out from within the house. Although a road ran in front of the U-shaped house, and the small dwelling sat in a large field, three tall buildings stood near, lording over the smaller structure, and blocking any other means of egress for the Marines. Kyle didn't like the look of these buildings and understood that if this was an ambush, the only means of escape would be to the rear of the house. There sat a large open field that ran for several hundred meters to a grove of trees at the riverbanks.

"Push out, disperse."

"What do you see?" Thompson asked.

The sun sank, and Kyle was unsure if his eyes were playing tricks on him. Shadowy figures shuffled about the rooftops and balconies, slithering across windows and doorways of the surrounding buildings.

"We got movement." Thompson followed Kyle's line of vision but saw nothing. "I got a bad feeling about this house."

"Ambush?" Thompson asked.

"Think so," Kyle whispered, flipping the switch of his M16 from safe to semi-auto.

"They're in the house." Jones watched as Ashmore and Black broke through the back door of the washroom. The small room was empty of personnel and tucked to one side of the tight room were a washer and dryer. Aligning the windowsill above them was a various assortment of cleaning supplies. Ashmore tried to look out one of the two chest-high rectangular windows, but scraps of paper covered them.

He pushed the door leading deeper into the house when Black's foot caught the bottom edge of the washer. Ashmore jerked and wheeled about at the loud bang as Black tripped but kept his footing. Shaking his head in disappointment, Ashmore laughed at the younger Marine.

"Come on, boot. Stay focused, or you might get your head shot off." Ashmore was still smirking and shaking his head as he threw the bedroom door open. An insurgent stood behind the bed in the center of the room, waiting for the foreign invaders. Ashmore ducked, expecting fire from the AK, and fell into the perfect prone position. He landed behind his weapon and pulled the trigger. The SAW erupted with a loud, 'brrrrrp.'

BANG, BANG, BANG. Recoil. Recoil. Recoil.

The insurgent doubled over behind the bed, riddled with bullet holes, and dead.

"Hell yeah, you see that shit," Ashmore said, but Black didn't reply. Blood sprayed the white machines, and Black's feet flapped like the wings of a dying bird. He clutched his throat, trying to suck in air and call for help. His eyes stretched wide with pain and horror, staring at Ashmore, wanting to ask what happened to him.

As the aching for air grew too great, he squirmed and thrashed, spasming out and kicking the machines. Ashmore didn't bother with calling for the new corpsman. There was nothing that could be done to save the young Marine, but Ashmore would not let him die alone. Although he didn't like the young guy personally, he was a Marine none-the-less, and for that, Ashmore waited until Black's movement ceased before moving on.

He popped a dip into his lip and shrugged his shoulders. Ashmore had no feelings of remorse for someone dying. That part of him was lost forever and he spat on the floor before muttering, "Adios amigo."

III

BANG. Recoil. Headshot.

The insurgent's head snapped back and his brains painted the books on the shelf behind him. Jack spun on his heel to find Sutherland tearing off his helmet and admiring the large gash in the side of his cover.

"Too close?" Jack asked, helping Sutherland to his feet. Sutherland rubbed the side of this throbbing head.

"For comfort, at least."

"Lucky prick." Jack patted his shoulder. "You still got your grape."

To the right of the desk was a door and when Jack flung it open, he found Ashmore on the opposite side of the room that connected the two wings. The two Marines spotted each other and then noticed the man standing behind the parlor couch. He shimmied up against the fireplace, pressing a .45 revolver to a trembling woman's temple.

"Put it down, motherfucker," Jack ordered. Sutherland maneuvered around Jack to stand in front of the couch and give commands in Arabic.

"Imshi." The man told the Marines, shooing them away with his hand as if they were children annoying him.

"La, shukran." *No, thank you.* Sutherland replied.

"Yaeni qutil almar'a." *I mean to kill the woman.*

"La. Almawt yakun maeak. La sahiid." *No. Death be with you. No Martyr.*

"Aibtaead 'aw arhul… Aibtaead 'aw arhul… iiraqat aldima." *Go away… go away… bloodshed.* The insurgent warned.

"Lak 'an tughadir min hadhih alhayati." *You to depart from this life.*

"Lak 'an tamut." *You to die.* The insurgent bit his lower lip at Sutherland.

"Shayyaan fashayyaan." *Bit by bit.* Sutherland shrugged his shoulders. He was growing more use to the idea that he was going to die, even if others couldn't accept it yet.

BANG. Recoil. Headshot.

The man's head ruptured and decorated the fireplace with his brain matter. His dead weight tripped the woman, and together they crashed to the floor. Ashmore stepped in closer, resting his rifle on his shoulder. His tobacco stained lips drew back as he admired his kill.

"You first, though." Sutherland stared into the man's eyes, trying to see if there was a soul in them. Jack moved quickly to free the screaming woman from the dead man's arms.

"Where's Black?" Sutherland asked.

"Smoked."

"Shit," Jack said.

"Oh well, the fucker never fired a shot."

"What?" Jack asked.

"This whole time, the motherfucker never once fired a shot. Pacifist motherfucker. I told him that conscientious objector shit would get him killed."

"Damn, didn't know that," Jack said.

"Yeah, whatever, but I tell you what," Ashmore looked out the windows at the surrounding buildings. "I'm starting to think this place is a trap."

"Me too." Jack hurried past Ashmore and headed to the front door.

"What's out this way?" Ashmore pulled the door next to the fireplace open, unimpressed with the patio arrangement and the dead insurgent in the corner. He closed the door as Jack stepped out the front.

"Kyle, get in here."

Before Kyle could give the order, the atmosphere changed to one of gunpowder explosions and adrenaline-fueled movements. Carlos and Harvey stepped back, returning fire at unseen targets as Thompson, Doc, and Jones charged the house. Small puffs of dirt rose from impacting rounds like micro nuclear explosions trailing the running Marines. Kyle shoved Harvey and Carlos, getting them to move, and turned to cover their egress. An insurgent appeared on a balcony, firing at the Marines, and Kyle postured and fired.

BANG. Recoil. Sucking chest wound.

The man launched back into the wall behind him, bounced off and stumbled forward, toppling over the railing like a stuntman in some 80's action movie. Kyle didn't wait to see the body fall before joining the Berserkers in the house. Jack fired at the enemy's positions, giving Kyle cover until he rushed across the threshold. Jack slammed the door, barricading it behind him, and then rounds peppered the house.

"Pals," Kyle said, trying to catch his breath. He held out his fist and Jack nodded his head.

"Pals." Jack bumped knuckles. The men took in heavy breaths, exhausted, but smiling and alive.

Chunks chipped out of the wall and window shards threatened to lacerate the Marines. Ashmore flinched and in three big strides, cleared the parlor floor and threw himself into the bedroom from which he had came. Carlos and Doc Brooks, hunching over to avoid shots, followed.

Jones and Sutherland shielded the dazed and terrified woman behind the parlor couch. Running out of options, Thompson dove into the study and came to rest an inch away from the insurgent Jack had killed. Jack and Kyle dropped to the floor as dust and debris floated in the air like specks of glitter. Kyle searched, half expecting to see some silk spirit of Skyler walking through the dust.

"Everyone stay down," Jack ordered.

"Oh, good call there, fearless leader." Ashmore bellowed from the bedroom.

Harvey's head jerked from side to side. His weight shifted awkwardly between his feet until he panicked and broke for the back door. His shoulder caught the edge of the brick fireplace, and he stumbled out the house. The last glaring rays of sunlight fading behind the river, blinded him, and caused him to shield his eyes with his arm. The wooden planks of the patio stressed and groaned under his weight. It was there he met a series of AK rounds.

Zip...zip...zip...zip. His guts tore open underneath his sapi plate, spilling out onto the deck. A punching shock of the 7.62 bullet mangled his left hand, splitting his palm in two as the round tore through the middle and ring fingers. Staring at it, Harvey saw not his hand, but an alien-like claw with eight-inch fingers. The deformed hand released his rifle as his upper right thigh vibrated with violence.

Harvey gasped in pain; his leg buckled and any hope of standing faded as he pitched to the side. He reached out to the table in front of him, caught it as the next round shattered his hip, dropping him to his knees. Before he could allow himself to fall, two more bullets punched his chest. One struck his sapi plate and the other nailed flesh. Harvey went down, knocking over a chair as the eighth round broke his shoulder.

The chair tumbled into a vat of water, spilling it out onto the wet dirt, and forming a small puddle in front of him. His left bicep tore down the middle, and the last round chipped away at the bone beneath. He stiffened before pitching forward and landing face down in the accumulated pool of water. Harvey choked on equal parts of blood, water, and mud as rounds struck the dirt surrounding him. He couldn't gather the strength to keep from drowning and died unable to take another breath.

IV

Sutherland, staying low to avoid enemy fire, snatched and slammed shut the patio. Each direction, every possible escape, the enemy had covered. The rapid fire of AK's dwindled down until they ceased altogether. The sky darkened and the approaching night grew still. Only Ashmore appeared elated by his potential death. The others held a look of worry, waiting for Jack to give an order.

A loud clearing of a throat disturbed the silence.

"Americans. We have surrounded you." Jack looked at Kyle, and both men peered out the windows flanking the front door. A man with only six fingers stood holding a bullhorn microphone, and at once, Kyle recognized him.

"Shit." Kyle slammed his fist against his thigh and slid back to the floor. "I had a chance to kill that motherfucker, and I didn't take it. Fuckin' cease-fires."

The number of insurgents tripled. They prepped AK's and RPK's and pointed them at the U-shaped house. The six-finger man stood at the opening in the gate with a bullhorn in one hand and a pistol in the other.

"You are…" He paused for a moment, trying to find the right words in the language which wasn't his native tongue. "…completely surrounded. Surrender or die."

Jack shrunk back down to the floor underneath the windows. Individual shots hit the house, and the men sank lower to avoid them. The bullhorn squeaked, and the loudspeaker rippled with another man's voice. A short man holding an AK stood on top of the perimeter wall, pacing back and forth, with the bullhorn to his mouth.

"Fuck you, Americans. You will all die. I will cut your heads off."

"Mohammad's mother was a pig farmer," Ashmore shouted over the others. At once, the house fluttered with AK fire, and the Marines ducked away. The barrage of fire continued uninterrupted for several minutes. Windows shattered and holes punched through the walls. Their ears rang with gunshots and a couple of the Marines released their weapons to cover them. The shots dwindled, reducing to pops until the clearing of a throat echoed from the bullhorn.

"You infidels will die. You sons of whores," the little man said.

"Come get some." A single shot knocked the short man off the wall and ended his life. Jack eased back down from the window with his smoking pistol.

The night grew eerie and the two groups of men waited for the other to take action. Nervousness overcame the men as their mortality flashed through their minds. Ammunition rattled in magazines held by unsteady hands. A few trembling lighters tried hard to ignite cigarettes. A grenade hit the wall and exploded outside, leading the way for a volley of insurgent fire.

As soon as the chaos started, it died down, disturbed only by a single word shouted from within the house.

"Bitch." The volatile atmosphere shifted to Ashmore, weighing the severity of his insult until a gasping chuckle broke the tension. Eyes danced about, landing on Thompson, whose hysteria soon infected the others.

"We're all gonna die." Thompson seized his side at the stitch of pain from his laughing. "Holy shit, this is crazy."

"Fuck them." Ashmore cackled. The Marines looked from one another, laughing as if it was all a joke. They were tired and hurt, but their moral was high and if Jack had to die with anyone, he was glad it was these Marines.

"Welcome to the zero hour, motherfuckers." Jack didn't hold back his god-like cheer and a hurrah pulsed through the Berserkers. Laughs withered, broken up with the occasional insult directed at the insurgents until a fury of rounds erupted and the Marines dropped to the floor. The silence returned, but the nervousness was gone.

"What do we do now?" Kyle asked. Jack gave no answer. He read the faces of his men: drained, tired, and hungry, but ready. Jack unbuckled his Kevlar, allowing it to roll to the floor next to him, and struck a match from a green MRE matchbook. He touched it to the end of a cigarette.

"Smoke'em if you got'em." Jack scratched at his dirty scalp. Outside, the volume of the bullhorn increased with static, then another man's terror-stricken threats. The Marines paid no attention to him.

"Jack, what do we do?" Kyle asked.

"I ain't got no answer. I led you in here and fucked you all. But let me break it down Barney-style for you. We're surrounded with only two options; we can either fight and die or surrender and die." Aside from Ashmore and Sutherland, the squad's eyes turned grim, and Jack could feel the disappointment radiating off them. Ashmore was still smiling, amazed that he was in this situation, and Sutherland stared calmly as if nothing new was happening to him. "Well, I don't know what you guys want to do, but I can tell you this, I ain't surrendering for shit. I've been a prisoner of war before and it ain't fun."

"Hey, Harvey, why don't you go out and talk to them," Ashmore called from the bedroom.

"Harvey's dead, Ash."

"Oh, my bad," he said, then chuckled.

Jack stood, staying clear of the window. Anger filled him but it was hate that fueled him. His teeth mashed together and his nostrils flared. "I ain't surrendering to these dirt worshippin' motherfuckers. You can, but I ain't. They might kill me, but I'm gonna kill as many of them motherfuckers as I can. We're Berserkers. Hell, I'd rather die here than go home all fucked up, anyway."

Jack paused to take a hard drag from his cigarette, trying hard to steady his shaking hand. His head swam with the rush of nicotine and he stopped to savor it.

"They may kill me today, but I'm gonna kill them back. I hate this fucking place. I feel sorry for you pricks that make it out alive. I'll be in

Valhalla, getting wasted and banging Viking bitches." Jack bobbed like a fighter preparing himself for a match.

Thompson crossed himself and said a silent prayer.

Ashmore beamed with excitement like a school-aged kid about to watch two big kids get into a playground fight.

Sutherland looked skyward. *What do we do now? What do we do now?* No longer sure who he was talking to.

Jack unsnapped his rifle sling and stood the weapon against the door jamb. His other hand tightened on his 9mm.

"This is your zero hour. Embrace it, motherfuckers." Jack roared, shoving his arm through the broken window. The ice-cold air rushed up his sleeve, and he unloaded the pistol. The insurgents paused only for a second, startled by the Marine's fire, then returned a volley.

The six-finger man fired his pistol. The bullet cut through the night and smashed through what remained of the window panel. The glass failed to slow the projectile's speed as it rotated to its destination.

Jack gritted his teeth and continued to fire his 9mm, only stopping as a round struck him in the shoulder. He didn't fall back but collapsed into the window frame. A second round dislodged him, sending him spiraling to the parlor floor as a large piece of his skull tore away with blood and a chuck of his brain deflecting outward.

V

"Lay down your weapons and surrender." The six-finger man's voice echoed. Doc and Carlos rushed to Jack's side as single shots of enemy fire broke through the wall. Kyle looked on in disbelief at his best friend lying immobile on the ground. "Lay down your weapons!"

Kyle's hands shook, his heart pounded against his rib cage, and a weakness sucked the life from his face. He gritted his teeth with the rage of the Berserker taking hold. Kyle leapt up in front of the window and shouted, "Come get some."

BANG. Recoil. Eyeshot.

One shot, one kill. The six-finger man buckled, and the Marines flocked to windows to exchange fire with the enemy. Kyle ejected his magazine and loaded in a fresh one as he slid across the floor to Jack. Blood stained Doc's hands while applying direct pressure to the head wound.

"You can hack it, Jack." Carlos kept repeating, handing Doc more gauze. Jack's body spasmed and his legs convulsed.

An image of Jennifer entered his head. She was in high school, a head full of curly blonde hair, and was bouncing in that unforgettable cheerleading uniform. The image glitched and her face glowed in the moonlight as he got down on one knee, asking her to be his wife. He recalled pacing the hotel lobby on the morning of their wedding. A trembling feeling working its way through his body.

They said, "I do" surrounded by a blanket of fresh snow. The light of the sun broke through the clouds and shined on them as if they were the only people in the world that mattered. He could hear her soft voice giggling at his father who had fallen asleep during their vows.

Their honeymoon: her hair floating out in all directions under the clear blue water. They held their breaths and each other. The memories jumped and there was her worried smile when she told him he was to be a father. There she was standing, crying as his bus pulled away. His heart felt hollow as these memories faded into an image he had never seen, but thought of on so many occasions. His wife and his son standing together, with heads cast down, staring at a grave with his name on it.

There were games he would never get to see his son play in and fatherly advice he would never get to give. He wouldn't teach his son how to treat a woman or how to be a good man. Jack couldn't show him how to fight with your mind and not just your fists. Fishing. He had only ever wanted to teach his son how to fish like his father had, and now that was gone too. In the span of a second, a single lead projectile tore all this away from Jack.

He blinked his eyes open, but with his brain scrambled, he didn't know what he was looking at. He knew the men hovering over him, but he didn't know why or how, or if they were real or if they were angels.

"You can hack it, brother. Stay with us." Jack saw Kyle's lips moving but couldn't hear him. Jack waited for a light, waited for some presence which seemed to be ever evading him. He waited for a sign of goodness or a looming darkness, but nothing revealed itself.

There came no shadow creatures, no devils nor angels, and mostly, there came no Gods. The chemicals in his damaged brain changed. Not only could he see himself holding his wife, but he could feel the pulse rushing through her veins as she wrapped her arms around him. He allowed himself to smile, releasing any guilt he once had; for guilt had no place in death.

Jack allowed the infinite absence of life to overtake him. He slipped into a nirvana state, absorbed in death with no fear of punishment and no hope of reward. Somewhere in the distance, Jack could have sworn he heard the sloshing of beer and the merry laughter of Vikings. The clock ticked down the seconds of his zero hour and he embraced it.

Corporal Jack Campbell

Killed in Action Fallujah, Iraq, Al-Anbar Province

July 16th, 1982 – November 15th, 2004

Private First Class Richard Black

Killed in Action Fallujah, Iraq, Al-Anbar Province

January 13th, 1985 - November 15th, 2004

Corporal James Harvey

Killed in Action Fallujah, Iraq, Al-Anbar Province

December 7th, 1984 – November 15th, 2004

CHAPTER FOURTEEN

SHIT STORM

You are the first Marines! Not all the communist in Hell can overrun you.

-Chesty Puller

I

A light mist funneled off the wind, forming a collective water that trickled in droplets off the house and down the windows. Emptiness gnawed at Kyle, and he sat motionless, staring at the outline of Jack wrapped in a green poncho liner. The pain hit him; they would never speak together again. The life they once had, the good times of drinking and laughing, were gone. There was no going back; nothing could reverse the hands on the clock.

If you can't make it, how can we?

He wanted to cry, to roll up into a ball, and be forgotten. Jack was gone and his death brought thoughts of Skyler. Kyle placed a cigarette between his chapped lips and put a flame to the end of it.

Rounds ricocheted against the house, but Kyle failed to register them. The nicotine eased the nipping pain in his stomach and the realization they were going to die. A small bark came down the hall, and Jones scurried flat across the floor, welcoming Cannonball with open arms.

"What are you doing here, boy? How did you get in?" The dog lapped at his face and his tongue warmed Jones's cold cheek.

"What now, Corporal?" Sutherland slithered across the floor, staying out of the enemy's view, and eased up next to Kyle. The sorrow in Kyle's eyes shifted to Sutherland before drifting back to Jack's body. He licked at the cracks on his lips, hoping to provide them with some moisture, but no relief came.

"I don't know what to do. I don't know how to save you guys. I just don't know. I'm not Jack. I don't have any moto speeches. I'm not the leader he was," Kyle said, white smoke funneling from his nostrils. Sutherland shifted away from Kyle as if slapped in the face.

"Corporal, all due respect, but fuck you." Eyes locked on the new lance corporal. Kyle didn't react to the disrespect, and when no response came from him, Sutherland continued, "I'm a Marine. I don't need you saving me. Like Jack said, this is my zero hour. I have to embrace it. I ain't gonna lie down and die for these hajji bastards. If they kill me, well fuck it, they're gonna have themselves a brawl."

Kyle puffed away on the filtered cigarette, countlessly rolling around his options in his head. Looking into the hardened face of Sutherland, Kyle knew the kid was right.

"Look at you, Sut. Man, I remember you didn't even want to drink with us and now look, you're one hard charger."

"Yeah, and if I gotta lead these men out of here, I will, but I'm not in charge. You are."

"I'm not Jack Campbell."

"No one's asking you to be. Stop comparing yourself to a dead man. You're in charge. Better him than us, right? We either die together, or we kill these bastards, but we need a plan."

"Yeah." Ashmore clapped his hands together, the noise jolted several of the men. "Fuck yeah. Let's kill some sonsofbitches."

Energy pulsed through the room again.

"What would Chesty say, we're surrounded and outnumbered." Sutherland stared back at Kyle. "Good, they can't get away from us now. We got these bastards."

Enemy rounds hitting the house increased as the Berserkers cheered. Kyle took a hard drag from his cigarette and flicked it across the room into the fireplace.

"I love this idea. We're gonna die, but we're gonna take a lot of them bastards with us. I love it; I love y'all for being here with me when I die." Kyle cheered at each one of his men. He checked the magazine in his rifle and then slammed it back in. "Jones, take that woman into the study. Berserkers spread out. Let's kick some ass. Show these bastards what kind of Marines you are."

Carlos glanced out the bedroom window and saw three men, mainly concealed in shadows, running along the concrete fence. He hurried back to the parlor door.

"Dig it, we got movement to our flanks."

"Ash," Kyle called out.

"I'm on it." Ashmore and Carlos stomped down the left hall. Kyle pulled out a single claymore mine from his daypack lying next to Jack. Opening the front door only two inches, he shoved the claymore out and to the side, trying to conceal it without being spotted.

"Spread out. If these fuckers get in this house, they better be stepping over your dead bodies. And Marines…" Their eyes locked on Kyle's skull-painted face. "See you all in Valhalla."

II

Carlos followed Ashmore through the first bedroom, passing through the bathroom, and came into the second bedroom. Ashmore stepped over the enemy combatant at the base of the bed.

"Your kill?" Carlos asked, pointing down. Ashmore looked at the dead man as if he hadn't noticed the body had been there.

"Yeah," Ashmore said. "He smoked Black. Let's move this bed."

They tossed the insurgent across the room and shoved the bed away from the high rectangular window. Carlos wondered who would build a house in such a strange design, but the thought vanished as he spotted

Black in the washroom. He pulled the door close and scooted the bed in front of it. The two Marines took post at the chest-high window, adjusting their eyes to the darkness surrounding the house.

"You know that door opens the other way. That bed ain't going to stop it," Ashmore said.

"I know, but if someone does run in there, it'll slow them down, you dig?"

"Good idea." There came a pause between the two as more dark figures shifted about. Carlos wondered if it was his mind playing tricks or if he was seeing the insurgents.

"Man, this is crazy," Carlos said, propping up his rifle to his sector of fire. A belly laugh escaped Ashmore, startling Carlos.

"I know. This is so jacked up; it's awesome. I'm gonna kill the shit out of these assholes."

Carlos stopped and looked at Ashmore. "You *actually* think we're getting out of here alive?"

"Sure, why not?" Ashmore was confused by Carlos's tone. He mindlessly searched his pocket until he found his can of dip and tossed a pinch in. Packing the dip with his tongue, he spat a stream onto the insurgent across the room.

"Have you not assessed the situation? We're surrounded by armed and very pissed off muj. We have no radio, we're miles ahead of where we should be, and no one knows we're out here," Carlos said, to which Ashmore smiled, a dribble of spit clung to the tip of his chin.

"I know. Ain't it great. We're gonna fuck up so much shit and not get in trouble for it. Nobody's gonna see us do it. I'm so throwing an incendiary grenade at someone."

"You do know these guys want to cut off your stupid ugly grape and kill every one of us."

"I know. They're so stupid to think they can kill me. Dumbasses." Ashmore brought the SAW up to his shoulder, resting the bipod on the ledge of the window. His eyes narrowed, and he leaned into his weapon. Carlos examined the darkness, trying to see what spiked Ashmore's attention.

"What are you gonna do if we get back, Ash?"

"I don't know. Maybe rob banks or some shit. No job calls for a SAW gunner." Ashmore said matter-of-factly, and Carlos believed him. The astonishment of his friend brought another fit of astonishment to Carlos.

"Well, Ash, I can tell you this."

"What's that?"

"I'm glad you're on our side, you crazy maniac motherfucker." Ashmore laughed, which quickly faded, and he tightened his grip on his weapon.

"We got movement," Ashmore yelled, his voice carrying to the other wing of the house. Thompson paid no attention to the warning as he threw open the dining room door from the study. Jones motioned for the woman to shelter in the corner, hoping the desk would protect her from any danger.

Doc Brooks pushed past Jones and posted in the dining room. He was happy the window wasn't full length. The chest-high windows allowed the men to stand, keeping their minds on the fight, and off the aches that come with crouching for long periods of time.

"What's up with these windows?" Doc asked.

"Yeah, I ain't seen a house with these kind of windows before," Thompson said.

"Yeah, but the parlor has two full-length ones. Like what the hell happened, did they run out of these weird rectangular ones before they got to the front room."

"No shit."

Doc Brooks' heart painfully pulsed and talking helped him suppress the urge to vomit. An ambush had never once crossed his mind, but now he feared he'd be among the dead. Doc Brooks crossed his heart and prayed for his survival.

Cannonball barked at Jones's heels, and he ordered the dog to hide under the chair.

"Jones." Thompson called to him from the dining room. "I'm leaving this door open. We might need you to back us up."

"Roger that."

III

Ashmore waited for two insurgents to straddle the fence before opening up with his SAW.

BANG. BANG. BANG. BANG.

Recoil, Recoil, Recoil, Recoil.

Both insurgents fell from the wall, dead, but several AK's beyond that came to life. Carlos didn't waste any ammo but picked his targets with well-placed shots.

BANG. Recoil. Headshot.

BANG. Recoil. Sucking chest wound.

BANG. Recoil. Sucking chest wound.

"And therefore never send to know…" Ashmore spoke in a deep voice as if reciting a prayer or a verse from somewhere deep within his memory. "…for whom the bell tolls; It tolls for thee."

"What the fuck is that?" Carlos asked.

"It's an old poem Hemingway used once. I always liked it."

"You fuckin' read Hemingway?"

"Yeah, what? Surprised?"

"That you can read? Yes."

Rounds sprayed into the night as he chanted out the poetic irony.

In the front parlor, Kyle and Sutherland traded off shots: firing and taking cover, taking cover and firing.

"Keep an eye on that door." Kyle gestured to the back by the fireplace. An insurgent darted into the front yard with a flaming bottle, arm cocked back like a quarterback with a football.

BANG. Recoil. Chest shot.

The Molotov cocktail met the pavement, bursting into a fountain of flames, and covering the insurgent. Within the bright glow of orange and red, a scream arose until the fire sucked the oxygen from his lungs.

From their side of the house, Doc and Thompson could see the light of the burning man.

"Where the fuck is that light coming from?" Doc asked, his sector of fire illuminating with the flames.

"Hopefully not the front of the house burning down. That would suck."

"No kidding. But we would have heard the other guys if that was the case."

"Unless they're dead," Thompson said. Doc's throat went dry and he found that swallowing was equal to the sensation of rubbing the soft tissue of his mouth with sandpaper. His eyes shifted from the door of the study to the window in front of him. "Eyes front, Doc. We got company."

Doc's jittery eyes looked at the perimeter wall as the enemy poured over it. That shaky feeling attacked his stomach and he was quick to empty his magazine before dropping to one knee to reload. As he chambered a round, the kitchen door flung opened, and an insurgent stepped into the dining room. He was young and just as surprised as Doc was to see someone standing there.

Both men hurried to fire their rifles.

BANG. Recoil. Chest wound.

BANG. Recoil. Sucking chest wound.

BANG. Recoil. Gutshot.

The insurgent fell in the threshold. Doc, delighted at having been the one to survive, reclaimed his spot at the window next to Thompson.

"Nice one. Keep an eye on that fucking door." Thompson didn't take his attention off the fight until, from the corner of his eye, he spotted Jones stumbling in from the study, his hand clutched to his neck.

"Shit." Doc sprinted to Jones. A flood of blood flowed through his fingers and Jones fell into the corpsman's outstretched arms. The woman loomed in the doorway with a bloody knife in her hand and Cannonball barked behind her. She lunged at Doc who had no time to run away, but Thompson quickly blasted her from this world.

BANG. Recoil. Headshot.

Jones's legs kicked about, and his eyes bulged in their sockets, struggling to draw in a breath. He squirmed; his back arched painfully, he twitched, kicked, and was no more. Cannonball strolled out of hiding, refusing to flinch at the gunshots around him. He pawed past the insurgent woman, growling as he did so, and made his way to Jones.

"Ain't nothing you can do for him now, Doc," Thompson shouted, firing at the enemy. His heart broke for his friend, but he would have to worry about that later. "Get back over here."

Doc laid Jones on the ground and got back to the fight. Cannonball watched the corpsman return to his fighting position. The puppy looked at the caring man lying motionless before him. In all the noise and quick movements, they were alone. Cannonball nudged Jones with his cold nose and licked at his tears, trying to revive his human friend.

Corporal Anthony Jones

Killed in Action, Fallujah, Iraq, Al-Anbar Province

May 31st, 1983 – November 16th, 2004

CHAPTER FIFTEEN

LEATHERNECKS

Courage is endurance for one moment more…

-Unknown Marine Second Lieutenant in Vietnam

I

The battle raged throughout the night with brief periods of cease-fires, allowing the insurgency to regroup. Each time they pushed for the house, the stubborn Marines held their ground and fought them back. The sky yielded its darkness to a purple hue which helped illuminate the blank landscape. Silence encased the house, both inside and out. Not even far away fights could be heard.

Each side waited for the other to act until Ashmore watched a burning bottle sail through the air.

BANG, BANG, BANG.

Recoil, Recoil, Recoil.

The man went down, but the bottle smashed against the house, engulfing the wall in flames. Another insurgent snuck into the washroom, ready to flank Ashmore and Carlos, who held their ground in the neighboring bedroom. The burst from the AK spooked both Marines and three rounds struck the windowsill next to Ashmore. Carlos pivoted, spinning into a crouch, and aimed at the insurgent standing over Black's body.

BANG. Recoil. Upper thigh wound.

BANG. Recoil. Chest wound.

The man stumbled over Black's body as two more insurgents entered through the back door. Before they had a chance to acknowledge the Marines, Ashmore threw a grenade over Carlos's shoulder. It bounced loudly off the empty washer and landed on top of Black.

POP. Flash, a puff of smoke.

Smoke clouded the washroom, and when it settled, neither insurgent was standing. They screamed and rolled, swatting at visible flames until they became another addition to the growing mound of bodies which stalled the advance of more insurgents. The washroom went ablaze.

The remaining fragments of glass broke free from the window as another Molotov cocktail flew into the room. It struck the wall behind the Marines and the cool night gave way to the increasing heat. Carlos grabbed the delusional Ashmore by the flak jacket.

"We gotta fall back."

"Yeah...yeah...yeah. Did you see that incendiary grenade burn those fuckers?" Ashmore joked as Carlos pulled him away from the window. They started for the bathroom door, but Ashmore halted him. "Did you see it?"

Ashmore wasn't smiling. His eyes burned with intense sternness and Carlos could see his jaw was clenched.

"Yeah, man. I saw it." Carlos pulled his arm away and the joyfulness returned to Ashmore's face. "You fuckin' psycho."

"Good. Just making sure," Ashmore said, pushing past Carlos. He entered the bathroom as an insurgent broke through the patio door in the bedroom and lunged at the two Marines.

A pineapple grenade sailed through the parlor window and landed with a thud in front of the couch. Sutherland scooped it up and tossed it back before it exploded. A Molotov struck the outside surface of the front door. *Bastards are trying to smoke us out,* Kyle thought.

As the fire peeked through the bullet holes in the door, Kyle fired three shots out the window. Sutherland tore a frag from his flak and tossed it into the front yard.

POP. Flash, a puff of smoke.

The fire climbed, leaping at the ceiling, and eating at the house in its gluttony.

"Sut, fall back to Thompson's position," Kyle ordered, firing at any target that moved.

The back door near the fireplace flung open, and a man tackled Sutherland. The insurgent landed on top and plunged a dagger at the young Marine. Sutherland dug his fingernails into the man's wrist, halting the blade's descent. The dancing light from the fires reflected off the knife above Sutherland.

The same light bounced off a machete blade in the bedroom, catching Carlos's eyes. He dove into Ashmore, pushing his friend into the bathroom and out of harm's way. His actions were heroic but inadvertently placed himself in the path of the blade. The machete implanted in Carlos's hip, tearing through flesh and muscle and striking bone.

Carlos captured the man's hand, preventing him from driving the blade to the hilt. The insurgent snarled, pushing Carlos back, and trying to shove the weapon deeper. Ashmore didn't have room to swing his SAW around. He released it and ripped his ka-bar knife free from the sheath. With one hard downward swing, Ashmore came over Carlos and drove the knife into the man's skull. The insurgent released the machete and dropped to the ground, where he coughed blood and died.

Carlos collapsed, holding his side, and breathing heavily. Ashmore stepped on the insurgent's face and pulled out his ka-bar knife.

"Dude, you got stabbed by a machete." Ashmore applauded, helping Carlos to his feet. "That's fuckin' crazy."

"Thanks, brother." Carlos was less impressed than his friend was. They limped into the parlor to find Sutherland on his back, under an insurgent. The Hajji bore down with his weight, trying to drive the steel into their friend's throat. Kyle turned, surprised to see the struggle going on near him. As Ashmore brought up his SAW, Kyle leveled his rifle as well. Before either man could apply pressure to their triggers, an RPG struck the house. The loud explosion produced a violent shake.

The concussion sent rocks and mortar flying, and Kyle jolted forward. He squeezed back on the trigger, but fired wide of his intended target, hitting the fireplace instead. As the blade inched closer, a canopy of dust settled upon Sutherland and the insurgent. Sutherland gritted his teeth and mustered all the strength he could to push the knife away. The insurgent, who outweighed the young Marine by fifty pounds, snarled, revealing a row of rotten teeth and the bitter odor of bad breath.

"Dude, I don't care if you kill me, just don't breathe on me," he managed to say.

Ashmore and Carlos were stuck at the door, unable to enter the parlor together. Ashmore held the SAW at his waist, aimed at the man hovering over Sutherland, and pulled the trigger. He feared he might hit his friend instead of the insurgent, but there was a click as Ashmore's weapon failed to fire. He looked down and found it empty.

The insurgent's breath stung at Sutherland's eyes. He pushed forward on his knees, bringing the majority of his weight over the handle of the knife. Sutherland's arms quivered and the tip of the blade poked at his neck, drawing a tiny trickle of blood.

A blurry, brown object moved frighteningly fast in front of Sutherland and he knew this was his zero hour. He hoped Jack's theory of Odin was correct so he could rejoin his friends for a drink in the mighty hall of warriors. The insurgent's head snapped back, blood and yellow teeth raining from his mouth. He rolled off Sutherland, who circled to his side, welcoming the freedom from the man's weight and the return of oxygen.

The insurgent landed on his back, his eyes closed, and coughed blood across the room. Through the spray of crimson mist, Ashmore brought his boot down. The man never saw the bottom of the boot until it connected with the center of his face. Ashmore's weight shifted from his shoulders down to his leg, planting firmly on the man's nose.

He didn't hear the man's skull crushing, but he felt it. Ashmore rotated off him, coming down into a fighting position like he learned in boot camp. From there, he delivered another skull stomp. The man didn't flinch as shards of his crushed skull tore his brain to shreds.

"Kill! Kill!" Words reminiscent of basic training. The blood seeping from the man's ears still didn't convince Ashmore that he was dead, and he stomped the skull three more times.

"Holy shit, that works," he said, smiling at Sutherland. "Happy to see me?"

"More than ever." With Ashmore's help, he climbed to his feet. Carlos limped to Kyle, holding the back of a parlor chair for balance. Against his wishes, the chair broke under his weight, and he crumbled to the floor next to Kyle.

"Damn, I'm hurt bad." Carlos hissed. Another RPG shook the house, bringing pieces of the ceiling and walls crumbling down. The fire intensified along with the insurgent's rate of gunfire. Ashmore grabbed Sutherland and dove into the bedroom before the chimney imploded. A large section of stones crushed the parlor couch in the center of the room as broken pieces of bricks peppered Kyle and Carlos.

"What do we do?" Sutherland asked, tossing his empty M16 aside and bringing up his shotgun. Ashmore pulled him along, retreating into the bathroom. No matter which room they ventured into, the fire found them.

"We gotta skin out of here, Sut." Ashmore kicked open the door to the next bedroom, but the heat repealed him.

"What about Kyle and the others?" Sutherland tried to turn back, but Ashmore jerked him along.

"They're all dead, son. It's you and me now," Ashmore shouted over the gunfire from outside. "Let's get to the river."

Ashmore squinted and ducked his head, running through the searing heat of the bedroom and shoving through the patio door. Smoke curled upward from the devouring fires, creating a screen for the Marines. Ashmore and Sutherland broke out. They rushed blindly into the smoke which disoriented Sutherland. Fear encompassed him as an unsuspecting insurgent, unaware of Sutherland's presence, materialized in the murky haze.

BANG. Recoil. Gut Shot.

The figure vanished without Sutherland seeing him fall. A short distance ahead, Sutherland could hear Ashmore's SAW spitting out bullets. Sutherland, unsure and in a complete fog of war, ran toward it.

III

Doc went for the study, but the second RPG stopped him from entering, tossing about books and stones. A massive section of the wall crushed the door leading into the study, blocking Doc's route to the parlor.

"Don't bother, Doc. We can't go that way. Let's get out of here," Thompson said. Clink. A grenade rolled over the surface of the floor.

"Grenade!" Doc screamed and threw Thompson down, landing on top of him. The pineapple grenade exploded, and the force felt like someone kicked Doc with a giant boot. Shrapnel cut through his uniform and equipment to which Doc hissed and collapsed without another word.

"Doc, Doc? Oh, you stupid bastard. Doc!" Thompson shook the motionless sailor, who failed to respond. *Please, God let me find a pulse. Please let me find a pulse.* He felt for and found a faint pulse as the kitchen door creaked open. Thompson spun on his knees, bringing up his rifle, and fired.

BANG. Recoil.

Something fell hard against the door, and as it slowly swung open, the body of a female tumbled in holding a rifle. Thompson didn't wait to see where he'd shot her as he hoisted Doc's body over his shoulder. Pinning Doc's leg under his left arm, he grabbed Doc by the wrist, keeping his right arm free to wield his weapon.

Doc was heavy, but Thompson managed to stabilize himself to carry the corpsman like a firefighter through the kitchen door. The house shook again, and more pieces of the adobe dwelling fell inward. Thompson made his way outside while Kyle made his way to Carlos.

"You with me, bud?" Kyle asked.

"I'm still here," Carlos replied. Kyle eased next to Carlos and helped him prop his rifle upon a pile of fallen chimney bricks.

"This is it," Kyle said. Carlos extended his hand and Kyle shook it.

"It was a pleasure, Corporal."

"It's been my honor, Mijo." Kyle lit two cigarettes and gave one to Carlos. The color faded from Carlos's face, and it took a lot of strength for him to smoke. His eyes closed and he slipped next to Kyle.

"No...no...no. Not yet, brother," Kyle said, shaking Carlos awake. "We got some killing to do before that."

"Oh, yeah," Carlos shook his head, feeling like a man who had been drinking all night. "I almost forgot."

"Well, if we're going to die." Kyle exhaled smoke and lifted his 9mm Beretta. "Let it not be in vain."

The fire raged around them as two insurgents filed in through the back door. Carlos shot but didn't aim. He pulled the trigger without remorse and didn't care who he hit as long as they were the enemy.

"You like that?"

BANG. Recoil.

"You like that? You like that?"

BANG. Recoil. BANG. Recoil.

"You like that, you fuckin' suckin' sack of rat shit. Fuck you," Carlos screamed as more insurgents poured in, dropping like flies in front of him. The blood and spirit were coming back to Carlos's face. Kyle could see a large group moving across the front yard.

"Suppertime, bitches." Kyle pressed the detonator's small button, exploding the claymore and killing several in its wake. The itch to move gnawed at Carlos, who struggled to stand, holding the wall to keep himself from falling. His body was growing cold, and his strength was fading. He limped to the back door, freeing two grenades from his flak jacket. Catching the pins between his teeth, he jerked both grenades downward.

"Dig it, always wanted to do this," he said without looking back at Kyle. He hobbled out onto the patio under a hail of gunfire before the two grenades went off.

Kyle sat silently in the parlor, watching embers spark and listening to the fire crackle. His heart sank looking around the empty room for his friends.

"Jack? Carlos? Anybody?" He spoke not to this world, but to the next. "If you're there, say something. Show me something. Please don't leave me alone like this."

Nothing moved except the embers popping from the flames. Kyle hung his head between his knees.

"I don't want to be alone," he whimpered. He felt the burn of the bullet grazing his earlobe ahead of hearing the whip-like crack. Kyle jolted to the side, clutching his ear, and kicking the air in front of him. "Motherfucker!"

He looked down at his red palm, and his heart turned cold and rage grew. His face contorted from his snarl. Over his shoulder, he eyed the outside world and said, "You think you're gonna kill me this easy!"

His teeth mashed together.

"You're gonna have to work a lot harder for it if you wanna kill me."

His blood pulsed and the energy excited his muscles.

"Where was the Marine Corps founded?" He found himself shouting, preparing to school the enemy on the history of his people.

"Tun Tavern, 1775. That's right, a bar. We started as drunken, fisted-fightin' motherfuckers." He answered himself. Kyle looked over at Jack's body lying under the poncho.

"Who was the most decorated Marine in history?" Kyle stayed low, crawling across the floor to Jack's body. A plan formulated in his mind.

"Chesty Puller. I hope you're watching, Chesty. I'm about to make you proud."

"Where did the Marines earn the nickname Devil Dogs?" Kyle pulled back the poncho liner. "Belleau Wood. World War I. The Germans couldn't stop us; you think you got a chance, bitches?"

"What does Semper Fidelis mean?" On Jack's hip was his 9mm ammo pouch with two clips inside; he removed them both. "Always faithful."

"What did Dan Daly say as he charged the Germans at Belleau Wood?" The heat from the fire increased as the flames stretched over him. Kyle removed his flak jacket. "Come on you sons of bitches; you want to live forever!"

"Who was the first enlisted man to win the Medal of Honor in World War II?" His blouse and green shirt were sweaty, so he removed them, leaving himself bare-chested. "Basilone."

"Who are the only two Marines to earn the Medal of Honor on two occasions?" Kyle shoved Jack's pistol down the front of his pants. He was alone. His friends were dead. Kyle wanted to give in, to surrender, but he wanted to take as many of them with him as he could. He picked up his M16 and fired. Rat... tat... tat. Rat... tat... tat. "Dan Daly and Smedley Butler."

"Do you know who you're fuckin' with?" Rat...tat...tat. Rat...tat...tat.

"You're messing with the United States Marines. I will unleash Hell upon you." Rat...tat...tat. Rat...tat...tat. He fired round after round, slamming his rifle to the ground when it ran empty. He tore the hajji bayonet off his flak jacket and stuck it in his belt on the opposite side of his own Ka-bar. Removing the last grenade from his flak jacket, he pulled the pin before heading to the front door. "Kill! Kill! Motherfucker!"

IV

Standing at the rear entrance of the gate, Sutherland stumbled upon Ashmore laughing madly as he cut the enemy down in his path.

"Shit, Sut, thought I lost you. This way." He waved Sutherland on and headed into the darkness with Sutherland close behind. The blanket of smoke prevented them from seeing Thompson running parallel to their flank. Thompson heard Ashmore's voice like it was on some distant plane of existence. He stepped in that direction, but the explosions caused by Carlos's grenades redirected him.

He made his way through a destroyed section of the fence, shocked to find two insurgents coming to the same spot. They had failed to see him as he fired his rifle with one arm.

BANG. Recoil. Miss.

BANG. Recoil. Miss.

Doc's weight pressed hard against his shoulders, causing his shots to go low. His two rounds embedded into the cement bricks of the fence, forcing the insurgents to dive for cover without returning fire. When they stuck their heads up a second later, Thompson had vanished like a phantom back into the smoke. He hurried down the slope, nearly tripping twice in potholes. Once he pushed past several trees, he came to a rest at the shoreline of the river in time to hear Kyle's grenade explode at the front of the house.

POP. Flash. A puff of smoke.

Kyle charged out the smoking ruins of the burning building, taking the enemy by surprise. He let out a war cry so fierce that it forced the Gods to open their eyes on him. For one moment, the universe watched only him, only one man on the battlefield. It didn't care about any man dying or being born at that moment. It didn't care for the starving or the fed.

His torso was pale. Like a nightmare to his enemies, his skull-painted face weaved through the smoke, stalking them. With steam rising from his head, he blew smoke through his nose, giving himself the appearance of a demon. Both hands filled with pistols, he fired at anything moving. The enemy closed in, trying to shoot Kyle, but Kyle evaded them, skipping and dancing across the front yard to avoid their gunfire.

Behind him, the rising sun blinded the enemy and the house created a concealment for him. A hand grasped his shoulder, and Kyle crumbled the man with a single pistol-whip to the head while shooting him point-blank with the other hand.

BANG. Recoil. Gutshot.

He didn't wait to watch the man double over in agony before moving on. Kyle punched his pistols at the insurgents aiming to kill the Marine with the death face. One sidearm went empty, and Kyle spun it around on his finger, catching it by the barrel to crack across a man's skull. The impact buckled the man's knees, and Kyle released the pistol, never stopping as he heaved up his Ka-bar.

He continuously shot and stabbed the enemy, moving about the front yard as an AK bullet sliced his thigh. With the hate and adrenaline, and all the rage and excitement, he barely felt the wound as he pressed on.

An insurgent charged with a fixed bayonet attached to his AK. Kyle sidestepped him, delivering a spinning back elbow, taking the insurgent off his feet. The man didn't open his eyes to see the pistol pointing at him.

BANG. Recoil. Headshot.

Kyle grabbed the AK, firing a series of bursts at several enemies making their way along the fence. He chunked the empty rifle at a running insurgent. The steel barrel struck the man in the head, causing him to fall painfully to the ground. Kyle stormed out the front gate to confront the enemy. He stepped over the dead that littered the streets while firing the pistol and slashing his knife. His death face popped in and out of existence, drifting through the smoke like the Grim Reaper.

Two men charged from behind him and he shot both. Tat...tat. Tat...tat; ending both of them before they hit the ground. He kept moving and more enemies advanced, more surrounded him. Kyle kept evading, all the while, with a cry on his lips that seemed to never stop even when he took in a breath. His vocal cords vibrated a deathly war cry which echoed the fears of the insurgents. They were being preyed upon by the death-like Marine.

His arm burned as a blade opened a deep laceration in it. Kyle didn't acknowledge the injury but hacked at the enemy with his Ka-bar. The insurgent took two slices across his chest before Kyle buffaloed him with the pistol. A bullet nicked the top of his shoulder, but still, he didn't falter. Kyle killed without mercy and the insurgents who didn't run, found death inside Kyle's warpath.

A machete lunged at Kyle, but Kyle eluded the man who held it, kicking out his knee and causing him to tip forward. The knee broke, and he dropped his weapon to clutch his leg. Kyle released the pistol, while simultaneously snatching the machete off the ground. He stepped to the left, shifting his weight from one leg to the other while bringing the machete around. With one swift swing of his blade, Kyle removed the man's head and cut his screams short.

An exploding grenade rocked Kyle, but still, he went headfirst at the enemy until the only thing he could hear was the savage howl of his own war cry.

Lance Corporal Jason Sutherland

Purple Heart Recipient

For Wounds Received on November 16th, 2004.

Fallujah, Iraq, Al-Anbar Province

HM3 Alan 'Doc' Brooks

Purple Heart Recipient

For Wounds Received on November 16th, 2004

Fallujah, Iraq, Al-Anbar Province

Corporal Kyle Dillon

Purple Heart Recipient

For Wounds Received on November 16th, 2004.

Fallujah, Iraq, Al-Anbar Province

Lance Corporal Roberto Carlos

Killed in Action Fallujah, Iraq, Al-Anbar Province

February 6th, 1983 – November 16th, 2004

CHAPTER SIXTEEN

SNAFU

Freedom isn't free but the Marine Corps will pay most of your share.

-Ned Dolan

The new dawn rising over Fallujah on November 16th, 2004, came in a silent breeze. Soot filled the frosty air and the gunfire died off long before the rainy mist extinguished the fire. Sutherland stood watching what remained of the roof as it moaned, then buckled, and finally crashed inward. Thompson kneeled next to the wounded but breathing Doc Brooks, and scratched Cannonball behind the ears. Cannonball, who sat on his hind legs, whimpered as he stared at the rubble of the U-shaped house, longing for Jones.

A few insurgents had followed the Marines to the palm groves, but their bodies now laid on the slope and their friends retreated into the city. Sutherland struck a match from an MRE and touched the flame to a cigarette. With his shotgun dangling in front of him, he walked toward the smoldering ruins of the U-shaped house. Thompson called out to him but gave little effort trying to stop him.

Most of the perimeter fence still stood, despite gaps blown into it by RPG's. Sutherland did register the destruction as he walked through the rear entrance. The parlor section of the house was gone, but the lower part of the chimney stood like a sentry over the wreckage. Ashmore hunched over a dead insurgent and stood upon seeing

Sutherland approaching. Smoke from an extinguished fire drifted up with the wind behind Ashmore.

Sutherland slowed his stride but didn't stop. Ashmore leaned over and picked up what Sutherland first perceived to be a ball.

"There can be only one," Ashmore shouted. Swinging high from his outstretched arm, Ashmore held a decapitated head. Sutherland didn't respond. He continued his march to the destroyed house. "What? Not a fan of Highlander?"

Ashmore threw down the head and returned to collecting various war trophies from the dead. At the foot of the patio, an insurgent squirmed at Sutherland's feet. Without glancing down, Sutherland took a hard drag on his cigarette, and with his other hand, blasted the man with his shotgun.

BANG. Recoil. Chest shot.

The kill did nothing for Sutherland, and he stepped on to the dilapidated patio. Carlos's body laid torn to pieces, but this didn't stop him. In the corner, a flame no bigger than that of a campfire, danced around an assortment of wood and bricks, fighting to stay alive. Sutherland paused only long enough to pull the Bible from his cargo pocket.

There was no regret, and no remorse as he tossed the book into the flames, allowing the fire to live a moment longer. He continued through the spot where the back door had once stood and traveled on toward the front of the house. Near the front wall, bunched up in a burnt mess, he found an empty poncho liner.

He picked it up, turning the warm material over in his hands, before dropping it to the ground. Three burnt bodies laid spread out on the floor, and the smell of cooked meat was strangely pleasant to Sutherland. There was no front door to stop him, so he strolled around the front yard, shocked to find dozens of bodies scattered about. The firefight had been intense, but Sutherland was sure they hadn't killed this many men. Mangled limbs, decapitated heads, and disemboweled bodies decorated the yard like scary ornaments.

Sutherland froze near the front entrance of the gate. A man sat motionless, hunched over the body of Jack Campbell and covered in blood. Together, they sat atop a mound of severed heads. Sutherland walked closer and etching out through the dried blood was the largest Berserker tattoo he had ever seen. The flesh appeared to be stripped away and each red muscle fiber was tattooed on with the utmost attention to detail.

Sutherland had never seen this tattoo before and was speechless at the design that seemed to be coming from within the body of the hunched over man. He stepped even closer. If Jack laid across this man's lap, then the man with the amazing tattoo had to be Kyle.

Two ravens circled overhead.

Sutherland proceeded cautiously, avoiding the bodies which clumped together near Kyle's little pile. Sutherland placed his foot on a burned bottle, and the glass broke. Kyle shifted at the noise, sending Sutherland's hair into a nervous position of attention.

Shit, he's alive, Sutherland thought as a soft whimper resonated from Kyle. He eased closer, trying to hear what Kyle was saying and skipped back when Kyle threw a wandering glance over his shoulder. The skull-face, once painted white, was now smeared red. His head rotated to the front and looked up at the sky as if he was praying.

Kyle rocked back and forth. With each breath, he nearly toppled over like a man hit with an uncontrollable hysteria. Sutherland had assumed he was crying, but the sound was Kyle's ever-growing laughter. Blood stained his body like dried sweat, and his head wobbled on his neck.

Sutherland reached forward twice to catch him, but Kyle didn't fall. He looked about the area and couldn't believe all the dead insurgents radiating out from Kyle. The skull face painting took on a horrid look in the morning light, and Sutherland wondered what it must have been like for the enemy to see. Lost in his thoughts, he failed to realize Kyle's bloodshot eyes looking at him like a stranger coming to interrupt.

Kyle gazed at Sutherland, with eyes seeing a part of this world and a part of the next. His chest heaved and his jaw opened to scream, but he burst once again into a springing laughter.

"Corporal," Sutherland said with a nervous ripple. Kyle looked around, still laughing as if someone were telling a joke only he could hear. Sutherland moved around to face him, and Kyle returned to his hunched over position. Getting closer, Sutherland noticed something moving in Kyle's hand. Fresh blood ran down Kyle's forearm as he worked the tip of the hajji bayonet into his flesh. Sutherland pulled the knife free from Kyle's hand.

On his arm, Kyle had carved a single word, 'PALS.'

His skull-painted face drifted from one side to the other, trying to understand where he was. Two lines of tears flowed from his eyes, which bulged in their sockets like the pressure in his head was reaching a dangerous level. Sutherland never heard the cries of nightmares like the ones hidden in the howling of Kyle. The rolling fits turned to a maddening scream and it was in the distorted face of Kyle that Sutherland learned the only real lesson he carried with him for the rest of his life. War does not create men, but yet produces shattered fragments of what could have been.

-And if the Army and the Navy, ever look on Heaven's scenes,

They will find the streets are guarded by United States Marines-

SEMPER FI

Author Biography

Chance Nix is a former Marine who did two tours of duty in Iraq. He is a Purple Heart recipient and a combat veteran of the Battle of Fallujah. He lives in Texas with his wife Jennifer and their two sons.